continued . . .

MYTHOS

"A smooth, flowing tale that entices the imagination."
—*Huntress Book Reviews*

CODESPELL

"A hint of cyberpunk, a dollop of Greek mythology, and a sprinkle of techno-magic bake up into an airy genre mashup. Lots of fast-paced action and romantic angst up the ante as Ravirn faces down his formidable foes."
—*Publishers Weekly*

"One long adrenaline rush, with a few small pauses for Ravirn to heal from his near-fatal brushes with the movers and shakers of the universe, all while trying to figure out how to survive the next inevitable encounter."
—*SFRevu*

"Imaginative, fascinating, with a lot of adventure thrown in . . . Mr. McCullough has followed his first two books with a worthy sequel. *CodeSpell* will keep the reader on edge."
—*Fresh Fiction*

"A fast-paced, energetic page-turner . . . Ravirn continues to be a fascinating protagonist."
—*RT Book Reviews*

CYBERMANCY

"McCullough has true world-building skills, a great sense of Greek mythology, and the eye of a thriller writer. The blend of technology and magic is absolutely amazing, and I'm surprised no one has thought to do it quite like this before."
—Blogcritics.org

"It's smoothly readable, vivid, and fun . . . Highly recommended."
—MyShelf.com

"McCullough has the most remarkable writing talent I have ever read . . . Not satisfied to write a single genre or to use a subgenre already made, he has created a new template that others will build stories upon in later years. But know this: McCullough is the original and unparalleled."
—*Huntress Book Reviews*

WEBMAGE

"The most enjoyable science fantasy book I've read in the last four years . . . Its blending of magic and coding is inspired . . . *WebMage* has all the qualities I look for in a book—a wonderfully subdued sense of humor, nonstop action, and romantic relief. It's a wonderful debut novel."

      —Christopher Stasheff, author of *Saint Vidicon to the Rescue*

"Inventive, irreverent, and fast-paced, strong on both action and humor."   —*The Green Man Review*

"[An] original and outstanding debut . . . McCullough handles his plot with unfailing invention, orchestrating a mixture of humor, philosophy, and programming insights that give new meaning to terms as commonplace as 'spell-checker' and [as] esoteric as 'programming in hex.' "   —*Publishers Weekly* (starred review)

"A unique first novel, this has a charming, fresh combination of mythological, magical, and computer elements . . . that will enchant many types of readers."   —*KLIATT*

"McCullough's first novel, written very much in the style of Roger Zelazny's classic Amber novels, is a rollicking combination of verbal humor, wild adventures, and just plain fun."   —*VOYA*

"Complex, well paced, highly creative, and, overall, an auspicious debut for McCullough . . . Well worth reading for fans of light fantasy."   —*Sci Fi Weekly*

"This fast-paced, action-packed yarn is a lot of fun . . . Weaving myth, magic, IT jargon . . . into a bang-up story."   —*Booklist*

"Kelly McCullough has the hacker ethic and the hacker mind-set down pat . . . The combination of mythos, magic, and technology is great fun."   —*Bewildering Stories*

"It has finally happened. Someone crossed the genres of sci-fi and fantasy to create a magical world that has modern (futuristic) computer hackers . . . McCullough has taken characters out from the darkness of mythology and brought them into the light of this modern digital age . . . Out-freaking-standing."

      —*Huntress Book Reviews*

CROSSED BLADES

Kelly McCullough

ACE BOOKS, NEW YORK

THE BERKLEY PUBLISHING GROUP
Published by the Penguin Group
Penguin Group (USA) Inc.
375 Hudson Street, New York, New York 10014, USA

Penguin Group (Canada), 90 Eglinton Avenue East, Suite 700, Toronto, Ontario M4P 2Y3, Canada (a division of Pearson Penguin Canada Inc.) • Penguin Books Ltd., 80 Strand, London WC2R 0RL, England • Penguin Group Ireland, 25 St. Stephen's Green, Dublin 2, Ireland (a division of Penguin Books Ltd.) • Penguin Group (Australia), 250 Camberwell Road, Camberwell, Victoria 3124, Australia (a division of Pearson Australia Group Pty. Ltd.) • Penguin Books India Pvt. Ltd., 11 Community Centre, Panchsheel Park, New Delhi—110 017, India • Penguin Group (NZ), 67 Apollo Drive, Rosedale, Auckland 0632, New Zealand (a division of Pearson New Zealand Ltd.) • Penguin Books (South Africa) (Pty.) Ltd., 24 Sturdee Avenue, Rosebank, Johannesburg 2196, South Africa

Penguin Books Ltd., Registered Offices: 80 Strand, London WC2R 0RL, England

CROSSED BLADES

An Ace Book / published by arrangement with the author

PUBLISHING HISTORY
Ace mass-market edition / December 2012

ISBN: 978-1-937007-84-3

ACE
Ace Books are published by The Berkley Publishing Group,
a division of Penguin Group (USA) Inc.,
375 Hudson Street, New York, New York 10014.
ACE and the "A" design are trademarks of Penguin Group (USA) Inc.

PRINTED IN THE UNITED STATES OF AMERICA

10 9 8 7 6 5 4 3 2 1

ALWAYS LEARNING   PEARSON

For Laura, simply because I love her.

And in memory of Lee Perish, friend, aunt, fan—
you will be missed.

Acknowledgments

Extra-special thanks are owed to Laura McCullough; Jack Byrne; Anne Sowards; my mapmaker, Matt Kuchta; Neil Gaiman for the loan of the dogs; and cover artist John Jude Palencar and cover designer Judith Lagerman, who have produced wonders for me.

Many thanks also to the active Wyrdsmiths: Lyda, Doug, Naomi, Bill, Eleanor, and Sean. My Web guru, Ben. Beta readers: Steph, Dave, Sari, Karl, Angie, Sean, Laura R., Matt, Mandy, April, Becky, Mike, Jason, Todd, Jonna, and Benjamin. My family: Carol, Paul and Jane, Lockwood and Darlene, Judy, Lee C., Kat, Jean, Lee P., and all the rest. My extended support structure: Bill and Nancy, Sara, James, Tom, Ann, Mike, Sandy, Marlann, and so many more. Lorraine, because she's fabulous. Jackie Kessler—she knows why. Also, a hearty woof for Cabal and Lola.

Penguin folks: Kat Sherbo, Anne Sowards's fabulous assistant; production editor Michelle Kasper; assistant production editor Jamie Snider; interior text designer Laura Corless; publicist Brad Brownson; and my copy editor, Mary Pell.

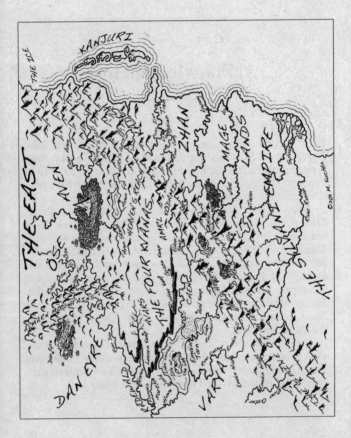

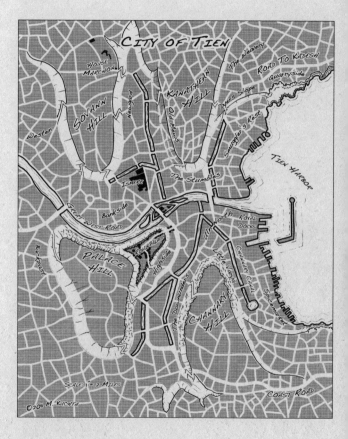

CITY OF TIEN

House Marchon

Sovann Hill

Westen

Kanathean Hill

The Weavery

Road to Kadesh

Wet's Slope

Quartyside

Newgard

Old Mews

Smuggler's Rest

Ismere

The Stumbles

Tien Harbor

Bankside

Great West Road

Hildrith

Royal Docks

Backrest

Palace Hill

Mauthen Palace

Highside

Channary Canal

Spicemarket

The Downrunners

Little Tien

Channary Hill

Coast Road

SCALE 1" = 2 MILES

© 2011 M. Kuchta

1

Today I saw a ghost in an old lover's eyes. I hadn't realized how much I would miss my face until the moment Jax looked at me and saw a stranger.

I was sitting in the Gryphon's Head, as I have so often in the past, and drinking too much whiskey—likewise. Only it wasn't my usual whiskey, and I wasn't my usual self. The bells of Shan had just sounded the sixth hour. The sun slanting in through the open windows of the tavern was still hot, but the first touch of evening had started to steal the worst fire of its bite. I'd taken a seat far from my usual table and ordered the Magelands whiskey instead of my favored Aveni to reinforce my recent loss of face.

I recognized Jax the instant she stepped into the Gryphon, though she had the sun behind her and shadow hid her face. First love is like that. It writes itself into your heart and your memory in letters that can never be erased.

Or can they?

The look Jax gave me when our eyes first met cut as deep as any sword could. Not for what it said, but for what it didn't. There was no recognition there, no hint of what had once been between Jax Seldansbane and Aral Kingslayer. No love and no loss, just the cold assessment of a professional killer sizing up a room for threats.

She gave me a single measured glance, alert for any trouble, then moved on when she didn't see it, just as I would have in her place. I should have expected that, should have remembered what I had become, but I hadn't, and that indifference from one I had once loved tore at me. I was invisible to her, a ghost in her eyes.

It's all right, Aral. Triss's familiar voice spoke directly into my mind, sweet and clear and wholly reassuring. *It's you who have forgotten your face, not Jax.*

As usual, my familiar was right. I felt a pressure on my shoulder like a friend's hand, squeezing briefly and then gone. I glanced at the shadow that stretched out behind me and gave it a wry smile. Him really. Triss is a Shade, a creature of living night. He lives in my shadow, quite literally.

Thanks, my friend, I sent back. *Even a month on, it's hard to remember what the bonewright did to my face.*

I reached up, rubbing a rueful hand down my cheek and across my chin. Not that different from my old face, really, not from the inside anyway, and not to my fingers. But I knew that no mirror would show me the face of Aral Kingslayer ever again, nor even the somewhat more haggard and haunted version that I'd worn for my years as Aral the jack. A *jack*, one of the underworld's all-purpose freelancers. Packages delivered, bodies guarded, the occasional contract theft. All in a day's work for that Aral, and oh what a very long fall from the days when the world had called me Kingslayer and the unjust had shivered when they thought of me.

I took another long pull on my whiskey, smoky and strong, just what I needed. Then, I reminded myself that my changed appearance was for the best, considering all the wanted posters showing my old face. I kept telling myself that, and until the instant Jax's eyes had passed me over unrecognized, I had mostly even pretended to believe me.

I've never had a particularly distinguished sort of face. Medium brown everything, from eyes to hair to skin. Not too pretty, not too ugly, the kind of face that's easy to ignore or forget. The masters and priests who raised me to be an assassin in the service of a goddess now dead had always told me it was one of my strongest assets.

My new face shared all the best aspects of my old face, improved on them even. I had deliberately reshaped skin and bone in a way that removed most of the markers of my native land, worked at making myself look like the product of a mixed heritage. It was the sort of face you might see in any of the eleven kingdoms of the East—never a native, but not a clear foreigner either. In so many ways it was the perfect face for what I had once been. Aral Kingslayer, Blade of Namara, the goddess of Justice. How ironic then that I put it on only after the murder of my goddess, her temple's destruction, and the death of all but a handful of my friends and fellows.

Easy. Triss squeezed my shoulder again—a shadow's touch—this time in warning. *Remember where we are and control yourself. They are hunting us still.*

Again, he was right. The Gryphon was a public place. One where I was known to have spent a good deal of time, before my second life as a jack of the shadow trades was exposed. Looking around the room, I could spy several tables worth of potential trouble. The place in the corner that I used to consider my regular spot, for example. A man and a woman sat there, both with their backs to the wall, both exhibiting the alert calm of the waiting hunter.

She was slender, tall, and long limbed yet muscular, and far from fragile. Ice blond hair and white skin marked her out as foreign, as did her hard blue eyes. Her quick precise movement made me think of some sort of giant praying mantis. The man was also tall, but broad where she was slender, with heavy muscles showing through the thin silk of his long-sleeved tunic. He was as dark as any of the locals, but the angles of his face and his thick black beard suggested a Kadeshi background, as did the short broad-bladed axes he had tucked into his sash.

He caught me looking at him and raised an eyebrow ever so slightly, touching one of his axes in a way that told me he thought I was a thief. I pretended to be intimidated, swallowing heavily before looking down into my drink, and he snorted and went back to talking to the woman. Trouble averted easily enough, but dammit, I shouldn't even be here. I should have walked away and found a different bar to haunt, a new place to start building myself a new identity to go with my new face. But I was deadly tired of running, and somehow I just couldn't walk away from the old me that easily. Not even the drunken wreck of a version that had earned his bread as a shadowside jack.

Which brought me back to Jax. We had grown up together at the great temple of Namara. She had entered the service of Justice a year after I did, barely four. A tiny girl with long dark hair, pale skin, and a winsome smile that had grown into a wicked one as the years transformed the girl into a beautiful young woman. Though she had never grown all that much in physical stature, she had more than made up for it with her skills as a sorceress and assassin in the service of Justice, coming third in our generation for the quality of her kills, after Siri and me.

Why had she chosen this moment to walk back into my life? I didn't make the foolish mistake of thinking her presence in the one place in all of Tien I was known to have frequented was any kind of coincidence. I also wondered where she had been hiding during the six years since the temple fell. Not in Zhan, I guessed by the lack of color to her skin. Nor anywhere else with brutal sun, unless she had become a creature wholly of the night.

Aven perhaps, or back home in Dalridia or the mountains of the Magelands. One of those, almost certainly. She would have had to hide someplace she could blend in, and someplace close enough that she could have reached Tien in four weeks or less. That ruled out Öse, Varya and Radewald.

The news that the Kingslayer had been unmasked would have flown fast and far on wings of magic. Everyone in the eleven kingdoms with any sort of governmental or shadowside connections would have heard *that* message within a week, two at most. Unless she wanted to spend a lot of money and draw the sorts of attention that one of our kind couldn't easily afford, Jax would have had to travel by more mundane means. No ship or horse could have brought her here from any farther afield so fast.

I knew that right after the fall Jax had spent time in the grip of the Hand of Heaven, the human instrument the gods had used to destroy the temple and Namara's worshippers. As the magical enforcement arm of Shan's archpriest, the Hand was known for its willingness to employ torture and the stake to achieve its aims. That, no doubt, explained the dozens of thin scars that threaded Jax's face and arms, white on white like fine lace on a marble table.

But where had she been since her escape? What had she been doing? Her clothes told me nothing. Like anyone both sane and in-purse who found themselves facing Tien in summer, Jax had opted for a vest and loose pants in the thinnest of silks—gray in this case. She had eschewed the more common sandals for light boots of the same sort that I wore for roof-running. The short, curved swords she wore in a double sheath on her right hip looked vaguely Dalridian in design, but they could have come from anywhere. No clues there. No clues anywhere really.

I wanted to go to her, to take her in my arms and tell her who I was and how very happy it made me to see her alive. But six years as a fugitive had taken its toll. I would wait and I would watch, and only when I was sure there was no trap would I make a move. Even then, caution must come before trust.

For several long minutes she chatted quietly with Jerik at the bar, obviously asking questions, though I couldn't make out specifics. He kept shaking his head no and shrugging, despite the fact that she flashed several heavy gold coins at him. Finally she seemed to give up, flipping her hair back with an angry snap of her neck that I'd seen too many times to count in the short, tumultuous year we had shared a bed. Without another word she stalked straight out the front door of the Gryphon.

It should have been funny watching hardened shadowside bonebreakers twice Jax's size getting quickly and prudently out of her way as she gave them *the look*. But she'd caught me so off guard with the suddenness of her departure that I barely had the leisure to notice. I was far too busy trying not to *appear* as though I was following her, when I knocked back my drink, and then rose to do just that.

What's the plan? Triss asked silently. *I thought we were going to take this slow.*

That was before she left so quickly. We have no way of knowing if she'll ever come back, and I want to know why she's here.

Point. How shall we play it?

Cross her shadow. Tell Sshayar to let Jax know to meet us somewhere private at midnight. Walk away.

It was an old Blade trick for passing secret messages one to another. Shades had a means of silent communication that would allow Triss and Sshayar to exchange basic information. Unfortunately, with the exception of my newfound ability to communicate with Triss, no Shade could bespeak their Blade companion mind-to-mind. That was another legacy of the magic that had reshaped my face, the breakthrough that allowed us to do what none of our kind ever had before: mindspeak. But it wasn't something that could be taught, so we would have to fall back on the older method of passing the message Shade to Shade for later verbal relay.

Great plan in theory. In practice . . .

I hate it when we do that, I thought at Triss. *Where the hell did she go?*

That way, replied Triss, unobtrusively nudging my right foot. *I can taste Sshayar's essence on the street, but only very faintly. She's hiding deep in Jax's shadow and the sun is strong today, burning away the traces of her passing. We'll have to move quickly if we want to keep track of her.*

Jax had been barely forty feet ahead of me leaving the bar, but by the time I got out the door, she'd vanished into the crowd. Some of that was simply height. At a hair under five feet, Jax stood a head shorter than the average citizen of Tien. Thousands of whom were out wandering the streets in search of dinner.

The Stumbles, where the Gryphon is located, is one of Tien's worst neighborhoods. The streets are narrow and poorly kept—there are cobbles down there somewhere, but you have to dig through a lot of filth to find them. At the moment it was hard even to see the filth beneath the swirling mass of people that filled the street.

As was so often the case with slums, the Stumbles was also one of the city's most heavily populated neighborhoods. The accommodations mostly varied from miserable to inadequate, but rooms and parts of rooms could be had for a few kips a day, and that meant that people who'd have been sleeping on the street in other parts of the city could put a door between themselves and the night while they slept. That meant a lot, especially in a place like the Stumbles.

As I threaded my way through the crowds, guided silently by Triss, I kept an eye out for Jax. But between her height and the fact that almost everyone in that poor neighborhood wore light browns and middling grays, I never caught sight of her. I did spy a half dozen pickpockets and cutpurses, and had to warn two of them off with a look when they got too close to me. That last was a shock. Another painful reminder of my lost face—people knew Aral the jack in the Stumbles and would have known better than to even consider picking his pocket— but they didn't know me.

No one knew me. Not the petty criminals, not Machim the beggar, nor Asleth the noodle vendor. No one. That should have made it easier for me to pass through the crowds, as people who would normally have wanted a piece of my time ignored me. It didn't. Aral the jack was a dangerous man, a drunk maybe, and down on his luck, but people knew to get out of his way. Nobody knew to get out of the way of . . . who?

I stopped in the middle of the street as the weight of that question hit me. Who was I, really?

Aral Kingslayer had died with his goddess. The man who wore that name had crawled into a bottle and not come out again. In his place a new Aral had emerged, Aral the drunk who had paid his bar bills by playing the shadowside jack. Doing things for money the earlier Aral would never have contemplated. Petty little illegalities, and all freelance, so that there was never a chance he'd owe any loyalty to anyone ever again. Never anyone he'd have to care about.

That had all changed a bit over a year ago when a woman named Maylien had found an echo of the old Kingslayer hiding under the skin of the jack.

For a little while I thought I'd found a new purpose in life, a new Aral who might have a chance at doing some good in the world again. That was the plan anyway. I'd even thought it was working, right up till the moment I realized how much of me I'd lost with my face. I didn't even have a name anymore. Not really. Not one I could wear in public. If your only name was a secret, was it even really a name?

Aral! Come on, we're losing Jax. Triss gave me a sharp slap on the side of my foot and I got moving again.

But I'd lost my hunger for the chase and I hardly even

blinked when we lost the trail as it left the narrow streets of
the Stumbles and plunged into the human river of Market
Street.

Fire and sun! Triss growled into my mind. *It's gone, and I
can't tell whether that's an effect of the sun or if Jax did something clever to break her trail.*

I found it very hard to care about the answer when what I
really wanted was to go back to the Gryphon and drink until
the world went away. I couldn't tell Triss that though, not with
the way he felt about my drinking. Instead I just stood and
stared at the passing parade, full as it was of walkers and riders,
carters and rickshaws, even the odd palanquin. Sandals and
boots and hooves and wheels, all of them grinding away at the
dust and dirt and . . .

Wait. Back up. Think, man!

There it was. So simple and elegant I had no idea why it
hadn't occurred to me before.

My guess would be she got into one of those. I pointed at a
passing oxcart. *If she made sure that her shadow didn't spill
over the edge of the bed, a cart would make a very good get-
away vehicle. That or one of those closed palanquins. Hell,
she could even have had a covered rickshaw waiting for her
here.*

I'm an idiot. Triss sounded shocked. *The idea of a shadow
trail is new enough to you that I can understand why you
wouldn't have thought of that before now. But, why didn't it
ever occur to me?*

*For the same reason it didn't occur to me, probably. Blink-
ered thinking. We both knew fire and sun and running water
can break a shadow's trail, so it didn't occur to either of us to
think beyond the big and flashy to simpler means.*

So now what? Triss asked me.

The Gryphon, I think. Maybe Jax will come back. Triss
didn't say anything, but I could feel his disapproval as he
thought about me having another drink. *I could also use some
dinner, and it's Jerik's cooking or go home where we'll have
to deal with Faran and Ssithra. . . .*

I guess one more whiskey won't kill you.

I thought you might see it my way.

Faran was almost sixteen and a problem and a half. She'd

been eight when the temple fell. A combination of talent, smarts, luck, and utter ruthlessness had allowed her to escape an attack that killed most of her peers and teachers. For six years she and her familiar, Ssithra, had lived completely on their own, spying and thieving their way across the eleven kingdoms to stay alive. Her last assignment had gotten away from her in a way that would probably have killed her if it hadn't also brought her to my doorstep. I'd had to abandon my old face as part of fixing that mess.

Now she'd become my . . . apprentice? Ward? Surrogate daughter? Faran and I were still working out the details of what we were to each other. So far, the process involved a lot of snarling and baring of teeth and I desperately wanted a little break before I faced the next round. Though Triss's relationship with Ssithra was harder to parse, the level of hissing in Shade that went on between the two of them suggested to me it wasn't any less fraught. In any case, the Gryphon sounded a hell of a lot more like home to me right at the moment than the rented house we shared with Faran and her familiar.

The Gryphon had started to fill up by the time I got back. Jerik just grunted and pointed me toward an empty seat at the end of the bar when I called out my order for whiskey and a bowl of fried noodles topped with shredded whatever-happened-to-fall-off-the-back-of-the-cart-today. His indifference stung a bit, since I was used to being treated like a regular. A few minutes later, he dropped off my bowl and a small loaf of black bread that I hadn't ordered along with my glass, then turned away before I could say anything about getting my order wrong.

I was tempted to throw the bread at his retreating back, but just sighed and took a sip of my whiskey instead. It tasted smooth and silky, like liquid magic. Kyle's eighteen, the special cask reserve if I knew my whiskeys. Nothing like what I'd ordered. As I paused before taking another drink, Jerik spun around to drop a beer in front of the smuggler sitting three stools to my right. I raised my glass ever so slightly in Jerik's direction as well as an eyebrow. Jerik responded with something that could have been the faintest ghost of a wink or perhaps nothing at all.

I took another sip. It was top shelf Kyle's all right, the spirit old Aral the jack had drunk whenever he felt deep enough in the pockets. Since I'd ordered nothing but Magelands whiskeys at the Gryphon since I changed my face, and the Kyle's wasn't sitting somewhere you'd get them confused, I had to figure the switch was intentional.

Which meant he'd recognized me, and wanted me to know it. I would have liked to believe that was impossible, but he'd been my landlord and bartender for five years and knew me as well as anyone in the city. It was hard to disguise a walk, and harder still if you were drunk.

But why was he letting me know about it now? To cover my confusion I took another sip of my excellent whiskey and then followed that with a mouthful of noodles. The hot pepper sauce almost covered the aging vintage of the fried bits of meat and vegetables. Almost.

I considered my bread then. Jerik makes a hard black loaf that will keep you alive for a long while if the effort of chewing it doesn't kill you first. It's cheap and awful, and over the years I've spent almost as much time living on it as I have avoiding it. This loaf looked more battered than most of its fellows, with several dents and dings and a wide crack splitting it nearly in half along one edge. Hmm. I jammed a thumb into the crack, then broke off a tiny corner of the loaf when I felt a bit of paper shoved deep into the bread.

As I was twisting the scrap of bread in my pepper sauce, Jerik slid back past me. "Tab?"

I nodded and he left. Jerik only runs a tab for serious regulars, and the face I was wearing now simply hadn't been around long enough. I suppose I shouldn't have been as surprised as I was that he'd recognized me.

Jerik's a damned clever man. He used to hunt monsters for a living, and mostly on crown lands, which adds dodging royal patrols to the list of dangers involved in the trade. The dumb die quick, and the smart can get rich if they live long enough. There's a good deal of money to be made by selling the bits off to various magical supply houses, and Jerik was at it long enough that he really didn't need to work for a living anymore.

He retired from the business after the gryphon he ultimately named his bar for ate about half of his scalp and one of his eyes. The scars are terrible and a good part of the reason he keeps the lights low, but I think he missed the thrill of it all. It wasn't too many years after he got mauled that he first opened the Gryphon's Head and nailed the damn thing's skull up behind the bar. I've always figured he bought an inn down here in the Stumbles among the shadowside players, when he could have afforded a better location, because he missed spending time around dangerous predators.

Despite a burning desire to read my little note right then and there, I knew better. Instead, I just nibbled another corner off my bread and took a long slow sip of the Kyle's. Golden, though I still missed efik. More now with the recent presence of another Blade to remind me of things left behind. Brewed or chewed, the effect of the beans was so much smoother than alcohol's. Of course, if I hadn't given it up I'd be dead by now. Or worse, a sleepwalker sitting in some alley and slicing my arms so I could rub powdered efik into the wounds for a bigger better ride to the place where nothing matters.

I pushed the thought aside. Thinking about efik made me want it, and that was the road to ruin. After I finished my noodles and carefully rationed out the rest of my Kyle's, I scooped up the loaf and headed out into the Gryphon's yard. I used to rent a room over the stables back there. Now, I took advantage of long familiarity to slip into the lower level and find an empty stall, before I cracked open my bread envelope.

By the time I'd gotten it split in half, Triss had defied the conventions that light normally enforced on shadows, by sliding up the wall to a place where he could read over my shoulder, and changing his shape. Most of the time, he pretends to be nothing more than light would make him, a darkened copy of my own human form. But when we're alone, he will often reshape his silhouette to assume the outline of a small dragon complete with wings and a tail. When he does that, he assumes some of the other aspects as well, and now I reached out to give him a light scruff behind the ears, where his scales always seem to itch.

He made a happy little noise at that, but then shrugged me off and jerked his chin at the tightly rolled piece of paper I held. *What's it say?*

Unrolling it revealed a folded sheet with a small blob of black wax sealing it. There was no imprint in the wax and no name on the outside of the letter, but magesight revealed the faintest glow of magic on the seal. I held it up to Triss and he reached out with one clawed finger and touched the seal. There was a hiss and the wax dissolved. I raised an eyebrow at Triss and he nodded. As I had expected, it responded only to the touch of a Shade. Any other attempt to open it would have resulted in the whole thing burning instantly away to ash.

I opened the letter. Inside it said: *Ashvik's tomb. Two hours past midnight. The anniversary of the day you broke my heart.* And that was all. No names. No signatures.

Clever, just a location, the time, and a date no one but I would know. The day I told Jax I wasn't going to marry her. The fifth of Firstgrain, one week in the future. The whole thing was smart, and I wondered how many of these she had handed out, hoping one would get to me. There had been six kings of Tien with the name Ashvik, and their tombs were scattered widely through the royal cemetery. Anyone who intercepted the message and didn't know it was intended for me would have to guess not only the date but which one was the intended meeting place. The tomb of Ashvik VI, the man who had died to give me the name Kingslayer.

2

My earliest memories are filled with darkness. When I entered the service of Namara at the age of four I stepped into the shadows.

From my very first day, I trained in the lightless depths below the temple, learning to operate without sight to guide me. By the time I turned seven I was at least as comfortable in utter blackness as I was in brightest day. Then I bonded with Triss, and a shadow became my closest friend.

Most people think of darkness as the simple absence of light, but we who share our lives with Triss's kind know that it can be a living presence. A Shade can take many forms. He can be a substanceless wraith hiding in the shadow of his bond-mate. He can command that same shadow, reshaping it to reflect his will, as Triss does when he assumes the form of a dragon or gives me claws to climb with. He can even become a thick cloud, like a black mist, and wrap his companion in a lacuna of darkness—the form Triss currently held.

The greatest advantage any Blade has is his familiar Shade. On the most basic level, the mage gift needs a familiar to act as a focus if it is going to function at all. A mage without a familiar who wants to cast a spell is in much the same position as a bird without wings who wants to fly. Beyond that, familiars shape the power of their bond-mates' magic. If you want to wield fire, it helps to have a salamander to back your play.

Then there's the power a familiar wields on its own. If you want to pass unseen in a world where any mage can see the glow of your invisibility spell, if not the person hiding within it, a familiar who can cloak you in shadow is the best bet going.

"Bide a moment," I whispered into the darkness that surrounded me.

"Why?" Faran's voice came from behind me, low and angry. "What are you worried I'm going to mess up this time?"

I wanted to bang my head on the rock face to my right. Instead, I released Triss from the dreaming state that allowed me to use his powers and senses as my own. It was possible to make use of the latter even when he was awake, but if I needed to use magic or shift the substance of his being around, I could do things *much* faster and more cleanly when I had direct control.

I replied, as calmly as I could manage, "I'm not concerned for you, Faran. I just want to look things over before we go in. It's been a long time since I tried to sneak past palace security."

"And I've been doing practically nothing else for the last few years. The Zhani variety doesn't look any worse than Kodamia's, at least not from up here. Why can't we just *do* this?"

"Because it's abysmal tradecraft," Triss said in a much sharper tone than I'd have used. "The target could be a lone shepherd asleep in the middle of an open field, and it would still be foolishness to charge in without thoroughly assessing the situation. Did you learn nothing from the masters at the temple?"

Faran let out a very noisy, very fifteen-year-old sigh, but she didn't argue. For some reason she took reprimands from Triss far better than she did the ones I gave her.

Thanks Triss. Could you uncover my eyes now?

If you wanted to see, you had to risk being seen. That was one of the first lessons a Blade learned. The enshrouding darkness a Shade could provide wasn't quite invisibility, though it came damned close in all but the brightest daylight. One of the few disadvantages was that while no one could see in, neither could I see out. Not with my eyes anyway.

The senses I could borrow from Triss when he surrounded me included a sort of otherworldly cousin to human sight, but it was so differently focused that even with years of training and practice it couldn't quite substitute for the real thing. It really paid to use my own eyes as a double check on what I was getting through my familiar.

Consider it done. Triss rearranged himself so that the shadows thinned away to nothing in front of my face, allowing me to look down on the night-wrapped city.

As so often happened when I got my sight back, the first thing I noticed was how beautiful the world could be. Immediately below me, the palace sparkled like a great triangular crown studded with a thousand jewels glowing in every color imaginable. Even at this hour, the magelights shone so thickly on the lanes and winding paths through the gardens that they almost erased the night in places. In the wealthy neighborhoods immediately beyond the palace to the east, the lights made a looser net, outlining the streets in ribbons of white and blue and bright green.

As you moved farther away, the effect took on something of the nature of a patchwork quilt. While richer areas made extensive use of magic's shining answer to the night, the bright hard points of magelighting became few and far between in poorer areas. Frequent thefts kept strapped neighborhood councils from using the expensive lights to illuminate their streets. But even in the true slums like the Downunders and the Stumbles there were lights. Small, dim, and too often the cheaper and more dangerous flickers of oil lamps or torches, but lights nonetheless.

What beauty the slum lights lacked in power they made up for with movement, flitting and flickering like ten thousand fireflies. When there were no streetlamps, people had to carry their own lights with them. Between the restless dead and the more common human predators, no one wanted to be without light. That necessity transformed static nets and ribbons of light into slow-moving streams where the sparks danced to the whims of the current and rippled with the wind. The lights of the city made a colorful contrast to the dimmer white stars in the lightly clouded sky above.

Regretfully, I pulled my focus back down onto the palace

complex below us. Faran and I perched on a narrow horizontal lip of stone, high up on the bare broken slope that stood behind and above the palace. In terms of a straight military assault this approach represented the palace's biggest weakness.

The top of the slope, which separated the spur of rock that held the palace compound from the taller Palace Hill behind it, lay a good fifty feet higher than the walls of the palace below. If you could get siege equipment up there you could bombard the compound with relative impunity. Of course, you'd have to fight your way through miles of one of the densest cities in the world to get there, and the royal family would long since have retreated to the island citadel or moved upriver to the great fortress of Kao-li.

The palace had been designed with the comfort and convenience of the Crown in mind rather than brute projection of power. The ruling family of Zhan had long preferred to keep their brass knuckles hidden inside elegant gloves. That didn't mean that defense of the palace was neglected completely, just that it was geared much more toward keeping out thieves, assassins, and the occasional peasant uprising. In the case of the back slope, that meant constantly burning off any vegetation that tried to gain a foothold among the rocks, and doubling the height of the wall.

Further protection was afforded by the fact that the slope was bounded on the upper edge by the extremely well-guarded estates of several of Zhan's greatest nobles including the Duchess of Tien. That was half of why I had chosen to come in this way. The combination of the massive rear wall and powerful neighbors who firmly supported the Crown meant the guards tended to pay less attention to this side of the compound.

Add in the fact that the royal cemetery stood tight against the wall—with many tombs actually burrowing down into the bedrock on which it stood—and you had one of the few places in the palace compound that a Blade could get inside with relative ease.

Which is exactly what we proceeded to do once I'd resumed control of Triss and his senses. Down the slope. Then wait for a gap in the guard patrols. Collapse the shroud to about half the optimum size. That freed up enough of Triss's substance to spin myself finger and toe claws out of hardened shadow.

Up the wall using cracks and crevices no unaided human could ever have hoped to find. Fully reshroud, and down the stairs from the battlements. Then up and over the low stone wall of the cemetery to drop into the shadows behind a free standing mausoleum, with every step mirrored perfectly by Faran and Ssithra.

"Told you it'd be easy," Faran said as we briefly settled against the dark granite wall of the tomb—the meeting wasn't supposed to happen for almost two hours yet, but I'd wanted to have plenty of time to scout and prepare the ground.

Triss's senses provided a full circle of view, so I didn't have to turn my head to look at Faran. Not that I could see her. Even a Shade's . . . call it unvision, couldn't see through the lacuna of another Shade. Faran and Ssithra simply registered as a deeper patch of shadow in a darkly shadowed world. Though the royal cemetery wasn't wholly devoid of illumination—each tomb had a small magical flame burning eternally on the altar on the right side of its door—it was one of the darker parts of the compound.

Still, I could imagine the smug look she now wore on that slightly too-angular face. Faran was going to be beautiful once she grew into her bones and put an adult's flesh on that lanky frame. Brown hair and eyes, skin a shade paler than my own, and nearing my own height. When people saw us together in the market they assumed she was my daughter.

"I never said that I expected it to be hard, Faran. Triss was absolutely right back there. A smart Blade practices caution even in the simplest of assignments, because it's the unexpected difficulties that will trip you up."

"With the exception of what happened with the Kothmerk, I've done all right for myself these last few years." She sounded defiant, edging into angry. "Certainly better than you have, playing the jack here in Tien's shadow world."

I sighed. The Kothmerk was a big exception and one that had led to three different governments all trying to kill Faran and Ssithra. But give Faran her due. "Yes, in many ways you have." After the fall of the temple she'd become a freelance spy, selling other people's secrets to the highest bidder. "Certainly you made more money in your years on your own than I have in my entire life." Which was why Faran was the one paying the rent on the small house where we lived on the skirts of the Kanathean Hill.

"Doesn't that bother you?" For the first time that evening she sounded like she was asking a question she didn't know the answer to.

"Not really. Before the death of the goddess I never cared about money. It was simply a tool the priests supplied me with when I needed it for a mission. Afterward, I didn't care about anything except for Triss and where my next drink was coming from."

I continued, "I don't know what all you went through when the temple fell, or in the days immediately after."

Faran didn't say anything. She'd been nine at the time, a child trained in the arts of killing and not much else. From the way that her eyes narrowed and she changed the subject every time it came up, I knew she'd suffered. But I hadn't ever pressed, and I wouldn't now. The world can be a very bad place for a lost child, especially a little girl. If she wanted to tell me about it she would.

"I only know what I went through," I said. "Almost everyone I'd ever cared about died that day along with my goddess and my faith. It hurt me that I wasn't there to die with them, that I was spared when so many I loved had died. With my goddess dead I wanted to die, too." Though he'd heard me talk about it before, I was still glad Triss was deep down in dream state for this conversation. It caused him a lot of pain when I spoke about it. "I'd probably have killed myself then if it wouldn't have killed Triss, too."

"That's why you started drinking, right? Because it eased the pain."

"That, and I rather hoped it would kill me, though I didn't even admit that to myself until quite recently."

Faran took a deep breath. "I got drunk once, maybe three weeks after the Son of Heaven's soldiers killed everyone. I knew the priests of Namara were against alcohol, but I'd run out of the efik I took with me when I ran away, and I didn't have anything else to dull the pain. And it hurt so very much to be me right then. I was hiding out in a charcoal burners' camp while I tried to figure out what I should do next. I stole a bottle of rum and I drank until I passed out."

Faran stopped speaking and there was a long silence, but I didn't think she was done, so I let it run.

"There was a man at the camp, older, kind. He'd been feeding me, though I had no way to pay for it. He found me there asleep and he touched me."

Faran made a tiny little choking noise, but then continued. "But not in a bad way, that would almost make what happened bearable. I was having a nightmare you see, about the soldiers at the temple and all the blood, and he was trying to wake me up. That's what Ssithra thought anyway. He was just trying to wake me up. I seized control of Ssithra and I tore out his throat with claws of shadow. I didn't mean to. I was still drunk and I was scared and . . . dammit!"

I heard the dull thud of a fist hitting a thigh, then there was another long silence.

"I'd never killed a man before," she finally said. "I had the opportunity several times when I was escaping from the temple. I could have slaughtered half a dozen of the people who killed my friends. I wanted to, but I was too afraid. I was too afraid I'd get caught and killed myself. I was too afraid that I'd do it wrong. But mostly, I was too afraid of what killing them would do to my heart. So, instead, I killed the first good person I met outside of the temple."

I didn't know what to say to that.

"It's almost funny how much that first death hurt me, when you consider how many I've killed since," she said after a moment.

"I'm sorry, Faran. I . . . just . . . I'm sorry."

"It's not your fault, Aral, nor any of the Masters, though you all made me what I am. I blame the man who calls himself the Son of Heaven. He's the one who sent the soldiers who drove me out into the world before I was ready, and someday I'm going to kill him for it."

While I sincerely hoped she got that chance, a sudden feeling of presence from somewhere off to our left kept me from saying anything about it. Instead, I just leaned in close and extended my shroud to overlap Faran's—a long established warning signal among Blades—so that she would know something was up.

I'm not sure what it was that aroused my suspicions.

Certainly nothing so blatant as a scuffing sound or a change in the light, but I felt certain we were no longer alone. Reaching through the shadows that separated us, I found Faran's shoulder and squeezed it once, before pressing gently to let her know which direction I wanted her to go.

Moving with all the exquisite caution that my years of training and experience could bring to bear, I rose and started moving toward that feeling of presence. Through Triss's senses I could see the deeper patch of shadow that was Faran and Ssithra vanishing around the back of the tomb behind me, following my signal. When I got to the front edge of the tomb, I stopped and spent a long couple of minutes doing a slow scan of the area.

I focused all of my senses as well as Triss's on the task, devoting a part of my attention to each sense in turn, as well as to the collective picture they painted. Touch was nearly useless at the moment, telling me little more than the hang of my clothes and gear or the way the carefully manicured lawns pressed into the thin soles of my boots. What it did give me was the direction of the faint and fading sea breeze—about a quarter turn to the right of directly into my face. And that led to smell.

Most of the news my nose brought me had to do with things rotting in the harbor and several hundred thousand people packed tightly together in the late summer heat. Underneath it all though was a strange and subtle touch like a ghost from some spice markets past. I rolled my tongue, trying to bring up the memory of a taste, but couldn't quite establish it.

Hearing brought me a much more densely layered picture. Farthest and faintest I heard the sounds of the city proper, muted now while most of her denizens slept, but still there in the occasional scream or deep bellow. Closer in, the palace noises carried more nuance; the scuff of a guard's boot on the wall above, a low moan that suggested an assignation in the shadows behind a convenient hedge, the metallic click of a groundskeeper's shears as they tried to fulfill the impossible charge of keeping things perfect, while never getting in the way of their betters. Nearer still came the faint tinkling of the tiny fountains on the left side of each tomb's door, balancing the altar fires on the right—part of the traditional display of the elements signifying that the very stuff of nature mourned the passing of each of Tien's rulers.

The final piece of my collage view of the world came from Triss. Shades "see" in full round. They use a sense organ we don't even have a name for, to pick up on changes in the texture of darkness in every direction. Bats "see" with their ears, screaming and listening for the echoes, or that's what I was taught anyway. What Shades do is closer to that than any human sense, but it's a passive process, with the dark-echoes provided by the interplay of light and shadow.

Each individual shadow takes on a sort of depth that isn't quite color, but still possesses all the subtle shading of that palette. Where my own eyes might have perceived a simple block shadow where the edge of the tomb across the way cut off the light from several altar fires, I now registered a whole gradient of shadow flavors. It gave me an extremely precise sense of things, like the way the three magical tomb-fires that cast the bulk of that shadow sat, and how their intensity varied over distance and with the flickering of the flame.

No single part of my mosaic of the senses was enough to give me what I needed, but together . . . together was a different thing entirely. As I moved deeper into the graveyard, flitting from shadow to shadow, I followed my nose and that faintest hint of exotic spices until a change in the quality of the light drew my attention to a particularly tall tomb. There, the flames burned a little brighter in the reflection off a couple of faint scuff marks where the moss on the fountain had been displaced. Moving around the back, I put an ear to the wall and waited . . . there, the quietest of grating sounds came through the stone. Unless the tomb's primary inhabitant was moving about, there was a lurker on the rooftop.

I squatted down to make an even smaller target and released my hold on Triss's will. *Wake up, my friend. We've got company of an unexpected nature.*

As I filled him in on what I'd learned so far I double-checked all of my gear. The pair of short straight swords I wore on my back in a custom built hip-draw rig hung light and loose. All I needed to do to release either of them was pop the catch with a thumb and let the blade drop a few inches to free the tip. Wrist and boot daggers were likewise properly aligned and ready to go, as was my little bag of tricks.

Who do you think it is? Triss silently asked me when I had finished both narrative and preparations.

I can't say for sure, but I've got a suspicion. It's the spice scent. I've only ever smelled it secondhand myself, but Master Kelos mentioned once that some of the Hand of Heaven's sorcerer-priests use a special ritual soap. It's supposed to help keep them pure in the face of the corrupt world out here beyond Heaven's Reach.

Triss let out an angry mental hiss when I mentioned a possible Hand presence. *Should I slide up and take a look? Maybe tear out a throat while I'm at it?*

Much as I'd love to let you, I don't think we can risk it yet. If there's one finger of Heaven's Hand trying to push the scales down here, you can bet there are more close by. Killing this one could all too easily alert the others.

Point. So, what's the plan?

Finish scouting. If it is the Hand, I want to know how many more of them are around and where they are before I make a move. I just wish we had some way to warn Faran. She's damn good, but the Hand are the people who destroyed the temple. They've killed a lot of Blades.

Faran and Ssithra survived then, they'll be all right now. When she's playing it smart that girl is one of the most promising young assassins I've ever seen.

And if she's not playing it smart?

Triss just hissed. Faran was good, but also ruthless and prone to kill first and worry about the consequences later. And she *hated* the Hand. It was a bad combination, but we couldn't do anything about it without giving ourselves away. Not for the first time, I wished that my kind had better methods of communication. But our powers simply didn't work that way, which was part of why Blades had always worked solo far more often than in concert.

What if it's not *the Hand?* asked Triss.

It would still be nice to know if there are more of them around before we start slitting throats. Either way, we'll have to come back and pay a quiet visit on our friend up there before we head down to meet Jax. What do you want to bet that roof-top has a clear view of Ashvik's tomb?

You know it does. Triss sent back, and there was a strong undertone of anger to his mind voice. He didn't like the way this was going any more than I did.

I'd rather say that I'm sure that it does, but yes, I agree with you. Somebody set us up. The question is who and why. I have a hard time imagining Jax doing something like that, but two years ago, I'd have told you Devin would never turn away from the order or our friendship either. Look where trust got me there. My best friend's betrayal of everything I'd ever held dear was a wound that would never stop bleeding.

I took control of Triss again and went hunting. But while I did verify the sight lines to Ashvik's tomb and my meeting place with Jax, I didn't turn up any more signs of watchers on the tomb-tops over the next twenty minutes. Nor anyone else for that matter. Whether that was because my first target's companions were that much better at concealing their presence, or because there was only the one, I couldn't say. Process of elimination wasn't much help either, there were just too damn many tombs with good sight lines for our meeting point.

I had circled most of the way back around to my starting point, so that I could make sure of my original target and that I hadn't hallucinated my initial impressions, when I crossed a Blade's shadow trail heading toward Ashvik's tomb. Two actu-ally. Bringing Faran into my life had given me the opportunity to use my borrowed senses to focus on what was—for me—a newfound Shade skill, as we practiced trailing each other around the city.

But I wasn't yet good enough at parsing the nuances of Triss's shadow-tasting ability on my own to identify these traces fully, or tell which came first or how far apart in time the two had been made. I was pretty sure one at least belonged to Faran, and I guessed the second was Jax, but I had to call up Triss to verify my assumptions.

Faran and Ssithra, with Jax and Sshayar trailing along behind—probably following the youngsters, though there's no way to be sure, Triss opined.

I still didn't know what Jax might be up to, but the fact that she was on Faran's trail worried me. Doubly so in light of our unexpected guest on top of the tomb, which meant it was time to make a ghost of the latter. This was going to be that very rare kill that I could truly take pleasure in. After what the Son of Heaven's people had done to mine, I felt not the slightest bit of pity for any of them. I planned my approach as I hurried back toward the tall mausoleum.

I was nearly there when a rather sharp darkening of the skies above drew my attention. Great reefs of cloud began to form in the skies above, blotting out the stars, while the wind from the sea kicked up sharply, cooling the steamy air over the city and bringing with it the lightning-burned air smell that always came with the truly brutal thunderstorms. If I was any judge, we were all going to get very wet before the night's business got much further along.

It might just have been the weather shifting with that shocking speed you sometimes get in coastal areas, but I made a dash for the tomb at that point because of the other possibility. The elementals most commonly known as the Storms or the Heavenly Host. They took a myriad of shapes, lightning bladed swords, lucent wheels, whirling cones of darkness, but they all shared two features. They all had dense wings of cloud, and they only ever companioned the priests of the Hand.

The polished black granite blocks of the tombs were tightly fitted with no finger or toeholds. I could still have climbed the back or side walls of one if I reduced my shroud. But I thought it better to keep it at maximum extension under the circumstances, so I took the same route the Hand had: fountain, doorframe, entablature, lip of the roof.

I chinned myself on the edge at that point, peering across the flat top of the tomb before moving forward. My target was right where I had expected her to be, kneeling in the shadow of the low wall that encircled the rooftop, and she was indeed a member of the Hand.

There was nothing particularly distinguishing about the loose dark robes the slight figure wore. Nor the long spell-lit rod she held like a crossbow, braced on the wall and sighted in on the front of Ashvik's tomb in the distance. But the cord holding her ponytail in place was tied with the ritual knot of those who served the Son of Heaven, and she had a Storm at her side.

This one took the form of a huge gemstone, like a star sapphire with wings the exact green of the swirling clouds that gave birth to whirlwinds. It was of middling size for the breed, with a central body maybe three handspans wide by five long. Its wings were furled at the moment and most of it lay concealed below the level of the parapet.

That would slow the thing down if it spotted me before I could kill its master, which was good since I didn't know how well my shroud would hide me from it. It had no eyes and no obvious way for me to tell which direction it was facing, but I knew from my training that its most important senses belonged to a family other than sight anyway. A creature of sky and storm, it relied primarily on the movement of air currents to bring it information.

I was downwind, which would help conceal me, and was another reason I'd chosen to come in from the direction I had. But I didn't honestly know whether that would be enough. Silently, I slipped over the edge of the parapet and started toward the Hand.

That's when I heard Jax's voice, low but clear and sounding far too close. "Aral, is that you?"

Reflex put my hands on my swords as I shifted my attention from the Hand's back to focus my unvision beyond her to Ashvik's tomb. Jax stood there, silhouetted by the altar flames just to the right of the door, her shroud lowered to pool around her feet. Dammit! What was she thinking?

With a flick and a twist I released my swords. Dropping them down and around to point at the roof just in front and to the outsides of my smallest toes. That kept them within my shroud but ready to use on the instant.

Jax spoke again, and I realized that the Storm must be picking up noises from the area of the tomb and making them louder somehow, or I could never have heard her that clearly. "I see a Shade there," she said. "Just beyond the fountain and—"

I never got a chance to hear what Jax would have said next. As the Hand in front of me started to shift her aim toward the place Jax had indicated, a slender lance of brilliant white light speared out from somewhere off to my right. It punched a neat hole through Jax's left side before it carved a deep pit in the granite face of Ashvik's tomb.

3

———◆———

Love may burn away to ashes, but it never lets us go. Despite all the years and all the pain that lay between us, it felt like I'd taken an arrow in the chest when Jax let out a quiet little cry and crumpled to the ground.

The sapphire Storm snapped its wings then, popping straight up into the air before diving toward Jax, and Ashvik's tomb. That was an opening I'd never expected, and I leaped forward to take advantage of it. But even as I moved, the Hand whispered a word of power.

The long rod she cradled in her arms flared and sparked in my magesight, briefly surrounding itself with a blazing azure halo. As I brought my right-hand sword around in a beheading stroke, the rod spat forth a lance of fierce white light, like lightning smoothed and shaped into the form of a bright spear.

In the distance I heard Faran's familiar voice yelp and say, "Motherfucker!" And then, "Somebody's gonna die for that."

I continued forward. Blood fountained from the Hand's neck as her head fell free, bouncing off the lip of the low wall before dropping to the grass below. It splashed my left leg, hot and sticky, as I leaped past her slumping body and put one foot on the parapet before launching myself out into the darkness beyond.

A giant flash of lightning ripped the air between me and the tomb, temporarily blinding my unvision in midleap. The death spasm of my target's familiar as its life spilled away with its master's. It left a brutally painful afterimage burned into my borrowed senses; like a splintered crack in the very stuff of the universe. With no other choice, I tore aside the veil of shadow in front of my eyes so that I could see the ground.

I touched down briefly on the balls of my feet before letting my knees go loose as I collapsed into a forward roll to bleed off some of the speed of my fall. Holding onto a pair of drawn swords added a significant element of risk to the maneuver, but with at least one more priest of the Hand about, I didn't dare let them go. Fortunately, the turf of the royal cemetery was deep and exquisitely tended. Instead of the badly ripped up knuckles and separated shoulder I half expected, I came back to my feet with little more than grass cuts and a few fresh bruises.

I'd taken barely two steps when a lance of white light speared past my head. The smell of burning hair filled my nostrils and I felt Triss shriek in his dreams as the light tore a hole in his substance. I threw myself sidewise into a cartwheel that cost me my left-hand sword when it stuck deep in the earth and I was forced to let it go.

More lightning hammered down from the sky, half blinding my mortal eyes at the same time that it burned away my returning unvision for a second time. Another cartwheel put the edge of a tomb between me and the source of the white beams— another Hand obviously. This one more powerful by far than the one I'd killed.

"Faran!" I yelled. "Get Jax clear!"

Then I turned and dashed along the wall of the tomb, sheathing my remaining sword as I went, to free my hands. The bastard clearly knew where I was, shroud or not. I needed to make my next move fast. I was just getting ready to dive into another roll when shouts came from the compound wall above, and the palace alarm bells began to ring. Not unexpected, but damned inconvenient. I froze for a moment. Go back to help Faran with Jax? Or ghost the remaining Hand and clear the field of at least one of the opposing forces?

That's when the wet hand of a god smashed me back against the wall of the tomb. Rain and wind as I had never even imagined them wiped away vision and unvision alike, blinding me utterly even as they deafened and washed away all scent, leaving only touch and memory to guide me. I turned back the way I had come, abandoning any hope of finding the priest as I dropped my shroud and my control over Triss.

He let out a series of sharp hisses, swearing in Shade as he awoke. *Fire and sun but that hurts. What happened? It feels like I had a starshine chewing on my left wing.* I couldn't see Triss in the darkness, but I imagined him stretching out on the wall beside me, obviously wincing as he extended his wings.

One of the Hand clipped you with some kind of tightly focused lightning blast or something, but we don't have time to go into it or go after him. We need to find our way to Ashvik's tomb. I pointed in the direction I'd last seen Jax. *I'm utterly blind in this, the alarms are going off, and the Crown Elite are certainly on their way.*

The Elite were warrior mages whose stone dog companions could swim through earth like a fish through water. The storm wouldn't even slow them down, and we had minutes at best to get clear of the area before they arrived along with several hundred of the less magical but more numerous Crown Guard.

Go.

Trusting Triss to guide me, I began to lope in the direction I hoped was the right one, moving quickly, though I had to bend nearly double to fight the wildly shifting patterns of the buffeting winds. Through our bond, I felt my shadow stretch out ahead of me, spreading himself thin as he searched out the path. I hated to go unshrouded like this, but I didn't have a choice.

Stop, Triss mindspoke. *Bend over, your sword's a few inches to the left of your forward foot.*

I reached out a hand and found the blade. I cut my finger in my hurry as I slid it along the wet steel, searching for the hilt in the still blinding downpour. As soon as I had a grip I started moving again. Faster now, as Triss spoke directions into the silence of my mind.

Left a bit, or you'll hit a tomb. You've a free twenty yards in front of you, go. Watch out, there's a divot here where the

*gardeners missed a slink's burrow, jump. There, just ahead is
the line of the cliff where Ashvik's tomb lies. Let me slide left
and right to find the way . . . got it! Jax is gone, but there's a
shadow trail.*

Lead on.

We caught up with Faran and the unconscious Jax atop a
long low tomb built half into the wall of the bluff.

"Faran," I called, "I'm coming up, try not to stab me."

I dragged myself up beside them, fighting against the teeth
of the wind all the way. Jax lay in a heap on her side, her face
pillowed on her limp arm—presumably to keep her from
drowning in the rapidly puddling water that was overwhelming
the drains in the low parapet.

"She's alive?" I asked.

"Barely," replied Ssithra, invisible in the darkness. "The
lightning lance pierced the bottom of her lung. Sshayar is very
worried. We need to get her someplace warm and dry."

"First, we need to get the fuck out of the palace compound
before the stone dogs show up," I said.

"That's why we're up here," said Faran. "I thought they
might have more trouble spying us out through the elemental
muddle of the tomb."

"Good thinking," said Triss.

It was, too. The stone dogs were creatures of earth with
powers of and over their element. The Zhani custom of invok-
ing all the elements to honor their fallen mighty created a
multielemental barrier between the earth under the foundations
of their tombs and the air above. Fire and water came in the
shape of the altar flame and the fountain; air and shadow surrounded the bier where the embalmed bodies lay in their sar-
cophagi within their tombs. Of the six great elements only light
was not included separately, though light's great ally, fire, made
sure it was not totally excluded. A stone dog would have to be
right underneath us to sense us through all that, an all too likely
circumstance if we didn't get out of there fast.

"Sshayar," I said. "It's Aral. I have to get Jax out of here
unless moving her will kill her."

"You do not look as I remember you, but there's no mistaking Triss." A barely visible patch of darkness lifted itself up
from Jax's side and I knew from long experience that I now

faced a shadow tiger, its stripes formed by subtle difference of shading and texture—Sshayar. "It's good to see you both alive after so many years when we had feared you dead. Do what you have to do, I will see to Jax's wounds. They aren't nearly so bad as I first believed, but I still need to pack them with cool shadows if they are to heal as quickly as possible."

Then the shadow collapsed, falling back down to wrap itself tightly around her stricken mistress. I bent and lifted Jax onto my shoulders, glad of how tiny she was. With her wounds, I would have preferred to cradle her like an infant, but that would have left me defenseless. None of us could afford that.

"Faran, you're going to have to lead the way back to the wall and over." I opened my trick bag and started digging for a couple of leather straps to bind Jax in place. "Kill anyone who gets in the way."

"Of course," she said, and a feral smile flashed briefly in the rain. "I've already ghosted my first ever priest of the Hand tonight—I think that's when the storm started. It sure as hell got worse when you killed that second one. Maybe I'll get lucky and bag a third to give us a triad. Let me just make sure the first stage is clear. I'll have Ssithra signal you when I'm ready." She dropped over the edge of the tomb and vanished in the dark and the rain.

I'd barely gotten Jax fastened in place when Triss spoke into my mind. *Faran says to follow now and hurry. She doesn't want to get too far ahead of us in case a stone dog comes up from below.*

That was a sentiment I could heartily support, though the steady worsening of the storm helped us there. The brutal pounding of the earth by wind and rain—or water and air, if you preferred to think in magical terms—would do much to cover both our passing and our trail. It made an unanticipated but welcome secondary payoff for eliminating the two Hands and their companion Storms.

I nearly sprained an ankle jumping down from the tomb with Jax on my shoulders, and had to drop to one knee to prevent it. Forcing myself back upright I pushed on into the storm, with Triss whispering words of encouragement and guidance into my mind. Even with all of her gear, Jax couldn't have weighed much more than a hundred pounds. But a hundred pounds gets heavy fast when you're jogging along with it on your shoulders in a giant thunderstorm.

By the time we reached the low wall separating the cemetery from the palace gardens, I was sweating despite the cold rain. Climbing up that wall with Jax on my shoulders made me feel about twice my age, as did climbing back down the other side. I normally would have jumped, but I'd learned my lesson there.

Maybe fifteen feet on, Triss had me edge over against the palace compound's outer wall to avoid tripping on the bodies of a pair of fallen Crown Guards Faran had slain. They lay at the base of the stairs leading up to the ramparts. By luck or fate or Faran's skill, those were the only agents of the Crown that I encountered. The first pellets of hail started hammering down around me soon thereafter, stinging when they hit scalp or skin.

Faran was waiting for me at the great tower that marked the corner where the wall bent sharply to the northeast, as it followed the spur of rock that footed the compound, a denser shadow in the murk of the storm. "You sure you still want to go out this way?" She'd already slung a rope over the outside wall.

"No," I replied, "but I don't think we've got a good alternative."

I glanced over the edge. Somewhere down there in the darkness was the river Zien. The plan had always been to make our exit via the Zien, though I'd originally expected to sail-jump off the wall and glide down to the river on shadow wings. The running water was supposed to do double duty, helping us to shake off any possible pursuit by the Elite and their stone dogs as well as breaking our shadow trail in case Jax had taken up with Devin and the other rogue Blades. Now . . .

"There's no way she can swim like this," said Faran.

"No," agreed Sshayar, speaking up for the first time since the tomb, "but I can keep her face out of the water and cover her nose and mouth when needed if you can tow her along behind."

"I still don't know," said Faran.

"I suppose we could—"

"Stone dog!" yelled Ssithra, cutting me off. "Coming up through the wall. Go!"

Dammit!

I leaped up onto the nearest crenellation and jumped outward, spreading my arms as I cleared the wall. It was that or face a stone dog biting and clawing at me through the stones while I tried to climb down a wet rope in a thunderstorm. Triss spun himself into great dark wings, extending outward from my arms. It was only the second time I'd ever attempted a sail-jump while carrying a passenger—a dangerous proposition—though at least I was able to use my arms to reinforce my wings this time.

As I glided clear of the palace wall, I heard a faint roaring coming from below and realized it must be the river, angry with all the water pouring down off the hills of the city. Again I regretted the necessity that drove us to this escape route.

Fresh lightning splintered the air less than a spear's throw in front of me. I was still blinking away the afterimages when the lightning came again, closer. This time it very nearly struck Faran, who let out a startled yelp, followed by swearing.

"Fucking Storm!"

It wasn't until the next bolt fell between us and I saw the cloud-winged scythe, hovering above like some blade-headed ibis, that I realized Faran had spoken of the elemental rather than the elements. The last Hand must have set their familiar to hunt for us, and when we entered the heart of its domain it had found us. Much easier here, since sail-jumping kept us from shrouding up—there simply wasn't enough Shade to manage both sail and shroud. More lightning fell around us and Faran folded her wings, dropping away into the roaring murk below.

Hoping that we had cleared the riverbank I mindspoke Triss, *Let us fall, it's our only hope of shaking the damned thing off.* Then we, too, plunged into darkness.

We fell perhaps forty feet before the snarling of the river filled the world and the waters swallowed us up. We plunged deep, cutting straight through the icy surface currents generated by the storm into the blood-warm waters washing off the sun-bitten plains beyond the city. Slowing but still moving down, we passed into the cool shadowed depths the sun never warmed,

coming to a stop only when my feet hit the bedrock beneath
the half yard of muck that floored the great river. I felt the
impact all the way up to my teeth, but pushed off again immediately.

Having Jax across my shoulders ruined my swimming
stroke, making it all but impossible to control my motion. The
wild flood currents tumbled and torqued me around until I lost
all sense of direction. If not for Triss's constant tugs and nudges
guiding me in the right direction I would never have found my
way back to the air. As my head broke through the foam-frothed
surface, I felt Sshayar cut the ties that held Jax to my shoulders
and briefly panicked at the thought of losing her in this madness.
I twisted wildly, trying to catch her as she slipped free.

It's all right, soothed Triss. *Sshayar and I have her. You
just worry about getting us out of the river in as few pieces as
possible.*

Then Sshayar looped some of her substance around my chest
and shoulders, snugging Jax in tight against my back like a
trader's pack.

I nodded my thanks. *Triss, can you see Faran at all?*

In this? Are you crazed?

Point.

Between the winds, the rain, the hail, and the whirling
masses of flotsam and jetsam that the storm had swept off of
the streets and out of the sewers, the normally placid river had
become a wave-wracked demon.

Most of the floating debris fell into the repulsive but harm-
less category of dead dogs and human waste, but there were
bigger and more dangerous items to be avoided as well, like a
jagged-edged broken cartwheel that nearly impaled me. I'd
only been in the water a couple of minutes and I was already
exhausted. The cold and the extra weight of Jax made for a
punishing combination as I fought toward shore.

The huge stone pier came at me so fast I didn't even have
time to try to avoid it. I just threw my arm across my face and
hoped for the best. A big eddy caught me at the last possible
second and twisted me around and down, briefly sucking me
under before it spat me out again beneath the bridge where the
growling of the sharply narrowed waters echoed and reechoed
like an angry dragon.

It wasn't until the current spat me out the other side that I realized I'd just passed the foundations of the Sanjin Island bridge. I'd covered half of the distance from the north side of the palace to the bay, well over a mile, and faster than a galloping horse. I needed to get out of the water fast if I didn't want to end up swimming home from Kanjuri with my ex strapped to my back. Actually, that sounded an awful lot like some Kadeshi vision of hell. But no matter how hard I swam across the current I couldn't seem to get any closer to shore. Not compared to how fast I was heading for the bay. I started to worry more and more about which way the tide was running. If it was in we had a decent chance of making one of the piers. If it was out . . .

I think we may be well and truly fucked, my friend, I sent to Triss. *Unless you've got something?*

I don't know, replied Triss. *I'm doing what I can to keep us afloat, but this isn't my element and the effort's draining me, especially after that hit I took from the Hand.*

A few moments later I started tasting salt in the water. I also had my first cramp threatening—my left calf where the scars I'd picked up along with the name Kingslayer ran deep.

It seems almost funny, I sent.

What does? Triss's mind voice sounded weary and worried.

Between the Son of Heaven and the King of Zhan the price on my head's over sixty thousand gold riels, enough to buy a palace with all the trimmings. That's without mentioning all the other folks who'd pay to see me dead, and you with me. Or Jax and Sshayar for that matter. Literal armies of people have worked to kill us all, and here it's going to be a storm that does the deed.

We're not going to die here, Sshayar and I can keep us all afloat for quite a while. The words sounded confident, but the mental voice behind them came through weak and thready.

It doesn't have to be drowning. This water is cold, and there's always exposure. Beyond that there's sharks, sea serpents. . . . My mind was starting to drift. Very bad sign. *I just hope we wash up where someone who really deserves the money can find the bodies.*

Stop that!

What? Triss sounded madder than he had since the last time I went on a bender. Speaking of which, I could really use a drink. *Kyle's. That's what I want right now, a big glass of Kyle's. Or better yet, a hot pot of efik or a couple of beans . . .*

Namara-dammit, Aral!

That cut through the fog. In our nearly twenty-five years together I'd never heard Triss use the name of our goddess to swear. I realized that I'd stopped swimming somewhere along the line and was just idly treading water as the swells rolling in from the deep water rocked me up and down.

You're better than this, Aral. Come on, don't give up on me.

Sorry, Triss, I'll try.

I dunked my face to clear out the cobwebs. Somewhere along the line we'd transitioned from salty river water to actual saltwater. The water had warmed a little, too. Not enough to stop it from killing me, but enough to slow it down. The hail had tapered off as well. I thought about Faran then and worried, but survival had to come first.

Shadow me up, Triss, I want to use your eyes and I need to try a bit of magic.

I won't be able to help keep you afloat. . . .

It won't be long, and out here in the bay—I hoped I was still in the bay—*the saltwater will help. Do it fast though, I don't know how long I can stay focused.*

I could tell he wanted to question and argue, but all he said was, *I trust you.*

We settled in the water as Triss went incorporeal and stopped pushing from below, but Jax's head stayed above the surface. Then I felt him sort of sink into my skin along the interface between us, and slowly spread outward from there.

Normally it felt a bit like someone wrapping me, head to toe, in tight silk, cold and sleek and vaguely sexy. This time it burned like sealing wax straight from the edge of the flame. He trickled his way along my skin under my clothes. Whether I had gotten so cold that Triss felt hot, or the nerves in my skin had just taken so much abuse that ice and fire met in the middle now, I couldn't say.

I welcomed the sensation, any sensation. My mind was drifting and unseated, and the pain would help keep me in my head. Even the most minor sort of magic requires intense focus and real energy, and I had very little of either left to give. The well of my soul was nearly drained.

That meant it was time to place my final bet, and it was a long shot. I had no prepared spells for something like this, no long practiced tricks to fall back on, just my entirely inadequate magical skills. Unlike some of my peers, I'd always preferred the sword and the shadow to the word and the wand. I was going to have to improvise and that's why I had Triss playing second skin.

Blade magic of any high order worked best when it was guided by a single will and executed within a cloak of shadow. We had now reached the point where I'd normally have centered myself with deep breathing and an attempt to wipe away all my cares. Instead, I just yanked out the long dagger that hung at my right hip and balanced it on the palm of my hand.

I picked the dagger because it had a teak grip as opposed to the slimmer knives at wrist and ankle with their simple leather-wrapped metal hilts. I wanted maximum sympathy. Focusing what little nima I had left, I strengthened and thickened the shadows on my palm. The dagger lifted free of my hand, floating within a ball of liquid darkness, as I pictured a lodestone seeking a mate.

The dagger slowly rotated widdershins until it pointed toward me and Jax and our sheathed swords—wood and steel together, and not unexpected. I shaped that finding into my working, made it a part of the sympathetic structure of my spell. The dagger's point slid away from my chest, continuing to rotate slowly leftward until it had made a full circle. Another. I had to use my other hand to brace the raised one to keep it from shaking as both physical and magical reserves started to fail me. A third rotation. I couldn't do this much longer.

The fourth round began and I didn't think I'd be able to manage a fifth. The dagger bobbled. Stopped. Rotated back the other way an inch or two and froze. It was pointing somewhere ahead and to my right. If I'd done everything right there would be a ship lying along that line. If I was also lucky, it would be close, and lying at anchor instead of drifting with the tides. If I wasn't lucky we were all dead. I released Triss and the dagger sank back down to rest on my palm.

Do you think you can keep us pointed in that direction? I asked.

I can try.

Good. I dropped the dagger and let it sink because I didn't want to waste the time to put it away.

Is there a ship there?

I sure hope so.

4

—•≫•+•≪•—

Pain is a hone. Give it a chance and it will keep grinding till there's nothing left but dust, but properly wielded it can create the sharpest of edges. I was starting to feel awfully gritty.

Every stroke of my arms or kick of my legs grated like stone rasping on stone and I knew that if I stopped I'd never start again. I'd been swimming a quarter hour at the most, but the rain and the cold and bearing the weight of the woman I'd once loved on my back had taken their toll. Soon, very soon, I would stop struggling, and that would be the end of me. But not yet.

Not quite yet.

Once again, I dragged an arm up out of the water and forced it forward, reaching out to take my next stroke. This time, something changed. I smashed my hand into rough wet planks, a ship's hull. My hand was so cold I had to flex my fingers and check it with my other hand to see how badly I'd hurt myself. It was stiff and I'd jammed a knuckle but I didn't think I'd broken anything—one small benefit of my exhaustion, I just wasn't swimming hard enough to cause much damage.

Triss.

Nothing. He was tired and hurting, too, worn out from keep-

ing me afloat and the hit he'd taken at the cemetery, though I
knew he'd never have admitted it.

Triss!

What? Wait, we're here?

We are.

I'd pushed myself out and away from the ship's side so that
I wouldn't scrape up and down against the rough surface with
every lift and fall of the swells. Despite the still brutal wind,
the waves weren't bad. Probably because the storm had blown
up so quickly right on top of Tien rather than rolling in from
the deeps. It hadn't had the time or impetus to build the sort of
waves that a big ocean blow brought with it.

Now we need to find a way aboard, I mindspoke. Just for a
little while really, until the storm blew itself out and we could
return to Tien.

Looks like they lost the anchor, or cut it loose, Triss replied.
So the easy way's out.

Damn. I couldn't see that well through the murk, but had
no reason to doubt him. *Maybe we can use the rudder somehow.* I turned and forced myself to swim slowly toward the
back of the ship.

Namara had never sent me to the islands, so I didn't know
a lot about ships. I mean I knew the things everybody knows,
like the pointy end goes in front, and right and left were called
starboard and port. Beyond that my knowledge was spotty, a
mix of the simple stuff you picked up hanging out in dockside
bars, and the esoterica one gleaned from the odd courier job
for smugglers.

It was a three-masted junk, and the thought of smugglers
gave me another idea. On the big ocean-going junks like this
one, there were often compartments, fore and aft, designed so
they could be rapidly flooded to help the boat stay upright in
strong winds and big waves. They called them ballast tanks
or something like that, and the design was very different from
the southern ships that came up out of the Magelands and the
Sylvani Empire.

I'd been in and out of ships of both sorts while dealing with
smugglers, and the tanks were great for that kind of work. If
you put a secondary watertight compartment inside the big

main one, and kept that main compartment flooded when you sailed into port, it made a perfect hidey-hole.

As I slipped around the back end of the ship, I was very happy to find a couple of flood ports at the waterline, along with a whole series of fist-sized ports slaved to the larger ones with magic. The main ports were just big enough for a man to slip through. They sat on each side of the rudder, just above a set of sailor's wards. Of those, the only one I really recognized was the one to prevent fires, though I could guess at a couple of others since they were variations of the sorts of protections you'd see onshore for repelling vermin and the like.

Two questions remained: Was this a smuggling boat? And, did I have the strength to get both Jax and me aboard? On the first, I figured the odds were pretty good. Despite the storm, there wasn't a light showing. Add that to the fact that it must have been lying at anchor out in the harbor instead of tied up at the docks, and the case was pretty damning. Either it was waiting for a fast cutter to come unload it, or it wanted to ride the tide out to sea before the sun rose. As for the latter question, there was only one way to find out.

Triss, hold us steady while I see if I can't get the ports open.

I sank in the water while Triss shifted around, but then he got a grip on both me and the ship and lifted me partway free of the swells. A band of solidified shadow like a crescent moon now passed around my waist between me and Jax, then extended itself forward to sink its horns into the tarred seam between two planks. By bracing my boot tips against another seam lower down, I was able to position myself quite steadily in front of the nearer port.

The port looked like a giant's closed eye. Starting at what would have been the outside corner of the eye, my magesight showed a line of silvery light running upward to the deck far above. Somewhere near the ship's wheel it would connect to a tiny glyph. A simple thing, so that even the least of hedge witches would be able to close and open the port. The trick would come in activating the spell without also lighting up the glyph for anyone with the eyes to see.

I could cut the line, but then the glyph above would wink out and that would be almost as much of a problem. If I had time, tools, and energy—or really, any two of those—I could have managed it a dozen different ways. As it was, I had to go for an ugly little improvisation. Flicking my right wrist, I dropped the knife sheathed there into my hand . . . where it slipped straight through numbed fingers and vanished into the depths of the harbor.

Well, fuck. Moving more carefully, I reached across and very gently pulled the knife out of my left wrist sheath. Then I stabbed it into a plank so that the edge just touched the line of silver light.

"Sshayar," I whispered, "can you take over for Triss for a moment?"

For a heartbeat or two there was no response, then Sshayar responded just as quietly, "If it's brief. Between packing Jax's wound and everything else, I'm very close to my limits. Holding the two of you up for any length of time is going to hurt."

I'd partnered Triss long enough to read the subtleties in a Shade's tones, and I could hear deep exhaustion and pain in Sshayar's. But I didn't have a lot of choice. "Do it."

Triss, I need you to let me take over again as soon as Sshayar's in position.

You don't sound much better than Sshayar, he replied. *Are you sure you can handle this?*

No. But it's this or climbing the rudder, and there's no way we're going to manage that without being spotted.

Triss sighed in my mind. *I suppose we can't just yell for help and trust to the goodness of people's hearts. Not with the likelihood that our soon-to-be hosts are smugglers, at least.*

To say nothing of the combined prices on my head and Jax's. Trust isn't something any former Blade can afford.

Not even with each other, Triss sent sadly.

No, not even that.

Then Sshayar was in place, and Triss vanished into dreams so that I could go to work. Placing my palm firmly against the center of the port, I reached for the well of my soul and found it . . . well, not exactly empty, but drained below the place where I could safely draw from it. Too bad I had no other choice. I could feel the drain in the deeps of my soul as I pulled energy from my core and fed it into the shadows that held me, extending the stuff of Triss's being to cover the port.

I pushed it further, forcing a line of shadow up the line of the spell to the place where my knife stood out from the planks. My ears began to ring and little sparks danced around the edges of my vision. It felt like taking a deep cut in a fight, the kind where the blood comes out in pulses and you can bleed out in a matter of minutes if you don't plug the hole.

I had seconds to act, and I did so, forcing the hatch with a brute application of magic. That sent a spike of light racing up the line of the spell toward the glyph above, light that burned away shadows, burned away the substance of my familiar, if only a little bit. When it hit the knife I forced it to shift course, forced it into the knife. There was a bright flare in my mage-sight, and the whole world went white for a moment as the knife softened and bent.

I lost control of my body and slumped forward, my feet slipping free of the planks. If not for Sshayar holding me up, I'd have smashed face-first into the ship's hull and that would probably have been it. But Sshayar held onto me, and I held onto consciousness. Only barely, but barely was enough. I released Triss and he slid down my skin, collapsing into my natural shadow.

Sshayer collapsed, too, dropping us back into the water, but not before I reached out with one flailing hand and caught the lip of the port. As I dragged myself up and in, Jax slid free, staying in the water behind me. My back felt suddenly cold and unguarded. Necessary but scary—I'd never have fit through the opening with her there, but for the next few heartbeats I had no way of knowing if Sshayar had let go of me because she wanted to or simply because she'd reached her breaking point.

After I slid my hips through the gap I twisted myself around, so that I could bring my legs inboard without letting go of the port. I didn't know how far up the inside wall the port would lie, and wasn't up for jumping games. Then I pivoted and hung over the edge, reaching out and down toward the water, hoping I would find Sshayar waiting there, ready to catch my outflung hands. A swell rolled in first, dipping my hands in the water then raising them high into cold air and the rain.

Nothing. Nothing. Noth—

"What the hell!" A harsh whisper came in a familiar voice.

"Hussh!" Sshayar hissed. "Just reach where I guide you, Aral's going to pull you up."

A hand met mine. Jax! Another. I eeled backward off the

lip of the port, losing some skin and nearly dislocating my elbows in the process. Turned out, the port was a bit higher than my shoulders, a fact I discovered as my feet splashed into calf-deep water. Up came Jax. I let go as her hands reached the lip, and fell back onto my ass with a splash. Jax hung for a moment on the edge of the port above me, still more out than in. Then another swell came along, and shoved her through, along with about a hundred gallons of saltwater. She landed beside me swearing. We were in.

"Where in Namara's name are we?" Jax demanded in a whisper—even injured and disoriented she knew better than to make too much noise before she knew how the shadows lay.

"On board what I very much suspect is a smuggling vessel. Or," I amended, "at least one with a smuggling compartment or two. We're stuck till the storm's over."

"All right. That's one. Here's two: Why do I feel like pan-fried shit on a stick?"

"Because the Hand of Heaven put a very neat little hole in your left side. Luckily they used a self-cauterizing spell of some sort or you'd have bled out before I could even get to you."

I heard something like a hand sliding along wet cloth. Then, "Son of a bitch, that hurts. The who did what now?"

But another swell slopped a big bunch of cold water in through the port just then. "Answer you in a minute. I need to close that before any more of the sea comes in to join us." I dragged myself back upright and grabbed the lip of the port.

Standing hurt. Everything hurt. I could feel my teeth wanting to chatter in my aching jaw.

"After that, we'll see if there's a nice dry smuggling compartment around here where we can collapse for a while," I said over my shoulder. "If not, I'm going to cut a hole in the nearest bulkhead and we'll figure it out from there."

"Triss, you still with me?" I asked aloud because I didn't want to let Jax know about our newfound ability to communicate silently. A part of me might still love Jax, but I knew damn well better than to trust her.

His voice was weak and came after a brief pause, but it came, "Yeah, I'm here. What do you need?"

"Can you reach out there and pull what's left of my knife free?" I asked.

In response, a tentacle of shadow slid past me. If I'd done this right . . . The hatch blinked itself shut like the great eye it had been painted to resemble.

I yanked my hands back just before it would have crushed my fingers. My knees buckled as I staggered back, and I went down hard, falling face-first into the water and sucking in a noseful. I came up gasping and coughing, glad it still barely topped my calves. Much deeper and I might have drowned. The irony didn't escape me.

"You all right, Aral?" asked Jax.

"Not really. No. I feel pretty much like I came out of that deep-fried shit pan you mentioned a minute ago. But we can't stop just yet."

I wasn't ready to stand, so I stayed on my knees as I pulled my trick bag around front and dug around inside. Everything water could hurt was a loss. So was some of the stuff I'd have expected to be fine. Fortunately, that didn't include my little thieveslamp. Slightly smaller than a closed fist, it was basically a metal box with a shutter on one side and a dim, red, magelight inside. The mechanism didn't much like all the time it had spent submerged in saltwater. It squeaked its unhappiness when I forced it open with my thumb, but it did open.

That revealed a large, flat, boxlike space with no apparent access other than the ports. Considering the size of the ship and the height of the ceiling, I didn't like the odds of a smuggling compartment being concealed up top. Underfoot was possible, but unlikely as it would be easier to intuit from a quick glance at the hull and much harder to keep dry. That left the forward bulkhead.

"I don't see anything," said Jax.

"That's kind of the point," I replied. "Now be quiet and let me concentrate. I need to do this before I keel over, and I don't think I've got a lot of time." With some reluctance and a great deal of difficulty I forced myself back up onto my feet and stumbled my way over to the bulkhead.

"If you'll tell me what we're looking for, I'll help." Jax was heading for the other end of the bulkhead on hands and knees.

"I don't know exactly. A loose joining peg maybe, or a knothole that can be pulled out, if we're lucky. If not, something completely invisible and devilishly clever."

Turned out to be a loose peg high on the starboard side of the bulkhead. Push it in hard and it popped back out far enough to reveal a release. Pull that and it exposed a gently glowing glyph. A moment in shadow's skin and a word of opening and a large section of bulkhead swung out and down, becoming a short set of stairs leading up into darkness. I poked my head through the opening. The compartment was about four feet in depth by eight high and it probably ran the width of the ship. I couldn't say for sure because they'd packed it tight.

"Here." I helped Jax up onto a seat on the steps to get her out of the water and handed her my light. "Hold this.

"Triss, see if you can't slip back into the depths and check for anything dangerous." I started pulling out enough of the stuff right around the hatch to make room for Jax and me, as he slithered through gaps that would have stymied anything bigger than a nipperkin. "Looks like they're on their way out of port."

"How can you tell?" asked Jax.

"This." I dropped a small bale of exceptionally fine silk regretfully into the water sloshing around the bottom of the bigger compartment. "And this." I added a tiny crate of tea stamped with the seal of the Duke of Jenua—everything had to be packed small enough to fit through the flood ports.

"I think I must have missed a step, Aral."

"You don't smuggle tea and silk *into* Zhan. Though *this* they might." I pulled out another small crate labeled with a familiar distiller's mark and set it on the top step—Aveni whiskey, though not my favorite Kyle's.

"How do you know so much about smuggling?" she asked as I pulled my remaining hip dagger out and jammed the tip of it under one edge of the crate's lid.

I pounded on the pommel with the heel of my hand. "I don't know what you've been doing since the temple fell, but I needed something to pay my rent and my bar bill." I leaned gently on the dagger—I'd lost three knives already tonight—and the lid started to lift. "Turns out the smugglers will pay pretty well for a courier who never gets stopped by the Stingers."

"Stingers?"

"City watch. That's what the underworld types call them because they wear gold and black. And . . . oh, there we go." I lifted out a bottle of Skaate's finest eighteen, sliced the seal, and pulled the cork with my teeth. "Beautiful."

And so very delicious. I took a long swig off the bottle.

"Aral, that's disgusting! Don't you remember what the priests had to say about alcohol?"

I pulled the bottle away from my lips and looked down to meet her eyes. With the way she was holding the thieveslight I couldn't see them clearly, but the way her lip curled spoke to the contempt I couldn't see.

"Every word, Jax. Every word." I lifted the bottle and took another long drink—damn but I needed that. "I also remember how much good all those words did when the Hand of Heaven came knocking on the temple door. There was a lot the priests didn't know."

"Aral's a little bitter," said Triss from the mouth of the smuggling compartment. "In case you hadn't guessed."

"So am I," said Jax. "But drinking that way? How could you?"

"I'll show you." I took my third drink in as many minutes.

I hadn't drunk like this in a while—Triss hated my drinking and I tried to control it for him even when I couldn't for me. In my better moments, I succeeded. This wasn't one of my better moments, and that felt fucking wonderful, though the booze hadn't hit me nearly as hard as it should have. In fact, I'd burned so much nima that it felt like it was mostly just vanishing. Too bad. Sticking the cork back in the bottle I set it beside Jax.

"It's there in case you want some." Her jaw tightened in an all-too-familiar anger. "Before you throw the bottle across the room, or start yelling at me, I've got two things to say. One, we're trying to stay hidden here. Two, 'spirits for the drained spirit.'"

"What the hell are you talking about, Aral?"

I was pleased to note that despite the obvious anger in her voice, she kept it low and quiet.

"Nima," Triss said to Jax. "It's something we learned from . . . another mage. If you've overtapped the well of your soul—as Aral did getting us all here alive—you can temporarily recover some of what you've lost by drinking. That's why Aral hasn't fallen over yet, neither from exhaustion, nor from drinking half a pint of cask-strength whiskey."

Jax's expression calmed and she bit her lip. "Really?"

"I take it there's nothing back in there that we have to worry about, Triss?" My question came out a lot grumpier than I'd intended and I knew the reason for that.

It hadn't escaped me that in the years after Jax and I stopped being an us, she'd continued to get along beautifully with Triss, and vice versa. I resented that, though it made me feel petty. When Triss didn't answer me, I went back to making space.

"That seems an awfully useful thing to know," Jax said after a while. "Why wouldn't the priests have told us about it?"

"Because it only works when you've pushed yourself too far," replied Triss, his voice low and worried. "And, if you do it very often, it'll hollow you out like a piece of old bamboo. Pretty soon you'll start to feel like the only thing that can fill that void is more booze. It works in the short term, and sometimes I'll even say it's a good idea, but what drink does to your kind, over time, is ugly."

I closed my eyes and bit back my instinctive response. Then I pulled out one last crate of expensive tea and dumped it in the water.

"And there we go. Your bower awaits, Master Jax."

She looked up at me and I was shocked to see tears on her cheeks. "I'm sorry I didn't come looking for you earlier, Aral."

"Why do you say that?"

"I waited until I needed your help. And because of that, I think I missed the time when you needed mine."

I felt my throat go tight, but I didn't have any good answer for that, so I turned away. I wanted to yell at her. Not because she was wrong, but because she almost certainly wasn't. Eight years on from the mess we'd made of what should have been the best thing that ever happened to me, and she still knew me better than I'd ever known myself. Two sentences and she'd cut straight through all the armor and all the cynicism and drawn blood. She had no fucking right to still be able to do that to me. Not anymore.

When I finally turned back around, she'd crawled up the stairs into the smuggler's stash, though I hadn't heard her move. A glance through the hatch showed her curled tightly in a hundred silver riels worth of silk and dead asleep. She'd left just enough room for me to stretch out beside her like I had so many times before.

I looked up at the shadow tiger keeping watch on the wall above Jax's head. Sshayar's subtle stripes just barely showed in the red glow of the thieveslamp. I knew she was looking back at me, but not even a Blade can read the expression on a shadow's face, so I didn't know what she was thinking. I reached for the bottle and took another deep drink. This one I felt all the way down to my toes, which was good. I needed it to get me to put my foot on that first step. But it wasn't quite enough for me to take the rest of that short walk.

If it weren't for the fact that I'd probably drown if I stayed out there, I don't think all the whiskey in the world would have put me in bed with Jax again, even if it was only for sleeping. I raised the bottle again, then paused with it against my lips as I noticed the shadowy dragon take a spot on the wall beside the tiger. I looked into the place where his eyes would have been, for several long seconds, then raised one brow in question. I knew I couldn't trust my judgment on the booze, so I left it up to him.

Triss looked down at Jax, then back at me, and finally he nodded ever so slightly, though I could see it cost him.

I took another drink.

5

---◆---

Intentions are ice. Results are diamonds. Both can be hard and cold or sparkle and shine, but intentions only matter as long as the heat doesn't melt them away to nothing. Results can't be gotten rid of half so easily. You can split them or polish them, even burn them in a hot enough fire, but you have to work if you want to change them.

Waking up with your ex and a hangover when you'd only intended to have a quiet conversation with her will bring that point home with stunning clarity. More so if you wake up wedged into a tightly enclosed space the gods have decided to use as a dice box. At least, that was how it felt, between the way the world had started to roll and pitch and the stuffiness of the air. Things had gone completely dark back when I closed the thieveslamp, so my eyes were useless unless I dug it out again. The heavy smells of tea and sweat and old whiskey in the air made me long for a fresh breeze.

Triss, how long have I been out? And what the hell is going on?

Maybe four hours. The storm's still hammering us. If anything it's gotten worse. We're getting serious waves now.

I hope Faran made it out of the river all right. There was nothing I could do about it now or anytime soon, but that didn't make me feel any better.

I'm sure she's fine, sent Triss. But he didn't *sound* sure.

I forced the thought aside, burying it in the back of my mind for the time being—mental discipline had always been at least as important as physical for a Blade, and *much* harder. I lifted my left arm—Jax was asleep on my right shoulder—and felt along the wall, finding the hatch closed tight.

What happened? I asked Triss.

When the big waves first started to hit, the captain or somebody opened up the outer ports to let the compartment flood. The back of the ship was practically underwater at the time and it came in so fast Sshayar and I barely had time to get the stairs closed. The seals are tight enough that not even a shadow can pass, but as far as I can tell the ballast tank is still full of water.

I nodded. *So, for the moment at least, the only way anyone is getting in or out is by cutting through the forward bulkhead into the hold. Not my first choice, but I guess I can live with that. Though it's a good thing I don't mind enclosed spaces, and that I'm not prone to motion sickness.*

The hidey-hole I'd hollowed out for us up at the top of the stowed contraband couldn't have run much more than two feet high by four deep and seven long.

I took a deep breath by way of a test. *I notice the air isn't getting any worse.*

The planks between us and the ship's inner hold are pretty tightly fitted, but the caulking's only good enough to make it look like a watertight bulkhead. Sshayar and I popped some of the seams to improve the air.

Sounds like you've got everything covered and I can go back to sleep.

I really needed it, but both the pounding pressure at my temples and a growing thirst that the whiskey would ultimately only worsen gave me doubts. The fact that Jax had put my right arm to sleep and that the whole world was pitching about like I'd had six drinks too many didn't help. I might have managed to get past all the physical discomfort anyway—I'd slept with worse—if only I could have quieted my mind.

But now that I was awake, the questions had started. Both

proximate: where was the ship going and how were we going to get off without being noticed? And, more remote: What had really been going on back at the cemetery? Could I even trust Jax? I massaged my forehead, but it didn't help, either with the pain or the thinking.

After a minute or so I gave it up only to have my hand replaced by a sudden cool pressure running from temple to temple like a damp cloth—Triss, doing what he could to ease my pain with a shadow's touch. That surprised me. It had been years since he'd been willing to help with any of my bottle-born and self-inflicted wounds.

You hit the booze pretty hard last night, on top of all the things that hit you. Triss's mental voice sounded cautious and worried, not at all his usual bitter morning-after demeanor. *How do you feel?*

I did a quick mental inventory, comparing the ache in my head and the rot in my gut to the cold and the exhaustion of the night before and came up with a mostly positive balance.

Less like I'm about to die, but more like I might be happier if I did, I teased.

That's not funny.

No, I suppose it's not.

Jax stirred against my side, then drew a sharp breath—probably when she felt the pain in her side. "Aral?"

"I'm here."

"Why is the world moving?"

"Storm."

"Then we really are stuffed in some tiny little smuggler's stash on board a ship somewhere off the coast of Zhan?"

I nodded in the darkness. "Yes."

"Damn. For a few blissful seconds there I thought I'd just had the longest and worst nightmare in the history of dreaming. But the goddess is still dead, isn't she?"

"Would that it *were* a dream."

"And you and I are not a we?"

"No. Not for a very long time."

Jax drew a ragged breath. "Well at least that's one small mercy, though I think getting back together would have been worth it if it erased all the other bad stuff."

"Jax!" I growled. I so didn't need this shit.

She gave my ribs a squeeze. "I'm sorry, Aral. I was joking. Well, not really joking so much as desperately trying to keep myself from going quietly mad. It's an ugly habit I picked up from Loris when the Hand had us. Laughing was the only thing that really seemed to put the torturers off balance. They hurt us all the more when we did it, but they didn't enjoy it half so much."

What do you say to that?

"You've changed," is what finally came out, though it seemed both inadequate and obvious. I thought briefly about digging out the thieveslight, but somehow the dark made it easier to say the things that needed saying. "And I guess it's my turn to be sorry. I wish there was something I could have done. . . ."

"You've changed, too," she said.

More than she could imagine. Another small grace of leaving the light closed was that it meant we didn't have to talk about my face quite yet.

"I think the old Aral would have tried to match my joke with one of his own," continued Jax. "Perhaps the Hand did something of a transfer there. If I got your sense of humor, what gift did the Hand give you?"

"I can't think of a single thing." It came out harder and flatter than I'd intended, and I felt Jax stiffen against my side.

"Rage," Triss said quietly—it was hard to hear him over the noises of the tossing ship.

"What?" I asked in the same breath as Jax.

"Anger is a terrible gift," said Triss. "It cuts the hand that wields it every bit as deeply as its target, but I think you needed it in the years right after the temple fell. Without anger, we would not have survived."

Sshayar let out a low growling chuckle somewhere in the darkness. "If so, it was a good choice. Jax has always had plenty to spare."

"Hey now," started Jax, but then I felt her shrug against my side, and then wince and put a hand to her wound. "I guess you may have a point there."

"Of course I do," replied Sshayar. "It's ironic really. If you had possessed more humor or Aral more anger, you might even have stayed together."

I didn't know how to respond to that, it came like another

punch in the gut. I closed my eyes, though it didn't matter in the dark.

"I doubt it," said Triss. "They were too much of an age to do well together."

"There is that," said Sshayar. "She does not fight with Loris half so much as she did with Aral, or with Devin for that matter."

"You're with Loris now?" I asked before I could stop myself.

Jax drew a deep ragged breath, then let it go as she pulled away from me. "I am. Our experiences in the dungeons of Heaven's Reach gave us a close bond. After we escaped, it grew from companionship into something more."

I couldn't see, but from the sounds of things, I guessed she'd taken advantage of her diminutive size to wedge herself in the far corner, probably in the cross-legged pose she'd always favored. I didn't say anything right away, because I needed time to process the idea of Jax with Loris.

It really shouldn't have surprised me. Loris was perhaps twenty years older than Jax, a large gap for the general run of humanity, but like all the greater mages, Blades measured their lives by the span of our familiars. A dragon-bound mage might last a thousand years if they were lucky enough. The longest I'd ever heard of a Blade living was three hundred years, but it wasn't old age that killed her, it was a bodyguard's sword. When Blades died, we died by violence in action, and mostly we died young.

Lifespan was part of the reason Blades tended to form partnerships across generations rather than within them, but lifestyle had a lot to do with it, too. Jax and I had literally grown up together. From the age of four on we had spent much of our waking lives together. What lay between us included every childish mistake and every adolescent cruelty as much as it included our onetime love. Little surprise then that it hadn't worked out, that it almost never worked out.

Thinking about it, better by far Loris than Devin. I wasn't looking forward to being the one to break the news of Devin's betrayal to Jax if she hadn't already heard it. I reached for the whiskey bottle, though I didn't yet twist the cork free.

"That's why I'm here, actually," Jax said, finally breaking the long silence. "The Hand has Loris."

"I'm sorry," I said. "That's terrible. Do you know if he's still alive?"

"I believe that he is, but I can't know without going after him . . . them actually, and I don't want to do that until I'm ready to break them out. I need your help."

"You'll have it," I said, there could be no other choice. There were very few situations that I could imagine where Jax would need help from anybody, but taking on the people who'd destroyed the temple and murdered so many of our brethren was definitely one of them. "But back up a moment, I think I may have missed a step. 'Them'?"

"After we broke out of Heaven's Reach, Loris and I tried to gather as many of the escaped journeymen and apprentices as we could find. We've been bringing them back to a sort of fallback we set up in Dalridia at Cairmor. It's a minor castle my brother owns."

"Your brother?" I asked. "I don't remember you ever talking about your family when we were together."

Jax sighed. "My father was the younger brother of the King of Dalridia. It never seemed like a great thing to bring up among a group of people dedicated to enforcing justice on the royalty of the world. Between my induction into the order and taking my journeyman's swords, the priests and masters made sure I had no contact with my family, nor heard any news of them. After though, I had the freedom to seek out that news, or even my family, I went out of my way to avoid it and them."

I could understand that. Though my own family had been merchants of some sort and lived within sight of the temple, I'd never sought them out, nor talked to them in the city those few times I encountered them by accident. It was simply not the way things were done.

"Then the temple fell," I said.

"Exactly. After Loris and I escaped from the Hand we needed a place to lie up and heal. Loris comes from the Kvanas where the Son of Heaven's word is as good as any of the great Khans, so Dalridia and my family seemed like our safest option. When we arrived, I found out my uncle and father had both died. That left my brother King of Dalridia, since my uncle had chosen to honor the commitment he'd made to his prince consort rather than succumb to the pressure to produce an heir, and thus had no children of his own."

"How did your brother feel about taking in a fugitive from the Son of Heaven?"

"It's been ten generations since Namara had to send a Blade after a noble of Dalridia, though not a few noble heads have fallen to the royal executioner. My family takes pride in that record. My brother, Eian, was likewise proud of me and what I'd become."

"But," said Sshayar, "after what happened to the temple, Dalridia must be cautious about being seen to be in opposition to the high church of the eleven kingdoms. Eian was glad to see us and to offer us shelter, but politics forced him to ask us to keep as low a profile as possible."

"That's why he put us at Cairmor," added Jax. "It's a royal retreat high in the mountains at the southwest end of the kingdom, far from the major passes and any foreign influence. The villagers are personally loyal to my brother, and no else ever comes there. It's served us admirably as we've slowly gathered up what we could of the surviving Blade trainees."

Jax shifted in the darkness, then let out a little gasp of pain. "Damn, but this hole in my side hurts. Cairmor is nothing like what we had at the temple, but we've made it more than just a place of refuge. We're trying to teach the old skills so they won't be lost . . . though I'm not sure if that can ever matter again."

"How many have you brought there?" asked Triss, and I could hear the eagerness in his voice, the longing.

The destruction of the temple and our years in hiding had been even harder on him than on me. I might have lost my friends, my goddess, even my faith in myself and my mission in life, but at least I still lived in my own world among my own kind. The familiar bond could only be severed by death. When Triss had tied himself to me, he had left behind the quiet deeps of his home in the everdark, never to return.

Here in the sunlands, his only possible connection back to the life he had been born to came from congress with his fellow exiles. We'd only encountered three other Shades in the past few years, and never since the fall of the temple had he had a chance to talk to more than one of his fellows at a time.

"There were twenty-one of us at Cairmor before this latest attack by the Hand." Jax's breath and speech sounded more labored now.

"And all were taken?" demanded Triss.

"No. The attack came in the city of Tavan, during a mission, not at the school. They got Loris and four of our eldest journeymen—they'd be masters by now if Namara had lived to name them so, Maryam, Leyan, Javan, and Roric."

That hurt. I didn't remember Javan or Maryam very well, but Leyan was a wonderful girl, and very good with the garrote. Too young for me to have spent much time with her, but I very much liked what I'd seen of her. Roric, too, a huge bearlike boy who still managed to move with a cat's grace.

"What were they doing in the Magelands?"

"We'd heard of a daring young thief and spy working out of Tavan, and it sounded like it might be one of our last four lost apprentices. Loris and the others went to see if they could find out more, but ran into a cohort of the Hand instead of the missing apprentice."

"Ugly," I said. "When did this happen?"

"A few weeks ago. I'd been considering trying to break Loris free with the help of our three remaining older journeymen, but I couldn't make the odds work no matter how much I wanted to. This is the Hand, the force that destroyed the temple and more than a hundred Blades. My students aren't ready to face that. They simply haven't had the real-world experience in dealing with the problems that kind of raid would encounter. That's why, when I heard about your presence here in Tien, it seemed like a sign sent by a kindly fate."

"Do you know where they're being held?" asked Triss.

"When I left to come find you and Aral they were in a large abbey on the plains east of Tavan." She spoke a brief spell and then drew a quick glowing map in the air between us.

"About here." She touched a spot. "There's a good chance they're still there. I'm sure the Hand wants them in Heaven's Reach, but moving religious prisoners around the Magelands is going to be damn tricky."

I nodded, though she couldn't see me. The council of Magearchs may pay lip service to the High Church and the Son of Heaven, but they're a nation founded by, and for, magical refugees from various sorts of persecution.

Sshayar spoke now: "Outside of the abbeys and their temple-cum-embassies in the cities, the forces of the Son of Heaven are probably weaker in the Magelands than anywhere in the eleven kingdoms, save only Kanjuri. Tavan is particularly tough, squeezed up against the border with the Sylvani Empire like it is. The Others hate our gods with an immortal passion, and would cheerfully skin any of the Hand they could get their hands on."

I looked at Jax's map. "I think you're right. There's no good way for the Hand to get them out. Tavan's on a river, but the outflow goes right past the Sylvani capital. Upstream runs into the mountains and ultimately Dalridia."

"The Son's greatest strength is all in the north," said Triss. "In Zhan and Kadesh on this side of the mountains and Aven, Osë, and the Kvanas to the west. The Hand's only reasonable option is to get the prisoners on a ship, send them north to Kadesh, and then over Hurn's Gate and down through Aven. That's going to take some doing."

"Huh," I said as a thought hit me.

"What is it?" asked Triss.

"I just realized something. The current Son of Heaven has really expanded the power of the church, but he's strongest in the kingdoms where mages are weakest. Zhan, where the rules and customs make it very hard for mages to hold a title of nobility. Kadesh and the Kvanas, where the mage gift will automatically get you disinherited. Aven and Osë don't have any formal antimage rules that I know of, but I can't think of a single major noble house that's headed by a mage in either."

"I never thought of that before," said Jax, "but you're right. My brother is a mage, if a minor one, and so was my uncle. Varya's nobility is lousy with them. So are Radewald's and Dan Eyre's. In the Magelands and Kodamia you have to have magic to hold a title at all. Kanjuri's the only odd one out. They have no true mages, but the High Church is all but disbarred from the islands."

"Maybe it's got more to do with familiars than magery," said Triss. "Any Kanjurese peasant who exhibits the familiar gift is automatically raised to the peerage, and they disbar those nobles who are born without it. But none of that will get Loris or the others free. We need to focus on the task at hand."

"Not at hand," said Jax. "Not yet anyway. We've got to get off this ship. Then we have to get to the Magelands, and none of that's happening in the next couple of hours."

"First, we have to get back to Tien," I added. "I have things I need to take care of before I can leave." For reasons I couldn't really articulate, I didn't want to talk to Jax about Faran yet.

"Ah, your hidden Blade," said Jax. "Who was that at the cemetery with you?"

Before I could even start to dissemble, Sshayar spoke, "It was Ssithra and Faran. I spoke to them while you were unconscious."

"She's alive then!" Jax sounded delighted, which made me feel the worse for doubting her but didn't remove the doubts. "How is she? How long has she been with you? I don't remember a second Blade being mentioned in any of the stories that made their way to Dalridia."

"She only joined me recently, and we've gone out of our way to keep her presence a secret."

There was obviously no point in my trying to conceal her name, not when Sshayar knew it. But I still couldn't shake the feeling that talking about her with Jax was a betrayal of some sort, which made me wonder what my hindbrain wasn't telling me about Jax.

"That might be harder than you think," said Jax. "Do you know about the shadow trails?"

"Or the apostate Blades?" Sshayar added with more than a bit of a growl in her voice.

"Apostate Blades?" I asked, though I thought I knew who she was referring to.

Sshayar coughed like the angry tiger she could so easily become, and I couldn't blame her. Damn, but I needed a drink, and there it was at my side. I pulled the cork and took a sip.

"Bastards and traitors," said Jax. "When they took us prisoner at the fall of the temple, the Son of Heaven offered us a deal through the senior surviving officer of the Hand. Any Blade, trainee or master, who would agree to serve the will of Heaven from time to time was offered the chance to walk away

free and clear. I refused, as did Loris and many others. That's
when the torture started. Every so often they would come by
and ask again, though I don't know how they could have
believed we could ever be trusted if we said yes."

"Spellbound oaths, I assume," I replied. "That or the Son
of Heaven believes that torture works and the switch of allegiance from Namara to Shan can be reliably achieved with
coercion."

Jax made a rude noise. "Was that last a joke? Because if it
was, it's almost funny. If it wasn't, I have to say that the drink's
starting to affect you. As for spellbound oaths, you know as
well as I do that there are a thousand ways and one to twist
them around if you've got the incentive."

"Maybe even more than that, but it also depends on the oath,
and the Son of Heaven has resources beyond the normal. Do
you know how many of our brethren took the deal?"

"It's hard to say. I only know of one for sure, Kayarin
Melkar. She and I were chained together immediately after we
were taken. She agreed to the bargain, right there in the yard
with a dozen slaughtered journeymen and priests lying within
a stone's throw. If I could have moved I'd have strangled her
on the spot, but the enchantments on the manacles barely left
me the strength to breathe through the pain."

"Speaking of which"—Jax let out a sharp little noise. "Does
alcohol work as well as efik for pain?"

"Better in some ways. It doesn't numb things up, but you care
a lot less. You've got to be more careful about dosage, and the side
effects get uglier faster. On the other hand, it'll help restore your
nima, at least temporarily, and that'll help both of you."

"Hand it over." She put a hand on my knee, so I'd know
where to pass the bottle.

I did, and I heard her take a long drink that ended in a rough
gasp. "Stuff tastes like horse piss, how do you stand it?"

"It grows on you."

"Not if you're lucky," grumbled Triss.

Jax took another drink, shorter this time. "Still piss, but
yeah I can already feel it taking the edge off. Thank you."

"You're welcome." I licked my lips, and managed not to ask
for the bottle back, just. Even if she finished it, there was probably more around.

She continued, "Later, I saw Kayarin's name listed among the dead on that obelisk the Son of Heaven had erected outside the main gates of the temple. I'm not sure if that means she recanted or if the traitors are all listed among the dead or what, though I suspect the latter. I do know that there are at least a half dozen of the apostates running around loose. We've encountered their shadow trails a couple of times."

You have to tell her, Triss said into my mind. *He was her friend as much as yours. Maybe even more. They were lovers for years after the two of you called it quits.*

"I can't speak to Kayarin specifically," I finally said. "But I can say for certain that at least some of those listed as dead are alive and well and making a great case for the twisting of spellbound oaths."

"You've encountered some of them, then?" asked Sshayar.

"I have, or one of them anyway. That's how I learned about the shadow trails. He used ours to set us up for a deathspark."

"A deathspark?" asked Sshayar. "Why didn't your sacred blades protect you?"

"For starters, they're sitting on the bottom of a lake beside the stone corpse of the goddess. I returned them to her when I left her service."

"What happened after you got 'sparked?" Jax's voice sounded low and dangerous, angry.

"I ended up on a big wooden glyph thing they called the 'pillory of light.' The straps bound me and the glyph bound Triss."

"They beat him," said Triss. "They hurt him and I couldn't stop them. Later, I killed them all, but I couldn't do anything about it until a friend rescued us." Even a year later Triss was slurring his sibilants in a barely controlled rage.

Jax put a hand on my knee again. "I'm sorry, Aral. I know a thing or two about being bound to the pillory. If I could have, I'd have come to get you."

"It wasn't anything like what you faced. I wasn't even there that long."

"Four days, though you *were* unconscious for much of it," Triss interjected in a voice made icy by anger.

"You said that you knew some of the names on the obelisk belonged to the apostate instead of the dead." Jax sounded just as hard and cold as Triss. "I assume that means that you know who set you up."

"I do."

"But you haven't said a name yet. I know you, Aral, and I know what that means. But you can't possibly hurt me anywhere near as much as I've already been hurt. Stop trying to protect me and tell me the bad news. Who set you up?"

"Devin."

"Oh." I heard the bottle tip back again, for a very long time, then a small cough. "Damn but that's awful stuff. Did you kill him?"

"No. I could have, but I chose not to. I let him walk away."

"I wouldn't have," said Jax, and there was no give in her tone.

6

———✦———

Love and hate are two edges of the same sword. The hilt can twist in your hand in an instant, and suddenly the sword cuts the other way. It's a simple twist, simpler than anyone can imagine until it happens to them, simpler by far than putting the sword aside, or letting it rust away to nothing. All the strong emotions are like that, easier to reverse than to transform or put aside, and every one of them can cut you to the bone.

Jax was bleeding now. I could hear it when she talked about Devin. Quiet and cold, barely audible above the noises of the ship fighting the storm. Again, I was glad that neither of us had chosen to unshutter our thieveslights. I didn't want to see the pain that went with that voice.

"You should have killed him, Aral."

"You loved him once," I said.

"So did you. I got over it long before the temple fell. Why didn't you? If not in the years before the fall, when he started treating you badly, then later, when he arranged to have you and Triss tied to a rack?"

"Because I looked at him and I saw what he used to be," I replied. "There was a greatness there once."

"No, Aral. There never was." I drew a breath to respond, but Jax preempted me. "Don't. I knew him better than anyone, I think. Better than you did, certainly."

Jax took another long drink—I could hear the sweet gurgle of whiskey leaving the bottle. "I *heard* the things that he'd never say to you, the bitter things he whispered in the dark, his angers and his envies, and how very much he resented playing the second sword to 'the great Aral Kingslayer.'"

That stung. "I know that it was hard for him to have me as a best friend after I killed Ashvik. I can't blame him for resenting the attention the masters gave me."

"Not just the masters," said Jax. "The whole world."

I felt my face heat. I never much liked the renown that came with killing a king. I was proud of what I'd done, ending the life of a monster in a crown. Proud, too, of my ability. I'd managed an execution that three senior masters had died attempting. For a little while I was the world's best . . . assassin—I still found that word uncomfortable. It wasn't what the goddess called us, nor how we'd thought of ourselves, but now, looking back, I had to admit it was what we were. I'd loved the work and knowing I was good at what I did, but I'd never felt comfortable with the adulation.

"He couldn't stand all the attention you got," said Jax. "He hated that you were Aral Kingslayer and he was plain old Devin Urslan. He hated you."

"I can't believe that. Envied yes, I know that. I'd have to be an idiot not to, but hate? No. He may have said things he didn't really mean, but that's all."

"Why the fuck are you defending him? He betrayed Namara and he betrayed the order. But long before that he betrayed you. He's a traitor through and through." Jax shifted and then drew in a harsh pained breath. "He told me how much he hated you, Aral, more than once, and he meant every fucking word of it. That's what drew us together in the first place."

"I—"

"No. Let me finish. This needs to be said. Just give me a moment."

Jax took another drink and I found myself wishing for the bottle again. I started quietly searching around for another and hoping Triss or Sshayar would get involved in the conversation, though I understood why they didn't. This was a human thing, between me and Jax and Devin.

"It's true, Aral. The whole damned order thought you walked in the shadow of the goddess. Everybody but Devin and, later, me. After you and I broke up, we both hated you. That's what put us in bed together. I thought it would hurt you more than sleeping with anyone else would. And Devin . . . well, Devin's motivations were more complex. I think he wanted to be you as much as hurt you, and he figured fucking me would serve for both."

"I was happy for the two of you," I said.

"I know, and damn but it pissed us off. It's funny really. You were what brought Devin and I together, but you were ultimately what drove us apart as well."

"How so?"

"I hated you for what you did to me. Devin hated you for what you were. Somewhere along the line I realized that as much as you'd hurt me, you hadn't done it because you wanted to cause me pain. You did it because you figured out we were never going to work as an us. And, quite simply, you were right. It took me longer to get there than it took you, but if we'd stayed together I'd have come to the same conclusion at some point. Probably a hell of a lot sooner than I did by being with Devin."

She chuckled ruefully and took another drink. I didn't remember my reasoning as being anything like that clear-cut, but I wasn't going to argue with her, I'd done that more than enough when we were together.

"Once I understood why you left me when you did, I fell out of hate with you. Devin noticed and it didn't sit at all well. We started to fight, a lot. More than you and I did even. And whenever we fought, there you were being sympathetic and trying to help out your friends. It reminded me of why I'd loved you in the first place. Though I was smart enough not to fall *in love* with you a second time, I ended up loving you all over again. That was absolute death to my relationship with Devin."

Devin had the chance to kill me when I'd encountered him last, more than once. He hadn't done it. Part of that was clearly self-interest—I was potentially valuable to him in his new enterprise. But there was more to it than that. Even if Jax was right and Devin *had* hated me for years, I think he still loved me, too. We'd been best friends for almost fifteen years before I killed Ashvik and I never had reason for a moment's doubt of our friendship in all that time. It wasn't until I became the Kingslayer that I first started to notice a distance growing between us.

No. It wasn't as simple as Devin hating me for what I had become. But again, I didn't want to argue with Jax. Hell, that was the main reason I'd left Jax a month before we were to be married—I didn't want to argue with Jax ever again. Nine years on, and the whole not-arguing-with-Jax thing *still* felt good.

"Damn." Jax sloshed the whiskey in her bottle. "This stuff is brutal. Here, it's all yours." I felt the bottle pressed against my thigh. "I need to take a little nap."

Jax let go and the bottle tipped, but if anything spilled out I couldn't tell in the dark and the damp of the smuggler's compartment—even with the tight seals around the hatch and between the planks there was no avoiding the wet salt air. By the time I'd picked Jax's whiskey up and wedged it upright between a couple of bolts of cloth, she was snoring. Sleep sounded like a good idea, so I closed my eyes and was gone.

The next time I opened them my head felt like someone had bent a hot iron poker around my skull at eyeball height. I started groping toward the bottle.

"There's a good idea," said Triss in his normal sharp, morning-after voice.

Apparently, I'd used up all of my drinking grace with Triss—not that I blamed him. Mostly, these days, I managed to keep the whiskey from dominating my life the way it had a few years ago, but I was a drunk. The murder of my goddess had broken something in me, something that nothing and no one would ever be able to fix. I had a hole in my soul where my faith had once lived.

Sometimes, on a good night, if I poured enough whiskey into that hole, it felt liked I'd filled it up. Like maybe I'd finally stopped losing bits of me down that hole. But it never lasted. I'd go to sleep and the booze would drain away, leaving things exactly the way they were before I started drinking. That's because there was no bottom to the hole, and all the whiskey ever did was hide that fact for a while. The next morning always came along and shoved the truth in my face so hard it hurt.

Even knowing that, I found myself grabbing Jax's bottle and drinking off a good solid inch of the whiskey before setting it aside. It didn't do a damn thing for my hangover.

"It's a terrible idea, Triss. Nine kinds of stupid and more, but today I needed it, and that's all I'm having." That's when I realized we weren't moving. Not at all, and we were sitting at a funny angle. "What happened to the boat?"

"We're aground somewhere east and north of Tien."

"What! When did that happen?"

"A couple of hours ago. It was surprisingly gentle. I've been slipping through into the hold to listen to the common sailors. I've only been getting dribs and drabs, but as I understand it we lost the rudder at the height of the storm. They tried to make do after that with something they called sweeps, but it wasn't really working and they were deathly afraid of running into some bad patch of reefs. So when they hit a lull in the storm, they beached us."

"What happens now?" I hadn't the vaguest idea of how they might handle something like that.

"Once the sun's up, they're planning on emptying the holds and refloating the ship. Then they're heading on to Kanjuri."

"Which means that even if they don't open up the smuggling compartments, we need to get ashore. I have to get back to Faran. What time is it?"

"Judging by the taste of the night, it's a few hours before dawn."

"So, thirty hours since the fight in the cemetery, more or less." I reached out a hand and touched Jax's ankle. "Time to get up."

She jerked at my touch, then said, "Ow! Shit, my head feels worse than my side. Is that normal?"

"It is if you drink like Aral," said Triss.

"Then why does anyone drink like Aral? Aral excepted, of course, because he's obviously a fool and madman. He'd have to be, to give up efik for this stuff."

"I have no idea," replied Triss, sounding entirely too smug.

"The priests were right. Drink is a demon. This is the worst I've felt short of actual torture. I'm never doing this again."

"Entirely sensible," said Triss.

"Then why in the name of all that's holy did you tell me it could be a good idea? I'd never have even tried the stuff if it was just Aral saying it."

"When did I say anything like that?" asked Triss.

"Right after Aral said 'spirits for the drained spirit.' "

"Oh right. Sorry about that, but it really can help under a very specialized set of circumstances, save your life even."

"Hmph, I think dying might be less traumatic. Never again. Hey, the boat stopped moving. What's happening?"

Fifteen minutes later, we were slipping out through the half-flooded ballast tank to the still-open ports. Half an hour after that, we were holed up in a patch of thornbushes on the shore—the best defense against the restless dead we could find there in the middle of nowhere. I was just telling Jax to wait and rest her wounds while I went to see if I could find us some sort of transport back to Tien, when she reached up and touched my cheek.

"Aral, what have you done to yourself? I *thought* you looked a little odd when we were trying to get the hatch open to get into the compartment back there, but I'd assumed it was exhaustion and the hole in my side making me see things. But it's not, and that's more than makeup."

"It is. The last job I took exposed my face to the whole . . . well you know all about that. The stories and wanted posters that came out of that mess are what brought you up here to look for me. Fortunately, the same job also gave me the tools I needed to reshape the bones of my face."

"I didn't even think that was possible." Jax ran a finger down my cheek to my jaw and then back up the other side, pressing at the corner of my mouth and the orbit of my eye before suddenly pulling her hand back as if she'd burned it. "I'm so sorry it came to this. There's hardly any of the old you left in your face."

There wasn't much of the old me left on the inside either, but I didn't have the heart to say it. "Things are better this way. It gives me a chance at a new start."

But Jax just shook her head. "I expected you to have taken on some sort of disguise—you'd have to—but I was sure I'd recognize you no matter what you tried. I was wrong. I could have looked you straight in the eye without ever knowing you."

"You did, at the Gryphon's Head. I was—"

"Sitting at the table in back by the door into the courtyard. You had your back half exposed to an open window—how could you stand it. I saw you there, marked you as a killer even, but I didn't see it was you. That's . . ."

"Remarkable," said Sshayar, "and potentially very handy."

"Awful," said Jax. "It's awful."

"You'll have to tell us the story," said Sshayar.

"After I see if I can find us a cart or something. You shouldn't be walking or riding with that side."

"**When** and where should I meet you?" Jax asked as we abandoned the cart on the outskirts of Quarryside.

From here on in, the city got steadily busier and it was going to be easier to walk. The hole in Jax's side was going to take weeks to heal fully, even with the spells we'd spun to help, but it wasn't much bigger around than an arrow puncture, and far cleaner. Not much fun for walking but not impossible either.

"I need to pick up my things and attend to a small matter or two before I can leave for the Magelands," she continued. She didn't invite me to come with her.

That was fine. I didn't want her coming with me either. I wasn't ready to trust her, or anyone else who knew who and what I was, with the location of my current snug. Especially not with Faran there—at least, I sure hoped she was there. I had no intention of exposing the younger Blade to any risks I didn't have to. Honestly, I suspected courtesy on that front was half of why Jax wanted to split up for the moment.

"How about we meet back down by the docks." I pointed south. "There's a tavern called the Spinnerfish in Smuggler's Rest. It's as safe a place to meet as any in the city. The owner runs it as neutral ground where sunside and shadowside can meet without any worries about ambush or betrayal. People who bring their outside fights inside end up dead. Also, the fish is as good as you can get in Tien. Say, a few hours before sunset tomorrow? That'll give us time to find a ship that's headed for the Magelands with the next morning's tide."

Jax rolled her eyes. "Oh goody, my last ride on a boat makes getting on another one sound like the best idea ever."

"Not my first choice either, but if time's a concern it's a hell of a lot better than riding. It's not like we have the resources to pay for the fastest magical transport anymore."

"Tell me about it. I had to borrow money from my brother to pay my way up here." She looked up then. "This is my turn. See you tomorrow."

I tossed her a wave and angled right while she turned left and headed south along the waterfront. When I got to the Kanathean Canal, I hired a boat to take me out to the river and up to Bankside. That took me a long distance out of my way, but a shadow trail can't be followed on running water, and sitting in the little boat gave me plenty of time to watch for tails.

By the time I hopped the fence and stepped up to the back door of the little house I shared with Faran, I was quite certain I'd lost any potential hangers-on. I hated to be seen entering the place in my working rig, especially during daylight hours when it was harder to fudge the details. But it had been three days and I just couldn't wait any longer to find out what had happened to Faran.

I pretended to pull a key out of my trick bag and bring it to the keyhole, but Triss did the real work, slipping a portion of himself into the lock and triggering the spell points there to release the mechanism. I kept lock and hinges carefully oiled, so the only sound the door made was the faint scuff of wood on wood as it slid across the threshold. Beyond lay a short hall with a second locked door at the other end, rather than the more typical direct entrance into the kitchen—part of the reason we'd chosen this house.

I took a short step inside then closed the outer door and locked it behind me without going any farther. Concealed now from the outside world, Triss slid up and around me, dressing me in a second skin of cool shadow. As he released his will, I took control, raising my arms and extending yards, long tendrils of shadow from the palms of my hands.

I reached down through the cracks between the floorboards, splitting the tendrils so that I could simultaneously touch the glyphs marking a dozen short steel posts distributed randomly through the space there. This temporarily disarmed the spells on the posts so that I could move forward to the next door without triggering the magical death that lay in wait for any trespasser. Just as with the outer door, the inner answered to the shadows of my familiar instead of a key.

When the lock clicked open, I reached up my finger, now free of shadow, and slipped it into a hole drilled above the frame on the left. It was invisible to anyone shorter than the door itself. Pushing down and twisting, I released the purely manual trigger on the heavy blade waiting to split the skull of anyone who relied on sorcery to get them past our defenses. Only then did I twist the handle and open the door to the kitchen.

Faran was waiting for me, no doubt alerted by the spell glyph carved into the top surface of the outer door. My profound relief at seeing her alive and in one healthy-looking piece lasted the two seconds it took to register the look on her face. Grim and cold, the controlled anger of the professional killer instead of the wild fury of the wronged teenager. Faran was both, and when the teenager lost the argument to the killer things were bad.

"What's wrong?" I asked.

"Besides you falling into a storm-wracked river and then vanishing utterly for half a week?" She spat the words out one by one, but I recognized it for the play it was.

"Yes, besides that." I kept my voice perfectly calm because I knew that would annoy her, and being annoyed might put her off stride enough to listen more carefully. "You're wearing the wrong face for the worried apprentice."

She snorted and a tiny bit of the grim went away. "I suppose I am, though I'm that as well. I really do care about you, despite all our arguing, and I *was* very worried."

"So was I."

Then, without really intending to, I stepped forward and caught her in my arms, squeezing her hard. For a long moment she remained stiff and angry, then she relaxed, dropped her head against my shoulder and squeezed me even harder.

"Terrible old man," she whispered.

"Dreadful little monster," I growled back.

We had a strange relationship, Faran and I. Part master and apprentice, part surrogate father and adopted daughter, part opposing duelists. We'd barely known one another at the temple and hadn't seen each other for five years after its fall. During those years I had diminished, going from being one of the two or three most feared professional killers in the world to a broken down jack who delivered smuggled goods for drinking money. Faran had grown from a terrified and half-trained eight-year-old into a professional thief and spy who killed with far less regret than I'd ever shown.

When I rescued her from a job gone horribly wrong, the adolescent who'd lost every shred of family she'd ever owned had wanted nothing more than to turn over the reins and the hard decisions to a respected authority figure dimly remembered from her past. That child's desire for security sat very poorly with the professional killer who had taken one look at our respective records over the last few years and found me wanting.

My own feelings weren't any easier to parse. I'd never wanted children. In fact, like many in the order, I'd chosen magical sterilization rather than risk any future potential conflicted loyalties between family and goddess. And yet, there was something about having Faran in my life, in the role that a child of my flesh might have held in a different world, that felt so very right. It didn't make for an easy relationship.

Time passed and Faran's death grip on my ribcage eased. I could feel the tension returning to her back and shoulders, so I gave her one last squeeze and then stepped back and away from her. On the wall behind her the dragon and the phoenix watched us as silently as shadows, reminding me that we were a family of four.

"Where the hell have you been, old man?"

"Shipwrecked," I replied.

"Seriously?"

"It's a long story," I replied before giving her the three-minute version.

"We have a major problem," Ssithra said when I'd finished. "Faran and I found it while you were gone."

I turned my gaze back to the girl. As I watched, the child

faded away and the killer settled back into the place behind her eyes.

"Tell me about it," I said.

"I'd rather show you," replied Faran, "and the sooner the better. I had trouble believing it myself."

"Lead on."

7

———◆———

Legends cast the longest shadows. From the day I killed Ashvik onward, I never had any hope of slipping free of the shadow of the Kingslayer. The name carried so much more weight than the one they'd given me as a child, that sometimes I could barely stand the load.

But even so, I wasn't the most famous of Blades. Mythkiller outweighed Kingslayer, and Deathwalker had eclipsed us both when he was in his prime. Kelos Deathwalker, two-hundred-year-old lord of assassins, a legend and an inspiration before he died with the fall of the temple. He had taught me more about the arts of death than all my other teachers combined. His death had felt almost as impossible as Namara's. Without hers, it would have seemed completely unbelievable.

That's why the scene in the room below our hiding place cut straight through my heart. Legends died, they didn't turn their coats. Yet there was Master Kelos, alive and well and practically bending his knee to a woman whose robes declared her the Lady Signet, Nea Sjensdor, preceptor of the Hand of Heaven. She was tall and slender and she moved like a praying mantis . . . just as she had in the Gryphon's Head on the day that Jax had walked back into my life, though I hadn't recognized her then.

I felt a little shiver at the memory. It was Kelos she'd been sitting with then—had to have been—though I hadn't recognized him at the time either. Not even when he made eye contact and warned me off. I wondered if he'd known it was me despite all the changes to my face. There was no clue in his gaze, and Jax hadn't, and she and I had been as close as I'd ever been to anyone other than Triss. But somehow I couldn't make myself believe I'd fooled Kelos.

Fucking legends. I knew exactly how hollow they could look from the inside, and yet I couldn't make myself stop believing in the Deathwalker's. Not even now when I saw him playing lackey to one of the people who'd destroyed us. How could I not have recognized him?

The Signet I could understand; I'd never seen her face before. This Signet had been promoted to replace the three layers of officers that had died in the fall of the temple. We'd made the forces of Heaven's Reach pay a price in blood for destroying us, especially the Hand and the Sword, but it hadn't been enough. It could never be enough.

Breathe, Triss whispered into my mind. *Tell me what you see.*

Sorry. Give me a moment to get myself back under control.

Faran had brought along both a hearsay and eyespy, so we were able to listen and watch without actually getting in close. I lifted my gaze from the big glass half sphere of the eyespy now to meet Faran's gaze—the device didn't work with Shade senses so we both had our faces unshrouded.

"Later," I whispered, "you're going to have tell me more about how you found your way here."

"Not much to tell. Ssithra picked up Malthiss's shadow trail and we followed it."

I didn't ask how they'd recognized who the trail belonged to. There wasn't a member of the order who hadn't studied under Kelos and Malthiss. Legends, dammit, and for good reason. Look at our little spy post.

The Hand had set up temporary headquarters in a riverside warehouse just above the Royal Docks. Judging by the seals on the crates where Faran and I had taken up our perch, it was owned by the Crown. That meant the Hand was there with the King's blessing. Which made me curious about why they had chosen not to set up at the high temple of Shan or one of its satellites. But there could be a dozen or more reasons for keeping their presence unofficial, not least of which was my known presence in the area.

Most of the huge warehouse was simply a giant open room studded here and there with pillars to support the roof. One large section in the corner had been partially cleared of crates in an obviously hasty manner to make space for the Hand to set up their operations. At the far end, where we were, a series of open lofts had been built against the wall, allowing for the segregated storage of goods that couldn't be stacked very high or that needed to be off the ground.

Our perch was on the second loft from the top in the corner farthest from the Hand. The crates there climbed to within a few inches of the bottom of the level above us except for one small gap. The angled supports coming off one of the pillars holding up the lofts had forced them to leave an opening, and that's where we were.

Someone—almost certainly Kelos—had cut a trapdoor from the much more sparsely packed level above to allow access to the niche, hiding it under a couple of crates. The route into the building was equally clever.

It involved a really challenging roof-run, a brutal spider walk, and a barred clerestory window that had been invisibly converted to a pass-through, among other things. None of it would have been impossible for a mage with the right skills, but all together it would be damned hard for anyone but a Blade to manage. Even most Blades would never have stumbled on it by accident.

That was why I wanted to talk to Faran about how she'd done so. It didn't *feel* like a trap, but the good ones never do. I'd have been more worried about the possibility, if whoever set up the spy hole hadn't also put together a damned fine emergency exit. That involved a series of shadow-triggered destructive spells that would open a half dozen bolt holes. I couldn't really test it without giving us all away, but I had very little doubt it would work as I expected it to.

Aral!

Sorry. On it.

I looked down into the eyespy again, and began to describe the scene below to Triss. The cleared space was divided into three unroofed rooms by walls of crates. The main living area held a couple of couches and tables where three of the Hand were studiously ignoring the score of Swords taking up most of the space. A sort of bunkroom with a bunch of pallets held about another dozen Swords and one Hand, all asleep—probably the night shift.

A smaller office and sleeping area stood off to one side, separated from the living area by a heavy velvet curtain. The room contained a platform with a proper mattress on it, several chairs, a cabinet for papers, and a desk with an intense magelight of the sort favored by those who dealt with large amounts of correspondence. A loose ball of white fluff, like an afternoon cloud fallen to earth, lay curled on the mattress, the Signet's Storm familiar. I couldn't be sure, because it was mostly hidden under one wing, but the Storm's head looked to be the blade of a scythe.

The Signet sat behind the desk, glaring up at Kelos, who had perched himself on the open side panel of a high crate. He was squatting on his heels, a pose that would allow him to move in any direction on an instant's notice, and one that I knew he could hold for hours if he chose.

Kelos had ditched the bushy black beard for an equally false red goatee, and swapped his glass eye for the leather patch he used to wear back at the temple. His arms were bare, showing off the deep black scaled tattoos that slithered around his arms and torso like a great snake endlessly curling back on itself. There was no obvious sign of Malthiss, which meant the Shade had chosen to add a few extra loops to the tattoo as he so often had in my memories. The sudden appearance of the Shade's head rising into a striking position from amongst the inky coils that beautifully camouflaged his presence had given more than one apprentice Blade nightmares.

"I still don't see why you insist on perching above me like some great vulture," said the Signet.

"I like the light here," Kelos replied in that deep bass growl I remembered so well from my youth—his training voice. He'd used a lighter, sweeter tone with those he considered his peers.

"Clever," said Faran, and I had to agree, though I didn't like the implications.

Kelos had chosen a perch where both the dying light from the windows and the bright lamp on the desk would only paint his shadow across the boards beneath his feet or into the mouth of the open crate behind him. At a guess, that opening led to some sort of passage that would allow him to come and go from the Signet's office without casting any stray shadows where another Shade might taste them.

That meant he was concerned about the possibility of other Blades finding out he'd been there. But who was he worrying about? Me? Jax? Someone else? He'd been careful at the Gryphon's Head, too, or Triss would have tasted Malthiss's shadow there. Was that because I was known to spend time there? Or because he'd seen Jax and followed her there? Or just on general principle since he was supposed to be dead? With Kelos it could have been any of those, or all of them, or something everyone else had missed entirely.

"It's disrespectful," snapped the Signet.

"How so?" Kelos grinned, exposing big white teeth. "You command the Hand of Heaven, I lead Heaven's Shadow. I'm pretty sure that makes us coequal in rank."

"I am the Son's chosen successor and you should treat me with the deference my eventual ascension demands."

"The Son looks mighty healthy to me, and you have a dangerous job. I wouldn't bet any money on you outliving him."

"Is that a threat, Deathwalker? Because you don't scare me."

This time, Kelos laughed. "Tell it to someone who gives a damn, Signet. I don't care whether you're too brave to be scared of me, or if anybody else is for that matter, haven't in more than a century. What's in your head is your problem, and threats are for villains in children's stories. I don't bother. Why deliver a warning, when it's just as easy to deliver a foot of steel?"

The Signet leaped up from behind her desk, but the curtain snapped open before she could say anything. A short man wearing the livery of the king barged in. Looking beyond him, I could see that the Swords on duty at the entrance to the warehouse were not happy. I didn't blame them. If the king's envoy pissed the Signet off, she was likely to take a piece out of their hides for it. But short of starting a war with their hosts in Tien, there wasn't a whole lot they could do about a king's envoy playing things hard.

I didn't recognize the man, but I recognized the type, a glorified message runner with delusions of grandeur. Every court has a few—officials of sufficient rank to be taken seriously when you send them to run an errand, but limited enough ability that a king can afford to leave them sitting around and waiting for orders most of the time. Lesser nobles of dubious intelligence were ideal for the purpose.

"The more the king learns about that mess you created at the royal cemetery the less happy he becomes," the envoy snapped without prelude. "What were you playing at there?"

"Playing?" growled the Signet. "Is that what you think this is? A game? Because this is a deadly serious business. I lost two officers of the Hand the other night, if you hadn't noticed. We're trying to bring down the Kingslayer and—"

"Doing a terrible job of it," said the envoy. "When His Majesty agreed to your presence here, he assumed you knew what you were doing. Since that's clearly not the"—the envoy glanced up at Kelos, apparently noticing him for the first time. "What's this, have you acquired a pet monkey?"

"Ook," said Kelos, his voice deceptively mild as he made a show of scratching under one armpit.

"Insolent," said the envoy. "And you're not wearing the Son of Heaven's badge, monkey. Does that make you some local creature that the Lady Signet has picked up for some reason? Or what? Come down here where I can take a better look at you."

"I think I'll stay where I am," said Kelos.

"That wasn't a request, monkey, it was an order."

I saw the Signet's back tense at that, but Kelos just shrugged and silently held his place.

"Who do you think you're dealing with?" The envoy stomped closer to the crates as he spoke, pointing from Kelos to the floor imperiously. "I'm Heela Sharzdor, personal representative of King Thauvik the . . ." His words trailed off and he froze for a moment before making a little squeaking sort of noise.

"Sorry about the mess," Kelos said to the Signet.

It took me a moment to figure out that the envoy had stepped between the magelight and Kelos, so that his shadow now fell across the old assassin and the crate, making it quite obvious that Kelos cast no shadow of his own. At that very moment, Kelos's neck seemed to lift and broaden as Malthiss's cobralike head slid out from under his bond-mate's collar and rose into the air above Kelos. Before the envoy could do much more than let out another squeak, Malthiss opened his wide mouth and spat.

A thin amber stream of venom struck the envoy in the face and eyes. Sharzdor let out the faintest of whimpers, went completely rigid and toppled over on his side. He landed with an audible clunk, still in the exact position he was in when the venom struck, falling more like a statue than a man. The illusion grew stronger as his skin took on a distinct stony gray cast within a matter of seconds. Malthiss dropped back onto Kelos's neck, sliding down to vanish among the tattooed coils.

The Signet sighed and looked up at Kelos. "Now, what am I going to tell the king when he asks about what happened to his envoy?" She sounded more annoyed than angry.

"Tell him the Kingslayer did it."

"The Kingslayer? Really? How could he possibly get in here without us catching him?"

Kelos let out a low chuckle. "Aral's a damned resourceful Blade. You'd be surprised where he could get without you ever knowing he was there."

He knows we're here, Triss whispered into my mind. *And he's playing the Signet.*

How could he know about us? But I couldn't help but think Triss was right, about both things. Malthiss could have moved much faster had he chosen to, I'd have seen him do it.

The Signet just shook her head. "*Of course* he could. Or at least that's what I'm going to have to sell the king now. That and that the Kingslayer poisoned the envoy? Do you think he'll really believe poison? That seems a bit out of character."

"More than a bit, but that's not what you're going to tell Thauvik. You'll say that Sharzdor here was beheaded, the way Aral ghosted your priest in the cemetery the other night."

The Signet stiffened briefly, then shrugged and visibly forced herself to relax. "What makes you so sure that killing was the Kingslayer and the other wasn't?"

"Slitting throats isn't really Aral's style. That'll be the third

Blade they had with them, the unknown one." Kelos jerked his chin at the fallen envoy. "You'd better chop his head off soon."

"Why me? And why does it matter?"

"I'm not coming down there, so it's going to have to be you. And, the longer you wait, the harder it's going to be to conceal the fact that it was basilisk venom that killed him. You've got maybe five minutes before it starts to go from plain old paralysis to genuine petrification. At that point not only does the process become pretty difficult to conceal, but it'll blunt your edge when you make the cut."

"He'll actually turn to stone?" The Signet sounded dubious.

"He will. The venom acts as a magical catalyst. It uses the victim's own life force to transform flesh into something very like granite."

"Well then, hang on a moment." The Signet drew her sword of office—a long straight blade that glowed bright blue in magesight from all the spells it bore.

Bringing it around in a precise vertical cut, she beheaded Sharzdor without scraping her sword's tip on the floor scant inches beneath his stiff neck. Blood fountained across the flagstones and she had to hop aside to keep it off her boots.

"He bleeds like he's still alive," she said.

Kelos nodded. "Of course. If the venom killed its victims outright, there'd be no residual life force to drive the petrification. For the magic to work, the victim has to stay alive right up to the point where they finish turning to stone."

"Is it painful?"

"The turning to stone part?" Kelos shrugged. "Once the magic sets in fully there's no known antidote or countercharm, which makes it a little hard to ask the victims. As for the poison? It burns like a motherfucker, but if you can rip your eye out fast enough you can stop it before it takes effect." He tapped his eye patch. "That stings a bit, too, but it's better than the alternative. Any more questions?"

The Signet blinked several times, looking genuinely nonplussed for the first time, then nodded. "I've got two, since you seem to be in a cooperative mood. First, why does everyone claim that basilisks kill with their gaze?"

"Myth. The venom works best if it hits you in the eyes, so basilisks usually kill face-to-face and at some distance, as

Malthiss just demonstrated. It's a pretty short jump from there to the whole deadly gaze thing. What's your second question?"

"Malthiss isn't really a basilisk. He's a Shade. So how can he spit basilisk venom?"

"Trade secret." Kelos smiled a very alarming sort of smile. "Now, don't you have an explanation to fabricate for the king?"

"Thanks to you."

"Then I'll leave you to it, as I've things to deal with as well, now that the sun's finally down. Also, unless I miss my guess, you'll be receiving another visitor shortly. One I'd rather not meet." He slid back into the open crate, pulling the side he'd been perched on shut behind him.

We should get out of here, said Triss. *We don't want him getting around behind us.*

"I think that's our exit signal," whispered Faran.

"You might have a point," I said, starting to rise. Then I took one last glance at the eyespy and swore.

The warehouse door stood open with Jax on the threshold.

What is it? asked Triss.

I told him, and he let out a series of angry mental hisses in Shade.

"Faran, Ssithra, can you play lookout? I hate to ask, especially when it's Kelos you'll be looking out for, but I need to see what's going on between Jax and the Hand, and I won't get a chance like this again."

"Isn't it obvious?" demanded Faran in an angry whisper. "Your ex is another fucking traitor."

"Probably," I agreed, though it hurt me to say so. "But I still want to know the details. Will you watch for Kelos? Because if not, we have to go right now."

Faran's face twisted angrily. "Yes, dammit, but under protest."

"Thank you. If you see any sign of him, any sign at all, activate the glyph that brings the house down and run for it. Don't hesitate for even one second. I'll be right behind you."

She didn't say another word, just shrouded up and vanished. I turned my attention back to the eyespy. In the meantime, Jax had crossed the distance to the Signet's office where she now waited between a pair of the Hand. A third Hand had stepped

through to have a quick and whispered conference with the
Lady Signet. Though none of them spoke a word, the tension
between the Hand and Jax was so palpable I half-expected to
see steel come out of scabbards at any second.

Before that happened, the Hand in the office waved Jax in
and then, with obvious reluctance, stepped out and let the curtain close behind him. The Signet had returned to her place
behind the desk. Her Storm, quiescent all through the discussion with Kelos, rose now to hover above and behind her left
shoulder. Its scytheblade head bobbed angrily as it glared eye-
lessly down at Jax.

"I'm not happy about what happened at the cemetery," said
the Signet, "not at all."

"Fuck you." Jax stepped over the corpse of the royal envoy
to put both hands on the desk and lean down over the Signet.
"*You're* not happy! You change the plan without consulting me.
You show up unannounced at a meeting you promised you
would let me handle my way, and alone. You personally mage-
blast a hole in my side, knocking me completely out of the
game. Then you have the fucking gall to tell me that *you're* not
happy? I ought to kill you right now."

The Signet didn't so much as blink, though her familiar
angrily flared wings which had shifted from fluffy white to
storm-cloud gray.

"Are you done yet?" asked the Signet.

"You'd better pray to your stinking god that I'm not," said
Jax. "Because the second I decide this is over and there's nothing more I can do, I'm going to cut your heart out and burn it
in front of your eyes."

The Signet shrugged and continued as if Jax hadn't spoken,
"I'm not happy and your lover will suffer for it."

"What are you going to do? Torture him extra hard?"

"I promised that Master Loris and your captured journeymen would remain unharmed as long as you cooperated with
me, Master Jax. Thus far I have kept my promise."

"Of course you have. However could I doubt the head of the
Son of Heaven's personal inquisition? Maybe because I've been
in your dungeons before, and I know what sort of people you
are. You may have ordered your people not to leave any fresh
marks, but like hell you're not hurting them. No, you can tell

me all you want that you've called off the torturers, but I know how much your precious word is worth."

"I can always rescind the order to leave no marks. I lost two fingers of Heaven's Hand because of that debacle at the cemetery, and then afterward you vanished for three days! You should consider yourself lucky that I kept sending the daily messages to keep them alive while I waited for your return."

"You didn't *lose* any priests, you murdered them yourself when you changed the plan without consulting me. Did you think all you had to do was get Aral out in the open and then you could throw me away and do this yourselves? He's the fucking Kingslayer. Even if he's turned into a drunken wreck, he's still one of the half dozen most dangerous killers in the entire world. How stupid are you to think that barging into that cemetery wasn't going to explode in your face?"

The Signet moved like coiled lightning, leaning forward and backhanding Jax so hard that she staggered back and tripped over the corpse. As she went over backward, Jax twisted and put a hand on the floor, turning her fall into a cartwheel that ended with her on her feet halfway across the room with both swords drawn. The Storm rose high into the air and buzzed toward Jax, only to try to sheer off at the last second as a shadow tiger leaped to meet it. But Sshayar was faster, catching the Storm with both front paws and dragging it down toward the floor.

The Signet jumped to her feet and shouted, "Call your familiar off, Blade! Do it now, or there's no message and Loris and the apprentices die in the morning."

Jax twitched, but she didn't otherwise respond.

8

―――――◆―――――

Choosing not to die can be the hardest thing in the world. Sometimes life puts you in a place where all of your options are bad. No matter what you do, you're going to make things worse. It's easy to let despair rule you in a moment like that, or rage, or simply the desire to let go of your problems and let everything fall on someone else's shoulders.

I'd been there myself, more than once, and quite recently. I was starting to climb out of hell now, had gotten a good way up the ladder even. But I could still see the fires below waiting for me to slip. I knew how easy it would be to fall back into them. I woke up some mornings imagining how much simpler things would be if I didn't ever have to open my eyes again. But then I thought about what my death would do to Triss, and I dragged myself out of bed and forced myself to keep moving until the urge to die faded.

I could see Jax fighting with that same suicidal impulse right now. Faran's eyespy was a damned good one. I could read the rage and despair in Jax's expression, could almost hear the voice in her head telling the Signet to go fuck herself, could feel her longing toward the peace of oblivion. The balance between life and death held for three long beats, and then Jax's eyes fell.

"Damn you. . . ." she said. And then, a few seconds later, "Sshayar, let it go."

The shadow tiger turned her head toward her bond-mate. "Jax . . ." But then she loosened her claws and the Storm popped free. "She's just going to betray us in the end. You know that, don't you?"

Jax nodded. "I do. But until that moment comes I still have a chance of finding us a way out of this." She turned back to the Signet. "I'm going to kill you. It might not be today, it might not be next week, but I promise you the day *will* come. I will be the instrument of your destruction."

The Signet just smiled. "You keep telling yourself that, my dear. As long as it doesn't interfere with what I need you to do, you can harbor whatever little fantasies will get you through the day. Now, I need you to set up another meeting with the Kingslayer as soon as possible, and this time we'll get him."

"No."

"No?"

"No. We're going to do things my way this time, the way I told you it had to work from the very beginning. That is, unless you *want* to kill a bunch more of your people? Because I could go for that, too. Every time one of you dies it makes the world a slightly better place. If that's really your choice, just say the word. Otherwise, I'm going to turn around and leave now, and I'll see you again in the Magelands in a couple of weeks where we will do this my way."

It was Jax's turn to smile, and if I'd been the Signet I'd have been backing away. But then, I'd seen that exact expression on Jax's face in the past and I knew how much spilled blood it portended.

"Fine," said the Signet, "we'll do it your way, but if it goes wrong, the consequences will all be on you. Now, get out of my office. Oh, and have my leech patch up that hole I put in your side. I'm going to need you in top condition for this."

"Fuck that, and fuck you. I got enough of that hurt us and heal us crap last time I fell into the grip of the Hand. At this point I'd rather die than let another one of your butchers touch me."

"If that's how you want to play things, it's your lookout. You won't find a better healer anywhere in Tien than mine, but you *will* find a healer and get that side patched up. I don't give a damn about you as a person, but as an asset I need you in good health. Now, get out of here."

Without another word, Jax turned and stalked toward the exit.

As she reached for the curtain, the Signet called after her retreating back, "Report in to the chief officer of the Sword of Heaven at Shan's temple in Tavan when you arrive. She'll have instructions telling you where and when to meet me after you contact her."

Jax threw a rude gesture over her shoulder and stepped through the curtain. The instant it fell behind her, I snatched up the eyespy and hearsay and tucked them into my pouch.

"No sign of Kelos?" I asked Faran as I joined her at the clerestory pass-through a few seconds later.

She indicated the glyph designed to bring the house down. "Does it *look* like I blew up the warehouse?"

"No."

"There's your answer."

"Awful child."

"Old monster."

I half expected her to demand that I give her a complete recap of what had happened then and there, but the professional killer had pushed the angry teenager aside once more. She didn't say another unnecessary word between the warehouse and Jinn's, a small cafe near the Ismere Library. It took us almost three hours to cross the two miles between the two because we more than doubled the distance traveled in an effort to prevent anyone from following us.

By the time we sat down on the riverside rooftop, I'd used every technique I'd ever learned to shake a hound off my back-trail. Of course, the hound I most feared had taught me the bulk of those tricks. It made for an itchy feeling right between the shoulder blades. That was half the reason I'd chosen to head for the cafe. Better by far to lead any hound there than home.

Jinn's had its own tiny dock, and we'd arrived by hired

sampan—our third boat ride of the night. That easy access to the water was one of the reasons I liked the cafe. Another was the rooftop seating, four stories up with a lovely view of the river. From our table, five running steps and a long drop put you in the water. Ten steps and a short jump in the other direction carried you up onto the chimney road.

A lot of Jinn's custom came in that way, though the staff pretended not to notice since roof-runners mostly walked the shadowside and valued their privacy. The food ranged from good to damned good, with most falling in the latter range. Faran ordered a plate of fried rice with clams and scallops and a pot of tea. I opted for gingered whitefish served on a bed of noodles, and small beer. I wanted something stronger, but my recent indulgence had reminded me of where that would lead, and besides, it would take my edge off. Damn but I missed efik at times like this, when I wanted to calm down but stay sharp.

Faran rubbed her biceps through the sleeves of her gray silk shirt. "Do you think he followed us?" She looked even more paranoid than I felt. "That he's out there somewhere watching us right now?"

"No. I don't think so, no matter what my gut keeps telling me. The man's good, none better, but even he's not so good that he could have followed us through all that."

Care to bet your life on it? Triss whispered into my head.

Haven't I? Then, *Why, have you seen something I missed?*

No. I even think you're right. It's just . . . Malthiss, and Kelos. How can I not worry about them?

"You're doing it again," said Faran.

"Doing what?" I replied.

"Going away into your head. You do it a lot, and sometimes when you come back you know things that you didn't before. You're talking to Triss when you do that, aren't you? Mind-to-mind."

I blinked several times while I tried to figure out how to answer that. As far as I knew, Triss and I alone among our peers had developed the ability to mindspeak. Certainly, the temple masters had always taught that such communication between human and Shade was impossible.

"Don't try to deny it," said Faran. "Ssithra and I have been discussing it for weeks now. That's the only answer that makes sense."

I nodded. "I guess I should have known you'd figure it out eventually." Faran *had* become a quite successful spy after the fall of the temple. "It's not exactly a secret." It's just that I didn't entirely trust anyone but Triss.

"How did you manage it? And why not tell us about it?" She held up a hand. "No, wait. I want to hear about what happened with Jax first. That's more immediately important, though I'll want to know everything about the mindspeech, too. If you could teach us . . ."

"I doubt it," I said. "The circumstances were *very* unusual, but you're right, Jax comes first. But even before that, I want to know about how you stumbled onto Kelos's trail."

"You think he set me up to find that warehouse, don't you?" said Faran.

"I don't know, but if he put together that observation post he went to a hell of a lot of trouble to make it hard to spot. That he then left a shadow trail leading right to it strikes me as potentially suspicious."

Faran shook her head. "I don't think it was a setup. You saw the route we had to follow to get in. Three sail-jumps and a couple of spider walks, and none of it on main paths through the chimney forest. Kelos repeatedly went a good deal out of his way to cast no shadows on commonly trafficked rooftops."

"So, how did you stumble across it?"

"It was the night after you vanished. I was searching along the edges of the river on both sides, hoping to find the place where you and Jax had come ashore. There'd been pretty brutal sun all day, so I didn't have much hope of picking up the trail at that point, but I figured that with two Shades there was a slender chance."

"What time was it?" I asked.

"About three hours after sundown. I'd wanted to go right at dusk, but Ssithra wouldn't let me."

"Why not?"

Faran blushed. "She insisted that I needed to get some food and a nap before I went back out."

"Back out?"

"I'd spent some of that day looking around, too." On the table, the shadows cast by Faran's hand shifted subtly, and she jerked, letting out a small "ouch" sort of noise. "All right, I'll tell it your way, there's no need to pinch me."

She looked down at the table and her blush deepened. "I hadn't eaten or slept since I lost you in the flood. The only way Ssithra talked me into taking a break then was by pushing hard and insisting that with the sun gone, any trail would wait for a while."

She glared at her shadow. "There, happy now?" Ssithra didn't respond, but then, considering the relatively public nature of our current circumstances, the fact she'd done so much as pinching Faran was quite unusual.

When Faran looked up at me, I raised an eyebrow and she blushed yet again. The food arrived then, and we both went quiet for a few minutes—it'd been a long time between meals for both of us.

When she'd finished most of her plate, Faran continued, "Sorry. Where was I? Oh, right, sneaking along the riverbank practically under the Royal Docks, maybe a quarter mile on from where I'd left off earlier. Under any other circumstances we'd probably have missed it, but we were going over every inch of ground and paying extra attention. It was such a tiny scrap of shadow trail, no bigger than a silver riel, and not connected to anything."

"Then how did you follow it?"

"We didn't. Not at first anyway. We searched all around that first trace and couldn't find anything, but Ssithra swore up and down that it had come from Malthiss. So we didn't dare let it go. We didn't want to leave off the search for you either though, so after about an hour of scrabbling around on the bank there, I marked the spot for later investigation and we went on looking for your trail."

"But I'd been washed out to sea, so you didn't find that either."

"Exactly, though we kept on looking all through the next day. It was getting close to sundown then when we pretty much decided you and Jax had drowned." She swallowed hard and reverted to looking like a frightened teenager for a few heartbeats before recomposing herself. Then she gave me a very hard look. "And don't you *ever* scare me like that again, or I'll cut your throat in your sleep and bury you out back just so I know where to find you."

I smiled at her. "I'll see what I can manage."

"Don't think I won't do it," she growled, but smiled shyly a moment later. "Anyway, we were just coming back past the place where I'd left that stone when it occurred to me how a bit of trail might have gotten out there on the riverbank all by its lonesome—it fell from the rooftops above. The long shadows made by the falling sun gave me the idea."

She paused as our waiter brought us a plate of sweet butter biscuits for dessert.

She ate one while she waited for him to get out of earshot, then nabbed a second and continued, "We had to pinpoint where it came from, but that was easy enough once I'd figured out the mechanism. There was a gap between a couple of chimneys that lined up nicely with the sun and the stone."

She paused. "You're looking worried again."

"It just seems like an awfully stupid mistake for someone like Kelos to make."

"I don't know. I looked around the rooftops there. It was a really tiny slip. You have to practically crab walk to get past that point without rising above the level of the roof peak, and the gap's less than an inch wide. All it would have taken was for the back of his collar to flare the tiniest bit as he ducked past."

"We're talking about Kelos. His shirts probably address him as sir and ask before they wrinkle."

"There's that," Faran said ruefully. "But how would he know I'd find the trail from a patch that tiny? It was already mostly faded when I got there."

"Kelos *Deathwalker*."

She sighed and nodded, then laughed. "He's probably listening to this entire conversation, isn't he?"

"I wouldn't bet my life that he wasn't, but you've got a point. If we don't at least pretend that he's not that good, we're never going to sleep again, much less go home. All right, the man's not perfect. He slipped up and it led you to that warehouse, which gives us a chance to get ahead of our enemies. So what do we do with it?"

"Depends, what happened with Jax?"

So I gave Faran everything that had happened at the warehouse after I sent her to keep an eye out for Kelos. Then she wanted me to tell her about what happened between Jax and me on the boat. I'd given her the brief version earlier, but she wanted the whole thing now. I skipped some of the more painful details about my conversations with Jax, but sketched in enough so that it didn't feel like I was lying to Faran by omission.

"I guess that leaves me with one question," said Faran.

"Which is?"

"Do you want me to kill Jax for you?"

I stopped with a biscuit halfway to my mouth. "What?"

"Well, she *was* your fiancée once upon a time. It seems awfully harsh to make you do it."

"Nobody's going to kill Jax."

Are you sure of that? Triss asked me.

Faran raised an eyebrow. "What does Triss have to say about that?"

"Never mind what Triss thinks. I'm making the call here, and no one is killing Jax. It's that simple." But really it wasn't. So, I added, "At least not anytime soon. She's not working with the Hand because she wants to, that's for damn sure. I don't know what Kelos's game is here either. And, even if it *is* a setup, somebody has to free Loris and the journeymen. Maybe we can find a way to make it all work out."

"Do you really believe that will happen?" Faran spoke with all the corrosive cynicism of a girl who'd had her entire life destroyed at the age of nine.

"I'd like to."

"That's all the answer I need." She touched the long dagger at her right hip. "Just say the word when the time comes."

I put my biscuit back on the plate. I was no longer hungry. When the waiter came by again I ordered a small bottle of sake. Neither Triss nor Faran said a word about it.

Jax turned and opened her mouth to say something to me, a smile on her face. That put her back to Faran, a fatal mistake. My apprentice stepped in silently and drove a short broad-bladed dagger into the place where Jax's skull met her neck. She collapsed at my feet, turning as she fell, so that her dead smiling face looked up at me.

Wake up! Triss shouted into my dreams, and I did.

For the fourth time in as many hours, I lay panting in my sweat-soaked bed, as out of breath as if I'd just finished a ten mile roof-run. I couldn't say which variation of the nightmare cut deeper, the one where Faran made the kill perfectly, or the one where she stepped on a squeaking board and Jax turned and neatly split her skull.

In either case, sleeping any more sounded like a terrible idea. My room occupied the eastern half of the second floor of the little house Faran had rented for us. Even through the thick mud-brick of the walls the heat of the morning sun had started to drive the temperature up toward unbearable. Without getting up, I cracked the shutters in hopes of catching an ocean breeze. The bright light drew bands of hot gold across my bed. For a moment it touched the shadow of a dragon stretched out atop my sheet, his chin on my chest, then Triss hissed and slipped around behind the headboard.

"Warn me next time," he said from his place in the dark. "This time of year the sun stings when I'm not ready for it."

"Sorry, old friend. I wanted to chase the nightmares away, not you. Thanks for waking me up."

"You're welcome, but it was self-defense. The images are so vivid they're spilling over into my dreams." He poked his head over the back of the headboard and peered down at me. "I find it deeply weird looking at the world as you humans do. You see things very strangely, and I may be the only one of my kind ever to view it so."

His wings popped into sight as he flapped them agitatedly. "This two-way mindspeech is not an unmixed blessing. I'm glad I only get the images when you are dreaming or intentionally projecting them. I'll have to discuss it with Ssithra now that she knows that you and I can mindspeak, see what she thinks of your bizarre view of the world."

"Just don't tell her about the contents of this particular dream. The more I think about it the less I like the idea of Jax and Faran spending two weeks in close proximity shipboard.

I'm going to have to figure out a way to leave Faran here. That'll be plenty hard enough without Ssithra giving her any reasons to be suspicious."

Triss shot out a long forked tongue, touching the top of it to my forehead. "It's funny, you don't *feel* feverish."

"What's that supposed to mean?"

"Do you really think Faran is going to agree to anything that prevents her from coming on this trip? She's a teenager. She's deeply devoted to you, even if she pretends not to be most of the time. She doesn't trust Jax, and has already offered to kill her for you. There's nothing you can possibly say that will convince her to meekly wait here for you."

"You're right. Which is why I to have to trick her into missing the boat somehow."

Triss sighed. "This isn't going to end well. You know that, right?"

"But you'll help me, won't you?"

"No, I don't think that I shall. Not this time. I see no reason to put myself in a situation where I have to apologize to Ssithra and Faran for trying to implement a plan so obviously doomed to failure."

"But I've got to keep Jax and Faran apart. You see that, don't you? I can't let Faran kill Jax, and I won't let Jax endanger Faran in any way."

"This is not the temple, you have no authority over Faran other than that which she chooses to give you. I know you want to shield her from the cruelties of this world, but she's nearly a grown woman and you can barely take care of yourself."

"She's fifteen!"

"And you're not yet thirty, and more an older brother than a father figure to her, no matter how you see things. She survived six years all by herself in the hard cold aftermath of the temple falling. Thrived even. She and Ssithra managed a hell of a lot more than we did in those years."

"But I've got to protect her. I've got to protect both of them."

"Jax is your age and twice as responsible as you ever were and I've already said all I intend to about Faran. Leave the job of protecting the women to the women. Or, if that's not enough of an argument, leave it to Sshayar and Ssithra. It's their job, not yours."

"But—"

Triss just shook his head and dropped down behind the bed again. "This is exactly the same sort of sentimental nonsense that kept you from killing Devin. You can't save the whole world from itself, no matter what they taught us at the temple. Now, I'm going back to sleep. Wake me when you get out of bed or come to your senses. No. Scratch that latter, I'd prefer to wake up sometime before the end of the century. Wake me when you get out of bed."

I reached for the book I'd borrowed from Harad, the librarian at the Ismere, but gave it up after a few pages when it became clear that reading wasn't going to be enough to push the nightmare images away. Still, I remained in bed. I had about fifteen hours till my meeting with Jax and I needed to figure out how to get Faran out of harm's way between now and then.

It's amazing how fast a day can pass when you would rather it didn't. I'd spent practically the whole time trying to find an answer to the problem of keeping Faran and Jax away from each other. Yet here I was walking into the Spinnerfish for my meeting with the latter without so much as a clue's ghost.

About the only thing I could claim to have accomplished on that front was convincing Faran to play the hidden ace to my faced jack. Instead of sitting in on the meeting, Faran and Ssithra were dancing a slow circle around the Spinnerfish looking for the Hand. I didn't think Jax would have changed her mind about how she wanted to run things with the forces of Heaven's Reach, but I trusted the Signet to keep her word even less than I currently trusted Jax.

My stomach twisted around on itself like a knotsnake with an itch. That I even had to think this way about someone I'd nearly married at one point was so beyond fucked, it made me want to crawl into a whiskey barrel and have someone hammer the top shut. At least I'd have a little fun before I drowned that way.

I half expected Erk Endfast to slide out from behind the bar when I came through the front door of the Spinnerfish and tell me to turn right the hell around and march back out. A onetime black jack, he'd given up the blood trade when he left the Magelands one step ahead of an official execution order. He said he'd had enough of living shadowside after that, but it didn't keep him from making a ghost of anyone who threatened the peace of his establishment. And, whether I wanted things that way or not, I threatened the peace of the Spinnerfish just by walking in the door.

But Erk just nodded hello and kept on puttering away at something below the level of the bar top. He'd known my old face back in the days before ever it got pasted up on wanted posters across the eleven kingdoms, but my new one didn't belong to anyone who mattered. I was finding that I liked being a ghost even less than I liked being a legend. When I got closer to the bar, Erk smiled vaguely.

"You meeting Captain Fei again?"

I'd been in maybe a half dozen times since the change, mostly to have dinner with Kaelin Fei, Tien's number one corrupt cop and one of the very few people in on my secret.

I shook my head and spoke with a deliberate husk, "Afraid not, but I will need a private booth for two. I'd prefer not to be seen while I'm waiting."

"You know your way back. Take the third table past Fei's on the right. I'll send your guest back when they get here. Who should I be on the lookout for, the kid?" Faran had joined Fei and me on a couple of occasions.

"No. A woman, tiny with pale skin and long brown hair. Pretty, too."

"Anything really distinctive about her?"

"Besides her height? She's got a net of thin scars on her face and arms like finest lace. She'll probably be wearing two swords in a double sheath on her hip. Oh, and if you get on the wrong side of her she'll give you a look that'd cut diamonds."

"Two swords, huh?" Erk gave me the second look he hadn't earlier, though his expression didn't change. "I knew a man who used to carry two swords once. About your height and build actually. I haven't seen him around in a while, and that's too bad. Dangerous man, but a good one on his sober days. I liked him." He smiled now. "If you see him, give him my best."

"Doesn't seem likely, but I'll keep it in mind." I started toward the back room.

"Hang on," said Erk.

"Why?"

"I think your friend's just arrived."

I looked over my shoulder and found Jax heading my way.

"Jax," I said quietly as I went to meet her. "Your timing is perfect, as always."

"Aral." She caught my hands in her own and pulled me down to give me a kiss on the cheek.

I couldn't help but glance at Erk out of the corner of my eye to see whether he'd heard her name me. But if he had, he didn't give any indication of it. Still, I frowned. What was Jax's play there? I didn't make the mistake of believing she'd slipped. She was better than that.

I pulled one of my hands free of hers and guided her around me with the other. "We've got a private table waiting. It's this way."

Like all of Erk's private tables, ours sat in an alcove off one of the many little halls that made a maze of the back of the Spinnerfish. Designed to seat no more than two people, the narrow table had built-in bench seats on either side. I let the shimmering green gold curtains fall behind us as we settled in across from each other.

Jax touched the fabric. "It's subtle, but these are spelled."

"For privacy, nothing more, part of why I chose this place."

"Nice. How did your business go?" she asked.

"Just fine. Yours?"

"Much the same."

Then, forcing the words to come out smoothly despite the tightness in my throat and back, I asked, "Anything I should know about?"

It was a test. Like all Blades, Jax had been trained to lie smoothly and seamlessly, but she'd never been good at lying to anyone she cared about. Not in the old days.

She smiled and looked me straight in the eye. "Not really. Routine stuff all, though I can go into it if you're worried about it." There wasn't so much as a flicker of her eyelashes out of place.

"No, that's all right," I lied back at her, though probably not half so well. "I'm more interested in planning for what comes next. This is going to be very dangerous, too dangerous for a half-trained girl like Faran. I want to leave her in Tien, and I'm going to need your help to make sure she stays here."

9

———————⟡———————

The rising sun spilled blood across the waves, red and wrathful and full of portent, like the dreams that drove me out into the light. I am a creature of the night, an assassin and companion to shadows. The morning sun is my enemy. I do not seek it out, it hunts me. Today it caught me high in the rigging of the *Fortunate Lamia*.

I had come looking for the winds, hoping they would blow away the thick cobwebs of my nightmares. I found only melancholy and the burning edge of morning. For perhaps the hundredth time I rubbed at my eyes, trying to scrub away the images of Jax and Faran, each dead at the other's hand. Even leaving Faran behind hadn't been enough to banish my dreams. Maybe because I still had no idea how to deal with Jax, much less evade the trap that was waiting for me, and get Loris and the others free. I couldn't see any way to make things come out right.

Things had been so much simpler before the temple's fall. I never had to figure out what was the right thing to do, the Just thing. My goddess told me what needed doing, and I did it. The world was black and white. Or, at least, it had looked that way at the time. Among the many things I had come to understand since then was that the world was rarely as simple as I wanted it to be. A fact that was very hard to forget with Jax and Faran murdering each other behind my eyelids every night.

I never thought that I would miss my old nightmares, I sent to Triss.

Excuse me? His mind voice sounded muzzy and unsettled—he likes the morning even less than I.

Usually, I dream my failures or the dead face of the goddess.

And that's better how, exactly?

I prefer the scar that aches to the fresh cut that has yet to start bleeding. These nightmares remind me of how much I have left to lose.

Not how much you have left to save?

I shook my head. *Since the temple fell my glass has always been half empty.*

Is that *why you keep adding whiskey?*

I snorted. *Perhaps it is, the need to fill that which can never be filled.* Then I shrugged. *I don't know.*

The lookout is very nervous about you being up here, Triss sent, tapping my arm by way of pointing at the man.

I'd taken a perch on the rope strung along below the yard of the big junk's foremast. The one the lookout atop the big mast had referred to as the "footrope" when he called out for me to use that instead of trying to walk the yard itself, "for Orisa's sake."

I snorted. *There's barely a wind and the swells can't be running much over three feet. I'm in no danger of falling.*

I know that, and you know that, but the poor lookout is practically in hysterics. The captain doesn't look any too happy either.

The captain? When did he come out on deck?

Just now, he's having some very harsh words with the steerswoman, and his face is beginning to turn red.

I suppose we ought to get down before he orders us down. That would be awkward, since I've no intention of setting the precedent of obedience. Maybe if we show him we're in no danger it'll help calm him.

Before Triss could argue, I braced hands and feet and vaulted up onto the yard. Then I ran lightly back to the mast and jumped to one of the ropes that ran from it to the deck, quickly hand-over-handing my way down. The *Lamia*'s captain, a small round fellow, was there to meet me when my feet touched down, his face red and swollen with anger.

He opened his mouth, presumably to start yelling at me. I gave him the look that I used on the occasional footpad foolish enough to follow me into an alley. It was something I'd learned from Kelos, and the captain, who had been leaning forward, closed his mouth and took a small half step back.

"What do you think you're doing?" he said a moment later, but it sounded more plaintive than demanding.

"Getting some exercise. I woke up too early and needed to work out the kinks before I get in a practice duel with my partner." I arched my back and put my hands on my hips inches from the hilts of my swords—I'd put them on as a sort of talisman against the nightmares. "Why, is there a problem?"

"You gave me a bit of a start is all. I thought you'd fall and hurt yourself, or mess something up, but you seem to know your way around a ship's rigging. I didn't know you were a sailor."

"I'm afraid that I'm not really."

"Then where'd you learn to climb like that?"

"You really don't want to know." I smiled a predatory smile and the last of his color faded.

He looked from my face to the well-worn sword hilts at the base of my spine and jumped to what was almost certainly the wrong conclusion. There'd never been that many Blades to begin with, and now we were all but extinct. "Maybe I don't at that."

That wasn't very nice, Aral.

No, it wasn't.

You don't sound sorry.

I'm not. Oh, I didn't really want to step on him, but it was that or take a lecture and stay out of the rigging thereafter, and I'm already feeling trapped enough on this damned boat.

I suppose it's better than having you hitting the bottle again. I winced as Triss's mental voice scored a direct hit.

While I talked to Triss, the foredeck quickly cleared as the captain and what crew were awake found things to do elsewhere. I was just wondering if I might not be able to go back to sleep when Jax came up the ladder from the lower deck. The sun highlighted the scars on her cheeks and I felt a little stab in my heart. She still looked every bit as wild and appealing as she had when we were together, but the gentler side of her beauty was gone. Her face was a battlefield, gorgeous still, but marked forever by blood and pain.

"Was that wise?" she quietly asked me.

"Probably not, but I'm in no mood for an argument."

"From him? Or from me?"

"Either, both. If I'd thought about it, I might not have climbed up above, but it felt damned good, and I'll certainly do it again. I had a rough night and I wanted to get away from my dreams."

"Feeling guilty about leaving Faran behind?" Jax asked with a lift of her eyebrows.

"No. That's one of the few things I actually feel *good* about. I don't want her involved in what's coming. This business is going to get damned ugly."

Jax turned away when I said that, walking to the rail to look out over the sea. "Yes, I'm afraid that it will."

Was she ever going to stop lying to me? But I couldn't ask her that, so instead I asked, "How much of my little chat with the captain did you hear?"

"All of it. I don't sleep so well myself these days." She turned back to me, resting a hip against the railing. "You woke me when you climbed out of your bunk. I followed you out of the cabin after I saw you put on your swords."

"Worried about what I'd do?"

Jax frowned. "No. More about what you might have heard that made you feel you needed to arm yourself." Her expression slid into something more melancholy and she hugged herself. "You have nightmares?"

I pictured her smiling corpse lying at my feet the way my dreams had painted it so many times in the last few days, and I nodded.

"I get them, too. Almost every night. The torturers coming for me, the fall of the temple, dead friends cursing me for living when they didn't—all my failures." She shook herself and forced a grin. "Were you serious about a practice duel?"

"If you're interested, yes."

"Good, it'll give me something to think about besides evil

dreams." She drew her swords, one overhand, one under and slid forward into a guard position.

I reached for my own, then froze with them half out of their sheaths. It was the first time I'd seen Jax draw her swords since she'd come back into my life, and I simply wasn't ready for the sight that greeted me now. The hilts and hip sheath had betrayed me into believing she had chosen to put aside the swords of Namara and make do with lesser steel, as I had. But those were temple blades in her hands.

"Are you all right, Aral?"

I nodded, completing my draw. "You had them rehilted." The words came out harsher than I'd intended, angry.

Namara's swords had simple oval guards that divided blade from hilt, all of it enchanted by the goddess to never break or wear. The guards were faced with lapis so that looking at them point-on you saw what appeared to be a blue eye widely opened—the unblinking eye of justice. Jax had replaced the oval guards and black sharkskin grips with traditional Dalridian style basket hilts. The cups and guards were shaped of bent steel, the grips surfaced with braided bronze wire.

But the short, lightly curved blades with their distinctive smoky blue steel that absorbed light rather than reflecting it, and their absolute unmarred perfection of line, were unmistakable. The swords of the goddess didn't look so much forged as wished into existence.

"Of course I did." Jax shifted a step to her right, and raised her right sword to point at my throat. "I couldn't bear to see the old hilts every time I looked down, and these are much less obtrusive in Dalridia. Would you prefer to spar with wood? I'm sure the captain must have some practice blades around here somewhere."

I snorted and shook my head, recognizing it as more of a tease than a serious offer. We'd both trained under Master Kelos, and while he might prefer that the apprentices and journeymen didn't cut each other to ribbons, he'd always been adamant that there was no substitute for working with live steel for the expert. With a practice weapon you always knew that a fuckup wouldn't really cost you. That changed the calculus of attack and response for the worse. It made you more likely to take stupid risks or deliver imprecise attacks.

"Do you want to do this or not?" I asked.

"Whenever you're ready then."

I feinted a cut at her left wrist, she parried and tried to catch my blade in a bind that I slipped. She flipped her underhand blade to an overhand grip, spinning in close as she did so with a cut that would have taken my feet off if I hadn't hopped over it.

"Not much of a jump," she said, as she flicked a thrust at my forward thigh. "The old Aral would have gone a good foot higher."

I parried and forced her sword down and out, opening up a line on her biceps. "The old Aral would have been wasting his energy." As I attempted the cut, she followed her out-of-line sword into a spin that put her arm out of my reach while bringing her other sword around to slice at my collar bone.

"Why should I move even a half inch more than I need to?" A strategy I implemented by twisting just out of reach of her blade. As I riposted toward her heart I found myself wondering whether I ought to stop my thrust if Jax didn't.

But she beat my blade neatly aside, and delivered a heel tap to the top of my forward foot. "That would have broken your foot if I'd followed through."

"Point," I said.

Stung by the ease with which she'd taken the point, I jumped out of the way of her next thrust, leaping back and up onto the rail that separated the foredeck from the drop to the ship's waist. Then, before Jax could adjust to my higher position, I did a front flip over her, slapping the flat of my left blade against the back of her neck as I went past.

"Point," replied Jax, "and much more the old Aral."

Nice, added Triss.

In other circumstances, he and Sshayar might have joined in with our sparring, making it a partners match. Or, Jax and I might have taken control of our respective shadows to attempt maneuvers impossible to the Shadeless duelist. With the ship's crew watching, that wasn't really an option, so they stayed out of it. Even though our reduced circumstances dictated that Faran and I practice without our Shades as often as with, it felt strangely lonely to do so against Jax.

Now we really picked up our game. Lunge, parry, thrust,

block, cut, bind, spin, flip, thrust again, cartwheel, slice, kick, and so on. I picked up a half dozen nasty bruises and three minor cuts in the exchange and inflicted a similar bill of damage on Jax. We kept it up for a good ten minutes before simultaneously throwing up our blades and stepping back. I think I scored more points, but I was gasping like an asthmatic dragon by then, and felt as though I'd just run the roofs from Westen to the Spicemarket and back without a break. Jax was sweating and breathing heavy as well, but she didn't look half so blown as I felt.

"More?" She flashed me that wicked smile of hers, daring me to pretend she hadn't run me into the ground.

"How about I take a turn," said a smug and all-too-familiar voice from behind me.

"Faran?" I wheezed, more than half in shock.

Not that anyone but a Blade could have hidden themselves in the tiny triangle of space at the front of the ship, or that I had any doubt who that voice belonged to. But she couldn't have picked a better moment to lay me out with a few words.

"Of course. You didn't really believe I was going to let you out of my sight that easily, did you, Master Aral?"

The "Master Aral" waved all kinds of warning flags. The only times she'd called me that since I first found her in the sewers of Tien was when she was well and truly pissed off.

I was still trying to find the wind to come up with a good response when Jax spoke up. "Oh, very nicely done, Faran! I presume you've been here this whole time, but I didn't catch so much as a hint of your presence. Later, I'd love to hear how you managed to get aboard at all. I'd swear no one else was riding that sampan Aral hired to deliver him to the ship right as we sailed out of the harbor."

"Maybe if you ask nicely, I'll even tell you," said Faran, and I could hear the hard cold undertone to her words.

"If you're half as good with your steel as you are with your shadow-slipping then you'll be a damned worthy opponent. Come on, give me a try."

"Done." Faran stepped past me to face Jax, and there wasn't a damned thing I could think to do about it.

Faran held a pair of cane knives instead of swords. She much preferred the heavy, forward-curved blades that fell somewhere on the range between a long dagger and a short sword with a side order of hatchet. The weapons had come out of Kadesh originally, where they used them to harvest cane and bamboo, as well as the occasional enemy head. They weren't a traditional weapon for the servants of Namara, and Faran had never talked about how she'd come to pick up a set, but she used them with a brutal efficiency that often scored points against my longer and more elegant Zhani dueling swords.

Now, as she squared off against Jax, I couldn't help but feel that I'd stepped right out of the real world and into one of the scenes from my earlier nightmares. I wanted to stop them, but couldn't come up with any way to manage it short of physically stepping between them. Worse, exhausted as I was from my bout with Jax, I didn't know if I'd be able to do anything about it even if I tried.

I was still dithering when Faran dropped into a crouch and spun a reverse kick at Jax's shins. Rather than hop over the attack, Jax simply sank one of her swords into the deck. I winced. She placed the sword flat on to Faran's kick, rather than setting it up for a sliced hamstring, but it was still going to leave a hell of a bruise.

Only, it didn't. Somehow, Faran shifted her kick, lifting it from a low sweep into a heel strike aimed at the big muscles in Jax's thigh. At the same time, she interposed one of her cane knives flat on between her calf and Jax's sword. Striking there, just below the hilt, the impact of Faran's kick forced Jax to let go of her sword rather than have it ripped out of her hand. That collision between blades slowed the heel strike enough so that Jax was able to hop back out of the way, but it left her leaning too far forward to avoid Faran's follow up a moment later.

I drew a sharp breath as Faran's second knife slid up and under, drawing a line straight toward Jax's throat, but there was simply nothing I could do but watch. If Faran decided she wanted to kill Jax right now, Jax died. Though I hated myself for it, I couldn't help but think of how much less complicated my life would be if she followed through.

"Sorry about that," Faran said, an instant later, when the tip of her second knife skidded across the skin under Jax's chin, leaving a bleeding gash. "I didn't turn the blade fast enough. You look taller than you are."

"Point, and I'm tempted to call it two," Jax said ruefully as she retrieved her sword from where Faran's blow had thrown it. "Or am I wrong that you *chose* a disarm over breaking my wrist?"

Faran smiled wolfishly. "You're not wrong. I couldn't slow my kick down at that point, so I decided I'd better not aim for flesh."

"Two then, and very well done. I wouldn't have believed how fast you move those heavy knives around if I hadn't seen it." Jax dabbed at the blood dripping off her chin and looked up at me. "She's good, Aral, she's . . . are you all right? You've gone awfully pale. And you haven't put your swords away. Did I push you too hard earlier?"

I shook myself. "No . . . I'm fine really. Just the lack of sleep catching up to me." I flipped my swords around and resheathed them—not sure why I hadn't done it before. What was I going to do with them, kill one of the women to prevent her from killing the other? "Nicely done, Faran."

"No worries about me losing control then, Master Aral?" She spoke sweetly, her voice making a sharp contrast to the anger in her eyes. "I did mark her pretty good, after all."

"An accident," said Jax who turned away from the main part of the ship and any watchers among the crew before applying a very minor sort of spell to staunch the bleeding. "And, hardly an uncommon one for live steel practice. Hell, I'm already oozing blood from four places where Aral nicked me today, and I've had much worse from him in the past." She laughed. "Remind me later, and I'll show you the scar that Aral gave me back in the days of our youth—it's nowhere I care to expose in public."

"I'll do that," said Faran. "Master Aral is concerned about my control, and it would be nice to see how well he did when he was my age. In the meantime, shall we continue?"

Jax nodded, before simultaneously cutting high and thrusting low. Faran blocked both blades, but had to twist hard to her left to manage it, leaving herself open for the elbow Jax drove into her right kidney as she stepped past her younger opponent. It wasn't a full force blow, but it still sent Faran staggering forward, allowing Jax to turn and tap her on the back of the head with the flat of her sword.

Faran growled, "Point." Then she pivoted to face Jax, assuming a low guard position.

There's really not a whole hell of a lot I can do here, is there? I asked Triss.

No. I don't like it either, but short of spilling blood or confronting Jax about the Signet, there's no way to keep them from what should be a friendly sparring match. Honestly, doing the latter's as likely to set them at each other's throats for real as anything. He sighed mentally. *Jax would already be dead if Faran wanted to kill her right now, so I think you have to let it go.*

While I reluctantly agreed with Triss, that didn't make it any easier to watch as the pair exchanged several more passes. Faran was more cautious now, and less vicious, and Jax was likewise taking extra care now that she knew her young opponent was no tyro. The pace increased as the two felt out each other's style. As the cuts and ripostes grew steadily faster and more potentially lethal, I had to practically nail my feet to the deck to keep from turning away.

But somehow I managed to keep watching. It was a rare chance to study Jax's present style from the sidelines and, as much as I hated to admit the possibility, I might well need any advantages I could get against her later. Faran drew blood again after a bit, though not as much this time. Then Jax put a huge slice in Faran's shirt, and a much smaller one in the skin along the lower edge of her ribs.

"Point." The growl was gone from Faran's voice, replaced by a cold flat emotionless delivery that worried me far more than the earlier anger had.

"Sorry," said Jax. "I twisted my grip a touch too late."

"Don't be. The mistake was mine. I let you in too close. I promise you I won't do it again. Ready?"

I really didn't want the bout to continue with Faran in this mood. Then, as if in answer to the prayers I could no longer make, the arrival of one of the *Lamia's* officers gave me the perfect opportunity to end things. The man had climbed the ladder from the lower deck and poked his head up over the edge of the foredeck but looked deeply unhappy at the idea of getting any closer to the two women and their bared steel. I couldn't really blame him.

I waved at him and stepped between Jax and Faran. "Hello, can we do anything for you, Master Sendai?" The ship's Kanjurese sailing master and first officer was a good-looking man, slender and tall like most islanders—though it was unusual to see one of them outside the archipelago.

Sendai swallowed but nodded and climbed the rest of the way up onto the foredeck. "Begging your pardon, sir, but we're just about to clear the mouth of the gulf, and the captain sent me to ask that you take a brief rest while we treat with the Vesh'An."

"Of course." Jax flipped her left hand sword back to an underhanded grip, then sheathed it and its mate. "Can't let the Vesh'An go waiting."

The tall man smiled a very fetching smile. "Thank you, ma'am. Much appreciated. If the three of you would like to watch, I'm sure the captain would be happy to have you as his guests for the wandersea ceremony."

"Wandersea?" asked Faran, who hadn't yet put up her weapons. "What's that like? I've heard the name, but I've never been out on the open ocean to see one before."

"It'll be easier to show you than to explain it," said Sendai.

"Fair enough." Faran slid her cane knives into the crossed sheathes on her back. "Show away."

The captain came up on the foredeck. A burly sailor followed along behind him carrying a pair of large brandy bottles. My mouth went dry as I stared at the bottles going by. A drink would make dealing with Faran and Jax so much easier.

As the captain climbed up onto the platform at the end of the foredeck, Sendai directed us to the portside rail for a better view. A few minutes later the ship cleared the headland that marked the mouth of the Gulf of Tien and entered the open ocean. Three fins broke the surface, veeing the water beside the ship.

"They look just like the dolphins I've seen in the fish market, except for the black and white markings," Faran said quietly.

"You won't *ever* see these dolphins in a fish market, nor

anything else with those markings," Jax replied just as quietly. "No sailor would be insane enough to try to net or spear a Vesh'An."

"Even if a sailor was crazy enough to try, they'd never make it back to shore alive," I added.

"It's strange seeing them in the flesh like this after hearing about them all these years," said Faran. "Will they really shift?"

Before either of us could answer, the captain trilled out something in a strange liquid tongue that sounded more than half like a series of whistles. It was nothing like what I'd heard of the languages of their Durkoth and Sylvani cousins, but the Vesh'An were the strangest of the Others who shared our world. The leader now leaped high out of the water and trilled imperiously back at the captain. He bowed deeply and responded in kind.

They went back and forth like that two or three times before the captain reached back and took the first bottle from the crewman. With another trill, he tossed the bottle far out over the side. The Vesh'An who'd been trailing along to the left of the leader shot forward and leaped high out of the water. Right at the top of its arc it shimmered and transformed into a woman, naked and inhumanly perfect, though still marked like the dolphin in black and white. She caught the bottle in one hand and plunged back into the sea in a perfect athlete's dive.

For another few heartbeats she streaked along beneath the surface in a woman's form. Then the shimmer came again, and she returned to dolphin shape, diving deep and vanishing. When she was gone, the captain repeated the trilling phrase and threw the second bottle. The Vesh'An who caught the tribute this time was male and, if anything, prettier than the woman had been. The captain bowed to the leader and spoke a final trilling farewell. The Vesh'An returned it in kind before disappearing beneath the waves. The captain left then, too, without so much as a nod for his passengers.

"The foredeck is yours again," Sendai said to us as he started after the obviously uncomfortable captain. "Please try not to scar it up too much." He flicked a glance at the deep gouge left behind where Faran had kicked Jax's blade. "He'll be ever so much easier on all of us if you don't." Then he winked at me.

"I'll see what I can do," I said quietly as he went down the ladder.

Good luck with that, Triss said into my mind.

"Do they always use brandy?" asked Faran.

Jax shook her head. "No, though it's almost always alcohol. What kind depends on what the local clans have been asking for. That'll be part of the exchange with the captain. When he next comes into port up this way, the captain will leave word at the harbormaster's office so that other ships will know what to bring."

"Why alcohol?" asked Faran. "That stuff is nasty!"

"There we are in perfect agreement." Jax gave me a speaking look. "But the Others invented distilling along with brewing and fermenting back in the days before the god wars, and it's one of the few things the Vesh'An can't do for themselves very easily in their watery halls. Since they've never lost the taste for it they need a source, so they get it in tribute from us or trade with the Sylvani."

Jax stretched and rolled her shoulders. "And now, I'm thinking that I should leave you and Aral alone to argue out your unexpected arrival. Hopefully, cutting me up has taken the worst edge off of both of your tempers, and you can do it without further bloodshed." Then she vaulted over the rail and dropped the eight feet to the deck below before heading back to our shared cabin.

"She's as nice as I remembered her," Faran said once Jax had closed the door behind her. "I see why you don't want to kill her." Then she turned back my way and her eyes went hard and cold. "Which definitely means I'm going to have to do it for you."

As she walked away, I found myself wondering where the captain stored those big bottles of brandy and how long it would take before anybody missed one.

Don't, Triss sent.

Don't what?

If you get drunk right now, you're not going to be able to stop Faran.

Just one drink . . .

It won't be one. Not when you're this worried, and you know how that'll end.

He was right but . . . "Fuck." I scrubbed at my eyes, trying to erase the vision of a big beautiful bottle of booze tumbling through the air, as though I thought it might work.

10

———◆◆◆———

Every assassin knows that beauty and death sometimes walk hand in hand. It's there in the perfection of the smith's art expressed in deadly steel, or in the night sky like a scatter of diamonds on velvet, seen from the side of a castle tower. Even spilled blood has a terrible beauty to it, rich and red and royal.

So it was with the oncoming Vesh'An hunting party that passed us on our tenth day at sea. Most of the clan's warriors slid through the seas in dolphin shape, leaping in and out of the water, weaving a wild pattern in the waves. A few, including the lord and lady and their leading knights, rode in human form astride the backs of great war-whales. There were ten of the black and white beasts, looking for all the world like giant brutish cousins to the dolphin-formed Vesh'An that danced around them. The nobles rode bareback, armored in seaweed and shell. They carried shining swords and deadly lances carved from the bones of dragons. Harder than iron, their edges shone green and gold and blue and silver—all the myriad colors of the sea.

The sailing master ran out onto the bow platform and waved at the Vesh'An as they raced past, calling out "Good hunting!"

The lord bobbed his raised lance in response, and one of the knights blew a conch horn. Master Sendai must have seen my curious look, because he crossed to where I was leaning against the rail.

Though the rest of the crew continued to avoid us, and the captain mostly pretended we didn't exist, Sendai had seemed almost fascinated by us, going so far as to watch our sparring practices from the foot of the bow platform the last few days.

"That's Clanarch Ekilikik and his people. They've done us a good turn more than once. They're going after one of the great sea serpents or a kraken by the look of their gear, which means some of them likely won't be coming back. The Vesh'An are the only reason the outer lanes stay open for shipping. Without them, we wouldn't dare sail beyond sight of land. If they pass again on the way back to their home waters around Ar, we'll throw them a couple of bottles of our brandy, though protocol doesn't demand it."

"How long till we reach Ar?"

I was slowly going crazy trapped between Jax and Faran on the tiny island of the *Lamia*. I wanted off that boat, but at the same time, our arrival in the Magelands would bring the moment when I had to make a final choice about what to do about Jax that much closer.

"If the winds stay as good as they've been so far, we'll hit port late tomorrow," said Sendai. "That's where you leave us, right?"

I nodded. "It is."

"That's too bad. I'm actually going to miss having you aboard."

"Your captain won't."

"No, but he's far too much of a traditionalist to be happy with landsmen who run the rigging like old hands. To say nothing of the fact that you frighten him. Hell, you frighten most of the crew."

"But not you?"

Sendai laughed. "Oh, you frighten me, too, but mostly in a good way. I'd love to get to know you better. . . ."

He let it hang there for a long moment, long enough to make sure I understood the offer underneath. I had to admit I was tempted, at least a little bit. He was an attractive man, both physically and emotionally. I generally preferred women, but had slept with a few men over the years, and Sendai appealed to that part of me. Also, it had been a long time since Maylien, and I hadn't shared a bed with anyone since.

But finally, I smiled and shook my head. "I'm sorry, we won't get that chance."

"Already committed elsewhere?" he asked lightly, though I could read disappointment in his eyes. "Or just not inclined my way?"

"Neither, actually. I've got no commitments and no objections, but my life's too tangled up at the moment for me to want to add another twist."

"I guess I can understand that, but you can't blame a fellow for trying."

"No, and another time I might have said yes."

"Well, if another time comes round at some point, look me up. We mostly make the coastal run back and forth between Tien and the Magelands." Then he turned and left me at the rail.

As I watched him walk away, I couldn't help but smile. There was something preciously normal about the exchange. No one trying to kill me or anyone under my protection, no one I needed to kill, just a simple proposition and no hard feelings when it didn't pan out. He waved at Jax and Faran as he passed them on the lower deck. The pair were perched atop a stack of barrels in the shade of the mainsail, quietly talking.

I was still smiling when Faran got up a few minutes later and came my way. Climbing up the ladder to the foredeck, she crossed to stand in the exact same place Sendai had.

"Did you know that Jaeris and Altia are alive?" Faran asked without any preamble.

I nodded. When Jax and I had been trapped by the storm, she'd told me the names of all the surviving apprentices and journeymen she and Loris had taken in.

"They were my best friends at the temple, along with Omira and Garret." Faran said rather wistfully. "Jax says she doesn't know what's happened to Garret but that Omira turned up on the list of the dead. She's really dedicated to her students."

"Having second thoughts about killing her?"

"No. The only reason I haven't killed her *yet* is that I don't want to have to deal with a body on the boat." Faran's voice came out flat and hard, but it didn't match her eyes. There, I could see the teenager wrestling with the killer.

"You know," I said quietly, "it's all right if you are having trouble with the idea. Better, really. I know that the priests taught us to kill without regret or remorse in the name of the goddess, but times have changed. If you do kill Jax, it won't be because the goddess ordered you to, it will be because *you* decided that you had to do it."

Faran opened her mouth, but I touched a finger to her lips. "Wait, let me finish. That decision, should you have to make it, might even be the right one for the moment. But it's not a choice you should make easily or lightly or without second and even third thoughts. In fact, nothing has ever been as simple as the priests told us."

Faran looked genuinely shocked. "Are you saying that the order was wrong to do what it did?"

"No, and yes. It's complex." I stood up from the rail and leaned toward Faran as I tried to organize my ideas into something I could express—ideas that would once have been bitter heresy, but had increasingly come to dominate my thinking over the past year.

"I don't think that Namara ever ordered me to kill anyone who didn't need killing. King Ashvik, in particular, was a monster, and killing him was certainly justice. But that's not *why* I killed him. I killed him for the simple reason that my goddess told me to. And that's not enough. Or, it shouldn't be."

Faran frowned. "I don't think I see the distinction. Namara was Justice personified. If she wanted someone dead, surely that meant that they should die. It seems pretty simple."

She's right, you know. Triss sounded almost as confused as Faran, which is part of why I hadn't been talking with him about this. Despite his shadowy nature, Triss didn't really think in shades of gray.

No, she isn't. I sent back at him.

Aloud, I said, "I imagine that the destruction of the temple and the mass murder of our order seemed a right and simple thing to the forces of Heaven's Reach." Faran let out a little gasp of outrage, but I shook my head. "No. Really. Think about it. Speaking through the Son of Heaven, the great god Shan himself, Emperor of Heaven, declared our damnation and ordered our annihilation."

"That's different," Faran said aloud at the same time as Triss declared, *But he was wrong to do so!*

"How *exactly* is it different? Their god, who also happens to have been our goddess's liege lord, told them what they should do, and they did it. You and I and every other servant of Namara may believe that what they did was wrong, but as long as the word of a god is all that it takes to define what is right for anyone, it's simply one god's followers against another's. The only way to make what the followers of Shan did wrong is to accept that there is more to making your choices than the word of any god."

"I guess I never thought about it that way before," said Faran.

In my head, Triss remained silent.

I plowed on, "Some days I miss the simple view and I want nothing more in the world than for things to go back to the way they were when Namara was alive. Then, I only had to think about how to kill someone, never why I was doing it. Other days, I wonder what I would do if Namara were somehow resurrected. Is it possible to go back to certainty? Even if it were, would it be *right* to do so?"

"Do you regret killing Ashvik?" asked Faran.

"No. Not at all. He oppressed and murdered his people, and even killed members of his own family. He slaughtered thousands of Kadeshis for no apparent reason, and tried to start wars with Kodamia and the Magelands. Ashvik deserved to die."

"Then why does the distinction matter?"

"Justice is rarely such a simple thing, no matter how much we might like it to be," I said. "Most killers aren't monsters. They're people who made the wrong decision for what might have seemed at the time to be perfectly good reasons. That's why we have laws, and why in places like the Magelands there are courts and juries who try to interpret those laws."

"But the courts can't or won't touch the high nobles in places like Zhan, or even the Magelands sometimes," countered Faran. "And there are no courts in the Kvanas or Kadesh, only the word of the khans and warlords."

"Which is where we come in, or did."

"I thought you just said you didn't want to go back to the way things were," said Faran. "You're not making any sense."

"Maybe I'm not," I agreed. "I'm not entirely sure what I want or don't. I believe that the world needs a way to handle the Ashviks and the dukes of Seldan, and I think that almost has to look something like what the Blades of Namara once were. But I also believe that doing things just because the gods tell us to has to stop."

"And what does all this have to do with whether or not I kill Jax?" Faran asked, looking more than a little frustrated. "Her working for the Hand seems pretty straightforward to me."

I raised an eyebrow. "You're smarter than that, Faran. The situation here is the most tangled I've ever had to deal with. Jax is my friend and was once much more than that. I care about her deeply."

Faran looked away, so I put my hands on her shoulders and gently turned her so I could look her straight in the eye. "I also care about you. I don't want to see the two of you in conflict, but I also understand that ultimately what Jax chooses to do in the face of pressure from the Hand is on Jax. She may put you, or me, for that matter, in a position where killing her is the only answer. I don't want that to happen. I understand that it might."

"You're trying to make me think again, aren't you?" she demanded. "Well, it won't work. And I won't feel bad about it if I do have to kill her." She sighed. "You really are a horrible old man." But then she gave me a hug.

"I try, my young monster. I do try."

Faran pulled free of my arms. And then, with a very thoughtful look on her face she crossed to the nearest section of the rigging and went aloft. I wasn't sure if I'd really gotten through to her, or if it would change anything even if I had, but at least she seemed to be considering it.

What do you *think?* I asked Triss, since it was the first time I'd run most of it by him as well.

I think that if the goddess were still alive you would be facing a heresy trial.

Nicely dodged.

He hissed something in Shade that sounded obscene, then sighed. *I don't know. Some of what you say makes sense, at least from the human perspective, but I'm not so sure that justice is as difficult as you make it out to be. We were right to do as Namara ordered. The goddess was just as well as Justice.*

What does that make Shan?

A legitimate target.

That made me blink. *Shan is a god, Triss. Even if I agreed with the sentiment, I think that Namara's death pretty well demonstrates that he is beyond the reach of justice.*

Some said the same about Ashvik after he killed the first Blade that came for him. More said it after he killed the second. Most agreed when he killed a third. That did not stop us from making an end of him.

Are you seriously suggesting that we try to kill Shan? I asked. *Because that sounds more like suicide than justice.*

No, I am not, but if the opportunity should ever present itself . . .

I'll keep that in mind, but now I'm confused about your position on gods.

It's simple. Namara was good because what she wanted to see done was good. Shan is bad because what he wants to see done is bad. Why is that hard to understand?

Who makes the decision?

Me. You. Anyone. The fact that they are gods only tells us that they are powerful. It says nothing about whether they should be revered or reviled.

I'm beginning to think that I'm not the only heretic in this partnership.

No. My thinking is perfectly normal for a Shade. You, however, are a very strange Blade, and a rather odd human on top of that.

I laughed, though I couldn't tell whether or not he was joking. Triss and I have been together so long that I sometimes forgot that he's not even remotely human. It's always something of a shock when I'm reminded of the fact. I was trying to decide what to ask him next when I noticed Jax coming up the ladder from the lower deck.

"Hello." I nodded as she got closer.

"That was very well done," she spoke cheerfully enough, but her expression was troubled.

"What was?" I asked.

"How you handled Faran, just now."

I felt my stomach clench. I hadn't seen any evidence of Jax pointing a hearsay our way, but I'd been too intent on paying attention to Faran to even spare a glance for Jax. Stupid. Really stupid. The kind of stupid that would have Master Kelos spinning in his grave . . . if he weren't still alive and a traitor. How the hell did my world get so fucked up?

Jax was giving me a very strange look now, so I opened my mouth and said, "I . . ." But that's all the further I got. What did she know? What should I say?

Jax laughed. "What a look, Aral. You'd think I'd caught you plotting to murder someone's puppy. No"—she waved me off before I could continue—"it's all right. I don't know what the two of you were talking about and I don't want to know. She's your apprentice and the two of you need a private space for that to happen."

"I'm confused. If you don't know what *we* were talking about, then what are *you* talking about?"

"I've spent most of the last six years gathering up and teaching the surviving students of the temple. It's not at all how I'd planned to spend my life, but I've found it enormously rewarding. I've also learned a few things about how to handle the youngsters."

"I have no idea where you're going," I said, feeling ever more lost.

"Faran is right on the line between child and adult and that's a very hard place. Not just for the child either, but for everyone around them. I couldn't hear what the two of you were saying, but I could see how you were saying it. She was upset after I told her about Omira and Garret, that was obvious. So she went to you. Am I right so far? I don't want details."

"Yes."

"You gave her your full attention and you treated her with complete seriousness. I don't know what you told her, but I could see from over there that you were talking about things that mattered to you. I could also see that Faran wasn't entirely happy with what you had to say, but that it made her think. The hug at the end reinforced that you care about her even if you don't always agree. In short, it was everything I try to do with my students."

"So why do you look so torn up?" I asked, though I thought I knew at least part of the answer, or hoped I did anyway. I didn't want to believe that the Jax I had once loved could be anything but torn up over the idea of betraying me to the Hand.

She looked away from me, then down at her feet. "Because I'm here, doing"—she flung her hands out to the sides—"this! I should be back in Dalridia taking care of *our* students, not feeling more than half jealous about you and yours. Fuck! I hate this."

"Jax . . ." I put a hand out to touch her shoulder, but she shrugged it off.

"I'm sorry, Aral. I should never have gotten you involved in this." She looked up into the rigging at Faran. "Either of you. She's good, Aral. Really, really good. She reminds me of the way you and Siri were at that age. But she's fey and fragile, too, poised on the edge of disaster with only you between her and . . . I don't know what exactly, but nothing good. It's easy to see how many scars the fall of the temple left on her, but not so easy to see how she's going to deal with them."

"You're not making a lot of sense," I said.

"I know, and I'm sorry for that, too. This whole thing with Loris and the journeymen just has me all messed up."

"Tell me about it, maybe I can help." I put my hand on her shoulder again.

This time she left it there for several beats before shaking her head and slipping free. Without another word, she walked off.

I think she almost told us just then, Triss sent.

But almost isn't enough.

No. It's not.

I don't want to have to kill her.

Neither do I, but if it comes to it, I'd rather it was us than Ssithra and Faran.

Sendai tossed a bottle to the Vesh'An just before we entered the harbor at Ar, and I hated that I couldn't look away as it sank into the water. Hated the way I was backsliding on the booze in general. I was better than this. I could control my drinking. I'd proved that over the last year, and more than once. But dealing with Jax and Faran and all the lies and tension in the confined spaces of the boat had me thinking about drinking all the damned time again.

I shook my head. It wasn't me, it was the situation. I just needed to get off the fucking boat and it would all be fine. But somewhere in the back of my head, a little voice was saying, *Yeah, you just keep telling yourself that, Aral.*

Jax joined me at the rail as we came into the dock. "Ready to go?"

I nodded. "Packed my bag an hour ago. Is there a plan? Or are we winging it from here?"

"I've got a snug on the west edge of town by the last of the river docks. I'd like to hole up there for a day or two while I check with a few local contacts about what's been going on in the month I've been gone. Then we hop a barge heading upriver."

"I'm getting awfully tired of boats, Jax."

"You and me both. I'm a mountains girl, both by birth and, more recent, experience. But in this case it beats walking. Come on, let's get our gear."

Faran was already grabbing her small bag out of the cabin when we arrived, and a few minutes later all three of us were crossing the gangway down to the dock. It felt damned good to be back on solid ground. I was going to walk back to Tien when this was all over. Assuming I survived the next couple of weeks, of course. No sure bet there.

I hadn't been to Ar in years, and I'd almost forgotten what a bedlam it could be. The Magelands had a more disparate population than the rest of the eleven kingdoms to begin with— since anyone from anywhere could become a citizen if only they possessed one of magic's gifts. Add to that Ar's status as the largest and most populated human port on the outer sea, and the kaleidoscopic whirl of people alone would be more than enough to bewilder the average traveler.

But there was more to it than that. Much more. Ar was a mage city, built around the magical university that both provided its reason for being and its government. In Tien or Kadeshar, or even Dan Eyre, one person in a thousand might have some modicum of the mage gift, and most of those were hedge witches at best. In Ar or Uln or Tavan it was closer to one in twenty. Magic was everywhere.

In magesight the streets of Ar flashed and twinkled in every shade of every color of the rainbow. Walking through the city felt like walking through the middle of the annual fireworks display Tien put on for the king's birthday. Windows bore charms that kept them forever clean. Canopies of light protected restaurant patios from the worst depredations of rain and sun. Even the sewer drains had glyphs inscribed on them to keep clogs from forming.

Much of the magic was ephemeral, minor spells that required constant renewal to keep them going. Permanent magic needed both expertise and significant expenditure of power. But the city had minor mages in plenty, and part of the training of young scholars at the university included maintaining the service spells that helped keep the city functioning. Nowhere but in the great university cities of the Magelands was magic so cheap and plentiful.

I had already developed a headache, but I knew from past experience that both the pain and the confusion would pass once my inner eye had a chance to adjust to the feast of light. Still, the visual cacophony of it almost made me wish I could shut down my second sight. Nor was I alone in my discomfort. A sidelong glance showed me that Faran was squinting as well, though Jax seemed more inured.

She leaned in close to Faran and said, "You'll adapt faster if you look around for the biggest spells and brightest lights and stare at them a bit. It makes the rest of it a bit easier to bear."

"I've been here before," Faran snapped back at her. "I know what I'm doing. I'm not one of your poor little lost apprentices." Then she stormed forward.

"Dammit," Jax said to me, "I didn't mean it that way."

"I'd better have a word with her," I said.

But Jax shook her head. "No, if we're going to be working together, she and I need to sort out our differences. I need to talk to her myself. Why don't we make the best of this. If you let us get a block or so ahead it'll give you a chance to see if we attract any undue attention."

"Start with a block, then go two and three, split and double-round?" I asked.

"Even better," said Jax. "It does double duty. If I tell Faran she's given us a great opportunity it'll make it easier for her to accept my apology. And a split and back around will definitely tell us if we've got a hound nosing after us. Keep going straight up this street till you hit University Way and then take a left. If we get separated we can meet back at the dock where we landed at sunset."

"Fair enough."

So, as Jax speeded up to catch Faran, I slowed down a little bit. One of the easiest ways to spot a hound is to split up. The hound has to decide who to follow, which makes the job much harder. It also gives you lots of options for circling around each other, and putting the hound in a trap. A good hound knows all that, but it leaves them with very limited options.

I didn't want to be too obvious about what we were doing, so I pretended there was something wrong with my boot. As I knelt to adjust things I did a quick top of the eyes scan of my surroundings. Perhaps inevitably, I spotted the nearest alehouse. As I stared longingly at the place, a magic light flared on the rooftop of the low building.

I probably would have missed it among all the visual noise if not for the fact that it was a very distinctive shade of orange pink—not a common color for magic, and one I'd been trained to look for from the age of six. I glanced up, and there, crouched in the shade of a narrow dormer, was Master Kelos. He held up a hand, palm out, and magical light flashed again, this time drawing words, "Here Midnight Alone."

11

———◆◆◆———

The past is never dead. It lives inside us, no matter how hard we might try to cut it out. As a child my parents gave me to the temple. Not long after that the temple gave me to Master Kelos. I had other teachers, other masters—we all did—but more than anyone else it was Kelos Deathwalker who shaped me into Aral Kingslayer.

Each of the children who went through the temple had a special master they answered to. For Siri and me, that master was Kelos. He taught me how to hold a sword, how to walk in shadow, how to kill. On the day the goddess made me a Blade and sent me after Ashvik, there were only two people at the temple who knew what I planned. Devin was one. He tried to convince me not to go. Kelos was the other. He wished me good hunting. I loved the man as you can only love the idols of your childhood.

Maybe that was the reason it didn't even occur to me to try to follow him. Or maybe it was simpler than that. Maybe it was fear. Kelos didn't want to see me right now, and for all that I had done in the years since I entered the temple, I was still afraid of making him mad at me because I knew all the way down to my bones that he could take me.

After sending his message, Kelos had nodded to me and walked away over the peak of the roof. I nodded back and I watched him go. And then, after he'd left, I walked away myself.

Are we going to do it? Triss asked as we followed Jax and Faran up the road in the general direction of the university.

What?

Meet Kelos tonight.

I stopped dead. It was only in that instant that it even occurred to me that I *could* decline to show up. Somewhere deep down below the level of conscious thought, I had simply assumed that I would meet him. Master Kelos had summoned me. Period. Nothing after that involved a choice on my part.

Only, it did. It's hard to describe what happened inside my head when I finally realized that. Even though I had seen Master Kelos talking to the Signet and heard him acknowledging the Son of Heaven as his master, it hadn't really sunk in. It didn't matter that I'd been filled to overflowing with a toxic mix of fury, betrayal, and a half dozen other awful emotions at the time. Somehow, down in the deeps of my soul, Master Kelos was still *my* Master Kelos.

In the hierarchy of my life it had always gone from Namara to Kelos to me. The high priestess of Justice had barely even entered into it. Now Namara was dead and Kelos was . . . what? A traitor certainly, but beyond that, he was no longer *my* master. Somehow, that was so much worse than things had been when he was simply dead along with my goddess.

Despite Triss's companionship, I suddenly felt alone in a way that I never had before, like I'd lost a layer of protection between me and the void. Maybe this was what it felt like for a normal person to lose a parent. I don't know. I wanted to scream or cry or send a pillar of magelightning blasting into the heavens.

I did none of those things. I couldn't. Discipline held me back and got me moving again. Bitterly, ironically, even poison-ously, the very discipline drilled into me by Kelos Deathwalker kept me from acknowledging the pain now inflicted by that same Kelos Deathwalker.

Aral? Triss spoke into my mind, but I couldn't answer him because I wasn't really there.

I was walking through the past at the same time I walked

up the street. The day I summoned Triss was the very same day the priests gave me to Kelos. I was seven.

"Greetings, young Aral." Always a big man, Kelos had seemed a giant to me, but one who now crouched down to put our eyes on a level. "The priests tell me that your bonding ceremony was successful." He extended his hand. "That makes you my brother as well as my student. Welcome to the order and our mission, young Blade."

I wasn't truly a Blade yet, merely an apprentice, but Master Kelos was treating me like a man and his brother. Kelos Deathwalker! The Blade that all the other Blades used as an example. Heady stuff for a child raised by the priests to believe nothing was more important than our sacred mission. I extended my own hand to shake his, trying as hard as I could to mirror the way that he had offered his.

"Greetings, Master Kelos." I wanted nothing more in the entire world than to justify the serious way Master Kelos treated me as he shook my hand and then released it. "The priests have informed me that you are to be my master and teach me the ways of the Blade."

"I am that, son, as well as your brother."

"I will try to justify the honor Namara has done me by giving Triss into my care today and me into yours."

My shadow shifted then, for the first time since the summoning ceremony ended, as Triss took on his dragon shape and folded his wings and bowed his head. "Masster Keloss, mosst honored Resshath Malthiss, I—" Triss's continued in Shade then, as he seemed to have exhausted his knowledge of the tongue of Varya.

Malthiss changed, too, assuming the form of a great basilisk coiled around Kelos's neck and shoulders. "Triss, Aral, welcome. We have much to teach you."

"And that ends the formalities," said Kelos, with a grin. "Now, let me get you a pair of proper swords and show you to your new room."

I half expected him to pick me up then, but he never treated me like a child. Oh, he gave me hugs when I needed them, as well as the occasional hiding. But from the very first day I entered his care to the moment I placed my Kila in the great orb of Namara and became a full Blade, he always accorded me the respect due to one of his full brethren. Perhaps more importantly, he was one of the very few who didn't treat me any differently after I became the Kingslayer.

Oh, he was proud of me, none more, and he told me so the very first chance he got. But that didn't keep him from pounding me in the salle the very next day, or scolding me in exactly the same way as he always had when I fucked up. It was a blessed relief, especially compared to the way the younger trainees started treating me after I killed Ashvik.

The funny thing was that it didn't occur to me until years later that he probably would have loved to have someone who treated him as just another Blade. Not until shortly before the temple fell, in fact. But he was still *Kelos Deathwalker* to me at that point, and I never quite worked my way up to it. And now, I never would.

Are we going to meet Kelos? Triss sent after a time. *You never answered my question.*

I shrugged. *I'd give you an answer if I had one, Triss, but I don't. I just . . . don't.* I didn't want to, but I wasn't at all sure that we had much of a choice.

"**Nice** place," I said to Jax.

The snug was a large open attic room on the top floor of a warehouse. It stood just above the river docks on the western edge of the city. Not a bad location, but not a prime spot either, not even for a warehouse. Most of those lay on the far side of the city, along the harbor front where you could easily shift things from the sea-going ships to river barges. But there was a secondary hub here where a spur of the Great Coast Road made a loop around the back of the city to give wagons and livestock a route that didn't run through the heart of the university district.

For reasons known only to the original builder, the place stood seven stories tall, which was two more than any of its neighbors. No one sane hauls crates up above the third floor even with a crane. For that matter, there was no real call for that much space, that many stories off the ground, so far out from the center of the city. All of which meant that Jax's brother had been able to pick the place up for about half what the floor space might otherwise have justified.

In addition to being the main port of the Magelands, Ar and its river provided the only real route for goods to move from the coast inland to Dalridia. That meant that the Dalridian Crown, in the person of Jax's brother, had significant interests in the city. Those included wanting some unobtrusive storage space for the odd bit of goods, or royal sibling for that matter.

Jax had taken over the entire southwest corner of the top floor, which mostly consisted of a big open room with lots of shuttered windows and a trapdoor that provided roof access. At the moment, the shutters were all flung wide, providing a beautiful view that took in the river, a good chunk of the coast road, and miles of farmland. The furnishings were sparse, a couch, a couple of chairs, a table, and a couple of rolled-up futons for sleeping.

Fully half the high-ceilinged room was empty save for a dozen or so large and badly mildew-stained rugs that provided some padding for falls in what was obviously an improvised salle. The sanitary facilities consisted of a closetlike room with a porcelain bucket and a small balcony that allowed it to be emptied unobtrusively into the river—as illegal here as it would have been in Tien. Baths could be had at a public bathhouse across the way, a fact Jax had mentioned to Faran as we passed the place.

I walked over to the nearest window and leaned out. "Really a nice place." Though what I was thinking was, "How the hell am I going to get out of here without having Faran and Jax follow me?"

"You mentioned that already." Jax gave me a rather suspicious look. "Are you feeling all right? Because you've seemed a little dazed ever since we left the waterfront area."

"I'm sorry. I don't generally like boats, but I'm finding it shockingly hard to get used to ground that doesn't rock back and forth under my feet."

"Right. Well, I need to go out, and I don't think I'll be back till well after dark. There's food and drink in the amphorae along the back wall. Is there anything more you two need to know before I leave?"

"It's barely past noon now," said Faran, joining the conversation. "What's going to take you so long?"

"Mostly a lot of very boring business for the Dalridian Crown, though there's also the odd bit of spymastering. Part of the way I pay my keep and that of my students is by helping out Dalridian intelligence. In service of which, I need to talk to a couple of people at the university, as well as a few at the docks. After that, I have to stop in at the Dalridian embassy to see what our local eavesmen have picked up."

Jax smiled. "You're welcome to join me for most of it, if Aral will allow it."

I raised an eyebrow.

"Oh, I couldn't bring you along, Aral. That would be out of character, but I've dragged my students through the city often enough that no one will remark on Faran if she wants to come." She turned back to Faran. "Of course, you'll have to wait outside for several of my stops."

"It's fine by me," I said. It would provide the perfect opportunity for me to step out without having to explain myself beyond a note on the table saying that I thought I'd seen something.

"I don't think that would be a good idea," Ssithra said quietly from within Faran's shadow.

Faran nodded. "Point. Besides, I already know all that I need to about the eavesman business."

Faran had made an extremely good living the last few years playing the independent spy for a number of Crowns and services. Without knowing in advance who Jax's contacts were, she'd be running the risk of bumping into past employers. Or worse, competitors.

Jax shrugged. "Makes no nevermind to me. Now, if you'll excuse me . . ." When neither of us argued, she waved good-bye and left.

We'd had lunch—mushroom and sausage kebabs from a street vendor—on the way across town, otherwise I'd have sent Faran off to find us food while I had a look around. I was just trying to think of some other way to get Faran out the door when she preempted me.

"I'm going to that bathhouse Jax showed us, and I'm going to take a good long soak," she said. "Two weeks of nothing but cold saltwater for washing up is two weeks too many. Do you want to join me? You need it."

"No, I'll get a bath in later." Faran gave me an odd look, and I realized that I needed to explain a bit more.

"I know I stink, but I don't trust Jax and I want to give this place a really thorough going over before we settle in. I also want to check out escape routes. All of that's likely to involve a lot of dirt and sweating. No point in having to take two baths in one day." All of which was true, though not primarily for the obvious reasons.

"Suit yourself. I'm gone."

That gave me something in the neighborhood of an hour alone. I spent it crawling all over the upper floors and roof of the warehouse and coming to one inescapable conclusion.

"We're going to have to tell Faran about the meeting with Kelos." I was looking out over the river from the southern windows for the third time as I said it.

A sail-jump would carry me down to the roof of one of the near continuous stream of passing barges. From there I could get aboard a water taxi to bury my shadow trail. It was a good plan . . . for stage two of my little trip to talk to Kelos, and it wouldn't work this side of sunset. Unfortunately, stage one—getting out the window without having either Jax, Faran, or their Shade companions see me go was a nonstarter.

"So, we're going then?" He didn't sound happy.

Neither was I, and I still wasn't certain, but I didn't see a good way to avoid it. "I expect that we are, yes."

Triss sighed, but he didn't try to argue with me—not then anyway. "If we're going, why don't we just leave now?" He had taken dragon shape, though he stayed on the floor beside me, where the sun would have put him.

I sat down on the window ledge. "If we go now, Faran will come looking immediately, no matter how clever a note we leave. We can't sail-jump in broad daylight without flashing a sign that says 'Blade here' for anyone who knows how to read it. So the chance she won't find our trail approaches zero. You saw Kelos's message when he signaled us down by the harbor. He told me to come alone, and he might react violently if I don't. That could get very ugly very fast."

"Then, leave from the baths in a couple of hours. Find some

reason to put off bathing till the sun's almost down. Faran's already soaked for nearly an hour, she's not going to want to go back so soon. That would give us a good half hour's head start. If we can't make that work for us, we're so far past it that we shouldn't even be in the game anymore."

"That might work, but there's also Jax to consider, *and* what happens if we leave Faran alone and vanish for hours. I don't think it's a good idea to have Jax show up and run into a Faran who's maybe thinking something bad has happened to me."

"Then, better yet, don't go. We don't have to meet Malthiss and Kelos at all. They have embraced the evil that destroyed Namara. They have no right to ask anything of us. You know that, right?"

"It's not that simple, Triss. We don't know what Kelos wants out of this whole situation and he's far too dangerous to ignore. I'd much rather run the risks involved with dealing with him face-to-face now, than skip out on the meeting and wait for him to show up behind us somewhere later."

Triss flicked his wings angrily. "I do not like this."

"I don't like it either, I'm just speaking of what is." I shrugged. "We have two options. One, we can deal with him now."

"When he and Malthiss have had plenty of time to get ready for us," interjected Triss.

I laughed. "Like they need it. Or, are you seriously suggesting they wouldn't be able to take us without a lot of set up?"

Triss turned his head away. "No. Even at our very best we could not have beaten them in a straight fight, and we have fallen a long way since then."

"Which brings us back to my original point. Now. Or later, after we've pissed him off. Those are the choices."

Triss sighed and slid closer, reaching up to put his head in my lap. "I guess we might as well get it over with."

I scratched behind his ears, in the place where his scales were thinnest. "Then we have to tell Faran. Speaking of which . . . Why don't you come in off the roof?"

There was a snort from above, and Faran's face suddenly appeared upside down at the top of the window. "How'd you know I was here? I swear I didn't make any noise."

"No, you didn't. But neither did you go to the bathhouse. I

made sure to be on the roof on that side of the building when you should have been crossing the street. That meant you were either following Jax, or hanging around here for some reason. Once I knew that, I just had to watch the right shadows to see if any of them were a touch too dark."

Faran reached down and caught the lintel of the window, flipping herself around to land neatly on the ledge. "I could have been sneaking off to do something entirely different. Maybe meeting up with some of *my* old spying contacts."

"Possible, yes, but given the circumstances, not likely."

"So the whole conversation you just had was entirely for my benefit?"

I shook my head. "No. I needed to convince Triss, too, and Ssithra for that matter. We have to meet Master Kelos. We have to do it tonight. We can't let Jax know about it, either before or after. And, we have to do it alone if we don't want Kelos thinking it's a double cross. For this to work, I need all three of you on my side."

Faran's shadow shifted, so that a phoenix now joined the dragon. "I am convinced," said Ssithra. "What is our part?"

Faran held up a hand. "Not so fast, Ssithra. I want to know more about Master Kelos's message."

"There's not much to tell," I said before giving her the details.

"All right," said Faran. "I don't like it either, but I think you've got to go to that meeting. So, what do Ssithra and I have to do about Jax?"

"Besides not trying to kill her while I'm gone? Not much. Just tell her that I was up on the roof about half an hour before she got back and that I thought I saw something suspicious. So I went to check it out. Then, when I get back, find a way to let me know when it was I'm supposed to have left."

"Really, that's it? You think she'll buy it?"

"If she asks for more than that, I'll tell her it was just a couple of none-too-clever thatchcutters looking for an easy nut to crack. After I warned them off, I followed them till they tried and botched a shutter job and then I headed home. On my way back from my meeting with Kelos, I'll break a set of top-story shutters a mile or two from here and do it loud and stupid enough to get the owner screaming for the watch."

Faran nodded. "Then if Jax has her people ask around there'll be a nice clean trail to corroborate you. That should work nicely. All right, now that I know what you're up to, I can go and get my bath."

"One question before you do," I said. "How did you know I was up to something?"

"You agreed to let me go off alone with Jax way too easily, considering how hard you've been working to keep me from killing her. The only reason I could think of for you to do that was that you wanted to get me out from underfoot."

"Point. I screwed up there."

"No wonder, you are getting awfully ooooold for this stuff."

"Brat."

"Geezer."

The university bells were ringing a quarter past ten when I dropped from the dormer onto the patch of roof where I'd first seen Kelos. I'd spent the better part of an hour circling around the place and looking for any signs of a trap, but I hadn't found anything. No surprise. Not with Kelos involved. If he were laying a trap for me I wouldn't see it till the jaws closed.

Damn but that's clever! Triss said into my mind.

What?

Kelos has left us a message that only a Blade could read.

Oh, how?

Kelos got Malthiss to concentrate himself completely on the tip of one of his fingers. Then he used that finger to write a shadow-trail message on the roof here.

That is clever. Why didn't we think of that?

No need for it, I suppose. I wasn't allowed to tell you about the shadow trails before the fall of the temple. It was a secret between the Shades and the highest masters. Afterward, I didn't have any reason to think about it, not until we ran into Devin. Now that we're dealing with other Blades again, I'm sure we'd have figured it out eventually.

What does it say?

Triss swore in Shade for a moment.

What? I asked.

"Aral, quarter after ten? If so, then you're exactly a quarter *of an hour behind me and I still know you well enough to predict some of your actions. I've left a trail for you starting on the round stone tower directly north of you. You should just be able to see it from where you're standing. Follow it. I know you don't trust me, and I don't expect you to. That's why the trail will take you someplace where we can talk without you feeling you have to keep looking over your shoulder."*

He signs it, *"Your brother and onetime teacher, Kelos."*

"He has no right to call me brother," I said in a shaking voice. "Not anymore." I closed my eyes then and clenched my fists so hard I half expected my nails to tear the skin of my palms.

We can turn back. Triss's mental voice was barely louder than a whisper.

No. We still need to do this.

I didn't know the chimney forest of Ar half so well as I knew Tien's, so getting around was just flat slower than it would have been back home. But the trail that Kelos had left me was clear. It led directly toward the university, which struck me as a little bit odd. As a rule, Blades avoid other mages where we can. Magical power is a huge wild card in any game, and going anywhere near a Magelands university is like playing cards with a whole roomful of people holding nothing but jokers. Even Kelos has to tread carefully around such people. So, I was more than a little surprised when the trail brought me straight to the university wall, without turning aside.

Are you sure? I asked Triss.

There's an arrow here at the end of the trail pointing straight across to the university. Also, I don't think you can see it with your eyes, but there's about a foot of black silk rope trailing over the wall by the pillar there across the way.

I'm surprised you can pick it out against the dark wall. Normally you don't do well with that sort of minimal contrast.

The rope has been treated so it stands out to my senses. I've never seen anything like it before, but it would be difficult for a Shade to miss.

A foot, you say. Is it tight against the wall? Or is it hanging out where I could grab it easily at the end of a short sail-jump across this alley here?

It's an easy grab, but you knew it would be.

I did, because it was there for me, and Kelos wanted to make things easy. I wondered what he had done about the wards. The entire top of the wall glowed with intense spell-light, every inch of the surface crawling with alarm and attack glyphs, including the area directly above the rope. I had no idea how Kelos had managed to leave the wards intact and unblocked there and still left a hole that I could pass through. But I had no doubt that he had.

At that point, even if I hadn't had other reasons to make the jump, curiosity would have driven me to it. I wanted to know what he'd done. So I asked Triss to give me control for a bit, took three running steps, jumped . . . and nearly fell out of the air when a huge bang and a flash happened at ground level about fifty feet to my right. I had just enough presence of mind to keep my wings out and make my grab when I hit the wall.

What the fuck was that? I thought.

Of course, Triss couldn't respond from within his dream state, so I got no answer. Swearing quietly but continuously to myself all the while, I reshrouded myself and hung quietly from the rope while I waited for my pulse to return to normal. I also tried to figure out what had happened. A couple of locals had gone to look around the area where the noise had come from.

"Looks like someone blew up Snurri's rain barrel," said the first.

"Damned university prank," said another. "There oughta be a law."

"Wouldn't do any good with these youngblood mages," replied a third. "They'd just see it as a challenge."

"That's the truth," said the first. "Guess Snurri'll have to complain to the proctors at the university. Won't catch the prankster of course, but maybe the administration will at least replace his barrel."

There was more grumbling over the next few minutes and much speculation as to whether the university would replace the barrel, but I shut it out. I knew damned well that no student had done the deed. It was Kelos providing a distraction for any watchers who might otherwise have chanced to look up and see me gliding across the alley.

When the neighborhood chorus left, I braced my feet on the wall and very carefully raised my head enough to look at the top of the wall where the rope ran. A thick piece of leather-backed black felt lay across the wards and spikes. They had done the latter up fancy with silver and steel both, not that any of the restless dead or creatures of wild magic were likely to attempt to enter a mage university. I poked at the mat with a fingertip. It was obviously a custom wardblack, but unlike any I'd ever seen before.

Normally, to make a wardblack, you lay a piece of enchanted silk across the top of the wards you want to fool and let it soak up a copy of the guard spells. Done right, it almost never sets them off. Then you attach that to a chunk of spelled felt that effectively mutes the wards for as long as you leave it in place atop them. In most circumstances, that's all you need. Either you cross the warded area fast and pull up the wardblack behind you. Or, if it's in a not terribly well-traveled space, you leave it in place for a cleaner and faster exit on your way out.

But most wards aren't attached to a university with literally thousands of mages inside. Here, the spell-light of the wards was almost as much protection as the wards themselves. If you left a wardblack in place for any length of time, someone would be bound to notice the dark patch it created. Kelos had gotten around that by sewing a bunch of fake wards into the top surface of the felt and enchanting them with a simple charm to make them glow in magesight. Add in the leather to provide a protection against the spikes, and you had a temporary doorway through the university's security that you could leave open behind you.

It was the easiest thing in the world for me to pull myself up atop the wall and then, following another shadow-trail arrow, drop down inside and head across the lawn. The trail led me from there to . . . *You're not serious. The fucking proctor house? He wants me to meet him on top of the offices of the university police department?*

Apparently, sent Triss. *Apparently.*

12

———◆———

Sometimes words cut deeper than any blade. Sometimes it doesn't even matter which words, only who says them.

"Hello, Aral." Master Kelos stood with his arms crossed and one hip leaning casually against the proctor house chimney. He was dressed in the full ritual clothing of the Blade—loose and flowing grays in a half dozen shades. "It's good to see you alive."

Without thinking about it, I found my hands on the hilts of my swords, my thumbs on their release catches.

"Don't." He said it quietly, not an order, nor even a serious request, but somehow I couldn't resist, and my hands fell away from my swords. "Oh, good, you're going to be sensible. I'd hate to have you start a fight up here. With a university full of mages around it wouldn't go well for either of us."

"What makes you so sure I wouldn't be willing to die if it meant taking you with me?"

"Nothing at all. In fact, I suspect that if you were sure that's the way things would play out, and if that was the only price, we'd already be fighting. But there's Triss to consider, and Malthiss. As well as all the many, many things that could go wrong along the way. That's why you weren't there at the fall of the temple, actually. Nor Siri either."

"What?" The word fell out of my mouth, barely loud enough for even me to hear, and it left behind a feeling of cold that made my jaw feel numb and useless.

"You don't think it was a coincidence that our best and most-talented young assassins were a thousand miles away when Heaven's Hand and Sword arrived at the temple, do you? You were both far too valuable to waste and too dedicated not to force them to kill you if you'd been there."

"But the goddess chose us for those missions. . . ."

"She did, yes. But she did so in consultation with the shadow council, her most senior priests and Blades. I requested that you and Siri and a few others receive assignments that would put you out of harm's way, in hopes that someday I would be able to bring you back into the fold."

"You knew they were coming? But that means that . . ."

"I betrayed Namara. Yes, it does, and it was the hardest decision I ever made."

The numbness in my jaw had spread to my whole body by then. I felt like I no longer had any real control over my limbs or actions. Sometimes, when you're drinking, there's a moment where you stop feeling like it's *you* that's drinking, where you feel completely disconnected from yourself. It's like you can see what's happening to you but it's not you that's doing it. This was like that, only without the alcohol. Without any drugs at all, just my own shock and betrayal slowly poisoning me from within.

So, it was doubly startling when Triss suddenly changed into dragon form and lunged toward Master Kelos. Kelos didn't so much as twitch, but before Triss had gone three feet, Malthiss was there, wrapped around Triss like a constrictor. The older Shade moved so fast I didn't see it, didn't see anything beyond a blurred impression of the shadows around Kelos's neck and shoulders flickering. It made a sharp contrast to the casual, almost leisurely way he'd acted against the envoy back in Tien.

The world blurred and flickered again, and I was standing a few feet from Kelos, my swords drawn, one point inches from his throat, the other hovering in front of his heart.

"Tell Malthiss to let Triss go, right now."

Kelos still hadn't moved. "Don't," he said in the exact same tone he'd used earlier. "I'd rather not have to hurt you."

"Kill him," said Triss. "It'll be worth whatever it costs."

I . . . couldn't. I tried, or at least I intended to, but the arm that I wanted to thrust the blade through his throat wouldn't move no matter how hard I thought at it that it should.

"Sensible," said Kelos. "I'm almost surprised. Perhaps the years have taught you some of the things that I never could. Now, I want you to move back to where you were standing before. Then Malthiss will let Triss go, and we can continue our conversation."

"I don't think so," I said. "You let Triss go first, and then we'll discuss the rest."

"I'm afraid it doesn't work that way," said Kelos. "Do be sensible again. We'll both be happier for it."

"No."

"Your choice."

Now, Kelos moved. I knew he was going to. I was ready for him. It didn't help, not even with my swords already in a position to strike. It was almost as fast as what happened with Malthiss. One instant Kelos was leaning casually against the chimney, arms crossed. The next, his arms drove forward and apart, using the knives in the wrist sheaths under his shirt as armor against my edges. He struck the blade of my swords, pushing my right sword to the left, and my left to the right as he slid toward me, putting my arms into a cross-bind.

I tried to backpedal, but he moved faster, shoving my own arms back into my chest with the weight of his body. Before I could recover in any way, I felt Kelos hook a foot behind my ankle and ride me to the rooftop. A moment later, I was flat on my back with Kelos kneeling on my chest and arms, gasping. He took the swords from my hands almost casually and flipped them around. Cold steel kissed my wrists as he slowly forced the blades down through the straps of my wrist sheaths and deep into the lead and planks of the roof, pinning me.

The most shocking thing about the whole maneuver was how quiet it had been. Even my fall had been controlled to minimize noise. If someone was in the room directly below us, the sword tips coming through the ceiling would have been much more likely to draw their attention than my landing.

"There," he said, "that ought to illustrate my point nicely." Then he was off me and stepping back to retake his place against the chimney. "That was very badly done, Aral. Once you drew steel you shouldn't have stopped to threaten. You should have gone for the kill. I might have been forced to hurt more than your pride, but you would at least have had a fair shot at spilling some of my blood in the process. This was beneath you."

Another flicker and a blur and Malthiss snapped back to peer at me over Kelos's shoulder as he had so many times in the past. With an angry snarl, Triss moved sideways to crouch on my chest, though he didn't try to attack either Kelos or Malthiss again. Instead, he just sat there, quietly but steadily hissing at them.

"But none of this is why I brought you here," said Kelos. "Jax intends to betray you to the Hand."

"Yeah, I'm on top of that. It's not going to happen. I won't let it, though I'm hoping she'll choose to come to me and talk about it rather than force me to stop her. And, yes, I do understand exactly how ironic that sounds coming from me to you right now."

Kelos smiled sadly. "It's not what I wanted, you know, not what I would have chosen if I could have seen any other way. Much like what I am doing now."

Triss's hissing rose and Malthiss leaned forward over Kelos's shoulder. "Triss, desist." Then he added something scathing in Shade, and somewhat to my surprise, Triss shut up.

"Why?" I didn't know whether I was asking about the temple or the current situation. I just knew that I wanted answers.

"Eleven years ago, you killed Zhan's king, Ashvik the Sixth. You were the fourth Blade to make the attempt and the first to survive the experience. Yes?"

I nodded and used the opportunity of that movement to shift my arms so that my sword's edges began to cut into the straps on my wrists.

"What good did it do? In the long run?"

I shifted to look Kelos in the eyes, working at cutting the straps with the same motion. "I brought him Justice. Isn't that enough? Isn't that what you taught me? That we have to show the people that not even kings are above paying for their crimes?"

"It's not enough, Aral. You know that Thauvik took the throne when his brother died, right?" I nodded. "Do you think he's one whit less of a monster than Ashvik was?"

"Well, I certainly haven't heard of him invading Kadesh, or murdering his own sons." Though Maylien had told me he was doing plenty of harm.

"That's true, but it's not because he's a better person. It's not because he learned that he mustn't do evil. No. What he learned is, 'don't get caught.' His first murder happened within hours of taking the throne, and he's quietly killed hundreds since."

"Thauvik being too scared to become a full-blown and highly visible monster means we've failed?" I demanded. "That we shouldn't even try? I don't see that."

"Oh no. That's not what I'm saying at all. Thauvik's stance means we were never allowed to go far enough. We were never allowed to go all the way."

"What are you talking about?" asked Triss. "Isn't killing a king going all the way?"

His talking now reminded me that Malthiss hadn't said a word since he told Triss to quit hissing. Though he'd never been the most talkative of Shades, this seemed more of a speaking silence. I just wished I knew what it was speaking of.

Kelos shook his head in response to Triss's question. "The pair of you weren't the first to kill a monster King of Zhan. I killed Ashvik's great-grandfather, who was a damned nasty piece of work, and Alinthide killed *his* niece when she played regent to Ashvik's grandfather and polo with servants' heads. In the service of the goddess I killed seven rulers and hundreds of lesser nobles and generals. But no matter how many times I administered Namara's justice, new monsters just sprang up to take their places."

He squatted down so that our eyes were closer to the same level. "It never gets any better, Aral. Not in any meaningful way. I've lived longer than almost any other Blade, and what I've seen is that when you stomp out evil over here, it just springs up again over there. Or it comes back again a few years or decades later. Killing kings isn't enough. I told Namara that more times than I can count, but she would never agree to do more."

"Like what?" I'd cut through the straps on my wrist sheaths by then. Though the swords still pinned my sleeves, that wouldn't hold me. But I still didn't move. Kelos clearly had more to say, and he was the one who'd taught me never to do something that will shut up a source of information until you absolutely had to.

"Get rid of the damn kings completely."

That was an argument I could almost agree with. "And replace them with what? Rulers elected from among the elite, like in Kodamia or the way the Magearchs of the universities are chosen here in the Magelands?"

"Why would I want to replace it with anything? The whole idea of one person having any kind of ruling authority over another is corrupt at its roots. I want to tear the whole system out of the ground and burn it. Injustice stems from inequality. The only way to eliminate it is to level the field so that no one person sets themselves up above the others."

"I'm not sure that's going to work," said Triss. "Your people seem to have a natural drive to rule over their fellows."

"That's why the order of the Blade will have to continue for at least a little while after we take down the nobility. We'll need to chop down those who would become kings until a new system of self-government can arise on top of the ashes of the old autocracy."

Part of me thought that what Kelos was saying had some merit, if only in a purely abstract sort of way. But I didn't believe it would work any more than Triss had. Real people didn't act the way that Kelos seemed to be saying they would. No, at the moment, my real question was whether Kelos believed any of it or if he was playing me. He certainly sounded serious; calm, collected, intense. But then, he always sounded that way. And still, not one word from Malthiss.

While Kelos *might* believe every word he was saying, there was no way for me to know that, this side of his implementing his ideas. He was perfectly capable of acting as though the total destruction of the ruling classes of the eleven kingdoms was his goal right up until whatever his real plan was needed him to act otherwise. I was very tempted to ask him how betraying the goddess to the Son of Heaven served any of those goals. But I thought I had enough now to make some good guesses, and time was passing. I had other, more important questions, and Kelos seemed in an answering mood.

"And what you're doing now? How does that serve your plans? Why did you set that trail for Faran to find?"

"You figured out that I left that for you? Excellent. I tried very hard to make it look like chance, but I needed you to see what was going on with the Signet and Jax. I got very lucky when you and she arrived so close together on the very first attempt. By the way, you might as well slice yourself the rest of the way free. It's not like you're going to take me by surprise when you do. But I would appreciate it if you left your swords where they are for now."

So I did, both. "I still don't know *why* you wanted me to know what's going on with Jax and the Signet."

"Because I need you to free Loris and the others without getting yourself or Jax killed in the process, of course. I've lost too many of you already. There were almost four hundred Blades and trainees once. Over three hundred of those died at the fall, with more killed since then. The Signet set this play up on the sly, so I didn't have a chance to block it in advance. If she had her way, every single one of us would be dead. I can't let that happen. I need all of you alive to help me once I take the system down."

"Why not simply kill the Signet yourself?" asked Triss. "Why involve us?"

"I . . . can't do it myself for a number of reasons. Not least of which, it would interfere with my longer-range plans. And I can't get Jax to do it. She's not ready to know that I'm alive again yet, not after what the Hand did to her and Loris. It would distract her too much."

"Don't you mean what *you* did to her and Loris?" I asked furiously.

Kelos's expression didn't change. "Not at all. I thought they'd been killed in the battle for the temple. It wasn't until months later that I discovered I'd been lied to. As soon as I found out where they were and what was happening to them, I arranged an opportunity for them to escape."

"How very nice of you to do that after arranging for the temple to fall in the first place."

"Don't be ridiculous, Aral. I didn't do it to be nice. You should know me better than that. Nice isn't a part of my character. I did it because I wanted them out and alive so that I could bring them back into the fold later, once they'd had some time to let the memories fade a bit. Neither did I *arrange* for the fall of the temple. The Son of Heaven was going to move against Namara one way or another. What I arranged was a way to salvage something from the ashes of our collective ruin."

What could I say to that? What could I do? When I was twenty-one, a building came apart around me in the middle of an escape. I got clipped upside the head by a chunk of falling beam in the process. It'd left me seeing double for a while and screwed up my thinking for days afterward. I felt that same sick confusion now, but instead of pain in my head I felt a vicious gnawing void in my chest and gut.

Aral? Triss spoke into my mind, and he sounded every bit as anguished as I felt. *What do we do?*

I don't know. I'm lost. One second I want to cut out his heart and feed it to him. But the next, I remember how much he did to make me who I am, and I want so desperately to have a reason to forgive him that I can almost believe that the only way he could save any of us was by betraying Namara.

Kelos reached into the trick bag at his side and pulled out a small package tightly wrapped in black silk. "I know you don't trust me. You shouldn't. You have no reason to. But I have to go now, and I don't know whether I'll get the chance to see you again before you have to deal with the Signet's ambush. You're going to need this. Here." He tossed it over.

As I caught it, Kelos shrouded up, vanishing into shadow. For a few beats I could still pretty much guess where he was by a combination of experience, intuition, and observation. But that quickly passed, and Triss and I were alone.

Silently, I opened the package and found two items. The first was a Shade stick—a short length of thick wooden rod with numerous holes drilled through it at a variety of angles. It would hold a message or, more likely, a map readable only with the help of a Shade. I put it aside for later perusal.

The second item was a small silver box with a piece of parchment across the latch that said "Do NOT remove the ring." Flipping it open, I exposed a gold signet ring still on the finger that had once worn it. Though I wanted nothing more than to close the box and throw it away—I've killed plenty of people, but the idea of keeping trophies turned my stomach—I forced myself to look at it closely. Where it had connected to the hand someone had attached a thick disk of bone or antler. Both the ring and the disk glowed brightly in magesight. There was a second, much smaller Shade stick tucked in next to the finger.

Grisly little package. Triss extended a tendril of shadow. *Let's see . . . the big stick's a map. The little one's a note about the ring, but I can't tell more without doing this properly and this is neither the time nor the place.*

Shaking my head, I carefully closed the box and rewrapped the little package, tucking it away in my trick bag. We needed to examine the contents more closely, but Triss was right. Then I stripped off my wrist sheaths and dropped them into the bag beside the package. Tomorrow, before we got on the boat I would have to buy some leather so that I could make new straps.

I'd have to be careful not to let Jax see them or the package, or she'd want to know what happened. That would pose a problem, since I wasn't yet willing to tell her about Kelos and didn't think I'd be up to making something up anytime soon. Next, I moved to pulling my swords out of the roof, which proved harder than expected. Kelos was an exceedingly strong man, and I ultimately had to get Triss to help me.

My final Kelos-delivered surprise of the evening came when I tried to pull the wardblack off the wall behind me. It was a clever piece of work, and I wanted to stash it somewhere for later study. But, as soon as it came free of the wards it had kept muffled, it became briefly too hot to touch, and then came apart in a puff of ashes when I dropped it.

All my elaborate planning with Faran went for nothing when Jax didn't make it home till after I'd gotten back. I told Faran enough of the story to satisfy her curiosity, though I omitted any mention of the finger. Before I could show her the map, Jax came in, deliberately making noise as she opened the roof hatch to let us know she'd arrived. After the others dropped off to sleep, I pulled out the tucker bottle of Kyle's that I'd

picked up on the way home and got quietly drunk. Triss didn't
say a word.

The day to day of travel is really only interesting to the par-
ticipants. The riverboat gave the three of us more time to spar
and train together, which was going to be key to making things
work if Jax ever came clean, or to dealing with her if she didn't,
for that matter. It also gave us plenty of time in too-close quarters to get on each other's nerves and inflict loads of mutual
misery.

I drank more than I should have and obsessed about Kelos
and his mysterious package—which I still hadn't gotten a
chance to examine privately in any detail. Jax spent much of
her time sinking into an ever more visible slough of despond.
Faran sharpened her knives and spent a lot of time staring at
the back of Jax's neck. The Shades quietly talked amongst
themselves, enjoying the trip far more than their respective
bond-mates. Whenever I asked Triss what they were talking
about he told me I wouldn't understand. Mostly, I believed him.

It took us nearly three weeks to travel against the current
from Ar to the landing stage where the road to Tavan met the
river at Fi Township. There, we rented a mule to carry our gear
and started walking south. Since horses are my next least favorite way to travel after boats, walking was just fine by me. The
road ran between low rolling hills covered with small copses
of trees and long stretches of farmland. This part of the Magelands provided the bulk of the food consumed in the big university cities: Ar, Gat, Tavan, Uln, and Har.

Periodically a small town or village straddled the road, and
even here, several days travel from the nearest of the universities, magic sparkled and shone a hundred times more densely
than anywhere in Tien. The spells were mostly small ones, just
as the local mages tended to be hedge witches and petty wiz-
ards. But every lock had a keytrue charm and every window a
shatternot.

The first night off the boat we stayed at an inn, delighted to
have separate rooms and more privacy than at any time since
we'd left Tien. That's when Triss and I finally got a chance to

examine the package in detail. We started with the big Shade stick.

First, I doused all the lamps in the room but one. Then I held the stick up to the light at an angle that cast its shadow on the wall precisely six feet away. Turning it slowly, I worked until I got the alignment just right, with light passing through two larger holes at either end to make pinpoints of brightness in the shadow. Then Triss flowed down my arm, completely covering the stick in darkness.

Projecting himself into and through the holes, he made cross connections following some formula only the Shades knew, and sketched out a three dimensional line drawing in the air. At its center stood a large multistory building with a half dozen major outbuildings around it, the whole enclosed by a high wall.

Looks like an abbey, I sent rather than said, in case one of the others was listening through the wall.

Yes, almost certainly the one where Loris and the others are being held. We'll have to memorize it.

I nodded. *Is there anything else?*

Yes. He shifted and the abbey faded away to be replaced by densely written text in Kelos's hand but the language of the Shades. *Looks like a list of the abbey's inhabitants, and another of the Signet's current entourage. Do you want me to read it to you?*

Later, after I've got the layout memorized.

Do you want to work on that first? Or should we look at the message that came with the finger?

Finger. Better to get it over with.

I shuddered at the thought of the thing Kelos had given me. Though I knew of a number of peoples who made trophies of their fallen enemies—skulls for cups and the like—it was not something that Blades did. Not sane ones anyway. Knowing Kelos, I doubted that was its main purpose, but I still really hated the idea of touching the thing. With extreme reluctance, I retrieved the box from my bag and opened it.

I can lift it out of there if you'd like, Triss offered.

No, I'll do it. I'm going to have to touch it sometime, and I might as well get it over with now.

I reached down . . . and promptly dropped both box and
finger, spilling the latter on the ground along with the smaller
Shade stick. I managed not to let out a shriek, but only just.
The finger was still warm. Somehow, against all logic and
reason, and after three weeks of riding around in my bag, it
was still warm.

In fact, it felt exactly as if it were still attached to a living
hand.

13

———————

Fear touches everyone. The soldier who panics at the sight of snakes, the torturer afraid of the dark, the murderer who abhors the deep blue sea. No matter how hard you think life has made you, no matter how many lives you've ended, no matter how many darkened alleys you've walked down, you have a breaking point. Apparently, a severed but still living finger was one of mine.

Aral! Triss wrapped himself around my shoulders, a cool but firm presence. *Are you all right?*

I nodded. *I will be. I just wasn't expecting it to still be warm.* I pushed at the finger with my boot tip.

I'm sorry, I should have warned you. I felt it when I first touched it.

It's all right, Triss. How is it . . . no, that's silly. It's magic, of course. But why?

Breathing deeply as I had been taught—by Kelos, ironically—I forced myself to relax. *Calm the body and the mind will follow.* He must have told me that a thousand times.

Once I felt like myself again, I reached down and picked up the finger. It felt disturbingly alive, and it took every shred of discipline I had to turn it so that I could look at the bone disk instead of flinging the damn thing across the room. I was so going to need a drink after this.

A silver nail head centered the disk, presumably driven through and into the bone of the finger on the other side. It was surrounded by a tracery of tiny glyphs and a single word carved in the runic alphabet of Aven—Kelos's name. I had to suppress another shudder at that. Though I hadn't yet parsed the spell's specifics, I instantly knew the only possible reason for Kelos to include his name like that. He had tied the functioning of the spell to the magical force of his own life, his nima.

The vast majority of magic happens in the moment, for the moment. What we call "low magic"—things like magefire, or summoning an item across a room—is the simple manipulation of forces. But even most high magic is temporary. Wards, for example, require regular renewal—weekly or even daily. Things like my thieveslamp or a window's shatternot are longer lasting. They might survive a year or more depending on who casts them, but those, too, will fade without regular renewal.

Permanent enchantments take a lot of power. Far more than any one spellcaster can muster in a single session. They need to be built one step at a time over days or weeks, layering in spell after spell to achieve the desired results. That's for the simplest of things. Greatspells take months or even years to build, though the most powerful sorcerers can collapse the process somewhat and a god can do even more.

Namara had created my temple swords in a seeming instant and those embodied multiple greatspells—though again, there were limits even to what a goddess could do. It was a rare year that saw more than a half dozen Blades become masters. That many usually died as well and their swords returned to the goddess, so she was able to use the power from the old to create the new, more often than not.

There are other ways around the time constraints, for those who are willing to find the price. Blood magic in all its forms is the most obvious. At the darkest extreme of that scale lies necromancy, which uses stolen life force to fuel magic out of all proportion to the caster's strength. What Kelos had done lay at the other end of the same line, tying his own life to a spell in a small but steady draw that would last as long as he did. No one was harmed by it except for Kelos, but it was still blood magic and fundamentally unclean.

Unicorn horn, said Triss.

What?

The bone plug on the end of the finger. It's a segment of unicorn horn. It's been carefully polished. But you can still see the spiral structure if you look closely at the edges, especially down in the bottoms of the glyphs carved around the outside.

I whistled low and quiet. Unicorn horn is fucking expensive, right up there with dragon bones and salamander blood. The original owners are magical creatures of enormous power and homicidal disposition, and they do not look kindly on corpse robbers. Still, I could see why Kelos had chosen it, no better medium existed for spells of vitality. It would make what had been done with this finger much easier to pull off.

Aral! Triss voice rang loud in my mind.

Yes?

Look at the ring.

I'd almost forgotten about it in my revulsion at the thing that wore it. Now, I turned my gaze on the gold signet . . . and nearly dropped the damn finger again. It was a starkly simple design. The band was watermarked in a cloud pattern, but otherwise unremarkable. The seal itself was an oval surrounded by a jagged band of lightning and imprinted with a six-fingered hand—the emblem of Heaven's Hand.

Is this what I think it is? I asked Triss.

I'm pretty sure that it is, but let's see what the Shade stick has to say.

We repeated the process we'd used earlier. This time there was no map, just a page or so of text in Shade. Triss read it, translating for me as he went along.

"Aral,

"This is the ring and finger of Eilif Uvarkas, Signet to the Daughter of Heaven and master of Heaven's Hand in the year 3130. I took his life of my own choice rather than at the command of Namara, though I think she would have ordered his execution soon enough had he lived. He abused his power and he deserved to die.

"This finger is the reason I could not wait for Namara's sanction. Had his life fallen to her decree, his body would have been left as a warning for others and the loss of hand and ring might have come to light. I refused to allow that to happen, sending the body into the everdark and burning a castle to hide its loss. Otherwise, the least response of the Daughter of Heaven would have been to change the spells on all the locks of all the temples of Shan, and that would not have suited my plans.

"As long as this ring stays on this living finger, the bearer has a key that will open any lock in Heaven's mortal kingdom. Do not let it fall into the wrong hands. Do not show it to anyone. I expect its safe return at the end of your present mission for me.

"Kelos."

I looked at the ring and finger again. Kelos had been holding onto this magical skeleton key for almost a hundred years. That led to a whole mess of questions. Like, why did he make it in the first place? And, what was he planning on doing with it when he got it back from me? Or, why trust me with it now?

I didn't think I'd much like any of the answers, though I knew that ultimately I needed to find them. Without saying another word, I put both ring and finger back in their box. The accompanying note from Kelos I destroyed. Then I asked Triss to show me the map again. The abbey was large and complex, and my memory was not what it once was. I knew it would take some hours over several sessions to really set it in my mind.

Fortunately, we spent the next couple of days traveling through populated country and our nights at inns, which gave me the time I needed. Our fourth day on the road found us high on a spur of foothills that came down off the Hurnic Mountains to the west. With so much good land north and east, no one had bothered to colonize these stony ridges, and we were, ourselves, alone and far from any inns or houses when the light started to fail.

The weather was fine and we had nothing to fear from bandits or any but the most fearsome of beasts. So, when we came to a small oak wood, we turned off the road and looked for a good place to lay in a fire and camp for the night. While I got the fire going, the women went out a-hunting. Faran and Ssithra killed a good sized huddle bird, and Jax and Sshayar turned up some lovely fat mushrooms and a few apples that we could roast along with the fowl.

The fire was merry and the Shades took delight in slipping in and out amidst the flickering shadows it created, playing a sort of dancing game of tag—phoenix, tiger, and dragon. The meal was excellent, and wanted only a bottle of wine or whiskey to make a real feast of it. But the small beer didn't taste half bad. After most of a skin—neither Jax nor Faran would touch the stuff despite how weak it was—I felt very nearly relaxed for the first time in more weeks than I cared to count.

I think Faran felt the same way, and we bantered back and forth for quite a while before I noticed that Jax had gone silent. When I shot her a questioning look, she quietly backed away from the fire and shook her head.

"Are you all right?" I asked.

"Stomach's not sitting quite right." She put her hand to her mouth. "I need to go off a bit and deal with it." Before I could say another thing, she turned away and hurried into the darkness beyond the fire.

Faran sat up and looked after her. "Do you think she's going to be all right?"

"No," said Triss. "She's poisoned herself, though it's not the mushrooms she fed you that did the job. It's bottling up fear and guilt and six years of unrelenting anger. I hope she figures out how to let it go before it kills her."

Faran cocked her head to one side. "Can something like that really kill you?"

Triss looked at me in a way that made me very uncomfortable before he spoke, "Oh yes. Not directly perhaps, but there are as many ways to die as there are stars in the night sky. If a person starts looking for their own death, they're bound to find it eventually."

Faran's face creased with a pain I'd seen there too often these last few months, and she turned to stare into the fire. Fifteen and full of bitter memory. I hated to see her hurting but I was too wounded myself to believe anything would help her but time.

She nodded lightly toward the flames. "They started with fire, did you know that?"

"No. I saw the scorch marks in the rubble, of course, but by the time I got there it was far too late to make any sense of the mess." I didn't have to ask what she was talking about—the fall of the temple was still a raw wound for me six years later. "The buildings were all shattered and the rubble had been pushed into the cellars. They'd plowed up the fields and sown salt in the furrows."

Faran nodded. "I saw all that when I went back a year or two after." She closed her eyes tight as a fist. "It started with lightning all around, igniting the orchards and the wheat in the fields. The Storms, of course, though we didn't know it at first. They came at noon and late in the summer when the sun is strong and the Shades are weak. The whole complex was ringed with fire in minutes, miles and miles of fire."

"That's why we couldn't take the little ones to safety," whispered Ssithra. "Between the fire and the sun, the heat and the light were simply too intense for us to do much of anything but hide in our bond-mates's shadows."

"Then the lightning started to fall inside the walls," continued Faran. "Master Tamerlen was leading a few of us toward the main building when she was struck. Her hair caught fire and her eyes boiled. I see it again and again in my dreams. . . . I don't think I'll ever be able to unsee it."

I got up from where I'd been lying with my feet to the fire and walked over to kneel beside Faran, putting a hand on her shoulder. "I'm so sorry I wasn't there." Faran didn't reply, but she did lean her head against my forearm.

"You wouldn't have changed anything, Aral." Jax's voice came from behind me. "You'd have died with so many of the others . . . if you were lucky. If you weren't you'd have been taken by the Hand."

I turned to look over my shoulder, but couldn't see Jax in the darkness. I realized that if Master Kelos were there right now, I wouldn't have hesitated to kill him. How could he have done this to them? To us?

I shook my head and started to answer Jax, "But—"

"But me no buts," she said quietly but firmly. "I know what I'm talking about. I dreamed about how things might have gone differently if you'd been there to help. You and Siri and Kaman. We were short a dozen of our very best that day."

A darker shadow slid out from between the trees, and Jax

continued, though she didn't yet show herself. "When they had me on the rack I fantasized about how you all might have changed things, and I hated each and every last one of you for not being there for us."

My throat constricted. "Jax, I . . ." What? What could I say that would make the slightest bit of difference?

"It's all right, Aral. Even then, I knew I was lying to myself, that your presence would have done nothing but increased the body count. I needed the lie then. Needed it for years afterward. I couldn't have done . . . well, a lot of things over the time since then without it. Most especially I couldn't have done what I've been doing since that day at the Gryphon's Head."

She dropped her shroud as she got closer to the fire and to us. "Without lying to myself, I couldn't have lied to you. But I'm done with the lies now. We need to talk."

"It's about damned time!" Sshayar twisted herself out of Jax's shadow and into the shape of a tiger slipping around in front of her. "I thought sure you were going to force Faran into killing you. Or worse, Aral."

"What?" Jax looked completely flabbergasted.

"Oh, Jax, I do despair of humans sometimes. You know how good Aral is, and you've seen a bit of what Faran can do. Did you honestly think that one or both of them wouldn't figure it out given time? I didn't even have to tell them, they already knew."

Jax looked from me to Faran and back again, her expression shocked. "You know that the Hand is using Loris and the others as hostages to force me into betraying Aral to them?"

I nodded.

Jax rolled her eyes. "Then why in the name of all that was once holy have you been sitting here with your faces to the fire and your backs to the shadows and me? And why did you let me feed you mushrooms of unknown provenance?"

I smiled at her, though it wasn't a happy smile. "Because I thought I owed it to you to give you the chance to do what you're doing right now."

"You are a complete and total madman, and infuriating to boot. You do know that, right?"

Triss said, "If he doesn't, it's not for lack of hearing it from me. But really, in this case I agree with him. Sshithra and

Sshayar and I have been talking it over, and contrary to Sshayar's worries, none of us would have let you harm each other. We've been quietly trying to figure out amongst the three of us if there wasn't some way we could get you to just get on with your confession so we could start working on a real plan."

"For that matter," said Faran, "we didn't let you feed us strange mushrooms. I very carefully watched you pick them."

"How did you manage to do that without me spotting you?"

Faran grinned and winked, burying her darker side under the brash teenager. "I thought we'd already established that I'm very, very good."

When she'd first appeared in my life I'd wondered which of the two was the mask. But the more time I spent with her, the more I realized that the two faces were equally real. Now I wondered if she'd ever be able to integrate them, or if one must inevitably give way to the other. Then Jax plopped herself down on the ground on Faran's other side and I pushed the question aside.

"All right," said Jax. "I give up. I'm apparently a lousy conspirator and a fool on top of that. So, now what?"

Sshayar put one large paw on Jax's lap and gave her a very hard look.

Jax blushed. "Oh, right. Thank you, Sshayar. Aral, Faran, I'm sorry. I should never have lied to you. I . . . I'd like to make excuses for my choices, but then it's not really an apology. Suffice to say, I fucked up completely."

"Apology accepted for my part." I grinned. "I knew you were a fuckup beforehand, but I'd be a hypocrite if I didn't forgive you that particular flaw. Faran?"

She nodded at Jax. "If you'll forgive me for spending the past month trying to decide exactly where and when I ought to cut your throat, I'm willing to call it even."

"Then, I guess we're going to have a problem," said Jax. "Because you haven't done anything that needs forgiving, and I have."

Faran shrugged and smiled. "Fair enough. You're off the hook as far as I'm concerned."

"Thank you, both of you." Sshayar coughed pointedly, and Jax looked at her and then winced. "Oh, bugger." She turned back our way. "Triss, Ssithra, my profound apologies, both for my behavior and the oversight."

The Shades accepted more gracefully than either Faran or I had, and we settled in to discuss what Jax knew about the abbey where the captured Blades were being held. It would have been the perfect time for me to bring out my map and the signet ring if it weren't for two tiny details.

First, I still didn't trust Jax any farther than I could easily throw her. She'd lied to me too many times and too easily over the last month for me to rely on her word now. Second, I agreed with Kelos that it would distract Jax to know he was still alive. At least, I hoped it was that I agreed with him and not simply that even now I had trouble going against his word. I had good reasons for my choice not to tell her.

I just wished that doing it didn't make me feel like such a bastard.

Shan had dandruff. I found that reassuring. I *knew* that the Emperor of Heaven never manifested himself outside the mother temple at Heaven's Reach, but the dandruff made me *believe* it. It also made me wonder about the devotion of Shan's servants in Tavan.

I wasn't really lying in a bed of dandruff, just the accumulation of dust and other detritus atop the huge sculpture of the god that dominated the temple's sanctum. But the fact that neither the temple's novices nor its servants had bothered to clean the area inside the enormous iron crown for what looked like the last several years, didn't speak well of their piety.

When Jax had checked in with the Sword of Heaven in Tavan she'd received orders demanding a midnight meeting with the Signet. At that point I'd absolutely insisted that I should go in ahead and set up where I could hear the whole meeting and cover her back if she needed it. Jax had resisted, but eventually given in.

Faran had supported me in my argument with Jax, then given me a serious chewing out once she could do so beyond the range of Jax's hearing. I had to argue long and hard before she grudgingly agreed to allow me to go alone. Of course, I was pretty sure that she was lurking somewhere close at hand, in case things went wrong.

I shifted Triss away from my face now and peered down through the gaps created where Shan's irregular stone hair met the lower edge of the iron crown. Nothing below had changed from the last time I'd checked, approximately two minutes ago. Neither had the careful positioning of my blowgun with its preloaded poison dart—I didn't want to have to move much if I needed to shoot someone. Same with my other equipment.

Everything was as ready as I could make it, and fidgeting with it wasn't going to help. I took a couple of slow breaths and for about the dozenth time wished that I had a couple of efik beans I could chew to take the edge off my nerves without dulling my wits. It was an old familiar craving and one I'd managed to beat by substituting booze for beans back when I returned to Tien after the fall of the temple.

It was the worst idea I ever had, and it probably saved my life. In responsible-sized doses, efik was a much less self-destructive sort of habit than alcohol, but the chances of my handling it responsibly were pretty much zero back then. I'd rather be a drunk in the gutter any day of the week than a sleepwalker cutting gashes in my arms so I could pack them with powdered efik and smile my life away in a filthy alley.

Alcohol might be slowly killing me now, but efik would have done for me in a matter of weeks back then. The switch kept me alive then, if for no other reason than how much I initially hated the booze. It took time and real effort for me to get to the place where I *needed* alcohol. Slow suicide is still suicide, but it gives you a lot more time to change your mind along the way.

I was very aware of time at the moment. The great bells of Shan ring on the quarters of the hour. His temples are the arbiters of time in most cities of the eleven kingdoms, though they compete with the universities for that distinction in the Magelands. Here in Shan's sanctum, I could hear the faint gurgles and clunks of the huge water-clock that the timekeepers of Shan used to measure time during the hours when the sun hid its face from the world. Every five minutes it rang a gentle chime, so I knew how long I'd been waiting for the arrival of Jax and the Signet—one hour, thirty minutes, and change.

If the Signet was prompt, I'd have another twenty minutes to contemplate the god's dandruff. If not, at least I'd be able to keep an eye on Jax while the Signet kept her waiting. For perhaps the dozenth time that evening I reached for the efik in my trick bag only to stop my hand halfway there when I remembered. The only efik I carried now was mixed with opium and packed in robin's eggs to make an easily delivered and quick acting knockout drug.

Patience, Aral.

Easy for you to say. What does time mean to a shadow?

Shade, and not all that much in the divisions you normally use. Though, I must admit, your twitching makes me more aware of its passing than usual. I—hold on, the door behind the statue is opening.

I flattened myself even more tightly against the god's stony hair, though I left the hole in front of my face unshrouded. I wanted to see if I could, and I didn't think the risk too great. A moment later, the Signet entered my vision, coming around the sculpture from the right.

Now would be a good time to hold your breath, Triss sent in a mental whisper. *The Signet's Storm is directly above us, and I don't know what it can and can't sense.*

I stopped my breath and slowed my heart as much as I could, which made me miss the efik all the more. With a few beans in me I could have easily gotten my heart rate down as low as thirty beats to the minute, and held my breath for as long as six or eight minutes at the same time. Without it, I would have trouble pushing it down much below forty, and holding my breath past three or four minutes was beyond me.

And the whole effort went for nothing when I felt the statue move beneath me and my heart rate exploded while my focus on not breathing gave way to an effort directed at not screaming.

The god wasn't supposed to manifest anywhere but the mother temple!

14

---◆--◆---

Flesh, like stone. The assassin's art calls for the mastery of stillness in the face of shock or surprise. Even in the face of the impossible. In this case, perversely, stone, like flesh. I forced myself to stillness as the giant statue on which I lay slowly shifted its position.

Shan had been carved with multiple arms, as the gods usually were—four in this case, though I had seen sculptures of him with as many as ten. As the Signet passed around in front of the statue, she touched the back of her left hand to the cross-legged god's knee. That's when Shan's lower arms began to move, sliding forward and down with a dull grinding sound like the world's largest knife being sharpened. Dust fell from the ceiling here and there, bringing with it the damp smell of rotting mortar. The whole thing made me want to shriek like a child and bolt for the exit.

Two things kept me in place. The first was a lifetime's indoctrination in the need for stealth. The second, and far more important factor, was that the statue didn't *feel* alive. I had witnessed Namara's arrival in her stone avatar many times after I became a full Blade. The living statue that housed her soul would rise from the deeps of the sacred lake to give us our assignments or accept our obeisance after a successful mission.

The bright burning core of that experience was the feeling of vitality that radiated out from her physical form in every possible way. When you stood before the goddess you were aware of her presence in the same way that you were aware of the heat and light when you stood beneath the summer sun at noon. You couldn't not *know* that it was there.

The sculpture of Shan had none of that *presence* to it now. In fact, when I thought to look for it, I could see a strong glow of magic about the arm that moved. The whole statue partook of the spell-light, but everywhere but the arm, it was more like the dim glow of a ghost fungus or honey mushroom. That was deeply reassuring. Divine enchantments, like that on my old temple blades, cast no spell-light. Which meant the statue's motion was driven by mortal magic.

The mill-wheel-like grinding noise should have been another clue, since Namara's statue had always moved with silence more perfect than any living flesh. The grate of stone on stone continued as the sculpture turned its lower hands palms up, bringing six-fingered hands together into a sort of cup. Climbing the toes of Shan's left foot like a set of stairs, the Signet now ascended to the god's knee.

From there she moved to seat herself in the lowered hands, taking possession of the religious throne they had formed. That gave me a perfect shot at the back of her neck—she'd even tied her ice blond hair into a thick braid and pulled it aside. It took a real effort of will on my part not to take the shot.

Do all of Shan's idols do that? Triss asked into my mind.

Maybe. I'd never had an assignment that involved the temple of Shan, and the subject of the other gods hadn't really interested me when it came up in my education. *Jax might know, or Faran, but I've no idea.*

Siri would have. She'd always been more interested in matters theological, which is why she'd ended up with the assignment that earned her the name Mythkiller. Well, that and the fact that she was probably the best mage in the recent history of the temple, Kelos not excepted. So good that she'd been sent to study at the magical university in Uln for a few years after she became a full Blade. She could do things with shadow and spells that made my head hurt to even contemplate.

I'd once seen her step into the shadow of one tree and out of the shadow of another almost twenty yards away. When I'd asked her about it, she said it was a magical effect she'd been experimenting with. Then she went off into a rather abstract explanation that started out with a discussion of the way the fringes of the everdark interacted with normal reality and ended with something she called geometrical mathimagics. My big take-away from the conversation was that she would attempt to teach me to do it if I really wanted her to, but that she didn't think she'd try it again herself since it felt rather like being frozen into a block of burning ice.

I'd never taken her up on it, though I was thinking it would be awfully handy right now if I knew I could use the shadow of the crown as my exit strategy if I needed to. The way the Signet's Storm kept darting here and there around the upper reaches of the temple and poking its scytheblade head into various nooks and crannies left me feeling very exposed.

Jax is here, Triss said into my mind, *near the front door.*

Thanks. I couldn't see that part of the room from where I currently lay, and moving to get a better view seemed like a particularly bad idea at the moment.

She's coming closer now. The Signet either hasn't seen her yet or is ignoring her.

She walked into the narrow semicircle of space I could see clearly, coming slowly toward the seated Signet. She stopped about ten feet short of the double-hand throne and silently glared up at its occupant. If she was at all curious about where I might have set up to keep an eye on things, she didn't betray it by so much as a sidelong glance. All of her attention remained focused on the woman seated above her, even when the Storm flew down to hover behind her.

"You're early," said the Signet.

Jax nodded, but didn't say anything.

"That's good. It speaks of obedience, and you need to learn obedience. I've had time to think over our last encounter, and it wasn't at all satisfactory. Our deal was that you would cooperate with me and none of your people would get hurt. You violated that deal, and there's a price to be paid for breaking your word to Heaven."

Jax stiffened. "What have you done?"

"Nothing irreversible." The Signet reached into her robe and pulled something out, flinging it to the ground at Jax's feet. "Five right ears. If you do exactly as I say going forward, I'll have one of my best leeches regrow them. If you take one more step out of line, the next thing I throw at your feet will be the head of the youngest of the prisoners. I know how you and your lover value your students, so I'll make sure to have her killed in front of Master Loris."

Aral! Triss barked into my mind.

I froze with the blowgun I hadn't even realized I'd picked up, halfway to my lips. Below me, Jax's hands on her sword hilts were shaking. Her face looked very much as I imagined mine must, twisted into a mask by a fury that burned in the blood and bones.

"If you draw your swords, Blade, one of your students will die. If you or your familiar attempts to harm me, all of them will die, as will you and your lover. If you kill me, the message that spares them will not be sent in the morning and they will die by torture. If you do the slightest thing to make me annoyed with you, I'll harvest you a matching packet of left ears. Do you understand me? A nod will suffice, but it had better happen damned quickly."

At a cost I could only imagine, Jax removed her hands from her swords and nodded her head once.

Are you sure I can't kill the Signet? I asked Triss.

Yesss, he hissed angrily in response—his loss of human speech patterns a clear sign of his own rage. *Too much remainsss at ssstake right now, but sssoon, I hope. Very sssoon, though I think Jax dessservesss firssst rightsss if ssshe wantsss them.*

I can't argue with that.

"Better," said the Signet. "I don't tolerate disobedience from my subordinates, and I certainly won't tolerate it from a slave like you. The only reason you or your precious charges have lived even this long is that the Son himself has ordered that the death of Aral Kingslayer takes precedence over everything else to do with your failed religion."

That left me blinking. What had I done to piss the Son of Heaven off that much recently?

"Here." The Signet pulled a packet from her robes and threw it down beside the string of ears. "Your marching orders. There's a map of the abbey with your route marked out and when you are expected. We set things up exactly as you suggested originally. Deviate one jot from the assigned path and your comrades die. You strike in two nights at moon-dark. Your Kingslayer should like that. Now, get out of my sight."

Jax turned around and walked away almost casually. I wondered how much that feigned nonchalance cost her, and admired her for her ability to pull it off. I don't know if I could have done the same in her place. Nor if I could have stopped myself killing the Signet on the spot. I'd barely been able to hold back with Triss speaking directly into my mind and infinitely less provocation. Loris was never my lover, nor the journeymen my students.

If Faran's ear had fallen on the floor at my feet, could I have walked away like that? What if Jax's had fallen with it? I had my doubts. Only the fact that my fellow Blades' lives depended on the life of the Signet prevented me from killing her even now.

The Signet rose from her throne, and walked down the toes of the great statue. This time I saw her ring of office flash as she touched it to the giant's knee. Flesh, like stone. Again I disciplined myself to stillness as stone moved unnaturally beneath me.

I didn't move until the Signet and her familiar had long since departed the sanctum. Then I rose and, slipping back out the way I had come, I went to find Jax and Faran. We had plans to make and blood to spill.

I caught up with Jax about halfway back to the snug at the inn. Or, maybe I should say, she let me catch up to her. Like all the great cities of the Magelands, Tavan was built around a university and magic was everywhere. Even most of Tavan's thieves were minor sorts of mages, so the chimney highway was rife with tangles and blinds and other sorts of charms designed to confuse the unwary and prevent pursuit.

If Jax had wanted to, she could easily have used that

environment to avoid dealing with me till we got back to the snug. Instead, she chose to dawdle along the main route leading from the temple quarter—the Magelanders confined the religious orders to one small area of their city—to the neighborhood that held our temporary snug.

"Jax," I called before I dropped down onto the roof behind her—I didn't want to startle her.

She turned and waited for me to get closer. "You saw?"

I nodded.

"I'm going to make the Hand pay for that, and not just the Signet either."

"I'll help."

"Do you think we can really save them?"

Don't you think we should take this conversation somewhere a little more private? Triss asked.

"Maybe," I said to Jax, "but we shouldn't talk about it here." I looked around for someplace we could speak without being overheard. "Come on." I pointed up to a small water tank on top of a tall apartment block off to our left. "How about there? It's close and it looks as isolated as anything around here."

She raised an eyebrow. "Faran?"

"Can wait till we've had this conversation."

"All right." She frowned but led the way.

Like most such tanks, the top was slightly dished to act as a collector for rain water. Since the building was also the tallest one within a half mile or so, that put the center of the roof out of line of sight for pretty much everything but the university bell tower—over a mile distant. With Triss and Shayar standing guard up at the lip, we had as much privacy as it was possible to have without using magic.

Jax settled into a cross-legged seat. "So, I know why I wanted to have this conversation now and just between the two of us. What about you? Why did *you* want to leave Faran out of it?"

"I could go for the half truth and tell you it's because you so obviously wanted a private conversation. And that I owed it you to honor that desire, since that's true enough."

"But?"

I took a deep breath while I tried to sort out how to tell her about Kelos. "But I have things that I need to talk to you about that are going to be hard enough for both of us without trying to include the junior division."

Jax laughed a bitter little laugh. "I'm not going to like this one little bit, am I?"

"Probably not, no, though it *will* improve our chances of pulling this thing off." I paused before asking, "How could you tell?"

"Because you're wearing the exact same expression you had the day you told me you were breaking our engagement." She straightened her back and shoulders. "Might as well get the hard stuff over with. Hit me."

I reached into my trick bag and pulled out the shade stick. "Here." I handed it across to her.

She turned it in her hands. "Looks like a map, and a fairly complex one, if I'm any judge. What's it for?"

"The abbey where Loris and the others are imprisoned. They're confined in a series of crypts underneath the sanctum. The only practical way in or out goes right under the idol."

Jax held up the map. "So, this is the good news. How did you come by it?"

"That's the bad news."

"I kind of figured. And?"

"Master Kelos gave it to me."

"That's not possible," Jax said flatly. "Kelos is dead. I've seen his name on the obelisk."

"Devin's name is there, too."

"But Devin's a traitor. You told me that yourself."

"So is Kelos. In fact, Kelos is *the* traitor, the one who set us all up."

"That's not possible," she said again. "Kelos could no more betray the goddess than he could cut his own heart out."

"Actually," I said lightly, "if anyone I know could actually manage to cut his own heart out, it'd be Kelos."

Jax ignored my half-assed joke. "It can't be true, Aral. Kelos *was* the order, the bedrock on which all of the rest of us stood."

"He claimed that he was trying to salvage what he could out of an inevitable circumstance. That that's why I wasn't at the temple when it fell. He sent me away along with Siri and Kaman and some of the others, because he knew we would choose to die before we'd take the Son of Heaven's deal. He wanted to save us for later use."

Jax's face slowly twisted into the same hate-filled expression I'd seen in the temple of Shan earlier. "You're serious, aren't you?"

"I wish to everything I ever once held as holy that I weren't. . . ."

"Then it's all his fault. The death of the goddess. The fall of the temple. All the ones we've lost then and since. Kaman, Tamerlen, Viera. My torture. The wreck you've made of yourself. Even what's happening to Loris right now. It's all down to Kelos, and you're working with him now?" Jax leaped to her feet and leaned down over me.

She's going to hit you. Triss's mental voice sounded dry, almost detached.

I know.

And then she did, a full-armed backhanded slap intended to inflict maximum pain without causing real harm. I rolled with the blow, but it still stung and it would probably bruise. It was exactly the same way she'd hit me when I broke our engagement. It told me two things. First, she was really mad at me. Second, she was fundamentally still in control of herself. She knew what she wanted to do to me and how far she wanted to go, and she'd chosen the exact tool she wanted to accomplish that task.

"Feel any better?" I asked. I kept my voice calm because I knew it would irritate her.

"No! And you're an asshole, you know that, right?"

"You're certainly not the first to say so. Are you going to hit me again?"

"No. I'm sorry, that was a stupid move."

"See, I told you she could be taught," Sshayar said from her place up on the lip of the water tank.

"And fuck you, too, dear," replied Jax, this time without the heat, then she laughed.

Quick to anger. Quick to cool down. Quick to move on to the next step. That was Jax all the way, and that's why I'd pushed her. I wanted her to hit the top and bounce back so we could move on. I wasn't one jot less furious than she was, but we didn't have time to waste on theatrics.

She flopped back down on the roof and gave me a hard look. "Don't think I didn't see what you just did there. You used to do the same damn thing when we were engaged. On the upside, the make-up sex generally made up for how much that calm mask thing you do used to piss me off. Do you ever miss that? What we had together."

"No," I lied, pushing aside memories of Jax naked and wanting to make up for the bad times. It wasn't easy. "I don't."

"You're lying."

"Probably," I agreed. "But it's still true. Can we talk about how we're going to make the Hand pay for what they've done?"

"Soon. You still haven't explained why you're working with the man who destroyed us. I'm not doing anything till you answer that."

"I think the Son of Heaven and his god probably have to take some of the blame for the fall of the temple, too."

"But Kelos was complicit. Without him . . ."

"Maybe." I held out my hands like balances. "I don't honestly know what would have happened if he'd tried to stop things dead instead of cutting a deal."

"You're starting to piss me off again. Answer the fucking question, Aral."

"I'm not working with him. I'm using him. I'm taking his help to do something I was going to do anyway."

"Don't give me weasel words. That's not what I'm asking, and you know it."

"Fine. I'm doing it because I don't see that I have a lot of choice. When I drew on him, he knocked me down and disarmed me as easily as I might do the same to some back-alley pinch-purse. He's *the* master, Jax. If he wants to help us, I'm not seeing any good way to get him out of the picture. Unless *you* think you can take him?"

Jax shook her head. "Of course not."

"Well then, what do you want me to do? Throw away the map? Give up the other advantages his help can give us in getting Loris and the others free?"

"No." She looked at her feet.

"How about blowing off the mission completely and letting them all die? Would that be better? Because that's the only other fucking option we have!"

I bounced to my feet and started to pace in a tight little circle. "Do you think I like that fact that when he called me I came to him like a dog? Do you think I like that I can't figure out how I should feel about the man who was the closest thing I had to a father? Do you think I like the fact that I don't have any clue if I'm doing this because he's our best chance, or just because it's Kelos telling me to do it? Because I sure as shit don't like any of it one tiny fucking bit!"

"Old man, you need to get a hold of yourself or you're going to wake the whole damned neighborhood." The familiar voice came up from somewhere below us.

"Little monster," I sighed. "Get your ass up here, Faran. How much have you heard?"

"Pretty much everything after the slap." She pulled herself up over the lip of the tank. "I figured that you'd both be hot enough for a bit then that you wouldn't hear my getting in close."

"Triss?"

"She's damned good. I didn't so much as catch a hint of her."

"Me either," agreed Sshayar.

"Have you told her about the finger yet?" Faran asked as she took a seat a few feet to Jax's left.

"No. Just the map. As I recall, I didn't tell you about the finger yet either."

She shook her head sadly. "That's right. I had to pick your pouch to find it, and I'm really quite hurt about that."

"I don't think I beat you enough. You are a most disobedient sort of apprentice."

"Probably because I'm only your apprentice for the assassin stuff. Where it comes to spying, I kick your ass."

I looked at Jax. "Are your students like this?"

She smiled. "Only the very best of them. Come on, Aral. Don't pull that obedience line with me. I know what kinds of crap you used to get up to. In fact, I'm pretty sure that you broke about six dozen rules by sneaking out to the sacred island and asking Namara to give you the Ashvik assignment a year before you were slated to become a full Blade. That was right before you vanished into the night without a word to anyone including the council, right?"

"I can verify that," said Triss. "Though, Master Kelos did wish us good hunting, and Devin knew about it even before we went out to the island."

"Thanks, Triss." I sighed. "Can we move on now?"

"Sure," replied Jax. "You were just going to tell me about the *finger*."

"Oh good," said Faran. "I've been wondering about it for days now. I mean, I've seen it. And I think I can guess what it's for, but if there were instructions that came with it, somebody destroyed them before I got a chance to read them."

I told them about the ring and what it could do, and while I was at it, I told them about the moving statue, and brought Faran up to date on what had happened at the temple. When I was done, they both wanted to see the finger. So I pulled out the box and opened it up.

"Damn," said Jax. "That could come in very handy." She poked it with the tip of her own finger and shuddered.

Jax didn't like touching it any more than I did, but Faran blithely reached over and pulled it out of its box, turning it this way and that to get a better look at the glyphs. She seemed completely blasé about the idea of a living finger preserved a hundred years after the death of the hand that had once worn it.

"That's one tricky little spell," she said after a moment. "I'm sure I could replicate it easy enough, but I don't know if I'd be able to cook it up from scratch." She shrugged. "No surprise, I guess. After Master Siri, Master Kelos was always the one who taught us the most about practical magic."

"That's a hit," said Jax touching a fingertip to her chest. "Point, Faran."

"Huh?" Faran canted her head to one side quizzically. "What'd I do?"

"You just made me feel incredibly old," replied Jax. "Siri is nearly a year younger than I am. No one should ever refer to her as Master Siri with the same tone as they refer to Master Kelos when talking about their teachers. It's wrong."

"Weird." Faran looked genuinely puzzled. "I can't imagine that. You all looked pretty much the same age from where I was sitting in those days. You know . . . old."

Jax's eyes widened and she started to open her mouth. Then she paused and scowled for a moment. "You're pulling my leg aren't you?"

Faran held her wide-eyed innocent look for one more beat, then dropped it for a wicked smile.

"No wonder you call her little monster," Jax growled at me.

"Oh come on," said Faran. "It was a fair point." She jabbed the Signet's finger at Jax for emphasis. "I mean, you *are* old, right? Maybe not as old as Aral, but then, he's half as old as Kelos."

"Not yet thirty!" I said.

"Children, please." Triss plucked the finger from Faran's hand and put it back in its box. "We've got things to plan. If we're done with the show-and-tell part of the evening, maybe we could move on to the main event?"

"I don't know how much planning we have time for," I replied. "The Hand will be expecting us the night after next. If we're going to have any chance at taking them by surprise we'll have to hit them tomorrow, and without surprise the hostages are all dead."

"Point." Jax's voice was grim. "We know the where, and our window really narrows down the when. We might manage a bit of extra surprise by coming in during the day, but that would cost us too much of our Shades's strength. It's still summer, which cuts down the available hours of full dark, and it's going to take at least a couple of hours to manage the job. So, sometime between full dark and the first hour after midnight."

"Agreed." Faran nodded. "These are the people who killed Namara and the order and they've taken people we care about, so there's no question of tactics. We kill everyone we see without hesitation or mercy. What's left to discuss; which door we use?"

"That and who goes for the prisoners," I replied.

"You do," Jax and Faran said in near perfect unison.

"Why me?"

"Loris is my lover and the others are my students," said Jax. "That's going to make my thinking less clear overall, and more so as I get closer to them. I *want* to be the one to free them, and we both know that means I'll be less professional and more likely to get them or us killed."

She closed her eyes for a second and her jaw muscles tightened. "It also means that if something goes wrong and someone dies, I'm going to regret it forever. I'd take point if I had to, but I don't know if I can hold it together if everything goes to hell. Not after what I went through when the temple fell. That puts me on eliminating the reinforcements duty."

I nodded, and didn't add that if things went to shit, it'd probably be better for her to have someone else to blame. Me, for example. "Faran?"

"You're too sentimental. You don't really like killing people who aren't directly in the way. If you're going after the hostages, everyone you meet will be directly in the way, and you won't think twice. But someone's going to have to do clean up on the periphery. That's going to involve cutting a lot of not obviously guilty throats. I won't hesitate. You might. End of story."

"I guess that means I'm going after the hostages."

"And we'll make corpses," said Jax, and there was a cold fire in her eyes. "Lots and lots of corpses."

15

Killing people. It's what I do best, my art as well as my craft. It's not nice. It's not pretty. It's not romantic. Any number of times I've found myself wishing for a world where it wasn't so often necessary. But in the end, I'm an assassin, one of the best, and I love my work even when I don't like it. But these were the people who'd destroyed the temple, some of them had killed people I loved. This time I would get to do both.

We arrived outside the high stone walls of the abbey just as the trailing edge of the sun kissed the horizon good-bye. We'd spent much of the day in a coach, which had allowed Faran and Jax time to memorize the map along the way, and Ssithra and Sshayar time to make copies just in case. We'd left the coach hidden in a ruined barn a few miles back, with the coachman inside wrapped in spells of sleep.

With sunrise, the spells would fade and he would be able to depart the barn with a much heavier purse. If anyone touched him or the barn before then, the whole place and all its contents would burn away to nothing in an instant.

"Last check," said a dragon-form Triss. "Everyone know what they're doing?

"We go in through the escape tunnel that comes out in the southwest tower," I said. It was about a third of the way around the abbey from the route that had been picked out for Jax and me by the Signet. "The ring opens the doors and the wards for us. There'll almost certainly be a guard in the tunnel proper." Under normal operations, there wouldn't have been, to help preserve the route's secrecy. But with the nature of the current situation, they'd have a trusted noncom down there.

"If we're lucky," I continued, "it'll be one of the Swords of Heaven, and he'll have some sort of alarm ward on him triggered by death because he'll be out of touch with the main perimeter. If we're not lucky, we'll be facing a member of the Hand. In either case, they go down, and they die as soon as we silence any death wards. Then we split up."

Blades rarely work together in close proximity. In the vast majority of situations over the many centuries of our history one of us has usually been enough to get the job done. Beyond that, our greatest asset is stealth. Working as a team throws a significant portion of that advantage away.

When you're functionally invisible, visual signals don't do you a lot of good. Add in that people tend to notice it when the shadows start talking to each other, and any attempt at communication significantly compromises your effectiveness. Shades can communicate silently to a degree, but with the lone exception of Triss and myself, that communication doesn't extend to their bond-mates.

Also, when you can't see your compatriots, you are much more likely to accidentally hit one with something lethal. So, on those rare occasions where it becomes necessary to act together, we generally prefer to split up and spread out. It preserves our advantages and reduces the chances of killing one another.

"Once we make the split, I'll take the most direct route possible to the crypt," I continued. "Depending on who and what Triss and I run into, I hope to have the first cell open somewhere between twenty and forty minutes from now. I'll arm the prisoners and we'll start cutting our way out. Once we're clear of the main building, I'll light things up to let you know we've made it."

"I'll start by heading back to the wall and clearing out the perimeter guards on this side of the abbey." Faran smiled a nasty little smile and Ssithra flexed shadowy phoenix claws. "Call it twenty minutes if nothing goes awry. Then I'll work my way inward with a goal of leaving you a wide-open path to freedom."

Jax rolled her shoulders to loosen the thick pack hung from her sword rig, while Sshayar stalked back and forth behind her looking every inch the hunting tiger. "I'll go straight for the guesthouse and set glyphs of destruction on the main supports and bindings on the doors. That's where the Hand will be quartered. Once we've prepared the way, Sshayar and I will bring the building down and try to kill the lot of them in their sleep. I'd prefer to slit throats, but . . ."

I nodded. For every Storm that died with their bond-mate, the weather was likely to get that much worse. That was going to wake people up sooner rather than later, which is why we'd picked up the destruction wards. That was one place where having this go down in the Magelands made our lives much easier. The destruction glyphs were devilishly tricky to make, and damned expensive.

Jax's brother was going to have palpitations when he saw the bill for that, but we'd had no choice. None of us had the skills to make them in quantity, even if we'd had the leisure. Time had foreclosed the theft option as well, that kind of play took serious planning. One useful side effect of the truly horrendous weather the destruction of the Storms was going to bring down on us was that it would make for a hell of a distraction once it hit.

Triss flexed his wings and looked at us all very seriously. "And if anything goes wrong?"

Jax snorted. "If it happens before Aral's signal, I try to make sure that if I die, I do it very quietly and take the bastards with me."

"Likewise," said Faran.

"I blow the roof off and holler for help," I added.

"Then we're off." Triss nodded and then collapsed back into my shadow.

From there he climbed my body, briefly covering me in a chilly skin of shadow before blossoming outward into a full shroud of darkness. The others followed suit, and we headed for the concealed entrance to the tunnel. According to our map, it was hidden in a rough outcropping of rocks in the side of a deep-carved creek bed that ran parallel to the nearer wall of the abbey.

We probably could have gotten in over the wall undetected, though it stood a good fifteen feet, and had both spikes and obvious wards protecting it. Those defenses were the kind of things that Blades dealt with all the time, and the abbey had been built more with an eye to holding off the occasional bandit attack or rampaging manticore than a group of assassins. But the tunnel had two major advantages.

First, it would get us past the outer wall and into the very heart of the abbey in one step. Second, the over-the-wall route was the way we were supposed to come in tomorrow, which meant there might well be extra layers of defensive spells in place at the moment.

"They really did a good job on this," Jax whispered when I finally came to a stop in front of a slightly higher section of the creek bank.

Without the map and accompanying instructions we'd never have found the spot. Even with it, I couldn't be positive we'd gotten it right until I actually got the door open. I reluctantly slipped the warm finger out of the little pouch I'd hung on the straps of my sword rig at chest level—I wanted it quickly and easily accessible.

Suppressing a desire to "accidentally" lose the awful thing in the stream, I stuck the finger and my whole arm into a deep hole half-concealed by the root of an old oak. It had a shallow bend about eight inches in, that prevented anyone from seeing the spell-light from the ward that was supposed to be at the back of the hole.

"I hope we've got the right spot and nothing poisonous has moved in since the last time someone did this," I said.

"Don't be such a worrier," said Faran. "There'll be a nest-not ward to keep the creepy crawlies out." She laughed. "Well, there will if you're sticking your arm in the right hole. If not, I'm sure we've got some antivenom around here somewhere."

"*Very* reassuring," I grumbled with my cheek pressed against the stone. "Why don't you stick your advice where . . ." But then there was a faint but definite sense of magical contact as I poked around the back of the hole with the severed finger. "I think I just got it."

"Yeah, we can tell." That was Jax. "I'm impressed."

"What?" I craned my neck back to see what she was talking about but didn't pull the ring out yet. "Oh. Wow. That *is* impressive."

Without making any noise or giving any other sign, a portion of the rock face had simply vanished. That bit wasn't all that unheard of. The fact that the door lay mostly below the stream's surface on the other hand . . .

About two feet of the low stone archway stuck up above the waterline. The rest extended down to the floor of the streambed. Opening the door should have filled the tunnel with water. It probably would have, too, if we hadn't used the Signet's finger or some other authorized magical key to open it—I imagined that the abbot's ring would have worked as well.

But not only was the water not pouring in across the threshold, it was actually flowing away from the hole in a very definite pattern. One that formed a flight of liquid steps leading down to the entrance. The entire shallow stairwell shone with a deep blue spell-light.

"Do you think we can actually walk on the stairs?" Jax asked rather dubiously.

"One way to find out." Faran jumped lightly down onto the top step . . . and didn't go through. "Huh." She scampered down the five remaining liquid stairs to the entrance. "Feels a bit like walking on planks laid over mud. I'll go ahead and look for guards."

Before either of us could say a word, she was gone.

"Jax," I said.

"I know, go after her." Then she, too, jumped down to the watery stairs and vanished.

"I sure hope this thing stays open for a while after I pull the ring away from the seal," I said aloud.

It wouldn't be a very well-designed spell if it didn't, Triss replied into my mind. *This is a very pretty piece of magic, I doubt they'd flub the exit.*

You're probably right.

No, I'm always right.

Smug shadow.

Silly human.

I think Faran might be a bad influence on you, Triss.

Just do it.

All right. I pulled the finger free of the seal and jumped down to follow the others.

The stairs did indeed feel like planks over mud, and I very much wished I had time to study the spell that made it work. But I kept picturing them suddenly collapsing, or the stone wall reappearing before I'd gotten all the way through the gap, so I hurried. I needn't have worried though. There was a rather obvious seal of opening and closing a few yards into the tunnel. When I touched the ring and finger to the seal, the dim light filtering in through the doorway abruptly went away. Hell of an enchantment that.

I took control of Triss so that I could use his senses to suss out the lay of the land. The tunnel was perhaps seven feet tall by three wide, and rough finished. From the entrance it sloped down and away from me in a none-too-straight line.

Jax and Faran were nowhere in evidence, but there was only one direction they could have gone. Adjusting the slender but heavy pack I'd strapped between the sheaths of my swords—it held weapons for our imprisoned brethren—I headed down into the dark after the women. I caught up to them after perhaps a quarter mile, at a sharp bend.

"About time you got here," said Jax when I came around the corner. She was waiting with her back against the wall, swords drawn.

"Finger," said Faran. She was squatting on the floor hunched over a cocoon of shadow, just beyond Jax.

I pulled the finger out of its pouch and leaned forward to hand it to her. She glanced back and neatly snatched it. Once she had the finger in hand, she pressed it against something inside the dark cocoon Ssithra had spun for her.

"Yes! It works." She pulled the finger free and handed it back to me.

Her shoulders bunched briefly, as though she were making some physical effort. In response, the cocoon gave a single pulse before flowing back to hide Faran in a lacuna of shadow once again. It left behind the body of a young man in the uniform of Heaven's Sword. A corporal, dying now as blood poured from his freshly torn out throat. Faran touched a dull brass badge pinned to his chest.

"Death ward, and completely deactivated by the old Signet's signet. That's a hell of a toy Master Kelos loaned you. I'm glad you're willing to share it with the other children."

I blinked several times—though no one could see it through my shroud. A sudden sense of wrongness was tugging at my mind. This magical key Kelos had given me went way beyond toy. Too far. The Shade stick would have been sufficient to set us up for this mission. More than sufficient. With a full map of the abbey showing all the modifications the Hand had made to hold our fellow Blades prisoner and three of us to carry out the task, we didn't really need the finger.

Oh, it would make things a good bit easier, but the most likely ways this could go wrong had never been about getting through the locks and wards. If we failed, it would be because we ran afoul of a too-alert Hand or Sword, not because bypassing some warded door took us an extra minute to open silently without the key.

So, if we didn't absolutely need the finger to make this work, why had Kelos loaned it to me? What did he want me to do with the finger that I couldn't do without it? He had to have a damned good reason to give me such a powerful tool to use against his new masters. Unfortunately, I couldn't for the life of me figure out what he wanted or why he wanted it. At least, not now, with the fate of so many of our remaining brethren at stake and precious minutes dripping away into the dark.

"Aral?" Jax touched my shoulder through the shadows that surrounded us both. "Are you all right? Because you didn't respond the first time I spoke your name."

"Sorry. Just thinking."

"About Kelos," she stated flatly. "And what his game might be. I've been wondering that, too, from the first moment I found out about his involvement." There was a definite reproach there. "But we can't worry about it right now."

"Can we afford to wait?" I countered. "What if he's setting us up for something right here, right now?"

"Then we're fucked," she said. "This is our one chance to get the others out alive. If we don't take it, they die. The Signet's deal has always been a lie, and tomorrow is too late."

"I know. But it just feels like we're walking into a trap."

"At least today's trap, if there is one, belongs to Kelos and not the Signet. Kelos wants something more than seeing us all dead, and that's a hell of a lot better than the Signet's vision."

She was right, and I knew it, but that didn't make my misgivings one little bit easier to bear.

"Come on, Aral, we've got to go on. Faran's already well ahead of us."

Jax didn't say anything more, and in the total darkness her shrouded presence was invisible even through Triss's borrowed senses. But I could feel her absence as she headed on down the tunnel. I followed after, wondering with every step what Kelos was up to, and coming up empty again and again, no matter how I looked at things. The passage ended at a narrow spiral stair where Faran waited for us with obvious impatience, her head unshrouded and a frown pursing her lips.

"About time," she said when I pulled my own shroud aside to let her see me.

"I'll go first," I said, holding up the finger.

Her frown deepened, but she turned sideways to let me pass, reshrouding behind me. There was another magical seal on the left hand wall at to the top of the stairs.

I turned to where I knew Faran must be standing behind me. "Did the guard have a token or a ring of some sort? I didn't see one."

"No, but I found a lunch sack, and a bottle of small beer tucked under the stairs. This clearly isn't a general use sort of escape tunnel, the Signet or the Abbot probably locked him in for the duration of his guard shift. The bottle was unopened and the sack full, so I don't think anyone's going to miss him soon."

"Good."

I released my hold on Triss and asked, *I don't see any cracks here, do you?* I was hoping that with his better command of Shade senses he'd see something I missed.

No, he replied. *No gaps at all. Same as at the other end. We're going to have to go through blind.*

"I'm going to open the door in a moment here. The map shows it opening into a meditation chamber in the library basement. Hopefully it's empty."

"If not, I've got it," said Faran, sliding up next to me.

"Then, in three, two, one . . ."

I touched the ring to the seal and the wall in front of me abruptly vanished. I felt Faran move past me into the room beyond.

"Clear," she whispered an instant later, not that I needed her reassurance.

The room was maybe seven feet across and shaped like an inverted bowl with a low domed ceiling of polished stone. The only things in it were a couple of carefully rolled prayer mats and a small hemispherical magelamp affixed to the exact center of the ceiling. The latter was currently shuttered, leaving the room in a near-total darkness. Only the dimmest thread of light showed at the base of a door a quarter of the way around the circle from where I stood.

A moment later, that line of light abruptly vanished, occluded by Faran's shroud. "I don't hear anything through the door. Shall I move forward?"

"Not yet," I replied. "I want to find the door seal on this side so we can close the tunnel."

"Gotta be in the lamp," said Jax, as she slipped past me as well. "Faran, keep the door shrouded. I'm going to open the shutters and have a look-see."

I braced myself, but even so, the bright white magelight hammered at my borrowed senses. After the near total darkness of the tunnel, the light smashed into the matrix of Triss's being in a quasi-physical way, forcing me to contract the area enveloped in the stuff of shadow. It took a good five beats of my heart for me to recover enough from the impact to really look at the magelight in any meaningful way. It was a particularly intense enchantment, blazing both with spell-light and the light of the world. Try as I might, I simply couldn't see inside the lamp.

"Damn, that's bright," said Faran.

"Too bright," replied Jax. "Though I bet several of the other meditation chambers are just as brightly lit to cover for this one. Hang on a second. . . ."

Her right arm abruptly emerged from the darkness of her shroud, and she stuck her hand in through one of the gaps in the rotating shutter of the lamp. The quality of the light changed as she covered the stone holding the enchantment with her hand, going dim and red. I stepped in close, and the comparative darkness allowed me to see another seal. This one was etched into the stone of the ceiling above the light proper. I used it to close the tunnel behind us.

Jax doused the light. "Everyone ready?"

"Of course," replied Faran.

"Yes." I drew my swords and resumed full control over Triss. This was going to be messy and bloody and the chances that there would be at least one or two fewer Blades in the world at the end of the night were very good.

"Then," said Jax, "Faran, if you'd be so kind as to get the door, we move. Aral goes first."

The door squealed as it opened, and I silently cursed as I ducked through. A monk was walking through the dimly lit hallway beyond. I took his head off before he finished turning to see who might be coming out of the meditation chamber. Without pausing, I leaped over his falling body and headed for the far stairs. Jax went for the nearer set that went past the passage that led to the abbot's house and thence to the guest complex.

Behind me, I saw the pale ball of the monk's head vanish into Faran's shroud as she picked it up and tossed it into the meditation chamber. I was just ducking through the arch that led to the stairs when Triss's senses showed me a dim flare of spell-light along the floor back by the door—Ssithra cleaning away the blood I'd spilled. Then I was fully on my own.

I went up two flights, passing another arch. Beyond it I could smell old leather and dust and all the other scents of a lot of books crammed into a confined area. I couldn't help but smile. At the next landing, I unlatched the window shutters above a reading bench and stepped through into the night. It was a short drop, no more than ten feet, and ended in grass instead of cobbles—part of my reason for choosing this route. I had to take the shock with my knees because my pack precluded rolling out of the fall.

"Who's there?" Another monk stepped out of the shadows beneath a willow, his too-wide eyes showing white in the pale magelanterns that stood at the corners of the small courtyard.

Dammit. I smelled the rum on his breath as I slid forward

to break his neck and I paused. He didn't see me, and I twisted aside without touching him. His corpse would tell a much more believable tale than anything he might say to a guard this side of morning, so I let him live and moved on across the courtyard.

On the far side I turned into a narrow paved way that ran between the locutory and the chapterhouse. The latter abutted the temple proper and helped support the larger building, so I went up one of the buttresses between two windows as soon as I left the courtyard.

From there I catfooted my way around the edge of the domed roof to the larger building where I killed a guard by slicing his throat. As I wedged him down into the darkest corner I could find, I glanced up the side of the temple while I decided my next move. The shortest path from here to the crypts went through the clerestory windows that lighted the sanctum, two floors above me. But there was certain to be some sort of guard on watch up among the bells in the tower.

If the guard in the tower was a Sword or Swords, it made sense for me to take the extra time to kill them and disable the bells. If it was one of the Hand, I couldn't afford to kill them now, for fear the death of their Storm would give warning of our presence. I hadn't yet decided when my ears popped and I felt a sudden chill breeze come rolling down from the western hills.

In response, lightning flashed in the tower above and a cloud-winged wheel of dark fire slipped out through the windows. Hand then, and nothing I could do about it. I braced myself in the shadowy corner between a buttress and the wall and started climbing as quickly as I could. I hoped the extra darkness there would hide me from the aroused Storm above, because I didn't have the time to do this gentle and quiet anymore.

Someone had started the killing before I was in position—probably Faran and probably not willingly. I didn't think it was Jax because I hadn't heard the sounds of a building coming apart. She'd had enough time to get at least some of the destruction glyphs in place by now, and I couldn't see her going for half measures in her current state.

I was just coming up on the level of the clerestories when

two things happened at once: A tremendous boom and crash sounded from the far side of the temple as the guesthouse came apart and took our plan with it. The Storm above dropped straight down toward me, the fiery wheel that formed its body spinning wildly between lightning laced wings.

16

---·---

Indecision is a luxury for the quiet times. If you let it become more than that, it will kill you.

Kelos had taught me: "Think ahead, act in the moment, dither later." In the split second I had left, I made the only choice that had any chance of keeping me alive. It might have been a stupid choice, but it was all that I had.

As the Storm dove on me from the bell tower, I discarded my shroud, collapsing the cloud of shadow-stuff down into a tight, quasi-solid ball haloing my left hand. With one foot braced on the buttress and the other wedged into the interstice between two of the huge stones that formed the temple wall, I reached my shadowed hand back to the hilt of the sword resting against my hip.

Leaning far out from the corner to give myself the room I needed, I drew the sword with a sharp snapping motion. The point dropped down in the beginning of a circle that took it past my ankle and then up and around to intersect the path of the diving Storm. I could feel myself overbalance as the sword came up past waist level—had known that was inevitable. I ignored the warnings of my stomach and my inner ear as I began to fall outward. Focusing my will on the sword and the shadow, I sent the head-sized ball of darkness up the length of my blade, which threw me even more out of balance.

Storm met shadow four feet over my head with an impact that drove me down and back into the wall. The base of my skull hit the hilts of the swords in my pack so hard that the whole world flashed bright purple for an instant. I ignored the pain and the way my right foot had started to slip, concentrating everything I had on that ball of shadow. It was pressed against the hub of the burning wheel that formed the central matrix of the Storm's physical form. With an effort that felt like it might tear a hole in my mind, I contracted the shadow sharply, folding it into a pinpoint and twisting. . . .

A giant pillar of lightning connected the sky and the earth, punching a burning hole through the dome of the chapterhouse. The noise and the light came as one, so close I could feel the heat. The thunder hit me like a giant's slap, shattering what was left of my hold on Triss. My right foot finished losing its toehold, and I pivoted into a weak jump, kicking off the buttress with my left. I caught the sill of the clerestory with my right hand as I smacked into the stones.

For a brief instant I dangled there, one-handed. Then, as I started to slip, I let my sword go and brought my other hand up and around. All the while I expected to catch a burst of lightning in the spine.

It wasn't until I was pulling myself onto the window ledge amidst the first spatters of rain that I had time to realize my gamble had worked. I would live at least a little longer. But with our presence now revealed, I had to move fast or the hostages wouldn't.

Triss? I sent, but there was no response.

That worried me more than a little, but I couldn't do anything about it. Not until I got my ass out of the gigantic storm that was about to hit and into some kind of shelter. As I started in on breaking the window, I quickly reviewed what I had just done, trying to set the memory in case I ever had to do something like it again. Shades are elemental in nature like the great dragons or salamanders. That makes them into a sort of living gateway to the everdark, the elemental plane of night.

A year ago, I had seen Triss open that gate in a fit of rage, sending men who had tortured me through it, into the dark and the cold beyond. It was probably the scariest thing I'd ever seen a Shade do, and to this day I didn't fully understand how it worked. That hadn't stopped me from trying to replicate the process.

I'm not much of a sorcerer. Oh, I can follow directions on the complex stuff and I do well enough with the basics of low magic like magefire and magelightning, but I'd known that none of that was going to hurt a Storm. Hell, most rough magic would probably just feed the thing. But I'd seen how Sshayar had taken on the Signet's Storm, and I figured that if I could pull something fancy with shadow magic, I might live to see tomorrow. And it had worked. I'd sent an eight-inch sphere of the Storm into the everdark, tearing a giant hole in its chest and killing it instantly.

The aftereffects of that death and those that had occurred when Jax took down the guesthouse had begun with the pillar of lightning. The rain, which had opened with a pitter-patter only seconds ago, was already rising into an icy and continuous hammering like a barrage of sling stones, while the building winds tried to tear me free of the ledge.

I wasn't done with the many-paned window, but if I stayed outside much longer I was going to take a long fall. Beyond that, I still had to get to the prisoners as quickly as I could. So I forced my head and shoulders through the jagged-edged and too-small hole, picking up a number of nasty gashes along the way.

What the hell? Triss's mental voice sounded muzzy and confused as I glanced around the dimly lit sanctum I was entering.

I was delighted and relieved to hear from him, but didn't have time to answer. *Later,* I sent as I pulled my feet free of the hole in the glass, pivoting into a momentary handstand on the inner ledge. *Right now, I need a skin!*

Triss didn't respond in words, just wrapped himself around me as he released his will once more. The cool shadows took the worst sting from my cuts and scrapes as they slithered over my skin. It felt wonderful, and I wished I had the leisure to enjoy the sensation, but I was already tipping forward and letting go. I somersaulted into empty space forty feet above the floor of the sanctum, spinning myself dark wings to break my fall as I went.

The window exploded above and behind me as a burst of lightning hit it from somewhere on the far side of the huge space—another Storm somewhere within the sanctum. Expected but wholly unwelcome. I half folded my left arm in response, partially collapsing the shadow wing it scaffolded, and sending me into a sharp spiraling downward turn. The next bolt sizzled through the space I'd have occupied if I'd continued my forward glide.

I hit the floor hard as I finished something that was not quite a straight forty-foot fall but well short of the gentle glide I'd originally intended. I let myself collapse, calf-knee-hip-ribs-shoulder, since the bag of swords on my back made a forward roll impossible. It hurt, but I didn't quite break any bones, so I had to call that a win. I rolled onto my chest and got my hands under me just as something came down on the small of my back with the metallic clash of steel on steel. Most likely a sword or an axe. Judging by the impact, it would probably have sliced me in half if it hadn't hit the blades in my pack.

The angle of the blow told me where to look for my attacker, and a glance to my right confirmed the presence of a pair of darkly clad feet and legs. I released Triss then—hoping he could give me some cover—as I snapped my right arm, sending the dagger from my wrist sheath into my hand.

Before I could do anything with my dagger, Triss shrieked in pain and my opponent's blade—an axe, glowing with spell-light—smashed into the stone of the floor a few inches above my head. Triss must have deflected it just enough, but at what cost I couldn't say. Sparks flew where the steel met the flags. I could hear a woman swearing in the tongue of Heaven's Reach, as the missed strike put her momentarily off balance. Twisting as far as my pack would allow, I drove my dagger sideways into the woman's foot, hitting just below the ankle bone and sliding back to sever the big tendon above the heel.

She screamed and her leg collapsed under her, so that she fell across my shoulders and head. I heard the axe striking the flags again as she came down on my back, though this time I didn't see where it hit. Lightning shattered stone off to my left, peppering my side with shards that bit and burned, but the Storm hadn't dared to strike me directly. Not while I was so tightly intertwined with its bond-mate. Before it, or she, could move again, I half rolled onto my left shoulder and flicked my wrist to put that dagger in my hand. Stabbing up and back, I slid the blade along the inside of her leg, slicing open the big artery in her groin.

Lightning rained down all around me then, shattering stone and temporarily deafening me, but not one bolt hit me—for which I thank the Hand that shielded me from her familiar. Within seconds, the fallen woman stopped thrashing as blood loss robbed her of consciousness.

Triss, can you see anything?

Not right now, no. Not with all the lightning. His mental voice sounded tight and pained. *But thanks for asking. Also, ow, ow, fucking ow!*

Right. What I really wanted at that point was just to lie there for a while and rest. Then, after I'd had my break, I wanted to take my poor tattered shadow and go the hell home. Instead I kept right on moving. By the time I'd twisted myself out from under the dying Hand and dragged myself back to my feet, she was all but gone and the indoor lightning had ceased to fall. Outside, the storm intensified yet again.

I had a couple of heartbeats of breathing space to look around then. The lightning-struck bodies of three or four of the Swords of Heaven lay close by, while another dozen or so were coming toward me from various places in the room.

With a roar like the world's biggest manticore complaining about a twist in its tail, the whole wall of clerestories above me blew inward. Shards of glass and twisted bits of lead fell like sharp-edged hail and I had to throw myself back against the base of the outside wall to avoid the worst of it. The rain followed, soaking the interior of the sanctum in instants, and I lost track of most of the soldiers of the Sword in that sudden chaos.

Time to shroud up again, I think, I sent.

Yes, and you're welcome. Shadow covered and concealed me.

Thanks, Triss! I forced myself out and away from the wall—I didn't want to move, but I needed to get clear of my last known position as a first order of business. *How badly are you hurt?*

I've had much worse, though the spell on that axe burned like a son of a bitch, he replied. *How about you?*

About the same. Nothing's broken and I'm in no danger of bleeding out, though I've a myriad of new holes in my skin. I really wish I had a couple of efik beans and that I dared to eat them. It'd sure take the edge off.

Triss snorted. *The first couple might, but we both know how that would end.*

Which is why I wouldn't dare take them. But a guy can dream, can't he?

The rain sheeting in through the ruined windows was playing merry hell with my ability to make sense of what I was getting through Triss's unvision. I knew where I wanted to go—the entrance to the crypt behind the statue of Shan—and I had long since learned to navigate blind. But it didn't normally rain inside, and the storm just kept getting worse. The roaring was so loud now I could barely think. At least it was washing some of the blood off of me. I'd gone perhaps twenty feet in what I believed was the right direction when the windows on the other side of the temple blew in as well.

I couldn't see a thing in the darkness beyond, but the only other time I'd ever heard a storm anything remotely like this bad was when a series of cyclones had ripped through the plains of northern Varya when I was a teenager. One of them had flattened a couple of the temple's outbuildings. Another had ripped a pretty big stripe out of the nearest town. Dozens were killed.

Thinking of it now made me wonder how that sort of damage had been avoided when the Son of Heaven sent his forces against the temple. Though they had won the battle that day, I knew that a lot of the Hand had died to do it, taking their familiars with them. Perhaps, given time to prepare for casualties, the other Storms could soothe the weather before it went wild.

Then I almost ran into one of the remaining Swords, literally—I didn't see him till I was practically treading on his toes. I no longer had time to think, only to react. I drove one of the knives I was still carrying into his belly, and then had to use the other on a companion drawn by the first's scream. A moment later, I left my right-hand knife behind when it wedged between the ribs of a third. I ended up throwing my left at a fourth, hitting her in the neck, but probably not fatally.

After that, I had a brief clear space. It lasted all the way to the entrance of the crypt, where another pair of temple soldiers stood waiting.

I had just drawn my remaining sword, when the farther of the pair quietly fell forward and landed on his face—dead, a knife sticking out of the back of his neck. The second turned to see what had taken her companion, and went down in a spray of blood as a line of steel flashed out of nowhere and sliced her throat. Knowing the cause, I was able to infer a faint dark lacuna mostly invisible amidst the craziness of the storm pouring in through every available opening. The curtain of shadow parted just long enough to show me Faran's face, then closed again.

Trusting Faran to cover my back, I stepped up to the crypt door and pulled out the finger. "I thought you were clearing the perimeter," I said over my shoulder.

"I had to change the plan rather abruptly. I was heading for the outer wall along the top of the buttery when the big winds first hit. Blew me clean off the roof of the building, and then halfway back to the temple proper when I opened a shadow sail to keep from breaking my neck. At that point, I was in the back courtyard of the temple and it was pretty clear the original play had gone in the shit. I figured getting the prisoners loose as quick as quick could be was higher priority than forcing my way back out to the perimeter through a wall of whirlwinds."

I nodded though she couldn't see me. "Sensible." Then the door to the crypt opened and I turned to the nearer of the two fallen soldiers. "Give me a hand here."

Together we chucked the body headfirst down the long steep stairs. As it tumbled down the last few steps, I more than half expected a burst of lightning to hit it, or a sheet of magefire. But nothing happened.

"Is that good or bad?" asked Faran.

"Hopefully good." If it signaled the absence of a lurking Hand and not clever restraint on such a lurker's part. "But there's only one way to find out." I shucked out of the pack holding the swords and passed it to Faran. "Block the light from the door." I wanted it as dark as I could make it before I started down.

Faran complied, filling the space with her shroud as I stepped onto the first stair. *Fast or slow, Triss?*

Slow might be smarter, but I don't think we have the time.

I don't either. Which is why I'd removed my pack. *This is going to hurt.* I reached through our link to borrow Triss's senses, but left him in full control and sent, *You can be my eyes.* The choice would impede my ability to perform magic, but it had other compensations.

Understood.

I shifted my sword into an underhand grip—less likely to accidentally stab myself that way—and dove headfirst down the stairs. I aimed down instead of out, staying low, and mostly skidded along on my chest until I hit the soldier's corpse, which tipped me into a roll. The entire front side of my body was screaming at me as I came to my feet in a low crouch just beyond the foot of the stairs.

I had at least one possibly cracked rib, but I couldn't afford to stay still. I immediately dove into a second roll, and then a third, moving down the narrow hall toward the nearest junction.

Soldier, on your right, hiding in the arch, six feet forward.

Though we were both sharing the same unvision, I simply wasn't aware of the soldier until Triss pointed him out to me. Which was exactly why I'd chosen not to take control this time.

Triss "sees" in every direction equally and thinks that way, too. I never will, though years of training and practice have taught me how to interpret what comes in through Triss's otherworldly senses via a sort of spot-sampling technique. For me it will always be like translating from a fundamentally alien language, whereas Triss speaks it as his native tongue. He can make sense of it far better than I ever will.

As I came out of my third roll, I flipped my sword around to a front grip and straight on from there into a backhanded lunge that took the soldier through the throat.

Drop! Triss yelled into my mind. I threw myself at the floor as a burst of lightning from the side passage passed through the place I had occupied only a moment before.

Storm right, Hand left! Triss yelled into my mind.

Then my shroud was suddenly gone as he collapsed into dragon form and leaped from my back to meet the oncoming Storm. That was the last I had leisure to pay attention to him, as a spear stabbed down at me from the left. I managed to avoid a skewering by rolling toward the spearman. But I didn't have enough room to dodge the thrust completely, and I felt the edge of the blade open a shallow gash along my right hip.

I swung my sword at my attacker's ankles, but he jumped back beyond the reach of my swing, pulling his spear back as he went. *Must be my day for facing death from above,* I thought as I braced my feet on the wall and kicked myself over into a backward roll. A spray of icy rain splashed across the back of my neck from the place where shadow fought Storm behind me when I came up onto my feet.

I barely had time to register it as the spearman lunged in again, this time with a thrust at my belly. A cross body parry deflected the spear a few critical inches so that it ripped a hole in my shirt instead of my side. I turned sideways to present the spear-wielding Hand with a narrower target, extending my sword forward and down in a high guard.

He stabbed at me again, going for my eyes. This time I had the leisure to make a much more careful parry, following on with a riposte at his forward hand—the only part of him I could easily reach. But the hand is a difficult target, and he neatly avoided my slice. The narrow confines of the hall and his much longer weapon gave him a brutal advantage unless I could get inside his guard.

Triss? Though I could feel through our link that he was heavily engaged, I wanted to check how he was doing and didn't dare turn to look.

Busy! Handle it.

Right. When the spear came at me again, I jumped forward with my parry, trying to beat the point aside and get in close before he could withdraw it. But my opponent was no tyro. Now that I was on my feet he'd shifted to a more careful sort of short thrust. That allowed him to easily hop back and put his point between me and where I needed to go. I drew the dagger at my left hip to give me a second weapon both for block and attack, but the next couple of quick passes ended with much the same result as that first. If I'd had a heavier sword, I might have been able to use it to hack the spear apart, but I didn't.

As we were dancing back and forth, I got the chance to study my opponent. He was tall, almost too tall for the low passages of the crypt, but not quite. As well as slender and well muscled.

His loose Hand's robes hung open, exposing partial armor—a cuirass and vambraces as well as shin plates on his boots. About the only good thing I could say about the situation was that we were both too separated from our familiars to make any use of magic. Otherwise, he'd probably have cooked me by then. I tried a couple of attacks, cuts high and low but he easily deflected them without offering me any openings.

Apparently that raised his confidence, because he laughed, "I sent my men to kill your fellows when the crypt door opened, Blade. All I need to do is keep you here for a few short minutes. You're too late already."

Fuck. If his goal was to provoke me into doing something desperate and risky, he'd just succeeded. Now we would see how that worked out for him. After I made my next parry, I raised my sword into a high guard again to give me chopping room. Then, I edged my left foot forward until it offered a more tempting target. I wanted him to come in low. He did. Rather than deliver a proper parry, I hopped aside while simultaneously bringing the edge of my blade down as close to in line with his spear shaft as I could, swinging with everything I had.

I hit the spear about six inches behind the head, edge on, with a motion that brought the sword down and back toward me. It was a very precise move and very fast, only possible because I kept my blade sharp enough for shaving, and it worked. My edge sank into the wood and stuck fast. If he'd known it was coming, he could easily have wrenched my sword out of my hand. But by the time he knew what was going on, it was already too late. I'd let go of my blade the second it stuck, and now I leaped forward.

He yanked his spear backward, trying to bring it into line to block my advance, but the trapped sword added a lot of tip weight and threw the balance off completely, twisting the shaft to the side. The effect wouldn't last long, but it didn't have to. I just needed long enough to get fully inside his guard, and it accomplished that. He was a veteran, and smart, letting the spear go the instant he realized what I'd done and reaching for his own belt knife. But by then I was on top of him.

I drove my knife deep into the flesh of his thigh, just above his knee, and left it there. As the pain momentarily doubled him up, I brought my now empty left hand up to catch his

descending chin. I'd already jabbed a spearfist at his throat
with my other hand, but he'd avoided the worst of it, twisting
to avoid the blow. That put my right hand next to the ritual cord
that bound his ponytail in place. Now I grabbed the knot and
yanked at the same time that I twisted with my other hand. His
neck broke with a dull wet crack, and thunder rattled the passage as his Storm followed him into death.

"Faran!" I yelled as I retrieved my blade. "Bring the
swords!"

There was no response, and I spared a moment to worry
about that, but only a moment. If the Hand hadn't been lying
to me, the prisoners might already be dying.

I didn't see her, Triss sent as he followed the line that connected us back to rejoin me in my mad dash down the hall.

She can take care of herself, I sent.

*Better than you can, in many ways, but that doesn't prevent
me worrying.*

Me either.

A metallic snap sounded ominously from around a corner
in the hallway ahead. It was followed by a flare of light so
intense that it burned. Wincing at the brightness I leaped
around the corner to find a pair of soldiers standing between
me and an iron door pried off its hinges. The light spilled
through from whatever lay within.

The closer of the two held a broken sword, the farther a
spear. A heart thrust killed the swordsman in the same instant
my thrown knife took the spearwoman in the eye. It hadn't
killed her—thrown blades rarely do, but she screamed and
dropped her weapon, reaching for the knife. A palm strike to
the back of her clutching hands drove the blade deep and finished the job, though it would take her a little while to figure
it out.

I went past her falling body and through the door into the
narrow tomb beyond. The light was almost unbearably bright,
despite the soldier who had preceded me blocking the worst of
it. All I could see was the silhouette of a head and shoulders,
but that was all I needed to drive my sword into the back of his
neck. He fell like a string-cut puppet, exposing me to the direct
assault of the light.

My shroud dissolved as the light forced Triss to collapse

back down into my regular shadow to protect himself, and the brilliance of it stabbed at my dark-adjusted eyes. I staggered a half step back at the sudden pain and had to throw up my free arm to cover my face.

"Who's there?" the voice was weak, barely a croak and totally unidentifiable, but it galvanized me into action and I began to grope around for the light. "It's Aral. Who am I talking to?

"Loris," and this time I could hear the pain as well as the weakness. "Jax?"

"Alive and well last time I saw her, but that was before this whole play blew up in our faces." My groping fingers found a metal rod hanging from the ceiling.

I slid my hand down the rod. As I reached the knob on the end the light dimmed. It was vibrating ever so slightly—in tune with the storm above—as was the floor now that I thought about it. If it got much worse it'd tear the whole abbey apart stone by stone. The cell stank of blood and piss and all the other horrible smells of torture and imprisonment.

". . . 's trap," said Loris. "She shouldn't have . . . *you* shouldn't be here."

"I know." I closed my hand around the magelight, darkening the room enough to allow me to open my eyes. My fist glowed red and I could see Loris hanging limp on a wooden framework at the back of the tomb. "She told me. I came anyway." I gave a yank on the rod, but nothing happened.

Summoning Triss to edge my sword in shadow, I snapped it around and cut the rod loose from the ceiling. Then I shoved the light under the body of the Sword at my feet. The light leaking out from underneath was still plenty to see by, but it was dim enough to allow Triss to slip back into dragon shape beside me.

Loris looked awful, naked and covered in bruises, bleeding freely from a deep wound in his side and minus his right ear. He was hanging on an elaborate wooden rack built in the shape of a glyph of binding. Heavy leather straps bound him at the wrists, elbows, throat, chest, knees, and ankles. The device was called the pillory of light. It was devised by Tangara, God of Glyphs, to hold captured Blades as a part of the war of Heaven against my goddess. I had spent some time on one a year ago, and the sight of it now set a fire in my blood.

The magelight that I'd just removed was the part that kept his Shade from acting. Now Issaru began to stir, appearing first as a tendril of shadow that reached around to cover Loris's wound and staunch the bleeding. Another severed the straps at ankles and knees. Loris hissed in pain as limbs that hadn't moved in who knew how long suddenly changed position. Remembering my own agony in a similar position I was glad that Issaru had the sense not to cut him free all at once.

"Let me help you—" I began, but Loris gave another sharp hiss.

"No. Cut the others loose. Issaru will take care of me."

"Aral?" the voice came from up the hall behind me, low but urgent. Faran.

"Here." I turned and went back through the broken door. "With Loris." For the first time, I noticed the broken-off stem of a heavy key in the door's lock. "Thank Nam . . ." But she was gone. "There's luck."

"Too much luck, I think," said Triss. My shadow licked out and touched the lock. "This tastes of tampering and . . ."

Before he could say more, Faran appeared at the corner, having dropped the shroud across her face—how long she'd been there I couldn't say. The bag of swords hung from her left hand.

"We've got—"

Before she could finish, there came an incredibly bright flash from behind her, then a boom like a dozen thunder bursts going off all at once. The floor jumped beneath me, and a wall of pressure and dust came shooting around the corner from the direction of the flash, turning out all the lights as it knocked me flat. Dull thuds and splintering cracks told of stones falling from the ceiling around us. The temple was collapsing.

17

---◆---

Spend enough time in darkness and you will discover that it has every bit as much variation as light does. The absolute blackness that surrounded me now had a soft weight to it, like lying under a blanket with six inches of sand pressing it down.

The air felt thick and hard to breathe, almost syrupy, heavy with mold and the stink of ancient stonework. I couldn't hear a thing. Not with my ears at least, though there was a buzzing in my mind that grew into words as I focused on it.

Aral! Aral, wake up!

It was Triss, but his mental voice felt as though it was coming from a terribly long way away. It had a sort of moist echo to it, like someone yelling in the depths of a sewer.

I'm all right. I tried to get an idea of my immediate surroundings from Triss's senses, but it felt like that part of our connection had temporarily closed down. *At least, I think I am. What happened? Where are we?*

I'm not sure yet. The big flash stunned me and now I can't see. I can still feel the hammering of the storm though—it makes the whole world shake—so we can't have been out too long.

I tried to move, but felt that same heavy resistance I had

before. This time, I pushed against it, trying to force myself upright—discovering only in that moment that I was lying on my stomach. For several long slow beats nothing happened. Then the silence fled before a deep ringing sound and I began to move, almost infinitesimally at first, but with a steadily increasing sureness. As I forced myself onto hands and knees, the ringing was interrupted by a couple of dull clunks, like falling stone. Then it slowly began to fade.

"Aral?" It was Faran, sounding more than half frantic.

"'M all right."

I felt hands on my shoulders in the same moment that I began to "see" things again through Triss's senses. I was lying three-quarters buried in a heap of dirt and small to midsize stones—fill the builders had packed in around the crypts and other foundations of the temple. Once I'd rubbed the worst of the dirt out of my eyes I could actually see better that way than through Triss. About half the dim magelights that had illuminated the passage before the collapse had fallen along with various sections of wall. But there was still so much dust in the air that Triss's unsight was practically blind from all the weird shadow echoes.

"How are you doing?" I asked as I finished clearing my eyes.

"Not bad considering," replied Faran. "I stayed upright and managed to avoid the worst of the collapse."

"Good plan, that." I rubbed the back of my neck where I could feel a nasty bruise rising—at a guess one of the bigger stones had clipped me. "I should probably try it next time a ceiling falls on me."

"Does it happen to you that often?" asked Faran.

Triss slid down into dragon shape and nodded sadly. "This is at least the fourth or fifth time. You'd think we'd be better at it."

I took a few steps forward. The passage that used to lead to the surface now ended in a pile of broken stone and rubble about ten feet in front of me. The blockage lay just this side of the corner where Faran had been standing. Behind me, the tunnel continued to another turn, though more wreckage half blocked the way there as well. Not that it mattered. I knew from the maps I'd memorized that there was no way out in that direction either. We were trapped, at least for the moment. Us and . . .

"Loris! You still with us?" I called.

"As much as I was before." He stuck his head into the hall, then followed it out, using the fallen soldier's sword like a cane. "What about the others? My students?"

"I don't know." I noticed he hadn't mentioned Jax, but I wasn't about to bring it up when we didn't—couldn't—know anything more about her fate. "I haven't had a chance to check on the others yet."

"Why not? And, who's this?" he asked then, looking more closely, "Faran?"

"Master Loris." She gave him a small formal bow. "I'm sorry the circumstances of our reunion aren't happier."

He gave her a warm smile and shook his head. "I presume you're part of Aral and Jax's rescue. All things considered, that ranks pretty high on my auspicious meetings scale." Then he turned and gave me a much more worried look. "Speaking of which, shouldn't you be opening doors?"

I nodded. "That and trying to figure a way to get us out of here." Though nothing came to mind. Dust was still falling from the ceiling here and there in response to the ongoing battering the structure was taking from the storm.

The tomb directly across from Loris's also had a newly fitted iron door on it, so I moved to that one first. The frame was badly sprung from the collapse and I had my doubts about whether we'd be able to open it in the conventional manner. But it never hurts to try the easy way first. While I was working on that door, Faran handed the bag of swords to Loris and headed for the next one down the line.

"Triss, if you would."

The shadow of a dragon climbed the door, and poked at the lock with a foreclaw. After a moment, he let out a little hiss.

"Having trouble?"

It's not that, he replied mentally. *This lock's been tampered with. Put a normal key in here and it's going to fuse the lock and weld itself in place in the process. A shadow on the other hand . . .* The lock opened with a sharp click.

Kelos? I reached for the handle and gave it a good solid yank. The door didn't budge.

Has to be.

How recently was he here?

No more than an hour ago, probably less.

Dammit, what's his game? And how did he get in and out of here past the guards without leaving a shadow trail? "The door's stuck," I added aloud. "Triss, see what you can do."

I glanced to my right, where Faran had started working on her door. Ssithra had slipped up to whisper something in her ear, and now she gave me the faintest of raised eyebrows, and indicated Loris with a flick of her eyes. I made a cutting motion with my hand out of sight of the older master. Faran shrugged and tapped the lock, sending the phoenix back to its task.

Meanwhile, Triss had risen up to cover a substantial portion of the door, pressing himself flat against the surface, and straining with an effort I could feel through our bond. I knew what was coming, and that it took both time and concentration. So I waited quietly for him to do what was necessary.

Another loud click came from Faran's lock then. Her door must have fared better than mine, because it opened with a sharp pull. Painfully intense light spilled out through the opening, and Ssithra let out a little shriek of protest before diving behind Faran to hide from the brightness.

"Who's there?" The feminine voice that came through the opening sounded weak and pained, but angry.

"It's me, Loris." He started to limp toward the door. "With Aral and Faran. We'll have you out of there as soon as we can, Maryam."

I remembered a shy, quiet young woman with black hair and big eyes. Tall, sweet, and absolute murder with swords or staff. Loris had reached the doorway by then. Though I could see how badly he wanted to go to his student, Loris stopped to one side of the threshold, just beyond the edge of the light pouring across it.

"Faran, kill that for me, please," he said.

His reluctance to do it himself made me wonder how bad the wound in his side really was—if he didn't dare let the light force Issaru away from it. . . . Faran pushed forward into the cell, which darkened a moment later. At the same time, I felt the effort Triss had been making crescendo. With a sudden snap of his wings, he contracted down into a tiny spot of absolute blackness. A good-sized section of the door went with him, vanishing into the everdark and leaving a dragon shaped hole into . . .

"Dammit!" No light spilled out of that opening, nor ever would.

"Aral?" Loris turned toward me, with a sick look on his face.

"The whole chamber's collapsed. Whoever was in here never had a chance."

Loris nodded and took a deep breath, visibly putting aside his loss. I did the same. We would all mourn when we could, but for now we had to wall away our pain and our worries and keep moving.

Just then, Faran came out of her door with Maryam leaning heavily on her shoulders. The older girl looked much as I remembered, if you didn't count the huge burn scar that started just below where her right ear had been and spilled down from there across her cheek and neck. Like Loris—or me when I'd been hung on the pillory, for that matter—she'd been stripped naked and was covered in bruises. I cursed bitterly, then headed toward Faran and Maryam, and the next prisoner's door which lay beyond them.

"Master Aral." Maryam bowed as much as her position allowed. "What's the situation? Faran says we're safe for the moment, but trapped. Give me two minutes and I can fight. Have you a sword for me?"

"We have a pair, over there." Faran indicated the bag that Loris held. "But you should sit down and catch your breath first. We'll find you some clothes, too. I know a couple of guards who won't be needing theirs anymore."

A hydra slid out from Maryam's feet to touch three of its noses with the dragon at mine, while its other heads kept watch. "It's good to see you most honored, Resshath Triss, Master Aral. Maryam is right, we are ready to fight. You need only point us at the enemy."

"I think we can afford to give you a little time to recover, young Vrass," replied Triss. "Rest and be ready."

The hydra bobbed a half dozen nods, then collapsed into Maryam's shadow as Faran helped the journeyman to a seat on the floor. Her eyes met mine over Maryam's head and they held tears and a murderous rage that I shared. I paused just long enough to examine the door of Maryam's cell before moving on to try my luck with the next one.

It was the first fully intact door I'd seen. I wanted to know why no light had spilled around the seams or through the keyhole, in case it turned out to matter for any of the others. It was tightly fitted to an extra-deep set of jambs with a similar set of seals at top and bottom, and a plate had been welded across the back side of the keyhole. The whole had clearly been designed by people who'd had plenty of practice at keeping even a shadow from slipping through the cracks.

The next door frame was sprung as well, but not as badly as the first. That gave me hope for what lay on the other side. Once I'd brushed aside the pile of debris along the bottom of the door to give me a better chance at opening it, I could even see a bit of light leaking through where the twisting of the frame had broken the seal. When I tugged on the handle, the door jiggled in the frame, but I could tell it was going to take some prying to get it loose.

I was looking around for a better tool than one of my daggers as Faran passed me on her way to the last door. A question of some possible importance occurred to me, so I caught her eye.

She paused. "Yes?"

"Why did it take you so long to catch up to me in the crypt?"

"I got hung up at the top of the stairs. You'd just ducked out of sight when a Hand ran in through the same door I'd come in by. She was leaking blood from a big cut over her eye and trailing five Swords behind her. I knew you could handle whatever you ran into down here, so I figured I should get back to my original job and clear the exits. It took me a little while to manage that lot. By the time I had, another Hand had come in and got the remaining Swords in the temple organized."

"Damn. I take it you decided to cut out then?"

Faran let out an evil little chuckle. "Oh, no. I was going to take a crack at that bunch, too, but the main doors of the sanctum blew in about then and the Signet came charging through the wreckage with several more of the Hand and a whole pile of Swords at her heels. *That's* when I decided it was time to head down here so I could play rear guard. I hadn't expected her to just drop the roof on us though, or I might have made a different decision."

Which meant the Signet and some number of troops were overhead right now, doing who knows what. Not good. But there was nothing we could do about it for the moment except get the rest of our comrades free and hope that the Signet thought we'd all died in the collapse. Glancing at the roof and the light but continuing fall of dust reminded me that we still could. We needed to pick up the pace. I spared a moment to hope that the Signet's presence with more of the Hand didn't mean Jax was dead, but only a moment. If Jax was gone, that would be one more thing to put aside until I had the time to mourn her properly.

The door finally yielded to my efforts, popping open all at once and falling half off its hinges in the process. Light jabbed at my eyes, coming unexpectedly from floor level and hitting Triss hard enough to make him squawk like a punted chicken before he jumped behind me. The collapse had knocked a few stones loose from the ceiling in the tomb-turned-cell, including the one that had held the magelight, which now lay half buried. The fact that the slumped figure on the glyph-form rack beyond wasn't moving, though he or she—impossible to tell through the glare—now hung mostly in shadow, was a very bad sign.

I scuffed some rubble in front of the magelight to block it further as I stepped over it on my way to the rack. I could see that the unconscious figure was male now. But whoever he was, he'd taken enough of a beating that I couldn't identify him beyond that at first glance. In addition to the missing ear, he had a split lip and flattened nose, and both his eyes had been blacked. He looked more than half-dead, an impression belied only by the faint rise and fall of his chest.

As I knelt and reached for the buckle of the strap on his right ankle, a shadowy talon came out of the darkness behind the glyph to slap feebly at my hands. I jerked back in time to avoid most of the blow, but still ended up with a pair of bleeding scratches across the back of my right hand.

"Thiess!" snapped Triss. "Stand down this instant!"

"Resshath Triss?" The voice sounded muzzy and confused. "Master Aral? Is that really you, and not more evil visions?"

"Yes," said Triss, his tone gentler now. "We're here to free you and Javan, and the others."

Javan, I remembered the name, but not much more about him than that.

"Truly?" The shadow of a huge horned owl hopped out from behind the glyph, turning his head this way and that as he looked around. "Free?" He jerked suddenly like someone waking from a nightmare. "The light's gone!"

In an instant he'd collapsed back into Javan's shadow, but only long enough to sever the straps that confined his bondmate all in an instant. Then, before Javan could fall forward off the rack, he'd flowed back out in front of him, retaining his human's shape so that he could catch the young man and ease him to the ground. I was about to suggest we move the two of them to the passageway when I heard a crash behind me followed by a sound like someone tipping a couple hundred gallons of water onto the floor.

Before I'd half turned around Faran called out, "Master Aral, we may have a problem here."

Another, weaker voice, spoke then, "Oh, thank Namara, I thought sure I was gonna drown."

The last cell lay across the hall and a few yards down from the one where I'd found Thiess and Javan. It stood wide open now with Faran standing in front of it in an ankle-deep puddle, with more water flowing out all the time. Fortunately, the floor of the passage sloped slightly down and away toward the bend at the back. So, the water was going that way for now. As I splashed across to see what was going on, Faran pushed forward into the flowing water and went to work on the light.

By the time I stuck my head into the cell, she had it tightly fisted, reducing it to a dim red glow. Another rack stood in the cell. It held a shaggy-haired young man built like a bog troll—deep chested and ridiculously broad shouldered, with thick arms that seemed too long for his body. Journeyman Roric, Avarsi by birth, and absolutely unmistakable. Remembering that he was almost as fast as he was strong, I didn't find it at all hard to believe he'd managed to survive the fall. As I watched, his Shade sliced the bands holding him to the rack, starting at his ankles and working up.

Behind him, water was fountaining out through a wide gap where the mortar had fallen away between two stones high on the wall. From there it hit the rack and cascaded to the floor.

Judging by the filthy high-water mark across his chest, Faran had gotten the door open just in time. Like the others, Roric was covered in bruises and scabs, and missing an ear. That didn't prevent him from stepping free of the rack without any help, or waving off Faran's offer of a shoulder to lean on as he staggered forward.

"Just let me get clear of this fucking ice water and aim me at the nearest Hand and I'm good," he growled, flexing thick fingers. "I've scores to settle."

The shadow that followed him out growled its agreement as it took on the form of a gigantic six-legged badger. Ssolvey, if I was remembering correctly. The Shade was another who'd never been much of a talker, which made it harder. But when I silently asked Triss, he reassured me that I'd gotten the name right.

"Give me a hand with the door," Faran said to me as she followed Roric out. "It was holding back the water as well as any dam before I opened it and I think that's going to become really important if this storm keeps up."

"Point." The ground was still gently shaking from the battering winds above.

As I moved up and put my shoulder to the door beside Faran's, Triss darted into the room and nosed around briefly before coming back to me. *Kelos touched this door last of them all. Though the water has erased any shadow trail he might have left, there's a stronger sense of his presence in that room.*

The water had gone down enough that we didn't have much difficulty forcing the door shut, though it did require Roric's help to hold it in place long enough to relock. As Ssithra saw to that, Loris joined us. He was limping badly, and looked even weaker than he had when I first found him. Fresh blood stained the lower edge of the shadows where Issaru had wrapped himself around his bond-mate's ribs.

"Roric, Maryam, Javan." He ticked them off on his fingers. "That puts Leyan and Ulriss in the caved-in cell." He closed his eyes and his jaw tightened. "She had a lovely touch with a strangling cord, and Ulriss was the sweetest Shade you've ever met. I will miss them both. But we have no time for mourning yet. What's the next step in the plan, Aral?"

"That would be for Jax to bring down the Hand's barracks

as a distraction and to eliminate as many of the enemy as possible while I lead you all out that way." I pointed to the collapsed passage. "Unfortunately, something went wrong and the distraction happened before I'd even entered the sanctum. And now, the Signet seems to have closed the only available door."

Loris frowned. "And the backup plan?"

"Still working on that one. Why don't you have a seat with the others and let Faran and I have a look down there to make sure my information about it being a dead end is correct." I waved at the other end of the passage and then started that way—we didn't have a lot of time.

Loris's expression shifted to one I'd seen a number of times when he was teaching me at the temple, the one he used whenever I'd said something particularly stupid. "I will rest when my students are safe. Not before. Is that understood, Blade Aral?"

It was a formal mode of address used only rarely by a senior master to a junior, and it carried a strong undertone of direct orders.

How bad is he, Triss? He might be my senior, but the goddess was dead and the hierarchy with her, and damned if I was going to let precedent kill an old friend. *Can you ask Issaru?*

I already did. Issaru says he's bad, but he'll live . . . if nothing happens to make him much worse.

I gave Loris a faint bow. "As you wish, Master Loris."

"Then lead the way."

The whole little power-play turned out to be moot when that part of the passage ended in another cave-in maybe thirty feet beyond the bend. Our world had shrunk to less than a hundred feet of narrow tunnel and a score or so of intact tombs including the ones which had been converted to cells. Add in the Signet and her troops above and we were well and truly fucked, unless one of us could come up with a way to move through solid stone . . . or shadow.

I had been idly staring at the nearest lock without actually seeing it for a good couple of minutes when the idea clicked in my head. How *had* Kelos gotten in and out of the crypt without leaving a trail or anyone seeing him? To the best of my knowledge there was no way to travel shrouded without leaving a shadow trail, and he couldn't have gotten past the guards without his shroud.

Not if he didn't want it reported, at least. Even if Kelos worked for the Son of Heaven now, I didn't think he'd want it getting out that he'd sabotaged the Hand. But what if he didn't come in through the front door? Then he wouldn't *need* the shroud. I had an idea of how he might have managed that, but it wanted a better head for magic than mine, or possibly someone who'd been a better listener back in the day. Loris answered to both descriptions.

"Master Loris." I knelt down next to where he was sitting to put us more on a level. "I once saw Siri step into one shadow and out of another without passing through the intervening space. She said it wasn't really a spell, more like a sort of side effect of the way the everdark overlaps our world or something like that. Did she ever bring it forward to the council?"

Loris's eyes went distant and then he nodded. "She did. It involved folding shadows like paper in origami. A couple of the better mages among us even tried it." He shivered. "I was one. It was very painful and extraordinarily dangerous. Master Thera walked in shadow and never returned, and none of the Shades who looked for her in the everdark could detect any hint of her presence."

"I always wondered what happened to Master Thera," I said. A service was held in her memory, but they hadn't told us how she died—unusual but not unheard of. Sometimes the council or the goddess sent a Blade out on a mission that wasn't shared with the rest of the order.

"Do you think it would help us now?" I asked.

Loris shook his head. "Even if I remembered the exact technique, I'd be extremely reluctant to attempt it. After we lost Thera, the goddess herself forbade us from trying it again."

"Why?" asked Faran. "It seems like it would be incredibly useful in certain circumstances, and everyone has to die of something. It's not like a whole lot of us ever expected old age to get us."

"It's less useful than you might think. The distance you can cover is short, no farther than a Shade can stretch and still have enough substance at both ends to form the doorway. Anywhere from five to fifty feet depending on the light, but never more that that. The pain factor is high enough that it renders the user unfit for much of anything for a good minute or two after they've passed through the everdark. But far more important is that Thera didn't just die. She was lost."

"I don't understand," said Faran.

"While she lived, Namara made sure to greet each of us on our way to the wheel of rebirth and thank us for our service to Justice. When Namara felt Thera's death through her spirit dagger, she went to the gates of judgment and waited, but Thera never arrived. Her soul was lost or destroyed."

"Do you have a better idea?" asked Faran.

"No, but neither do I really remember how to do it."

Faran nodded, but the look on her face was one I knew well, and it wasn't acceptance. I remembered then that when I'd first found Faran hiding in the sewers under Tien, she'd performed a very intricate bit of shadow origami. She'd used it produce an item she'd been hiding in a sort of shadow tuckaside in the everdark.

"You think you might be able to figure it out, don't you?" I asked her.

"I might." She nodded again, thoughtfully this time. "It can't be all that different from the trick I use to stash things in the everdark, just larger in scale. Though I can't imagine doing it with something as irregular as a tree's shadow. Siri's a far better mage than I will ever be."

"And it's far too dangerous for someone barely old enough to be a journeyman," said Loris. "I forbid it."

Faran's eyes flashed with sudden anger. "Namara's dead, old man, and the order with her. I don't answer to you. Nor even entirely to Aral, though he is *my* master as much as anyone ever will be again." She looked at me now. "Do you want me to try?"

I didn't. Not one little bit. But if we didn't find a way out of here, and quickly, every one of us would die. If it were *my* life and soul on the line, I wouldn't have hesitated to make the attempt. Now, I wished that I'd never thought of it.

Triss spoke into my mind, *She's only a little younger than you were when you killed a king. As I recall, that involved you defying the council and asking Namara to make you a full Blade ahead of your time.*

That's different!

Why, because she's more mature?

Point.

I reached out and put my hands on Faran's shoulders. "This isn't the sort of thing that you ask someone else to do. And it's certainly not the sort of thing you want to see someone you care about attempt. At the same time, I know what you can do and some of what you have survived. I care about you. I don't want to see you risk yourself this way, but after all the dangerous things I've done, I can't pretend I have any right to tell you not to do it."

Not bad, not perfect, but you're getting better at this.

"Would you do it?" she asked.

I nodded, though I really would have preferred not to.

"Thank you."

"For what?" I asked, genuinely surprised.

"Not lying to protect me this time."

I remembered my efforts to keep her from coming along on this trip and I was ashamed. "I'm sorry about trying to keep you off the boat. It was wrong. Thank you."

She quirked an eyebrow. "For what?"

"Showing me that I was wrong."

Faran hugged me. "You're still a dreadful old man, but you're my dreadful old man."

"And you'll always be my young monster."

Much better. Triss chuckled in my mind, but his mental voice was more indulgent than mocking. *Of course, if you're going to thank everyone who points out when you're wrong, you're never going to have time to say anything else. Why, the thanks you owe me alone . . .*

Faran stepped back away from me. "If there's any chance that I can get us out of here, I have to try."

"I know you do."

18

───◆───

Standing by and letting someone you love risk their life requires significantly more power of will than resisting torture. I've done both, and I'd far rather take the torture. It's doubly difficult when they're risking themselves because you weren't able to get the job done.

When Faran opened the gate of shadows for the first time I wanted to forbid her to step through, or better yet, to simply go through myself if anyone had to try it. She wouldn't hear of the latter for reasons that had to do with the structure of the magic, and Loris backed her up. He'd wanted to try it first himself, but with his wounds he simply wasn't strong enough to manage such a trip more than once.

I gave her a quick hug and a kiss on the forehead. "You take care of yourself."

"I'm only going fifteen feet, and the technique isn't all that different from my little shadow tuckaside. I'll be fine. Now, I need to go."

I'd never been more frightened for her, nor more worried. Or proud for that matter. But I just nodded, smiled as best I could, and stepped out of her way, all the while wishing desperately that I had a drink to hand. The portal didn't look like much, just a sort of deepening of the shadow cast by the broken door of Loris's cell. The off-kilter rectangle was slightly darker than it ought to be and vibrating gently in time with the beat of the storm. Another thread of shadow ran from it down the hall and across to vanish into the open cell that had held Maryam.

Without another word, Faran reached out a hand to the shadow gate, touched it, and vanished. I hadn't watched nearly as closely when I'd first seen Siri try it all those years ago. Hell, I probably hadn't watched *anything* so closely in the years since I last looked on the living face of Namara and took my final assignment.

Initially, the shadow seemed to resist her, bending to the shape of her hand like she was pressing on a silken sheet. Then the surface broke with a sort of pop and, a—for lack of a better word—flash of darkness, short but intense. Sort of like reverse lightning. In that instant, Faran had turned black and appeared to become two dimensional, like a paper doll painted in midnight. Then she was gone.

I started counting. One. Two. Three. At thirty, or about three times as long as it would have taken her to slow walk the distance, the portal vanished and Faran's voice emerged from the other cell, "Shitshitshit . . . hey it worked."

I covered the distance in a dash. Faran was leaning against the wall at the back of the cell, hugging herself and looking pale and cold. I wanted to hug her, too, but I could tell she needed the breathing space right now.

"Are you all right?" I asked. "You were gone a long time."

She bit her lip but nodded. "Hurts. So cold it feels hot, and the distances aren't the same at all. You're walking, but you're falling, too, because there is no up or down. I understand why Thera got lost." She shivered.

"You don't have to do it again," I said.

"Yes. I do." I could see how much the words cost her and I wanted to argue.

"We can find another way."

She shook her head. "Not fast enough. No, this will work and we can do it now. We don't have time to mess around anymore. Not with the Hand above. And not with the storm trying to tear the whole building apart." As if to punctuate her words, a large chunk of mortar fell out of the chink between two of the stones forming the barrel vault over the little tomb. "We have a way out, we have to take it."

"All right," I said. "Show me how to manage this little trick."

She shook her head again, even more firmly. "That's not going to work. If you don't have the basics, I'm not going to be able to get you there in any reasonable amount of time, *and* I've got a better idea. I'll create the way and hold it open, and you can all pass through on my heels. I think it will work better anyway."

A shadow phoenix appeared on the wall behind her. "Faran is right. I didn't fully understand what was needed until we actually did it, but now I see. It's a sshssithssha way. Each soul that passes along it will make it stronger for a time. That way the strong can lead the weak and, with us to guide you, all are more likely to make the passage alive."

Triss?

Sshssithssha, that makes sense.

Can you explain it?

Not in human words no. But Ssithra is right that each passage will make it easier for the ones who follow.

"It's your play," I told Faran. "We'll follow your lead."

"Thank you. Then we only have one thing left to do, and that's to find a shadow's path out of here." She jerked a thumb toward the nearer of the two cave-ins. "That looks far too solid for even the thinnest wisp of darkness to get through, and the other was just as bad. I'm hoping you have an answer for that."

"I've got it covered, I think. I wouldn't have brought the idea up in the first place if I didn't already have an idea."

"What is it?" Loris looked over my shoulder, inserting himself in the conversation for the first time.

"Ever stand on the bank of a clear stream with the sun behind you?" I asked.

"Of course . . ."

"Then you know that shadow can pass through clear water as easily as it passes through the air." I nodded toward the closed cell where we'd rescued Roric from the flooding. "If the water can get in, we can get out."

Loris frowned. "That water was coming in awfully fast and we don't have anywhere for it to go. *And* it wasn't anything like clear. If you're wrong, we may have trouble getting the door closed again, and that could become a major problem. What makes you so sure the distance through the water is short enough?"

"I'm not." I couldn't tell him that I believed that was how Kelos had come in without revealing a whole bunch of things I didn't want to have to explain or argue about just yet. "It's a gamble, but it's the only one I can think of that might pay out."

Not bad, Triss said into my mind.

"Madness," growled Loris. "Dangerous madness, at that. The water could kill us all."

"If we don't try it we'll all die down here anyway," I replied. "Later if not sooner. I'm no happier about the idea than you are, but it's all we've got."

Faran held out a hand abruptly. "Maybe we could extend our range." She had a very thoughtful look on her face. "Two Shades together might be able to reach farther than one. You've done this before, Master Loris, if long ago. What do you think?"

Loris's eyes went far away and he blinked several times. "I . . . maybe. I don't know. Tell me what you're thinking of doing."

Faran explained in detail, talking about shadow folds, and everdark warps, and nima sharing, and other details that I'd probably have understood a whole lot better if I'd listened closer in my high magic lessons.

"That might work," Loris said when she'd finished. And then, "Where did you learn all that? You weren't old enough to have gotten that kind of instruction before the fall of the temple."

"Here, in the Magelands. I spent two of my lost years in Har. I couldn't take classes at the university without letting them know what I was. But I was able to use my powers to eavesdrop on quite a number of lessons. Mostly at night, and mostly for the advanced students because of that." She looked suddenly wistful. "It's not really an education, but I learned a lot. I'd like to come back someday."

She shook herself. "But that's a wish for another time. We've already been down here too long."

A few moments later, Triss and I were standing ready to open the door, with Roric, Maryam, and Javan lined up behind me. While I was getting the others ready, Loris and Faran did something complicated with Ssithra and Issaru. When Triss triggered the lock, the door slammed open, smashing against the stones so hard that I half expected it to pop the hinges. A wall of filthy water fell through the doorway as a couple of thousand gallons emptied into the hallway in a matter of seconds.

We were all briefly up to our knees, and Faran waded in before it had fallen to ankle height, with Loris struggling along in her wake. I followed them into the doorway and waited there as Ssithra spun herself into a cord of shadow and slithered into the gap between the stones. Loris and Issaru stood in reserve, the former looking even paler than Faran had after her trip through the everdark. If Faran could avoid drawing on them, I knew she would, and I was at least a little bit hopeful. If Kelos had come in this way, then the distance should be possible for a single Shade to bridge.

Ssithra returned after a few minutes and resumed the shape of a phoenix. "I don't think I can do it alone. It's not that far from here to the place where the water is pouring into the channel, but it's some distance from there to anyplace big enough for a person to come out that isn't underwater. Also, the water's awfully murky. That means I have to put extra substance into maintaining the link."

"But if Issaru and I help, you can get my students out of here?" asked Loris.

"And you," said Ssithra. "Yes, I think so."

"Then let's do it."

"Resshath Issaru, are you up to this?" asked Ssithra.

The shadow bound around Loris's ribs shifted to form a hawklike face. "I am. But for Loris's sake we must act quickly once I remove myself from my place here."

A shadow hydra peered around the door frame from behind me. "Resshath Issaru, if Maryam and I go last before you, I can bind Master Loris's wounds for you until it is our turn. Would that help?"

The hawk face nodded. "A great deal, young Vrass. Come here."

They did, and the hydra wrapped itself around Loris's ribs over the top of Issaru. Once she was solidly in place, the older Shade slid out from underneath and briefly formed itself into a shadow hippogriff to bow thanks to Vrass. While they were doing that, I half buried one of the bright magelights in debris on the ground beyond the room's door. From there it cast a good dark rectangle of shadow on the wall, providing a frame for the gate.

The hippogriff climbed the wall next to the rectangle, then reared back onto his hind legs in the classic heraldic pose. From there he shifted down and back, assuming the shape of his bond-mate, sans only the sword Loris had adopted as a cane. The shadow Loris knelt and produced a flat sheet like black paper from somewhere near his belt. Streamers of green spell-light like fiery thread shot from Loris to his shadow mirror, visible only in magesight. It connected them at ankle and wrist, knee and elbow, almost like a marionette's strings.

Though Loris didn't move, the shadow did as the strings grew longer and shorter. Working quickly and carefully, the shadow Loris folded the black rectangle again and again. With each fold, a line of differently colored magical light extended itself from his fingertips to lie along the crease. When he had finished, he had built a rectangular three-dimensional box covered with faint angular lines of color where the creases lay.

It was weird to see it there, a rainbow-edged bulge of pure darkness sticking out from the wall where the shadow play had happened. Leaning forward, the shadow Loris placed the box at floor level in the exact center of the door shadow and pushed it into the wall. Where it had bulged inward before, now it bowed outward, giving an impression of a small but darkened opening extending into some other space. A mouse hole to the everdark.

As shadow Loris withdrew his hand, the hole began to grow and shrink simultaneously, thinning toward two dimensionality at the same time it expanded in height and width to match the shadow of the door. When it was done, the two outlines were in near perfect alignment and it only extended a hairsbreadth into other space. The glowing thread connecting shadow Loris to actual Loris faded as the former twisted into Issaru's hippogriff form again, leaving only a single narrow strand of shadow to connect him to the door.

"This end is ready," said Loris, and I could hear a heavy weight of fatigue under his words. "But it's taking a lot out of me. We need to hurry. I wish I could have done that half so quickly as Siri did it when she first showed us the trick."

"Issaru?" asked Ssithra.

In response, the Shade collapsed down into a thin cord of darkness to match the one that Ssithra now formed. Faran closed her eyes and spun a thread of green spell-light out from the center of her forehead. Together, the two strands of darkness and the one of light slid into the hole in the wall, spiraling around each other as they went, like the strands of a rope.

Seconds took hours to pass as we waited for them to establish the gate on the other end. From what I'd seen when Faran created one earlier, work on the far end was both much less dramatic and faster. It probably took less than a minute, but it felt like days. I spent most of the time trying desperately not to think about how very much a couple of efik beans or a big glass of Kyle's would have eased my nerves.

You'd regret it, Triss sent into my mind.

I didn't say one word.

You didn't have to, not when you want it so badly. I can feel you longing after it like a canker in my soul.

Me, too, but I won't give in to the wanting. And then, because I wouldn't lie to Triss, *Not today, at least.*

That's when the gate opened. I hadn't seen it with the last one, but this time I did. The back of that hairsbreadth of depth the shadow possessed suddenly acquired a sort of reverse translucency, as though darkness was shining through from the other side.

"Follow me." Faran stepped up to the portal. As before, there was a moment of resistance, followed by a flash of darkness. Then she was gone.

I went next, putting my palm out to touch the shadow. I was expecting to feel something like the press of cold silk against skin when you touch a bolt of fabric in the market. Instead, it grabbed onto me, and I realized the resistance didn't come from the portal. It came from a soul recognizing the hungry darkness. I tried to pull back, but it pulled me in with a sharp jerk.

My perspective rotated as I passed through the membrane between the worlds. I wasn't stepping forward into the everdark.

I was falling face-first into eternity. And it was cold, so very, very cold that it burned.

I had gone with my friend Devin to Aven once, the country of his birth. It was deep winter at the time and Devin had insisted on reliving one of the few experiences he remembered from his childhood, a steam bath followed by an ice water plunge. I don't know how cold it was that day. Cold enough so that in the quarter of an hour we spent in the sauna a good skin of ice formed over the hole we'd cut in the lake.

After my time in the steam bath I was so hot I felt light-headed and I was dying for a chance to cool down. The edge of the ice lay barely two long steps from the door of the sauna, a distance crossed so quickly I barely felt the cold. I leaped out and down, breaking the skim of ice and plunging into a sort of ecstatic agony of cold. My skin felt frozen and on fire by turns. In deeper water I could easily have drowned as sensation buried thought. The passage through the gate of shadows was like that, only more so.

If not for Triss, I'd have been lost then—overwhelmed by the cold and the pain and the utter lack of light, much as Master Thera must have been. Where I couldn't make any sense of my entry into the everdark, Triss had come home. He caught my hand and tugged at me, telling me to walk. Though I was falling and there was nowhere for my feet to find purchase, I followed his command and found that it made a difference.

No up. No down. Nowhere. Nothing. No when, even. Yet, walking moved me. Maybe it was the intent to move that mattered and not the motion, but whatever the reason, I suddenly knew that I could choose my path through the eternal falling darkness. And I did, following a strand of green spell-light that I could sense but not see—walking through pain, but walking still. I felt better then, but Thera had been companioned by a Shade, too, and she had never come back. I knew I couldn't relax until I came out the other side.

The distance felt simultaneously infinite and yet no farther than the one might casually walk between one breath and the next. I tried to count my paces, but I found that I had lost my ability to comprehend numbers. Then, just as suddenly as it had begun, I passed through the other end of the gate. My left foot trod nothing. My right came down on rough flags tilted at a bizarre angle.

Up and down reasserted themselves, and I tumbled forward onto hands and knees to empty my stomach through a stone grate in the floor. Sound came back then, as the roar of the storm hit me like a falling wall, brutal even indoors. It was so loud I could barely hear the rush of the water below the grate.

Clear the way. Triss gave me an order and I obeyed, rolling to one side when I found I hadn't the wherewithal to easily return to my feet. The action reminded me of my bruised or cracked rib—painfully.

We were in a low wide space with a steeply angled ceiling/ wall combination that hosted the gate. It was too small and strangely shaped to be called a room, more like a stone lean-to. The air smelled of damp rock and old dust and the burned air that comes with lightning.

"Where the hell are we?" I asked, my voice a ragged croak.

"Underneath a flight of stairs, I think." It was Faran, speaking very quietly and sounding even worse than I felt. She was sitting on the floor to one side of the shadow gate. "That grate there opens into a drainpipe. It's where we came in. Check around the corner, but do it quietly, I think the sanctum's just beyond. I have to stay here to anchor Ssithra."

I started to slowly crawl off in the direction she was pointing just as Roric fell through behind me. He was swearing quietly, or at least he was until Faran gave him a gentle shove with her boot. But then I was at the place where our weirdly shaped little alcove met the world with a flattening out of the ceiling at about chest height. I had just enough sense left to use a cornerbright to do my looking.

It took me a moment to make sense of what I was seeing, as much because of my perspective and the horrible disorientation I'd carried forward from the everdark as anything. We were indeed under a set of stairs. The shadow gate opened from the back of the first course. The corner where I lay was underneath a landing where the stairs turned back on themselves. From there, they continued up toward the second floor gallery at the back of the sanctum behind the great sculpture of Shan.

The area under the landing and stairs acted as a storage

space for religious paraphernalia which blocked much of my
view. What little I could see was further occluded by the half-
open door and the raised dais where Shan's sculpture sat. The
floor was visibly wet inside the doorway, and the door—
obviously blown inward by the storm—kept banging against
a bronze chariot built in an ancient style.

I looked back over my shoulder just in time to see Maryam
and Javan fall through the shadow gate in a heap. Javan was
unconscious again and lying across Maryam's shoulders.

"I bumped into him," she said as Roric helped her shift
Javan aside. "Tripped over him, really. Vrass saved us both
then, kept me upright and pointed us in the right direction."

"Fuck!" Faran snarled. "Fuckfuckfuckdamnit!"

"What is it?" I started to crawl toward her.

"Master Loris just closed the gate."

"What? No!"

A tiny hippogriff appeared on the angled ceiling where the
gate had been, all of himself that Issaru could project so far.
"Loris is dying. The effort of holding the gate open was too
much for him, was always going to be too much. He'd never
have made it through the everdark and we both knew it going
in. Get them home, Aral. He told me to tell you he was counting
on you." The shadow wavered and started to fade. "Avenge us."

And then he was gone. They were both gone. One more pair
of Namara's champions fallen to the Hand and the Son of
Heaven. Two if you added Leyan and Ulriss buried in the
cave-in below. Tears burned down my cheeks, and I promised
myself that I would make my old teachers's final requests into
reality whatever the cost.

19

When someone important to you dies, they take a little of you with them into the grave. Though we'd never been all that close, Loris took the last vestiges of my childhood with him. I was now the oldest living Blade. There were no more generations between me and the void.

I didn't count Kelos and Devin or the other turncoats. They'd lost any right to that name by betraying our goddess. All the priests were long dead, too. That left me the senior heir to the tattered remnants of Namara's once great legacy. The weight of it fell heavily across my shoulders and heavier still on my heart, as I tried to figure out how the hell to get Loris's students and mine free of the trap that currently held us. Perhaps fortunately, those students didn't yet seem all that interested in looking to me for answers.

Maryam worked busily at restoring Javan to coherence, while Roric leaned in close to Faran to say something. He spoke quietly, and it was impossible to hear him from even a few yards away over the roar of the winds, but the gist of his words became obvious when Faran handed across a small knife. He used it to cut shallow slices over his cheekbones.

When he was done, he caught me looking at him and gave

a grim smile. "A custom from my childhood in Avars, before the priests took me. They would not approve, I think. But they're gone now, and Loris was more than my teacher. He was my clan chief."

I nodded. "Blood for mourning. Blood for vengeance." I knew the custom well.

"And blood for blood," he finished. "You don't object?"

"No. I understand and I sympathize."

Roric nodded in turn. "I see that you *do* understand. It's in your eyes." His expression went very thoughtful and he flipped the knife over so that he held it by the blade, offering me the hilt. "In your heart, too, I think."

And, because it was, I took the knife and I slashed my cheeks as well.

Faran leaned forward as I finished and extended her hand. "Mine."

I handed the knife across, and she, too, cut her cheeks. Then she offered it to Maryam. The tall lanky young woman took it and shook her head.

"Madness," she said. "Primitive, superstitious madness." Then she cut her cheeks and passed the knife to Javan, saying "Blood for blood."

She's right, Triss said into my mind. *Both her words and her actions.*

Roric's Shade, Ssolvey, shifted into his giant badgerlike form and gave us a very formal bow. "Master Aral, Resshath Triss, what are your orders?"

Javan nodded. "With Loris dead and Jax missing, we are yours to command. What's the plan?"

What I wanted to say was, "A giant fucking mess." This was the point where we were supposed to go over the wall and head for the hills. Of course, that failed to take into account the fact that anyone who stepped outside right now was going to get blown clear to Kanjuri, on top of all the other stuff that had gone wrong.

Triss?

Your call, Aral.

We hadn't properly factored the winds into our thinking. Oh, we'd known there was going to be a big storm, planned to use it to help cover our tracks even. The fight at the cemetery had served as a recent reminder of the immediate consequences of killing the Hand and their Storm bond-mates. But we simply hadn't anticipated the scale and killing ferocity of it. Until the winds calmed, we were all trapped in the temple. Faran raised her eyebrows at me then, and I realized that I'd run out of time for thinking. Besides, there was only one possible answer.

"The plan is simple, Javan. We shroud up, we go out into the sanctum, and we kill everything that moves. Hand first, Sword as it's convenient."

"Now, that is a good plan." Roric's grim smile returned. "I like it. Blood for mourning."

"Blood for vengeance," I added.

"And blood for blood," which we all spoke as a chorus. Madness.

Then, one by one, we vanished into darkness.

Though I had assumed full control of Triss and his senses, I took the risk of leaving my eyes uncovered as I slipped out into the sanctum. I wanted to give myself one clear human-eyed look at the field before I surrendered my sight. The skies obliged me with a huge bolt of lightning that momentarily lit the whole place in a brilliant eerie light. I was pretty sure it was the last clear picture I was going to have of things for some time to come, so I set it in my memory.

The temple was more than half destroyed, with all the windows blown in. Portions of the vaulted stone roof had fallen, and rain was coming in every which way. One of the cave-ins had happened over the altar and the giant sculpture of Shan. Falling rubble had torn off the arms of the god on the left side, and left the ones on the right cracked and dangling. Bodies and debris lay everywhere.

No matter what happened in the next few minutes, the Son of Heaven had suffered losses here that he would be a very long time in replacing. It wasn't nearly enough for me.

Then the lightning was gone, and the battle began. Five Blades, all of them wounded, against a half score of sorcerer-priests and a hundred soldiers in the dark of a ruined temple. I lost track of the others in the first seconds, as my world narrowed to a series of fleeting impressions and momentary flashes of clarity.

The rain pounds and the wind hammers. Lightning tears

giant holes in the sky and rips irregular stripes out of Triss's unvision. The shadows of the raindrops create a million false dark-echoes that drown out the real ones. Blind fighting. I am forced to push aside the shroud over my eyes, risking visibility so that I can see.

I kill the first Hand I encounter with a thrust from behind. She falls away from me, leaving her blood on my sword. A giant bolt of turquoise lightning spikes down through one of the holes in the roof, incinerating her body in an instant funeral pyre. My shroud compresses almost to nothing, and Triss shrieks agony in his dreams with the intensity of it. The heat shatters the stones beneath her, and a wave of pressure edged with bits of hot rock throws me back and away.

I roll up onto my feet, only half dodging the spear thrust of a soldier who has taken advantage of the momentary reduction of my shroud. He misses anything vital, but I come away with a long shallow slice across the front of my right hip bone. I'm hunting the Signet and I don't have time for a Sword, so I throw a burst of magefire that sets his clothes afire and move on.

A half dozen more Swords die at my hand over the next couple of minutes before I spot my real target. Nea Sjensdor, Lady Signet, right hand and heir of the Son of Heaven, a potent symbol of the forces that destroyed my goddess and my life. She stands at the base of the altar. Her back is pressed tight against the stone facing, and there is a loose pile of rubble above and behind her, guarding the rear approach. I will have to take her from the front.

That's good on one level. I *want* her to know what killed her, and I want to see the look in her eyes when she dies. But it will make my task harder. Though her sword of office lies in its sheath across her back, she is armed with a pair of the short scythes called kama. Spell-light paints them a deep purple with some sort of combat enchantment, and the handles are steel instead of the more usual oak. I can see from the way that she holds them that she's an expert in their use. With the hooked blades extending her reach, she looks ever more mantislike than when I first saw her back at the Gryphon in Tien.

I can't spot her familiar—a Storm hiding in the chaos of the greater storm, but it has to be someplace close. The rain and the lightning continue to make it impossible for me to use Triss's senses, but I want to get in tight before she becomes aware of me. I look at the thirty or so feet of debris-strewn ground that lies between us, and set it in my memory. I shroud my face before releasing my hold on Triss. Magic won't win this fight for me, and having Triss awake to cover my back might.

I tell him, *I've found the Signet,* and I quickly fill in the details as I start forward.

For Loris and Issaru, he says when I am finished.

For Namara and the temple, I add.

This was not the Signet who commanded the forces of the Son of Heaven that day. That Signet died in the battle, slain by Master Illiana and Resshath Ssuma in a suicide attack, or so I had been told. But Nea was there, third in the line of command. The most senior of the sorcerer-priests to survive the battle, she was made Signet on her return to Heaven's Reach.

The changing sound of the rain as it strikes the statue of Shan and the feel of the floor under my feet tell me that I am within striking distance.

I need my eyes.

Triss parts the veil that covers them and I swing a low cut at the Signet's ankles with my left-hand sword in the same instant that I drive my right at her throat. The blades are cloaked in shadow, and yet somehow, the Signet anticipates them. She snaps her own right-hand weapon down in a flat block, while sweeping her left around to hook my thrust aside.

I have a brief moment to remember that her Storm had shown an uncanny knack for spotting us back at the cemetery, too. Perhaps it can read the patterns of the winds in weather like this in the same way that Triss sees dark-echoes. Then, with a twist of her left kama where it engaged my sword, the Signet points the end of the rod directly at my face. Reflexes buried far below the conscious level scream at me, and I bend sharply backward without having time to think why.

A blast of pure magical force passes through the space where my face had been only an instant before. I feel my nose break in response to the pressure wave, as I realize the kama are battle wands as well as blades. Avoiding the blast has forced me to take my eyes off the second of the Signet's weapons. I hop back awkwardly, hoping to avoid the blow that I know is coming.

Pain sears along the outside of my left thigh as the hooking slice finds my leg, and Triss grunts in sympathy as the enchantments on the blade cut him, too, but I'm lucky. The combination of shroud and my jump back is enough to keep her blade from leaving me with much more than a long deep scratch. I snap my free sword down and around, batting the kama aside before she can bring it in line for a magical attack. I can feel the blood trickling down my leg, but none of the big muscles is badly damaged.

I want to move out and away from the Signet, reshroud, and then come back in, but I don't dare. Not with the battle wands extending her range to as far as she can see. I have to stay close and keep her from getting them in line again. I move into a more defensive posture, focusing my eyes on her center but tracking the flickering shifts of her kama so that I can bat at them whenever one looks as though it might point my way. It's a weak position, but all that I can think of in the moment. Before I can even begin to formulate a new strategy, I feel my shroud leave me.

Triss!

Storm above!

Tiny lightnings flash overhead and Triss's words dissolve into a series of hisses and snarls. But I don't dare take my eyes off of the Signet, not even for an instant. If there are any of the Sword close at hand, I'm going to die in the next few minutes. I cast a prayer to a dead goddess, knowing it's futile, and yet still hoping that Faran or Roric or one of the others is close enough to act as its instrument.

Over the next few seconds, the Signet and I exchange a dozen quick blows and counters, and no one runs a spear through my back. I can hear Triss fighting with the Storm as a sort of continuing angry snarl in the back of my mind, and I can only hope that he's doing better than I am. I don't dare look up to check. The Signet's damned good. Too good for me to take her quickly, or possibly at all. Not unless I get lucky, or my prayer comes through.

That's when Jax whispers in my ear. "Aral, can you hear me?"

Her voice is low and faint, full of pain and exhaustion. To me, she sounds like a goddess. I nod, hoping that she can see me from wherever she is projecting her voice, and not wanting to speak for fear of giving her away to the Signet.

"Good," she replies. "I'm hurt, badly. Very badly. Dying maybe. I can't do much, but I can probably give you one split second of distraction. Make it count."

"Wait!" I shout.

An idea has come to me, inspired by where we stand, or where I think we stand anyway. Maybe I don't have to be lucky. Maybe I just have to be smart. I glance upward to see if I'm right. Storm and shadow tumble and twist around the remaining arms of the great statue, the scytheblade head of the Storm mirroring the paired kama of its bond-mate.

"Wait for what?" It's the Signet, responding to my yell and looking at me like I'm a madman. "Is the great Aral Kingslayer going to give himself up?"

I look her square in the eyes, I want her to think that I'm talking to her, even if what I say doesn't make a lick of sense. "No, what about you? Where are you? Where do you stand?"

The Signet shakes her head, but doesn't say another word, just lashes out with her left kama, aiming for my wrist.

"Leaned against the intact side of the altar," replies Jax. "Why does it matter?"

"Because Shan himself is about to strike you down," I say to the Signet, hoping Jax will understand what I want.

"You're mad," replies the Signet.

"Oh, I think I see," says Jax. "But how—"

Before she can finish the question, I flip my left sword into an underhanded grip, an insane shortening of my reach considering the circumstances. But I can't afford to lose it, and if I don't want to cut my own nose off, it's going to be a much safer grip for what I need to do. The Signet takes advantage of the maneuver to press the attack, and I'm in serious danger of losing the fight then and there. Twisting and turning like a madman, I manage to hold off the blades and dodge the blasts long enough to get my hand in the right position.

With a sharp yank, I rip the pouch free of my chest where it hangs off the straps of my sword rig. I use the same motion to flick the pouch and its contents to the place where Jax lies in shadow. Then I go on the offensive, pressing the Signet with everything I have. She knows something's up, but good as she is, she's not good enough to pay attention to anything but staying alive for the next few seconds. It's exhausting and I can't hope to sustain the pace, but I push her back and to my left, waiting for the sound of the first crack.

When it comes, I throw myself backward, rolling desperately as I hit the floor. The Signet gets off two or three blasts, none of which connect, but I pick up a lot of bruises and a couple of burns from the near misses. Then comes the noise I've been hoping for, an enormous crash that ends in a scream. I bounce back to my feet and see that Jax has come through.

She's taken the finger I threw her and pressed it to the side of the altar, triggering the movement of the giant statue's mighty stone arms. Its *badly cracked* stone arms. With my last attack, I pushed the Signet back just far enough to put her under the hand of her own damned god.

I don't know if Namara's ghost heard my prayer. I don't know if she answered me in the voice of the woman I once loved. I don't know if this struck her as the perfect justice for one of those most responsible for the destruction of her temple and her legacy. All that I know is that the five-thousand-pound fractured stone hand of Shan has fallen from its broken wrist as I hoped it would, crushing the Signet like the mantis she so resembles.

She's been touched by the hand of her god, Triss said into my mind. *It doesn't seem to have worked out for her.*

He's got the Storm pinned now against the chest of Shan's statue. It's still struggling, so I know the Signet isn't dead yet, but it's only a matter of time. No one survives the kind of injuries she has now. The entire right side of her skull is dished in and covered in blood, that and one arm is all that's visible under the broken stone, but it's enough. The Storm jerks violently, and there's a sharp crackle like carefully sequenced miniature lightning.

I'm letting it go, says Triss a moment later. *It wants to go to her and it promises not to attack us.*

If you're sure.

He doesn't answer, just releases his grip on the thing. It flits down to hover over the great stone hand, a wild woeful keening coming from somewhere in the vicinity of its head. I dismiss it from my mind and move toward Jax as Triss reshrouds me.

I can't see her, but there's a deeper patch of shadow near the front of the dais.

"Jax?" I don't like that I can't see her and her injuries. "How bad it is?"

"Later." Her voice comes out of the shadow, sounding even weaker than it had in my ear earlier. I wonder how she did that but this isn't the time to ask. "Now, you need to finish this."

"You're right." She is, but I need to tell her about Loris. Especially if she's dying.

"That may be the first time you've ever told me I was right."

I relax a little. If she's up to giving me a jab, she can't be quite at death's door.

"It may be the first time it's been true. Look, I have to go back to the fight, but . . ." There's no gentle way to say it. "Loris is dead." I hear a sharp hiss of indrawn breath, but Jax doesn't say anything, and I can't stay. "He saved us all, but he didn't make it."

Faran screams then—an agonized sound—and I turn and run back to the fight. I can't find her in the darkness, which is good. It means she's still shrouded and not dead, but it doesn't reassure. As I'm looking for her, I see a Hand swing an axe low and fast into a patch of shadow. The scream is deeper this time, Javan to judge by the foot and calf left behind when the shadow rolls aside. I split the Hand's skull down to the teeth, losing my sword when it wedges in bone. A small group of Swords rushes me then.

Killing them takes me more time than it has any right to— I'm exhausted. More keep coming, drawn by the little knot of fighting perhaps. When it stops, I realize that I can't see any movement anywhere. I turn a slow circle there in the middle of the sanctum floor and still don't see anything but the falling rain and flashing lightning.

Unshroud me, Triss. I need to find the others.

He doesn't say anything, just collapses, first to a thin skin of darkness, and then down into my normal shadow.

Are you all right? I ask.

Have to rest a bit. That's all. Wake me if you need me. I can feel him letting go then, dropping almost instantly into sleep, and wish that I could do the same.

"I've been watching your back." It's Faran, speaking

through gritted teeth from somewhere close by. "They're all dead. We won."

She releases her shroud and I feel a sick weight in my stomach. The entire left side of her head is covered in blood, and she's got a strip of cloth bound across her eye.

"It's better than it looks," she says. "At least I really hope it is."

Roric appears at her shoulder, close but beyond easy stabbing range—sensible under the circumstances. "Let me see it, Faran. Master Loris was training me in healing magics."

I want to help, but I can see that Roric's got it under control, and I've just remembered Javan. "Thiess!" I yell. "Where are you? It's over."

"Here! Hurry!" The Shade's voice is shaky with fear.

As I head in that direction, Maryam steps out of shadows in front of me, coming from the other direction. Judging by the stains on the shirt Faran had brought her from the dead Sword earlier, she's got a deep gash across the ribs under her right breast. Probably some broken ribs, too, but she seems to be handling the injuries all right. In a moment she's kneeling over the suddenly visible Javan. He's pale from loss of blood and covered in sweat, but still breathing.

"Can you handle him for the moment?" I ask. "I left Jax by the altar and she's badly hurt, too."

"Go," says Maryam, and I do.

I'm halfway back across the sanctum floor when it really sinks in that we've won. My knees go soggy, and I can suddenly feel every bruise and cut. My nose feels like some demented squirrel has been using it to hide walnuts. I'm going to have to get one of the others to set it for me, but that will have to wait. Jax first.

By the time I reach her, I've started to settle back into something resembling a normal relationship with my sense of time and space. The Signet's storm is curled against the fallen stone hand. Tiny lightnings are still occasionally crackling here and there in its wings, but faintly. They're taking a long painful time dying, but it won't be long now. If I were a better person, I might feel badly about that. I'm not and I don't.

"Jax? It's over."

"My students?" She dropped her shroud.

I winced at the sight of her—she'd broken her left leg and arm at the very least, judging by the angle of the one and the sling holding the other. There was probably more I couldn't easily see, but I knew better than to ask about her injuries before answering her question.

"Roric and Maryam are mostly fine but Javan's lost his right leg below the knee. I don't know if he'll make it, but Maryam's trying."

"Leyan?"

"Dead, crushed in a cave-in engineered by the Signet."

"Bastards. Faran?"

"All right, I hope. She's bloodied up pretty badly and she's got a bandage over her left eye."

"Why are you here with me then?"

"Roric's taking care of her, and I was the only one who knew you were even present. How bad are you?"

"Leg's broken in two places, arm in one. Cracked some ribs and I was coughing up blood earlier, but that seems to have settled down, so it's probably not going to kill me right away. Worst is my left hand." She touched the sling with her other hand, and I noticed the blood soaking it for the first time. "I'll be shocked if I don't lose a couple of fingers."

"The Son of Heaven is going to pay for this!" The words come from somewhere deep down inside me, and it felt more like they were speaking themselves through my mouth than that I was saying them. "I'll *make* him pay for it."

Before I could say anything further, there was a tremendous flash from behind me and another enormous crash of thunder as the Signet and her bond-mate died. Good. It was a start. Then a thought occurred to me, but if I was going to make it a reality, I would have to move *very* quickly.

"Jax, can you hold on a few minutes more? I've business with the Signet, or what's left of her."

She gave me an odd look but nodded. "Do what you have to."

20

I stared at the mountainside and saw my soul. The snow above the old Dalridian castle burned white in the sun, hurting my eyes, but I couldn't turn away. It perfectly reflected the cold anger I felt in my bones, frozen, deadly, and utterly unmelting even here at the tail end of summer.

More than three weeks had passed since the debacle at the abbey in the Magelands. Three weeks spent mostly in traveling to this place, Jax and Loris's refuge in the mountains. We'd started out on the river coming up from below Tavan to Uln by barge and boat, the gentlest transport we could find for our wounded.

We'd had to hire porters to carry the stretchers that held Jax and Javan over the goat tracks above Uln that were the only way into Dalridia this far south. Roric and I had ended up trading off carrying Faran for a good part of that leg, too, when she went delirious on us. We'd made the final passage of the journey by royal Dalridian coach which provided some luxury, but we'd never once stopped moving.

We all would have liked to rest and recover a while in Tavan, at the healer's hall attached to the university, right at the beginning. But we didn't dare risk staying longer than it took them to treat the worst of our collective injuries. It was just too dangerous to stay anywhere there was any chance the Son of Heaven's people might find us. We had hurt him as no one had since Namara's fall.

More than three hundred followers of Shan had died at the abbey, nearly a third at our hands, the rest in the great storm and the flood that came with it. The temple proper was the only building that had even two walls standing at the end of the night. Not long after the end of the battle it had lost the rest of its roof when the main vault gave way. We'd have been crushed if we hadn't already retreated to the storage space under the stairs to get out of the worst of the wind and the rain.

Roric and Maryam and I had spent most of the next morning digging our way out of the wreckage with the help of our three Shades, where muscle simply wouldn't do the trick. The devastation we found when we finally broke through into the daylight was like nothing I'd ever seen. The abbey had been destroyed utterly and the bodies of most of its inhabitants would never be found. For that matter so had a huge swath of the surrounding countryside.

For several miles in every direction it looked like the aftermath of some mad cyclonic country dance. Great slithering tracks of destruction crisscrossed the landscape in a pattern centered on the temple's sanctum. Not a tree stood unbroken in the surrounding orchards, nor a single stalk of wheat in the fields. Death had taken everything that lived, a death that I had brought with me into this place.

The sight filled me with a sick anger that I hadn't felt in such measure since I saw my goddess lying broken and dead on the bottom of the sacred lake. If I'd had a bottle of whiskey or anything else with alcohol in it I'd have drunk it down without a thought. But I didn't, I had to face that destruction sober and without anything to blur my understanding of my part in it.

I think that's what cemented my decision to kill the Son of Heaven more than anything. Faran was right when she'd accused me of sentimentality. I didn't like killing anyone I didn't have to. For most of my career as a Blade I'd managed to avoid ghosting very many people who didn't deserve it, mostly keeping the deaths confined to my targets and the people who guarded them. Probably no more than a couple of score total, and most of those in self-defense. Till now.

I didn't regret the Hand or the Sword, the people we killed directly with steel and magic. As far as I was concerned, they had earned their deaths on the day my goddess died. But the clergy and the lay brothers and sisters who made up the bulk of the abbey's regular inhabitants had done nothing directly to me or mine. If they were not quite innocent of the blood of my brethren and my goddess, still they hadn't done anything to deserve this. That was without counting any farmers or other bystanders taken by the storms or the floods as they flowed away downstream.

Those deaths now belonged on my tally, and I would answer for them when I faced the lords of judgment. But I would not answer for them alone. Not one drop of blood would have been spilled here had not the Son and his Signet struck the first blow by taking Loris and the others prisoner. The Signet I had already taken to account—absently, I touched the pouch at my side where two beringed fingers now resided in near matching boxes. But the Son had yet to pay his share of the butcher's bill. Both for the deaths at the abbey last month, and for the deaths at Namara's temple six years ago.

It was time Shan's chief priest faced justice. And if it was a justice tainted with that ideal's darker cousin, revenge, than that, too, was something I was willing to have on my account when I faced my own judgment. The priests and Blades who raised me had taught me that revenge was not the province of Namara, that it lessened her glory when the two commingled. But Namara was dead, and her priests with her, and my frozen heart wanted hot blood spilled to warm it.

"Master Aral, are you up here again?" It was Faran's voice, still weak and weary nearly a month on, and the sound of it made the ice in my heart burn a little colder.

I turned back to the stairhead where Faran had just poked her nose out the door. She looked gaunt and pale, and the scar that ran from her forehead down under her eyepatch and out onto her cheekbone stood out red and raw. The healers had saved the eye, though they said she had at best even odds of recovering her vision or of ever seeing the end of the headaches that had started in the days after the injury. She was under strict orders to rest as much as she could, and oughtn't have been climbing the stairs to the castle's highest tower, but I had no one to blame for that but myself.

"I'm here," I said. "Just looking at the mountains again."

"Well, Jax was asking after you, and I said I'd come find you, though Roric tried to take the task for himself. Will you come down?" She sounded sad and quiet, unsure of herself in a way that was utterly out of character—more ice around my heart.

"Tell her I'll be there in a few minutes."

You should go now. Triss sounded more than a little sad and unsure himself. *Don't send Faran away alone. Not again.*

He was worried about me, and not without reason. I hadn't touched a drop of alcohol since the abbey. Not because I hadn't wanted to. Damn me, but I wanted a drink. Wanted one more than almost anything I'd ever wanted before. Wanted to surrender to the bottle and let it blur away some of the pain.

But I didn't want it more than I wanted to hand the Son of Heaven his own heart before he died. And I was *not* going to let anything get in the way of that goal, nor let go of one shred of the pain and anger that drove me toward it. If I lived through the experience, there would be plenty of time to get drunk after the Son of Heaven was dead. Until then, nothing could get in my way.

She's still waiting, said Triss, *and you owe her more than the Son of Heaven's heart served up in a pretty package.*

He was right, of course. I shook myself free of the cold rage, or at least as much as I could.

"Come here, Faran. I've been neglecting you, and I'm sorry for that."

She crossed the short distance from stairhead to tower wall to stand beside me. "It's all right, really. I've been spending time with the other students. Altia's here and she was one of my best friends back at the temple. Jaeris, too." Her face clouded even more. "We've grown apart though, since then. Their experiences were so different. Especially Altia's. She was one of the first Loris and Jax found. . . ."

I put an arm around her shoulders and squeezed her in tight against my side, though I didn't have any comforting words.

"For her it's almost like the fall of the temple was a brief nightmare between safe havens, horrible but fleeting," continued

Faran. "She doesn't understand what I went through or what I had to do to survive. I think she believes I've betrayed my training a little. It makes me feel like some sort of actual monster, where you calling me one never did."

"You aren't and never have been any kind of monster but mine. You've done nothing that you should be ashamed of, and if Altia says that you have, perhaps I should have a few words with her . . . my young monster."

She wrinkled her nose, then smiled and squeezed me back. "You really are a horrible old man, and thank you for offering, but please don't. She hasn't said a word. It's just the way she looks at me, and I think that it will pass with time. We were good friends once." Then she settled in against my side and was quiet for a little while.

I'll deal with it, Triss said angrily into my mind. *Olthiss knows better than to let her bond-mate get away with that sort of judgmental rubbish. And if she doesn't, she will when I'm done with her. Probably best if you don't tell Faran though. Some things are better handled among Shades. We don't have silly illusions about our companion's better natures.*

Thank you. We're going to have to go after the Son of Heaven soon, and I want Faran to feel at home here while we're gone.

Triss made a sort of mental tut-tutting noise. *Speaking of not having illusions, I'm a bit worried about the state of the Blade you've chosen for this mission, companion mine. While I approve of parting the Son of Heaven from this life as soon as ever it becomes possible, making it personal makes for mistakes.*

That's Kelos talking, I replied. *And right now he's only sitting a tiny jot below the death mark on my list himself. If he'd done more than just jam those locks, Loris and Issaru might still be with us along with Leyan and Ulriss. I still don't know what his game is in all this, nor his exact role in the death of Namara, but I don't trust him as far as I could toss a stone dog, and I don't like what he's become one little bit. If he gets in my way, I may have to kill him, too.*

Or die trying, Triss sighed.

Or die trying, I acknowledged.

At least he hasn't come after that finger yet. I half expected

*him to show up at the abbey as we were digging out and
demand it back.*

*Me, too, which is why I made the second one from Nea's
hand. I just wish I'd done half as good a job with mine as Kelos
did with his. I don't know if it'll even work.*

*You had a few distractions to deal with, and less time to
prepare.*

There is that.

Faran sighed, gave me another squeeze, and then slipped
out from under my arm. "We'd better go. Jax was already
sounding pretty irritated when she first asked after you, and
that's a while ago now."

"I don't doubt it. She doesn't like being laid up any more
than you do, and she's a lot less capable of getting around
right now."

Bones took forever to heal if you wanted to make sure they
did so fully and properly, even with magic speeding the process. And Jax's left leg was broken in four places, not the two
I'd initially thought. She was lucky she hadn't lost it at the knee
the way Javan had. She couldn't use a crutch yet either, not with
that arm broken and almost half her hand gone—her luck had
failed her there, though she'd probably be able to hold a sword
again in a few months.

One more thing to add to the bloody bill I intended to deliver
to the Son of Heaven. My broken nose and couple of dozen
stitches barely even figured into it compared to the others. Only
Roric had come off lighter in the battle, though the torturers
of the Hand had done him enough injury to balance us pretty
evenly. If the temple yet stood, we would both have been
cleared back to active service, with Maryam perhaps a week
or two behind us while she waited for her cracked ribs to finish
healing.

I helped Faran down the stairs, though she claimed repeatedly that she was fine. Judging by the sheen of sweat on her
forehead when we hit bottom, I probably should have insisted
on carrying her. She led me to the solar where Jax was taking
her lunch, then vanished, obviously on earlier instruction. That
left just the two of us and our Shades once Jax sent away the
servant who'd carried her up from her rooms.

I raised an eyebrow. "You wanted to see me?"

"Obviously. Are you still planning on going after the Son of Heaven?"

"Yes." It wasn't the first time she'd asked, nor even the fifth, and I didn't much feel like talking about it anymore.

She looked at my shadow. "Triss, what do you think of this?" It was the first time she'd put him on the spot about it.

He shifted into dragon form to speak, and Ssithra matched his change out of courtesy. "I think that the Son of Heaven needs to die," he said.

Jax rolled her eyes. "So do I. So does everyone in this whole castle not excluding the grooms and potboys. What I want to know is what you think about Aral doing it, and insisting on doing it right now."

"I'm not leaving for a week, Jax. I'd put it off longer than that if I wasn't worried about an early snow closing the passes."

"Dammit Aral, what's the hurry?" asked Jax. "It's going to take you two months to get there no matter when you leave. Why can't you at least wait till next spring?"

I sighed. I didn't want to tell her the truth, but I didn't think she was going to stop arguing with me until I did. "I'm afraid I'll lose my resolve."

"That would be fabulous, as far as I'm concerned," snapped Jax. "This entire plan is crazy, and we need you here. With Loris gone, I'm alone now. You're a full Blade, and a better one in most ways than I ever was. You have so much to teach my students, why can't you stay here and do it?"

"Because I'm not going to do your students one damn bit of good as an alcohol-soaked sponge sitting in the corner and drooling! And that's what's going to happen to me if I lose my resolve. I want a drink right now, Jax. I wanted one when I got up this morning, and when I went to bed last night. I want one like I haven't in more than a year."

"You haven't had one drink since we got here," she said.

"That's because I have a goal that matters to me more than my soul right now. The only way I'm holding it together is by picturing the look on the Son of Heaven's face when I feed him his own liver. That's what the fucking fight at the abbey did to me, Jax. It pushed me right back over the edge, and now I'm clinging by my fingernails. I have to go, and I have to do it soon or I'm going to fall apart."

"But it's madness! You don't even have a real plan beyond traveling to Heaven's Reach and using the key that Kelos the traitor gave you to sneak in."

"Not yet, no. Because I have to see the lay of the land. I've never been to Heaven's Reach and I don't have the goddess to conjure me up a map anymore. Besides, you know as well as I do that all a plan does is give you a starting point. Not once in all the missions the goddess sent me on did the initial plan survive more than about halfway through to the goal. Most of the time it went to hell the minute I actually started encountering the reality on the ground. It's not having a plan that made me a good Blade, it was being able to revise the plan to suit the conditions as I found them."

"He's got a point," said Triss.

She threw up her hands. "You know, that's half of why Devin hated you. He used to say that no matter what the plan was, you always fucked it up, and *still* came out on top."

"That's because Devin, as much as I once loved him, is an idiot. Success isn't making a good plan and following it no matter what. Success is understanding that a good plan is step one on a long journey, and then moving on to step two when the time comes."

"We need you here, Aral. To take Loris's place." I raised an eyebrow and Jax blushed angrily. "I mean at the school, not in my bed."

"I know what you meant," I said, more gently this time because that's not what I'd intended to convey. "But you don't need me. Not the me you've got at the moment, at least. I have to do this, Jax. If I don't, I'm going to crawl into the bottle again. I can feel it."

She looked away. "The Son of Heaven is a harder target to crack than the King of Zhan. Four Masters have died trying to make him pay for what he did to us at the temple. Four. Not counting the turncoats, that's more than there are left of us. You're going to die if you go after him, Aral."

"I might. But if I don't at least try, you won't recognize me in six months. More importantly, I think I can do it." I pulled out the pair of little silver boxes. "This gives me an edge like nothing any other Blade has ever even dreamed about. It's not a magic panacea, but I think it'll get me in close enough."

"Maybe, but will it get you out again? That's always the harder part."

I shrugged. "I'm less concerned about that at the moment, but yes, I hope that it will."

"Don't think I've given up on this yet," said Jax. "I've still got a week. But assuming you can make this play work, will you come back here to help me with the school afterward?"

"Maybe. I'd like to, if I can beat the bottle. I don't know if killing the Son of Heaven will be enough to get me back on the right path. What I do know is that not doing it sure as hell won't."

"Again, not giving up, but if you have to go, won't you at least take Roric with you? You've got two of those fingers, and having some backup might make all the difference."

Triss's "No" beat mine. "I agree that Aral and I have to try this. But I won't let anyone else risk themselves with us."

Jax smashed her good hand down on her thigh. "That's because you don't believe you're coming back, isn't it?"

"I believe we can kill the Son of Heaven," replied Triss.

"That's not an answer," said Jax.

"It is, you know," said Sshayar. "Just not the one you want." She sat back on her haunches and gave Triss and me each a small bow. "I wish you success and good hunting. I will pray that you come back to us, but even if you don't, know that I agree that the target is worth the cost." Then she collapsed into Jax's shadow.

"Well, I damn well don't," she said.

"Neither do I," Faran added when I slipped back out into the hall. "But I've seen you drinking where Jax hasn't, and I think I understand you better than she does. If this is what you need to do, I'm not going to fight with you about it."

"But you'd follow after me if you were well enough, no matter what I said."

"Of course I would." There was no heat in her voice, but I could see it burning in her unbandaged eye, and I thought that her not being up to coming with me on this might be the sole good thing to come out of her injury. "You need someone to watch your back."

"Little monster."

"Horrible old man."

After that and my conversation with Jax there wasn't much

more to say but good-bye. I left the castle on foot a few days later, though Jax offered me a horse or a coach. A man afoot is much less obtrusive than a rider, and he can go as fast or faster over longer distances if he's willing to push and keep pushing day after day. There would be horses later, and boats, but only as necessary.

I was riding when I finally arrived at the border of Heaven's Reach. The shortest route took me through the high grasslands of the northern Kvanas, and they're a horse people. Anything else would have looked suspicious. I'd joined a group of Radewalder pilgrims coming east to see the great temple of Shan and pay tribute to Heaven's Son. With my new face I blended right in, and I'd learned the accent long ago and well enough that they believed I was a countryman well met in foreign lands.

I had a few tense moments when the border guards looked through our packs. But they didn't dig deep enough to find the fingers or other bits of magical gear. I'd hidden those in a concealed bladder in a fat water skin that I'd had a Dalridian smuggler make around them. Without my old temple blades, none of my other gear was strange enough to draw any real comment. Not when I'd strapped my swords to my saddle and disassembled the rig that normally held them into its component straps and rings.

Heaven's Reach, the domain, is small, one long valley running west to east along the border between the Kvanas and Aven. It's also rich, both in terms of the land, which is very fertile, and the tributes it draws from satellite temples and pilgrims across the eleven kingdoms. Shan is the Emperor of Heaven and all the other churches pay him tribute. We were coming in on the western border, so it took us three days of gentle riding to reach Heaven's Reach the city.

We took rooms in one of the many overpriced inns the church has built to fleece the pilgrims, and I pleaded a bout of illness when the others went to visit the outer shrines the next morning. It was an obligatory tour for the truly devout, but of no interest to me. While they were gone, I reassembled my rig and trick bag then hid them in the floor of my room. I spent the next three days playing pilgrim with the others as they went through the inner shrines and lesser temples that lay within the sacred boundary of the temple precinct—an enormous and extremely well-guarded stone wall.

I feigned a return of my sickness on the final day when they went to the great temple itself. I would have loved to do a thorough scout around with my newfound friends providing moving cover, but I couldn't justify the danger it would put them in. The risk of one of my traitorous brethren stumbling on my shadow trail was just too high. I hadn't run into anyone else's shadow trail yet, but if the Son of Heaven had any of my former comrades around to help provide him with security, he'd keep them close at hand.

By begging stories of the wonders of the great temple from my "fellow" pilgrims, I was able to assemble a pretty good map of the public parts of the inner complex of buildings. They were quite happy to make corrections to my charcoal sketch, showing off their new knowledge of this holiest of Shan's temples— but sad that we would be parting ways on the morrow. They were heading back to Radewald as soon as they could, to beat the snows, and I'd long since told them I was going on to Aven for business reasons.

I spent another night and day at the inn, to give my erstwhile companions time to move on. I wanted to give them a good. head start so they'd run a lower chance of getting into trouble if I was caught. I spent the bulk of that time wandering the outskirts of the temple precinct, studying my map, and putting together a plan for my initial approach. After I passed beyond the limits of the map I was going to have to improvise, but there was nothing I could do about that. Finally, I paid my bill, hid the bulk of my traveling gear on a rooftop, and strapped on my swords.

It was time for the Son of Heaven to die.

21

———————

You can inscribe a lie in letters of gold, but that won't make it into beautiful truth. The temple complex was supposed to provide a sort of imperfect reflection of the gods' own Celestial City here in the world of man. It *was* gorgeous, even I had to admit that, but for me it was like the beauty of a will-o'-wisp—a pretty falsehood meant to lead the unwary astray.

According to holy writ, the Celestial City's streets are paved with ivory and pearl, its walls carved from jade, and its buildings roofed with purest gold. Not even the Son of Heaven could afford to counterfeit that kind of wealth, nor had he or his predecessors tried. To do so, they claimed, would have been blasphemy. No, Heaven's Reach must only reflect heaven, not strive to imitate it.

So the streets were paved with plain stone, but crushed shells had been sprinkled over them and fixed in place with magic, so that they shone silver and white under sun and moon, and blue and gold by magesight. The walls were faced with pale green marble, and the rooftops covered in terra-cotta tile that was sheathed in silver foil enchanted against tarnishing. A thousand slaves came out at night to polish every surface so that it all shone and sparkled like a ghost of the city it was supposed to reflect.

I could easily have gone in through the gates with the rest of the pilgrims during the day. I chose to go over the wall after the sun went down instead, though it required more initial effort. I had the best reason in the world.

After I'd left the inn and parked my gear I'd conducted a small experiment that I'd been itching to try for the better part of two days. I split my medallion.

Every pilgrim was given a little cast pewter medallion when they made their "voluntary" donative at the gate shrine and was told to wear it openly for their time in the city. Of course, you didn't get a medal if you didn't donate, and no one without a medal got to enter the temple precinct. Even the priests wore them, though theirs were cast in silver.

The spells that bound the medallions were very slickly done. Wrapping each one in permanent self-sustaining spells would have been prohibitively costly of magical resources. What they'd done instead was enchant the major gates at the entrance to the precinct and between neighborhoods within it. When a medallion passed through any of these gates, powerful enchantment, built into the very stones of the arch, activated and energized the medallions.

When they placed the medallion around your neck at the gate shrine it looked like nothing but a cheap bit of religious jewelry of the sort any moderately prosperous and devout peasant might be able to afford. Magesight revealed nothing more about it than the regular sort, and it remained apparently ordinary until your group knelt on the threshold of the temple precinct and recited the prayer after the priest. There, each medallion flashed bright blue for a moment, and not just to mages' eyes.

For the rest of the day, it would flash each time you passed through one of the "holy gates" that divided the sacred city into a series of individually defensible baileys or wards. In between, the medallion was infused with a very faint blue glow visible only to magesight. That remained after you left the temple precinct, but had visibly faded by the next day.

I couldn't figure it out at first, not until I'd thought to split my medallion open along the casting seam. The medallion was actually two medallions, the outer religious piece, and the inner magical tracking device and key. There were four glyphs inscribed within. Finding, binding, sympathy, and identity.

From back to front, each medallion had a unique signature, each one keyed itself to its wearer, and would sound an alarm if separated from them, each one could be tracked using a simple spell. If you had a medallion, the temple could tell who you were, where you were, and probably where you'd been. If you didn't, anyone who saw you knew you were an invader. It was a slick system.

Very slick. Roughly fifteen minutes after I broke mine open, a Hand and five Swords were sniffing around the well I'd thrown it down. A few minutes after that, the Hand had said a few words over the well and the broken medallion had flown up out of the depths to land at her feet.

I couldn't hear what she told her escort from where I was perched on a nearby rooftop and I didn't think it was worth risking a hearsay, but she didn't seem too alarmed by the find. I figured I was probably not the first irreverent pilgrim who broke his shiny little toy and then panicked afterward. Triss agreed with me. Still, I was very glad I'd given the gate shrine attendants nothing but lies about my name and my business. Likewise the Radewalders, though I hoped no one would bother to go after them for questioning.

Getting over the outer wall wasn't all that difficult. It never is. All it took was patience, climbing skills, a shroud, and the judicious application of tried and true magical techniques to the basic security wards. I was just moving from there toward the center of the precinct via one of the curtain walls that divided the baileys when a very unpleasant thought occurred to me.

A smart and paranoid magical architect might well have built the gates to do double duty: charge the medallions *and* scream bloody murder if someone without one passed through, or even over one. Since the mage who'd designed the security for Heaven's Reach was clearly both paranoid and smart, it gave me more than a moment's pause. I released Triss from his dream state and brought him up to date on my thinking.

Seems likely, given the circumstances, he sent back. *What do you want to do about it?*

We could go down and head inward at ground level, staying away from the gates, but that's going to slow us down a lot.

Not to mention the fact that there may be other places besides that gates that have the same spells on them. Probably are, actually. He made a sort of mental "hmmmming" noise then that I didn't like.

What is it, Triss?

As much as you or I may find the thought repulsive, the Son of Heaven is the representative of Shan here in the mortal realm.

And?

Do you suppose some of the gate spells are god magic?

As in, invisible to magesight? Oooh, that's not a happy thought at all. It means that if there are some of them in places other than the gates, we'll have no way of spotting them.

Exactly. Which brings me back to my original question; what do you want to do about it?

I guess now is the time to see if our secret weapon is going to work. I pulled out the finger that Kelos had given me—I still didn't trust mine, though I found the idea that I had a backup reassuring. Looking at it closely I found the glyphs of binding and sympathy inscribed on the bezel, though not the ones for finding or identity. *At least this way, we have a much better chance of running for it if it fails.*

We do if it fails in a way that's visible to us.

Have I ever told you that I find you too much the optimist?

No.

Good. A faint mental laugh tickled the edges of my mind as I resumed control over my familiar.

Moving very slowly and with the beringed finger well out in front of me I slipped forward along the top of the wall. A few yards shy of the nearer gate pier, the ring's bezel began to glow very faintly blue in magesight. Reluctantly, I extended my shroud to cover the ring, blocking my own view. It was more important that I not attract the attention of any fortuitously placed guards than that I keep an eye on it. As I got closer still it began to glow with the same sort of worldly light as the medallions had earlier.

The pressure of the light coming off the ring prickled uncomfortably against the shadows that hid it, like a light sunburn late in the day. That amped up to a real burn that had me wishing I could uncover the damn thing as I passed over the central arch—normally Blades go out of the way to avoid carrying lights of any kind inside a shroud. Fortunately, it quickly faded again on the far side.

I could only hope that the lack of a finding glyph on the ring meant that the Signet was an important enough officer of the church that the monitoring system had been designed not to track and inconvenience whoever held the post. I did have an important secondary bit of positive evidence for that idea, if you assumed that Kelos had been keeping the finger close at hand over the few years since he'd changed his allegiance. If not, well, if not, I was probably going to die without ever getting anywhere close to my target.

I tucked the finger back into the divided bag I'd made for it and its mate, and moved on. The temple precinct was shaped a bit like a nautilus shell, spiraling inward through a series of walled baileys, each with its own shrines and temples, toward the central complex. My next check came as I crossed over another curtain wall, this one part of the encircling wall dividing the first of the inner rings from the next one in.

No sooner had I stepped from the transverse wall between two baileys to the larger ring wall, then I felt an intense flare of light from the pouch holding the Signets' signets. Even through the thick fabric, the light chewed at my shroud and continued to do so as I made my way from there to the next transverse wall. It dimmed, but continued as I moved across to the next loop of the ring wall where it flared again.

At that point, I hopped down to the roof of a lesser temple and squatted in a sort of alcove made by the intersection of the two walls. Facing into the corner, I shifted the shadow away from my face and chest, moving it back and up to create a pocket of darkness before releasing Triss. When I opened the pouch, I could see the ring still glowing, but very dimly—I wouldn't have been able to see it even by moonlight. Pulling out the finger, I moved it closer to the wall.

In response, and as expected, the glow brightened dramatically. Whatever magic tied the rings and the medallions to the gates was present in all of the major walls here in the depths of the precinct.

I don't know what we'd do without this ring. I tapped the signet with my thumb. *If Kelos hadn't given it to us for the abbey attack, I don't think we could have gotten even this far.*

I don't either, and I don't like it. It makes things too easy, and it's magic that's not under our direct control. This is tied to Kelos's life force. If he died or chose to sever the connection while we're here, we'd be in the shit deep.

That's why we made one of our own. I touched my free hand to the pouch at my breast. *In fact, why don't we check it?*

I put the first Signet's finger away and pulled out the one I'd made, moving it close to the wall. It was slimmer, coming from a woman's hand, and the ring dimmer—its glow wasn't even visible initially—and almost as much green as it was blue, but it did light up. The finger felt colder, too. Warm, but not quite blood warm, which might account for the dimness and green tinge.

But then, I wasn't the mage that Kelos was, and I hadn't had a slice of unicorn horn handy when I made it, nor a silver nail. I'd had to make do with a wedge of dracodon ivory and a bent sliver of silver, both pried loose from the altar furnishings beneath the stairs at the abbey. Not to mention that I hadn't been able to harvest it until a few moments after the Signet's death.

I liked touching it even less than the other one. It was bound to *my* life force, a connection I could feel as sort of a feathery tickle at the back of my mind. Most of the time I could ignore it, but when I actually handled the finger, that feathery feeling grew stronger and extended a line to the point of contact. It felt like a ghostly string running from the finger through my hand and up my arm to the back of my neck where it spiraled around my spine and on into my skull. Very disconcerting. I put it away as quickly as I could after I'd verified that it, too, glowed.

What do you think? I asked Triss.

It's certainly connected with the magic of the precinct, but I wouldn't want to bet my life on it actually working.

Me neither. Let's hope it doesn't come to that.

For that matter, I don't much like betting my life on the other one either. It's a shitty choice, really. With yours I trust the man but not the magic. With Kelos's I have the reverse problem.

Does that mean you want to turn back?

No. I still think we stand a decent chance of killing the Son of Heaven, mostly because of the ring. That's worth the risk. Go.

I took control and shrouded up again. Between gates and guards and places where I had to double back on myself, it took me almost another two hours to get to the part of the complex that held the great temple and the Son of Heaven's apartments. It was difficult and dangerous to get that far, but I never really faced anything that shadow and the Signet's ring couldn't get me past, and that made me deadly suspicious. It couldn't possibly be this simple.

Oh, I made up reasons to explain the ease of my passage. The relative absence of the Hand was high on that list. I'd passed at least a dozen guard posts that had obviously been set up with a single watcher in mind, but which currently held three or four or even five of the Sword of Heaven's soldiers. I couldn't help but think that they would normally have been staffed by one of the Hand with a Storm hovering close by.

I would have liked to believe that, that weakness in the sorcery department was on account of the nearly three dozen members of the Hand that we had killed at the abbey. It was probably even true to some extent. No ruler, not even one as powerful as the Son of Heaven, could easily cover the loss of that many elite mages. But somehow I was certain that wasn't all there was to it. Some other need or force was pulling the Hand away from the city and the temple complex, though what, I couldn't say.

Whatever the reason, I soon found myself looking down on what had to be the several balconies that fronted the apartments of the Son of Heaven. It was the splendor that gave it away, which was one of the fundamental elements that had always made the work of the Blade easier. No matter how security conscious they were, the kinds of targets that drew the attention of my goddess and my brethren couldn't resist the temptation to make their power manifest in their surroundings. In this case, a huge garden courtyard roofed entirely in spell-hardened glass to keep out both elements and assassins.

The cost of the glass alone was staggering, without adding in construction or the magic and the staff to maintain it. The garden itself was filled with all manner of tropical rarities that had no business growing here in the north, on the cold side of the mountains.

Here, too, was that counterfeit of the Celestial City that the Son of Heaven claimed was blasphemy. The garden paths were strewn with chips of real ivory and bits of pearl, the balconies railed with jade that matched the jade tiles facing the walls. There was even a small gold-roofed pavilion beside the fishpond. The security was very tight here, with every pane of glass and tile on the roof marked by wards of alarm.

Without the Signet's ring finger I would never have been able to approach from the rooftops. With it, not only was I apparently invisible to the wards, but I had a key that allowed me to open an access panel in the garden's glass roof. From there it was no work at all for someone with my skills to make his way down onto the balcony to the left of the garden terrace—the most logical one to be attached to a bedroom or withdrawing room.

Peering through the curtains, I found that I had arrived outside the latter. The presence of a pair of the Swords of Heaven on either side of the doors to the inner chamber told me all that I needed to know about whether I'd found the right place. I paused then to set one of the few spells that I know well, a cantrip that would create a zone of silence around me for a quarter of an hour. I used that quiet to kill the Swords where they stood.

Then I was alone. Nothing but one door and at most a few short yards stood between me and the bed where the Son of Heaven lay sleeping. I was seconds from making the man responsible for the death of both my friends and my dreams pay for his crimes. I reached for the handle of the door and found that I was shaking. I backed up and took several deep breaths. I wanted to be calm for this, to completely occupy the moment so that I wouldn't miss the slightest nuance of this most deserved of deaths. As I tried to recenter myself, I forced myself to look away from the door, and really see the room, and . . .

Aral, are you all right?

What? I had no memory of releasing Triss. *I mean, of course I am. I just want to treasure this moment.*

Then why are you standing with your back against the wall as far from the Son of Heaven's door as you can get?

Am I. I blinked, forcing my eyes to focus, and realized that I was. *So I am.*

What's wrong?

I looked around and once again my eyes fell on the large wooden plaque on the wall just to the left of the balcony door. This time I made myself take in the sight and think about what it meant.

It was a display mount of a sort more typically seen in the audience hall of a castle than the bedroom of a high priest. Someone had sawn a ring out of a giant ebony, trimming the edges to make it into a perfect circle, perhaps six feet across. It was polished to a brilliant sheen that showed off rings marking hundreds of years of growth. Spaced around the edge of the ring were iron brackets each of which held the hilt of a sword of my goddess, its point directed inward, so that they formed a sort of pinwheel.

Looking at it made me want to vomit, but now that I had really seen it, I couldn't look away. Without any conscious thought, my feet took me slowly across the room toward this proud display of purest sacrilege against my goddess. As I went, I remembered the rumor that the soul daggers of the remaining living Blades, mine included, were supposed to be imbedded in the wall of the privy that lay beyond the bedroom where the Son slept now. That way, he could start each day by pissing on them.

Somewhere in the back of my head I had the sense that Triss was calling my name, but I couldn't really hear him over the buzz that filled my mind with pain. I just kept walking forward, stopping only when I physically bumped into a small table standing directly in front of the ring. I hadn't even seen it until I put my hand down to catch myself on its edge.

When I did, and looked more closely at what it held, I let out a screech of pure rage. Fortunately, my cantrip had not yet faded, and though I could feel the force of my scream tearing at my throat, no sound of it reached my ears. You see, on the table was another display, smaller, simpler, a low rack, designed to hold two swords. Loris's swords. Nothing could have hurt me more just then, and no better tool for the death of the Son of Heaven could have been delivered into my hands.

Turning, I crossed the room in a couple of quick bounds before silently kicking open the inner door. The room beyond was huge and opulent with a great canopied bed at its center.

The Son of Heaven lay on his back in the middle of the bed, his arms crossed on his breast as though someone had laid him out for burial. Though I had not seen his face in person since before the fall of my temple—and that at a distance—I had viewed its likeness in a thousand places. There was no mistaking the man . . . the monster.

In a moment I was standing over him, Loris's swords raised for a double beheading stroke. Now, he would pay for all that he had done to me and mine.

I paused then for one brief instant, to savor what I was about to do. A mistake perhaps, for in that moment I began to do something I had not since I first entered the Son of Heaven's suite. I began to think instead of simply reacting. By doing so, I missed my chance to kill the Son of Heaven from within my armor of rage, missed the moment when his death would have been the sweetest release.

Aral?

Yes?

Kelos?

One lone word. Nothing more, and yet, once he'd uttered it, I recognized the truth, and what had been driving me toward this moment, or rather, who. Still, I was here, and I needed to finish my business with the Son of Heaven before I dealt with my old master.

I did what needed doing, but I took no pleasure in it. It wasn't my triumph at all. It belonged to Master Kelos. And when I was done with the Son of Heaven, I left the apartments and climbed back up the wall, passing through the glass panel to the roof. Once it was closed, I dropped my shroud.

"I know you're here, Kelos. Come out where I can see you. We need to talk."

Even knowing to expect him and what to look for, he surprised me, seeming to simply fade into existence a few yards directly in front of me.

"It's done?" he asked.

I nodded.

He cocked his head to one side. "You don't have Loris's swords. I'm surprised. I expected you to take them back to Jax in Dalridia."

"I'll get them some other time. Them and all the others. I

won't take them to Jax, though. I will return them to the goddess as I returned mine, as they used to return themselves at the death of their owners. It's the honorable thing to do, and I will always choose honor over revenge. It's what I was taught by the man you once were."

He raised the eyebrow of his good eye in a gesture I suddenly realized I had learned from him. "So it was honor that filled your heart when you killed the Son of Heaven?"

I smiled then, and I could see from his expression that Kelos didn't like the color of my expression. Which was exactly as I wanted it.

"Oh, I didn't kill him. He deserved it all right, and you gave me more than enough reasons. But then I stopped to think, and that was your undoing."

"Aral, what are you talking about?" He spoke sharply, but his expression looked more curious than concerned.

"Everything I needed to know to figure it out, I learned in that little play you staged for me with the Signet back in Tien. I'm not sure if that was the one mistake on your part, or if she said something she wasn't supposed to, or what. In any case, you won't become the next Son of Heaven today. The throne still has its current ass to keep it warm. Actually, I don't think you'll become the next Son of Heaven at all."

"It's not like that," said Kelos. "I don't want the throne for the throne's sake. I want the power it will give me to make things right in the world, and I *will* have that power even if you're not the one who gives it to me."

"No, I don't think that you will. For a number of reasons. First, you can't harm the Son yourself, nor any other member of the church hierarchy. Not directly. You're bound by a mortal geas—harm so much as a single hair on the head of the least priest and you die. That's half of why you just wedged the locks at the abbey, because you *couldn't* act more directly. The other half, of course, was so that some of the prisoners would die, because you wanted me angry. Too angry to think or hesitate. You needed me to kill the Signet to make you the Son's heir, before I killed the Son himself."

"Very good, boy." And he smiled, like he was proud of me, and damn me to hell but it still felt good to see him do it. "Very good. But you always were the best strategic thinker among my students. So, I can't kill the Son of Heaven. Nor any of his servants. Funnily enough, that even includes my fellow apostates in Heaven's Shadow. What else have you figured out?"

"That you need *me* to kill the Son of Heaven for you."

"Why? Why can't I just set up that brilliant young apprentice of yours to do the job? She's got the hate for it, and once she recovers from that head injury—she will, you know—she'd do the job up very prettily."

"I don't know the why yet. Not that one nor some others that are important, like why the Son doesn't like to have the Hand too close to him, though I'll figure it all out, given time. No, it's me you need. Well, needed. Killing the Son won't put you on the throne anymore. Not now."

"Really? What makes you say that? What could you have possibly done to prevent me?"

"I left Loris's swords in the Son's bedroom—sunk into the head of the bed to be specific. When he wakes he's going to cut his face on them unless he gets very lucky."

"And a couple of swords are going to turn the Son against his personal Shade."

"Is that what you call yourself now? Really?"

Kelos shrugged. "I don't much like it either. The head of the Hand of Heaven is the Signet. The chief of Heaven's Shadow is the Shade. It's a little cute for me, but then I intend to change it. I intend to change everything."

"It's not going to happen."

"What makes you so sure of that, Aral?"

"Because the Swords weren't all that I left him. There's a note, too. It's short, and insulting, but I think the paperweight I used when I set it on his chest will get the point across."

"What have you done?" And, for the first time in all my years of dealing with the man, I finally saw him look alarmed. It was a tiny thing, barely a widening of his one good eye, but it was there.

"I think you know, but I'm going to tell you anyway, because I want to tell you I've beaten you, not just have you figure it out. I left the Son of Heaven a finger along with the warning, a living finger that's connected unmistakably to your life force. Even a half-witted hedge wizard would be able to tie the magic in that thing back to you."

"How did you get through the wards on your way back out?" he asked.

"You are not the only man to kill a Signet."

Kelos nodded, but didn't say anything.

"When the Son wakes," I continued, "and I expect that to happen any minute now, the first thing he's going to see are the sharp edges of a pair of swords. The second is incontrovertible proof that you've been playing him. And you can't even raise your own sword to defend yourself against his soldiers. If I were you, I'd start running right now."

Kelos nodded again, and then he did the last thing in the world that I might have expected. He threw his head back and he laughed. Not just a little laugh either, a full-throated roar that was probably loud enough to wake the Son of Heaven all by itself.

"I don't understand. . . ." I said, and I really, really didn't.

Don't you? Triss asked. *He's proud of you.*

Before I could respond, Kelos raised a hand. "Oh, very good, lad, very good indeed. I've been waiting two hundred years for someone to beat me fair and square, and you're the one who's finally done it. I can't tell you how pleased I am that it was you."

"You're mad, you know that, right? Completely mad."

"A little, certainly. But not completely. You are my child as much as any Blade I ever trained. I don't know if you can understand what that means yet, but you may someday. When you killed Ashvik you showed the whole world that you had become exactly what I wanted to make you, a perfect weapon in the hand of the goddess, and I was damned proud.

"But this, this is so much more." He smiled and shook his head, spreading his hands in a gesture that indicated all of me. "You have become the hand that wields the weapon, the mind behind the blade. That takes you beyond what I had hoped for you to someplace I can't predict. That's more reward than I expected to see this side of the grave."

Now he was crying and so was I, and I wasn't sure whether I wanted to cut his throat or hug him. Perhaps fortunately I was spared the decision when an alarm bell started ringing.

Kelos laughed again, more softly this time. "I believe that means I need to start running. You, too. Shall we run together at least as far as the edge of the temple precinct? It would be an honor."

And damn me if I didn't fall in beside him. "To the edge of the precinct, and not a step farther."

"Done."

You're as crazy as he is.

You might just be right.

Epilogue

◆━━━◆━◆━━━◆

A man walks into a bar. It's the beginning of a thousand stories and the end of a thousand more.

This time the bar was a hole in the wall in a tiny town in western Zhan and the man was me. The passes to Dalridia would long since have closed for the winter and I had business yet in Tien, so I was taking the long way back to Faran and Jax and my new responsibilities.

Three weeks had passed since I said good-bye to Master Kelos at the edge of Heaven's Reach, and he'd told me he was proud of me again. I still didn't know how I felt about that or him. He hadn't said where he was going, and I hadn't asked.

He'd given me a message for Jax, too, but I wasn't at all sure I was going to deliver it. No matter how much Kelos might have meant it, I don't think Jax was going to be ready to hear that he was sorry about Loris. Not once she heard the rest of what I had to tell her.

Aren't you going to find a seat? Triss asked.

It was only then that I realized I'd frozen just inside the door. It wasn't the first time in the last couple of weeks, and I didn't think it would be the last. With Triss's prompting I headed deeper into the bar, finding a seat beside the fire, where I could put my back to a wall and keep an eye on the door.

The talk was all about the Son of Heaven and the two parallel slices the Son now bore on his forehead and cheeks. The news of strange goings-on at Heaven's Reach was traveling faster than I was. This time the story included a new detail: that nothing anyone could do would heal the Son's wounds. That was a fresh variation on the story, and though I doubted it, I hoped it was true.

When the boy taking orders came to get mine, I asked for a plate of noodles and a pot of tea, and I could feel Triss smiling through our link. I've never liked tea and I still wanted whiskey, had even ordered it and gotten falling-down drunk a couple of times in the preceding days, but I wasn't doing it every night, nor even most of them. It was a long battle and I had no idea if I was going to win it.

But for today, and just for today, I wasn't going to drink. And when tomorrow came, well, maybe I would be able to say the same again. If I didn't, I wasn't going to beat myself up over it. I would just move on to the next day, and the next.

The tea that came with my meal was just as lacking in appeal as I'd expected it to be, but I drank it anyway.

I'm proud of you, said Triss when I paid the bill and didn't order anything more, and unlike my confusion with Kelos I knew exactly how it made me feel when Triss said it.

Proud.

Terms and Characters

———◆———

Alinthide Poisonhand—A master Blade, the third to die making an attempt on Ashvik VI.

Altia—A onetime apprentice Blade.

Anyang—Zhani city on the southern coast. Home of the winter palace.

Ar—Main port of the Magelands, home to one of its five great mage universities.

Aral Kingslayer—Ex-Blade turned jack of the shadow trades.

Ashvik VI, or Ashvik Dan Pridu—Late King of Zhan, executed by Aral. Also known as the Butcher of Kadesh.

Athera Trinity—The three-faced goddess of fate.

Balor Lifending—God of the dead and the next Emperor of Heaven.

Black Jack—A professional killer or assassin.

Blade—Temple assassin of the goddess Namara.

Blinds—Charms of confusion and befuddlement, mostly used by thieves in the Magelands.

Cairmor—A Crown castle in Dalridia.

Calren the Taleteller—God of beginnings and first Emperor of Heaven.

Caras Dust—Powerful magically bred stimulant.

Caras Seed-Grinder—Producer of caras dust.

Caras Snuffler—A caras addict.

Channary Canal—Canal running from the base of the Channary Hill to the Zien River in Tien.

Channary Hill—One of the four great hills of Tien.

Chenjou Peninsula—The peninsula to the north of Tien.

Chimney Forest—The city above, rooftops, etc.

Chimney Road—A path across the rooftops of a city. "Running the chimney road."

Clanarch—Formal title for a Vesh'An clan chieftain.

Coals—Particularly hot stolen goods.

Cornerbright—Magical device for seeing around corners.

Dalridia—Kingdom in the southern Hurnic Mountains.

Deathspark—A piece of magic that turns a human being into a trap triggered by their own death.

Devin (Nightblade) Urslan—A former Blade.

Downunders—A bad neighborhood in Tien.

Dracodon—A large magical beast, renowned for the ivory in its tusks.

Dragon Crown—The royal crown of Zhan, often replicated in insignia of Zhani Crown agents.

Drum-Ringer—A bell enchanted to prevent eavesdropping.

Durkoth—Others that live under the Hurnic Mountains.

Dustmen—Dealers in caras dust.

Eavesman—A spy or eavesdropper.

Eian Elarson—King of Dalridia and brother to Jax.

Eilif Uvarkas—Lord Signet and preceptor of the Hand of Heaven in the year 3130.

Ekilikik—A clanarch of the Vesh'An.

Elite, the—Zhani mages. They fulfill the roles of secret police and spy corps among other functions.

Emberman—A professional arsonist.

Erk Endfast—Owner of the Spinnerfish, ex–black jack, ex–shadow captain.

Eva—With Eyn the dual goddess worshipped by the Dyads.

Everdark, the—The home dimension of the Shades.

Eyespy—A type of eavesdropping spell.

Eyn—With Eva the dual goddess worshipped by the Dyads.

Face, Facing—Identity. "I'd faced myself as an Aveni bravo."

Fallback—A safe house.

Familiar Gift—The ability to soul-bond with another being, providing the focus half of the power/focus dichotomy necessary to become a mage.

Faran—A onetime apprentice Blade.

Fi—A township upriver from Ar.

Fire and sun!—A Shade curse.

Fortunate Lamia, the—A trading vessel.

Garret—A onetime apprentice Blade.

Ghost, Ghosting—To kill.

Govana—Goddess of the herds.

Gram—The name of the world.

Gryphon's Head—A tavern in Tien, the capital city of Zhan. Informal office for Aral.

Guttersiders—Slang for the professional beggars and their allies.

Hand of Heaven—The Son of Heaven's office of the inquisition.

Harad—Head librarian at the Ismere Library.

Hearsay—A type of eavesdropping spell.

Highside—Neighborhood on the bay side.

Howler—Slang name for the Elite.

Huddle Bird—A game bird native to the Magelands and the Sylvani Empire.

Illiana—A Master Blade, killed in a suicide attack at the fall of the temple.

Ismere Club—A private club for merchants.

Ismere Library—A private lending library in Tien, founded by a wealthy merchant from Kadesh.

Jack—A slang term for an unofficial or extragovernmental problem solver, see also, shadow jack, black jack, sunside jack.

Jaeris—A onetime apprentice Blade.

Javan—A onetime apprentice Blade.

Jax Seldansbane—A former Blade and onetime fiancée of Aral's.

Jenua, Duchy of—A duchy in Zhan.

Jerik—The bartender/owner of the Gryphon's Head tavern.

Jindu—Tienese martial art heavily weighted toward punches and kicks.

Jinn's—A small cafe near the Ismere Library.

Kadeshar—Chief city of Kadesh.

Kaelin Fei, Captain—Watch officer in charge of Tien's Silent Branch. Also known as the Mufflers.

Kaman—A former Blade, crucified by the Elite, then killed by Aral at his own request.

Kanathean Hill—One of the four great hills of Tien.

Kao-Li—Fortress retreat of the Zhani royal family, upriver from Tien.

Kayarin Melkar—A master Blade who joined the Son of Heaven after the fall of the temple.

Kelos Deathwalker—A master Blade who taught Aral.

Keytrue—A charm to prevent lock picking.

Khanates, the Four—A group of interrelated kingdoms just north of Varya. Also known as the Kvanas.

Kila—The spirit dagger of the Blade, symbolizing his bond to Namara.

Kip-Claim—Pawn shop.

Knotsnake—A poisonous snake found in Zhan and Kadesh.

Kodamia—City-state to the west of Tien, controlling the only good pass through the Hurnic Mountains.

Kuan-Lun—A water elemental, one of the great dragons.

Kvanas, the Four—A group of interrelated kingdoms just north of Varya. Sometimes referred to as the Khanates.

Kyle's—An expensive Aveni whiskey.

Leyan—A onetime journeyman Blade.

Liess—A Shade, familiar of Sharl.

Little Varya—An immigrant neighborhood in Tien.

Loris—A former Blade.

Magearch—Title for the mage governor of the cities in the Magelands.

Mageblind—Mage term for those without magesight.

Mage Gift—The ability to perform magic, providing the power half of the power/focus dichotomy necessary to become a mage.

Magelands—A loose confederation of city-states governed by the faculty of the mage colleges that center them.

Magelights—Relatively expensive permanent light globes made with magic.

Magesight—The ability to see magic, part of the mage gift.

Mage Wastes—Huge area of magically created wasteland on the western edge of the civilized lands.

Malthiss—A Shade, familiar of Kelos Deathwalker.

Manny Three Fingers—The cook at the Spinnerfish.

Marchon—A barony in the kingdom of Zhan. The house emblem is a seated jade fox on a gold background.

Maryam—A onetime journeyman Blade.

Maylien Dan Marchon Tal Pridu—A former client of Aral's.

Meld—The overarching consciousness of a Dyad.

Mufflers—Captain Fei's organization, so known because they keep things quiet. Officially known as Silent Branch.

Namara—The now-deceased goddess of justice and the downtrodden, patroness of the Blades. Her symbol is an unblinking eye.

Nea Sjensdor—Lady Signet, preceptor of the Hand of Heaven.

Nest-Not—A ward to prevent vermin infestations.

Nightcutter—Assassin.

Nightghast—One of the restless dead, known to eat humans.

Night Market—The black market.

Nima—Mana, the stuff of magic.

Nipperkins—Magical vermin.

Noble Dragons—Elemental beings that usually take the form of giant lizardlike creatures.

Old Mews—An upscale neighborhood in Tien that burned to the ground.

Olen—A master Blade who taught Aral.

Olthiss—A Shade, familiar of Altia.

Omira—A onetime apprentice Blade.

Orisa—God of sailors.

Oris Plant—A common weed that can be used to produce a cheap gray dye or an expensive black one.

Others—The various nonhuman races.

Palace Hill—One of the four great hills of Tien.

Patiss—A Shade, familiar of Master Urayal.

Petty Dragons—Giant acid-spitting lizards, not to be confused with noble dragons.

Poison—Gutter slang meaning toxic or too hot to deal with.

Precasts—Active spells kept precast and at the ready.

Qamasiin—A spirit of air.

Quink—Slang word meaning, roughly, freak.

Rabbit Run—An emergency escape route.

Resshath—Shade term of respect meaning, roughly, teacher or sensei.

Restless Dead—Catchall term for the undead.

Riel—Currency of Zhan, issued in both silver and gold.

Risen, the—A type of restless dead, similar to a zombie.

Roric—A onetime journeyman Blade, Avarsi by birth.

Sanjin Island—Large island in the river below the palace in Tien.

Seldan, Dukes of—Varyan nobles, two of whom were executed by Jax.

Sellcinders—A fence or dealer in hot merchandise.

Sendai, Master—The sailing master and first officer of the *Fortunate Lamia*, Kanjurese.

Serass—A Shade, familiar of Alinthide.

Shade—Familiar of the Blades, a living shadow.

Shadow Captain—A mob boss.

Shadow Jack—A jack who earns his living as a problem solver in the shadow trades.

Shadowside—The underworld or demimonde.

Shadow-Slipping—The collective name for the various stealth techniques of Namara's Blades.

Shadow Trades—The various flavors of illegal activity.

Shadow World—The demimonde or underworld.

Shan Starshoulders—The god who holds up the sky, current Emperor of Heaven, lord of stability.

Shatternot—A charm to keep windows from breaking.

Sheuth Glyph—A glyph for the binding of shadows.

Shinsan—A water elemental, one of the great dragons.

Shrouding—When a Shade encloses his Blade in shadow.

Silent Branch—The official name of the Mufflers.

Siri Mythkiller—A former Blade.

Skaate's—A premium Aveni whiskey.

Skip—A con game or other illegal job, also a "play."

Sleepwalker—An efik addict.

Slink—Magical vermin.

Smuggler's Rest—The unofficial name of the docks near the Spinnerfish.

Snicket—Alley.

Snug—A resting place or residence.

Son or Daughter of Heaven—The title of the chief priest or priestess who leads the combined religions of the eleven kingdoms.

Sovann Hill—One of the four great hills of Tien.

Spinnerfish, the—A shadowside tavern by the docks.

Sshayar—A Shade, familiar of Jax.

Sshssithssha—A Shade word denoting a sort of path through shadow.

Ssithra—A Shade, familiar of Faran.

Ssolvey—A Shade, familiar of Roric.

Ssuma—A Shade, familiar of Illiana.

Starshine—Elemental being of light.

Stingers—Slang term for Tienese city watch.

Stone Dog—A living statue, roughly the size of small horse. The familiar of the Elite.

Straight-Back Jack—A shadow jack who gets the job done and keeps his promises.

Stumbles, the—Neighborhood of Tien that houses the Gryphon's Head tavern.

Sunside—The shadowside term for more legitimate operations.

Sunside Jack—A jack who works aboveboard, similar to a modern detective.

Sylvani Empire—Sometimes called the Sylvain, a huge empire covering much of the southern half of the continent. Ruled by a nonhuman race, it is ancient, and hostile to the human lands of the north.

Tailor's Wynd—An upscale neighborhood in Tien.

Tamerlen—A Master Blade killed in the fall of the temple.

Tangara—God of glyphs and runes and other magical writing.

Tangle—Charms of confusion and befuddlement, mostly used by thieves in the Magelands.

Tavan—One of the five great university cities of the Magelands.

Tavan North—The Magelanders' quarter of Tien.

Thauvik IV, or Thauvik Tal Pridu, the Bastard King—King of Zhan and bastard half brother of the late Ashvik.

Thera—A Master Blade, killed in a magical experiment.

Thiess—A Shade, familiar of Javan.

Thieveslamp/Thieveslight—A dim red magelight in a tiny bull's-eye lantern.

Tien—A coastal city, the thousand-year-old capital of Zhan.

Timesman—The keeper of the hours at the temple of Shan, Emperor of Heaven.

Triss—Aral's familiar. A Shade that inhabits Aral's shadow.

Tuckaside—A place to stash goods, usually stolen.

Tucker—Tucker bottle, a quarter-sized liquor bottle, suitable for two or for one heavy drinker.

Twins, the—Eyn and Eva, the patron goddess or goddesses of the Dyads. Sometimes represented as one goddess with two faces, sometimes as a pair of twins, either identical or conjoined.

Ulriss—A Shade, familiar of Leyan.

Underhills—An upscale neighborhood in Tien.

Urayal—A Master Blade, killed in an attempt on Ashvik.

Vangzien—Zhani city at the confluence where the Vang River flows into the Zien River in the foothills of the Hurnic Mountains. Home of the summer palace.

Veira—A Master Blade, killed after the fall of the temple.

Vesh'An—Shapechanging Others. Originally a part of the same breed that split into the Sylvani and Durkoth, the Vesh'An have adopted a nomadic life in the sea.

Vrass—A Shade, familiar of Maryam.

Wandersea Ceremony—A ceremony propitiating the Vesh'An and asking for their protection.

Warboard—Chesslike game.

Wardblack—A custom-built magical rug that blocks the function of a specific ward.

Westbridge—A bridge over the Zien, upriver from the palace and the neighborhood around it.

Worrymoth—An herb believed to drive away moths.

Wound-Tailor—Shadowside slang for a healer for hire.

Zass—A Shade, familiar of Devin.

Zhan—One of the eleven human kingdoms of the East. Home to the city of Tien.

Currency

—————

Bronze Sixth Kip (sixer)
Bronze Kip
Bronze Shen
Silver Half Riel
Silver Riel
Gold Half Riel
Gold Riel
Gold Oriel

Value in Bronze Kips

~0.15 = Bronze Sixth Kip
1 = Bronze Kip
10 = Bronze Shen
60 = Silver Half Riel
120 = Silver Riel

Value in Silver Riels

0.5 = Silver Half Riel
1 = Silver Riel
5 = Gold Half Riel
10 = Gold Riel
50 = Gold Oriel

Calendar

<hr />

(370 days in 11 months of 32 days each, plus two extra 9-day holiday weeks: Summer-Round in the middle of Midsummer, and Winter-Round between Darktide and Coldfast)

1 *Coldfast*
2 *Meltentide*
3 *Greening*
4 *Seedsdown*
5 *Opening*
6 *Midsummer*
7 *Sunshammer*
8 *Firstgrain*
9 *Harvestide*
10 *Talewynd*
11 *Darktide*

Days of the Week

---

1 *Calrensday*—In the beginning.
2 *Atherasday*—Hearth and home.
3 *Durkothsday*—Holdover from the prehuman tale of days.
4 *Shansday*—The middle time.
5 *Namarsday*—Traditional day for nobles to sit in judgment.
6 *Sylvasday*—Holdover from the prehuman tale of days.
7 *Balorsday*—Day of the dead.
8 *Madensday*—The day of madness when no work is done.

Read on for an exciting excerpt from
the next Fallen Blade novel

BLADE REFORGED

by Kelly McCullough
Coming July 2013 from Ace Books!

Trouble had a new dress, and it looked damn good on her. But that was no surprise. The Baroness Maylien Dan Marchon Tal Pridu always looked good, tall and lithe with long brown hair and a lovely set of curves currently sheathed in green velvet. My sometime lover, sometime client, and the unacknowledged heir to the throne of Zhan was a beautiful woman . . . and trouble. Lots and lots of trouble.

"Have a seat." I gestured to the open chair across from me with the half-empty bottle I'd found in the wreckage of the Gryphon's Head. "Let me pour you a drink."

"I don't think either of those would be such a good idea, Aral," said Maylien. "In fact, I was rather hoping I could convince you to leave with me so we could have this conversation someplace else. Someplace safe."

"But I like it here"—I swung the bottle around to take in the whole of the dark and empty bar, with its boarded-up windows, tumbled and broken furniture, and thick layers of dust over everything. "It's one of the few places I've ever felt at home." I was slurring my words. Not a good sign, but I didn't care. "Or at least, I used to, before whatever the hell happened here happened. Speaking of which, I'm guessing you showing up here right now, means you know something about that."

Maylien sighed and directed her attention to the dim shadow I cast across the table in front of me. "Triss, is there any chance of you talking some sense into Aral? Or do I need to play this out here?"

The shadow shifted, transforming itself from a darkened mirror of my own form into the silhouette of a small winged dragon.

It, or rather, he, flicked his wings angrily. "If I could talk sense into Aral, would he be sitting here drinking and waiting for the fucking Elite to show up and nail his hide to the wall and mine with it? But why would he listen to me? I'm just his familiar. It's not like I'm right nine times out of every ten that we disagree. Or, wait . . . no, it's exactly like that." Triss shook his head. "He's hopeless."

"You may have a point there." Maylien pushed her dueling blade to one side and sat down on the dusty chair across from me, doing untold damage to that fancy dress. "What do you want, Aral?"

That was a good question. What did I want? Once upon a time, I could have answered that question with ease, I wanted to be the instrument of Justice. That was back in the old days, when they called me Aral Kingslayer and I was among the most feared assassins in the world, one of the fabled Blades of Namara, goddess of Justice. But that was before the other gods murdered her and ordered her followers put to the sword. For a long time after that, what I most wanted was to turn back time to the days when Namara yet lived, to restore the temple, and to return my friends and fellows to life. To undestroy my world. Some days I still wanted that more than anything, but life wasn't as simple as I'd once thought it was. Or maybe I wasn't as simple. These days I couldn't even mourn the me I'd once been without second-guessing everything.

Fuck it. I took another drink. The whiskey tasted of smoke and honey as it burned its way down my throat. Damn but it was good. Even so, I sighed and set the bottle down because I didn't really want to drink myself unconscious either. Not the way I would have even a year or two ago.

I snorted, then looked Maylien square in the eyes. "I

honestly have no fucking idea what I want, but why don't you start by telling me what happened here."

The Gryphon's Head was a sleazy tavern in the depths of one of Tien's worst slums, or it had been anyway. Now it was a boarded-up ruin. For years after the fall of the temple I'd lived in a room over the stables. I worked out of the taproom then, paying my bar bill by playing the shadow jack, a freelancer on the wrong side of the law. But that me, Aral the jack, was gone, too. Not as dead as the Kingslayer, but sleeping certainly.

"Well?" I prompted, when Maylien didn't answer me right away.

"My uncle happened here," she said finally, her voice sad.

Maylien's uncle was Thauvik Tal Pridu, current King of Zhan and successor to the one I'd slain for my goddess all those years ago. Not one of my biggest admirers. Despite shedding no tears over the assassination of his half brother, he'd set the biggest price on my head of any of my enemies. He seemed to feel that letting me live after my removal of his predecessor from the throne would set a bad example. His involvement told me all that I needed to know about the destruction of the Gryphon's Head.

"What you mean," I said, "but are entirely too polite to say, is that *I* happened here. The king would never have even known this place existed if I hadn't made it my home."

"My *uncle* did this, not you—" Maylien began hotly.

But I cut her off. "He did it because of me, because he wanted to punish those who'd once given me shelter, whether they knew who I was or not."

She shook her head. "He did it because he's a monster, Aral. Just like my father and my sister. In case you hadn't noticed, the poisoned apple doesn't often fall far from the Pridu family tree."

The shadow of a dragon suddenly rose up between us, flapping his wings angrily. "How about we actually *do* something about the problem instead of sitting here and playing guiltier than thou until the king's men show up to cart us all off to the headsman? I know that's less dark and brooding and 'oh the world is an awful place' than either of you like to do things, but I've had about all I can take of that shit for the moment."

Maylien's answering grin was pained but genuine. "You sounded just like Heyin there."

I didn't smile, but I had to admit that Triss might have a point. Heyin, too. The chief of Maylien's baronial guard didn't like me much at all, but that didn't make him one bit less wise. Quite the contrary. He disliked me because he felt that I made a wholly inappropriate bedmate for his baroness. He was absolutely right. Maylien had more than enough strikes against her in the eyes of her fellow nobles without adding a broken down ex-assassin to the list.

First off, she was a mage, which meant that she had certain advantages that undermined the entire central structure of the Zhani hierarchy—the formal duel of precedence by which anyone of noble blood could challenge any relative for their titles. Secondly, her brand of magery was particularly scandalous, as she'd once been a member of the Rovers, a traveling order dedicated to keeping the roads free of brigandage. She'd spent most of her formative years as a homeless wanderer rubbing elbows with the sorts of people most Zhani nobles wouldn't deign to spit on.

Just then, a harsh squawk sounded from the kitchen—where both Maylien and I had entered. It was followed a moment later by the advent of a miniature gryphon. Bontrang. The little tabby-patterned gryphinx was Maylien's familiar, and now he flew straight to his mistress. Landing on the thick pad sewn into the shoulder of her dress, he mrped worriedly in her ear.

She nodded and rose from her seat. "The guard is on its way, Aral. We have to leave. Or, I do, at least. I can't draw the shadows around me like a cloak the way you can." She looked pointedly at Triss. "Will you come with me? I can tell you more of what I know about what happened if you give me the time."

"Is Jerik dead?" I asked. The owner of the Gryphon's Head was . . . well not exactly a friend, but I owed him.

"Not the last I heard."

"Will you help me find him?"

She nodded. "I know where he's being held."

"I'll come."

Jerik looked terrible, sallow and pale with loose skin on his cheeks and neck where he'd lost weight, and red blotches all across the old scar tissue where his left eye and much of his scalp had been ripped away by a gryphon. The fact that he was upside down, or rather, that I was and he wasn't, didn't help things. No one looks good that way.

There's just no getting him out of there, I mind spoke to Triss.

Not from here, no. We'll have to try another route, but why don't we talk about it later, someplace a bit less hazardous?

Point.

I bent double and caught hold of the rope looped around my right ankle, hand over handing my way up the few yards that put me in the shadow of the overhang. I'd set a pair of spikes into the gaps between blocks there. Anyone watching from a distance would have seen little more than the merging of one shadow into another, larger one. That's if they saw anything at all in the dim light of the waning moon.

The greatest advantage the Blades of Namara possessed was our partnership with the Shades, elemental creatures of darkness bonded both to our souls and our shadows. Semi-corporeal shapechangers, they were capable of expanding into a cloud of darkness to hide their human companions. In a world where spells cast their own light for those with eyes to see it, a Shade's penumbra was the closest thing there was to true invisibility. Triss had uncovered my eyes so that I could see Jerik for myself, but other than that I was entirely contained and concealed within an enveloping cloud of darkness.

Once I had a grip on the line connecting my spikes, I reached down and slipped my ankle free. Then, bracing myself between two of the corbels that supported the overhang, I started working the spikes free. Whether I ended up coming back this way or not, I didn't want to leave any traces that the guards might find.

Below me, the surf snarled as it slithered through the miles of jagged coral that surrounded the little island where the prison stood. The noise more than covered the quiet grating of steel on stone as I pried my anchors loose. The next bit was going to be tricky, so I reached through the link that connected me with Triss and gave him a gentle nudge. In response, he let go of consciousness, sinking down into a sort of dream state as he released control of his physical self to me.

My world expanded to include the darkened cloud around me as I added Triss's inhuman senses to my own. Light and shadow took on something like taste where they directly impinged on the diffuse blob of shadow that was Triss's substance. The effect was intense and visceral, with bright spots registering as a spice too hot for the tongue, and the deepest bits of darkness reminding me of the richer notes in a good whiskey. For dealing with greater distances, Triss possessed something I called unvision.

His field of view encompassed a complete globe, looking outward in every direction, but dimmer than human sight and darker. He had no real ability to distinguish color and only a limited sense of shape. Light intensity and textures dominated. Was something flat and reflective, or nubbly and absorptive? Those were the questions that Triss's unvision answered best. Once I'd grounded myself firmly in Triss's changed worldview, I reached out and found the edges of my larger self, pulling inward until what had been a broad spherical cloud of shadow contracted to little more than a second skin a few inches thick.

That freed up enough shadow-stuff that I was able to form thin claws on finger- and toe-tips. Drawing nima from the well of my soul, I poured that life energy through the familiar link that bound us, hardening shadow claws into something truly corporeal. Moving quickly, because it was no trivial drain on my soul, I reached out and up, inserting points of congealed darkness into the narrow gap between stones in the overhanging wall. Like some wall-crawling lizard, I made my way past the bulge that underlay the crenellations and up onto the battlements of the prison fortress known as Darkwater Island.

Jerik's cell stood high in the easternmost corner of the prison, facing the open ocean and continually hammered by wind and wave. A giant magelight topped the tower that rose up from where I slipped onto the wall. It warned ships away from the jagged reef lying inches below the surface and stretching for miles in every direction. I paused briefly in the lee of the tower to release Triss. He returned to full shroud form, leaving only the thinnest slit for me to see out. While he was doing that, I mapped out my route back to the supply ship that had brought me here. It was docked at a narrow pier extending out from the landward side of the reefs about a half mile from the prison proper. At the head of the pier a small building stood on stone pilings anchored deep in the coral—the same construction used on the prison.

On a calm day, a lucky man might be able to make his heavy-booted way from the base of the prison wall to the pier by walking carefully along ridges in the submerged coral. More likely, he would slip and fall into one of the many deeper channels that ran through the reef. Between the currents, the razor-edged coral, and the colony of demon's-head-eels the crown had encouraged to infest the reefs, it wasn't the best place to go for a swim. The only reliable way to get from the dock to the prison was by riding in one of the long narrow baskets that traveled back and forth along an enchanted cable between the two points. Or, in my case, *underneath* the basket.

I had to avoid several guards walking the rounds as I made my way back to the cable-head, a trivial task given their general lack of interest in their surroundings. It was sloppy, but not surprising given the isolation and reputation of Darkwater Island. No one escaped from the island and very few were released. Mostly it was a place the Crown sent prisoners to die slowly. And to suffer.

The latter came home rather forcefully when one of the doors that led down from the battlements into the prison depths opened and spat out one of Thauvik's torturers. Through the narrow gap in my shadow covering I watched him come toward me. The stylized laughing devil face paint made him look utterly inhuman, matching appearance to soul by my lights. The Ashvik whom I had slain had mandated the masklike paint when he first created the royal office of agony. The official reason was to increase the fear the masters of pain instilled in their victims. If it also served the purpose of effectively masking the identity of Ashvik's pet monsters from those who might be moved to retribution, well that was just fine, too.

I hopped up into the darker shadow between two merlons and crouched down as the torturer passed, briefly closing my eyes to avoid reflections. Triss hissed angrily but silently into my mind as he went by, and I found myself in hot agreement with the sentiment. While this man might not be one of those who had tortured my fellow Blades after the fall of the temple—that distinction belonged to the servants of the Son of Heaven and the office of Heaven's Hand—he was of the same monstrous breed. There is never any excuse for torture.

The man continued another dozen yards past my hiding place and then slipped into the limited shelter offered by a bend in the wall to light a small pipe—most likely some blend of tobacco and opium. He settled into a gap like the one I currently occupied to smoke. I might have simply moved on then if he hadn't chuckled in the manner of a man enjoying a recent memory, perhaps replaying a bit of his handiwork. It was a small noise, barely audible above the wind, and his makeup hid any smile that might have gone with it. But it was that one step too far.

I crossed the intervening distance without really noticing I was doing it. Before the torturer had time to even register the sudden darkness that had cut him off from the safety of the prison walls, I formed my fingers into a spear and drove the tip deep into his throat. He let out a brief gagging cough as he spat out his pipe, but that was all. It's hard to scream with a crushed larynx. Harder still when you're falling a hundred feet onto jagged coral at the same time. One twisting punch in the chest and he was gone.

Fire and sun, Aral! Triss yelped into my mind. *What was that?*

Justice. I turned and continued toward the cable-head.

I could feel my familiar's startlement echoing down the link that connected us. *I can't say that I disagree, but Namara preferred to aim at the masters that held the reins of that sort, the ones the law couldn't touch.*

I'm not Namara.

No . . .

And if you think the law was ever going to touch one of Thauvik's personal abominations then you've learned nothing of humanity in your years among us. I was absolutely spitting mad, and not entirely sure how I'd gotten there.

Calm down, I didn't say that. You're right enough about the chance of any normal sort of justice finding the likes of that one, and I'm not at all sorry to see him die. It's just that I'm . . . surprised to see you act on that sort of impulse.

. . . So am I, actually. It needed to be done, so I did it.

Something that had been lying beneath the surface of my thoughts for a couple of months suddenly broke through into the light then. *Namara's gone, Triss. She's not coming back. I've known that for years, but I think I've been avoiding thinking about what that* meant.

I had been groping toward what it meant to be a Blade without a goddess for more than a year now, ever since Maylien first hired me and forced me to confront what I'd become in the absence of the goddess. I think I finally had a big piece of it.

I can't just let the world go to hell because I don't have someone telling me how to fix things, Triss. Kings and high priests didn't stop going bad when Namara died. They just stopped having to worry about paying for it.

Are you taking this where I think you are?

Maybe. People like that torturer shouldn't be certain that they can make a life of hurting others without ever having to worry about paying for their crimes.

And you're going to fix that?

I stopped moving to let a guard go by and shrugged. *Maybe? Sometimes? When I can? I'm a homeless drunk and I don't know that I'll ever be able to see the world in the same black and white way I did when I was a young Blade, but sometimes the right thing to do is pretty clear. Not acting when I know what I* should *do is a kind of cowardice. I don't think I can bear to indulge my fears anymore. Take the torturer back there. I knew that if I didn't act to stop him, he was going to finish his pipe and go back downstairs to hurt and kill people. Could I really afford not to act in that circumstance?*

While I applaud the sentiment, sent Triss, *I do wonder where it's coming from. Faran was right when she said you were sentimental for a Blade and that you didn't like killing people who weren't directly in your way. That was only a few months ago. What happened?*

When we rescued the lost apprentices at the abbey we killed a couple of hundred of the Son of Heaven's people. A lot of them weren't in the way.

And?

It very nearly broke me, but it didn't quite. I survived and I made the people who put me in a position where I had to kill like that suffer. I feel stronger now than I have in years, since before the fall of the temple. I think all that death was a fire that burned away some of the sentiment. I think it burned away a lot of the old me, actually.

I'm not sure I like the sound of that. Triss's mind voice sounded worried.

I'm not sure I like it much either, or whether what's left of me is going to be someone I can live with, but I don't see that I have a whole lot of choice in the matter.

I knew that I sounded hard and cold, and to some extent that's the way I felt. At the same time, I didn't think I was going to forget the crunch of the torturer's throat under my fingers or the sight of him falling away to his death anytime soon. That was good. I had just killed a man, and it's not something I ever wanted to do lightly, no matter how much someone deserved it.

I guess what I'm saying is this, I continued. *I'm an assassin. I kill people. It's what I do, and I'm very, very good at it. Talent, training, calling, they all point in the same direction. The world is an ugly place and it needs people who can do what the goddess made me to do. Her death doesn't change that. By pretending it did, I've been betraying her memory, and, perhaps more importantly, I've been betraying what I am.*

By then, we'd reached the cable-head and needed to get back to working our way out of the prison. So, as he so often did, Triss got the last word in.

I think that you may have finally found your way back to what you once were. It's what I've wanted for years, and yet, now that it's come, I'm not sure that I have been wishing the right thing for you.

The Marchon baronial great house stood atop the Sovann Hill in the northwest corner of Tien proper. It bordered the royal park, occupying some of the most expensive real estate in the city, and if I lived a thousand years I would never grow comfortable with the sort of wealth and power expressed by the building and its grounds, beautiful though they were. I had been raised to *kill* the sort of people who owned places like this, not have tea with them. Namara's priests brought us into the temple at the age of four and trained us in the arts of death for the purpose of bringing justice to the corrupt nobles and crooked priests who were too powerful to receive it in the courts or at the hands of their fellows. Royal monsters, too, like Maylien's sister and father, both of whom had died by my hand, the latter in front of this very house.

Aral? Triss spoke into my mind, and I realized it was the second time he had done so in as many minutes.

I blinked and mentally stepped back into the moment, refocusing my attention from the Marchon estate of the past to that of the present. I stood on the third floor balcony that opened off the baronial sitting rooms. Below me, a few lonely flowers bloomed here and there, testament to the mild winters of Tien and the dedication of the gardeners.

Sorry, old friend, I sent. *I was far away.*

And long ago, he added. *I could see you wandering the streets of the past, and didn't want to interrupt, but I think Maylien will be joining us shortly, and we have things to talk about before that happens.*

I grinned. *Not while it's happening?*

Our ability to speak mind-to-mind was a relatively recent development and, as far as we knew, unique in the history of Shade/human pairings, though I, too, often took it for granted. The living shadows had provided my order with familiars and companions since our very inception, and when I remembered to think about it I rather enjoyed being the first of my kind to share such a deep bond with his partner.

I felt Triss's answering smile. *Not if you don't want Maylien to spend the evening giving you hard looks because you're distracted. I would have thought that when Faran caught us at it, that would have been enough for you to want to be more cautious about when and where we speak so.*

Before I could respond, the balcony doors opened and a pair of servants brought out a tablecloth and tea service. I noted that they only set two places, which meant that Maylien had won her argument with Heyin about this first conversation since my return from Darkwater Island. There were two pots as well as two cups, plus assorted plates and all the other paraphernalia that the nobility dragged into the simple act of having a cup of tea. That was because I really didn't much like the stuff, so my pot was both cooler and much milder than the rich smoky green that Maylien and most of her fellow Zhani preferred.

She commented on it as she came out and took a seat at the table, placing Bontrang on a perch beside her. "Really, Aral, are you sure you wouldn't prefer tea, instead of that lukewarm water you favor?"

I dropped into the chair across from her. "I don't actually favor it. It's just that it's better for me than the whiskey I'd prefer, and the less I can taste it, the better. I'd prefer plain water or fruit juice, but the latter's out of season and drinking city water without tea in it's a sure recipe for spending the next three days in the privy." Though, to be honest, I was with those who thought it was the act of heating the water rather than adding in the tea that prevented disease.

Maylien shook her head, but poured for me anyway, an action that would have given her footmen palpitations if she hadn't already sent them back into the house. "At least stir it properly, so I can pretend that I'm not serving you slop."

I sighed, but picked up the little brush and mixed the powdered tea at the bottom with my lukewarm water, giving it just the faintest yellow green tinge. The action made my teeth itch because it always reminded me of a hot cup of efik—the taste, the smell, the way it smoothed the harshest mood without the jangling of the nerves that accompanied strong tea. Mostly I didn't think of it anymore, except when I had tea, or wanted a drink and couldn't have one, or the muscles in my back knotted up over a mission, or . . . well, leave it there.

I had just taken my first sip when Maylien leaned forward and touched her fingers to my cheek. "I think I liked your old face better, though this one's more handsome. I understand why you had to make the change, but I wish you hadn't erased all the old lines when you did it. They gave you character."

"An assassin doesn't want character," I replied. "Character makes people remember you. That's a good way to get caught and killed."

"I didn't think you liked that word, 'assassin.' I'm not sure I do either. I still think of you as the 'last Blade of fallen Namara.'" That was what she'd called me in the letter where she asked me to help her kill her sister and take the baronial seat.

"I don't like it," I replied. "Not really, but it's more honest than the other. I'm no Blade anymore, and, truth be told, what was any Blade other than an assassin in Justice's name?"

She dropped her hand away from my face and leaned back in her chair. "You've changed since the last time I saw you, and far more than your face."

"I have that, and I think I'm not the only one." It'd been over a year since the last time I'd seen Maylien, and she hadn't looked half so comfortable with the trappings of her high state then. "But talking about what once was and is no more is not why I asked to see you today."

Maylien nodded and her expression lost its wistfulness as she put on the face of a peer of the realm. It was . . . instructive, and for me, more than a touch off-putting. Maylien the Rover, whose bed I'd shared more than once, vanished underneath the surface of Baroness Marchon.

She picked up her tea and took a careful sip. "You have the floor. Tell me about Darkwater."

"I was wrong and you were right. It's impossible. Staging an assassination is nothing like breaking someone out of prison. Getting into Darkwater was actually much simpler than most of my old assignments for the goddess. I was able to get in close enough that I could have easily killed Jerik without ever being in any real danger of getting caught. But there's simply no way I can get him out, especially not as weak and sick as he looks."

Maylien nodded. "I told you as much."

"You did. The prisoners are too closely watched. I wouldn't have ten minutes from the time I cracked the wall and broke his chains to the alarm being sounded, and that assumes I kill the guard who's in charge of the eyespy watching the cell and the one that's stationed outside his door beforehand. Then I'd have to get him down to the water and out across the reef to a waiting boat."

"Which wouldn't set off nine and ninety alarms why?"

"Exactly," I said.

"We could probably come up with a way of concealing the boat," said Triss, shifting out of my shadow and into dragon shape to insert himself in the conversation. "Tie it to a landmark in the coral and leave it sunk till we get there, or something, but there'd be no way of hiding it that wouldn't involve significant time to undo."

"I'd be willing to support you with money and men," said Maylien. "I still have ties to the underworld from the years I spent hiding from my sister. But I don't see that they'd help enough to make this work."

I shook my head. "They wouldn't, and I could put together my own team if I thought it would do any good. I may have changed my face since my jack days, but I know who to talk to if I need hard things done shadowside. But there's really no way to get Jerik out of there short of a major assault on the prison, and the chances are pretty good the main result of that would be getting him and a bunch of the others killed. All of the important prisoners have death wards inscribed on their manacles. Any guard can snuff out any of their lives with very little effort. More important guards, like the fellow watching the eyespys, can murder whole cell blocks with the touch of a ward. No, there's only one sure way to get Jerik out."

Maylien canted her head to one side. "That's one more way than I can see."

"It'll need your full cooperation."

She straightened her shoulders, and inclined her head ever so slightly. "I owe you my life and my honor, not to mention my coronet, and I pay my debts. If it's in my power to give, you shall have what you need from me."

"Don't agree to this blind, Maylien. It speaks well of you that you feel that way, but you're a baroness now. You have obligations that outweigh anything you owe me."

For the first time since she'd found me in the boarded-up remnants of the Gryphon, Maylien looked something other than confident, but only for a moment. "I don't think you'd ask anything of me that would compromise what I owe my people, Aral."

"I guess that depends on how you see things."

"Do get on with it," she said, more than a little exasperated.

"All right. I'm going to kill your uncle and, if you agree, I'm going to help put you on the throne of Zhan in his place. Then, you will release Jerik as well as most of the other prisoners. You will also shut down the office of agony and all the other abominations your uncle has slowly been reviving from the reign of the last King of Zhan I had to assassinate."

"You're going to what?" demanded Maylien.

Have you thought this one through, Aral? Triss asked into my mind.

"I'm going to assassinate your uncle Thauvik. If we do this right, you will be the one to assume the throne when he dies. That's going to take more than a little risk on your part, and, if we fail, your head is going to get nailed up over the traitor's gate."

From
BENEDICT JACKA

cursed
An Alex Verus Novel

Since his second sight made him infamous for defeating powerful Dark mages, Alex has been keeping his head down. But now he's discovered the resurgence of a forbidden ritual. Someone is harvesting the life force of magical creatures—destroying them in the process. And draining humans is next on the agenda. Hired to investigate, Alex realizes that not everyone on the Council wants him delving any deeper. Struggling to distinguish ally from enemy, he finds himself the target of those who would risk their own sanity for power . . .

Praise for the Alex Verus novels

"Harry Dresden would like Alex Verus tremendously—and be a little nervous around him. I just added Benedict Jacka to my must-read list."
—Jim Butcher, #1 *New York Times* bestselling author

"Benedict Jacka writes a deft thrill ride of an urban fantasy—a stay-up-all-night read. Alex Verus is a very smart man surviving in a very dangerous world."
—Patricia Briggs, #1 *New York Times* bestselling author

penguin.com
facebook.com/AceRocBooks
benedictjacka.co.uk

M1078T0412

From *New York Times* Bestselling Author
SIMON R. GREEN

THE BRIDE WORE BLACK LEATHER

A Novel of the Nightside

Meet John Taylor: Nightside resident, Walker—the new representative of the Authorities—and soon-to-be husband of one of the Nightside's most feared bounty hunters. But before he can say, "I do," he has one more case to solve as a private eye . . . which would be a lot easier to accomplish if he weren't on the run, from friends and enemies alike.

And if his bride-to-be weren't out to collect the bounty on his head . . .

penguin.com

Explore the outer reaches
of imagination—don't miss these authors
of dark fantasy and urban noir who take you
to the edge and beyond . . .

Patricia Briggs	Anne Bishop
Simon R. Green	Marjorie M. Liu
Jim Butcher	Jeanne C. Stein
Kat Richardson	Christopher Golden
Karen Chance	Ilona Andrews
Rachel Caine	Anton Strout

penguin.com/scififantasy